T0128946

# Unwonted Spellweavers

Unwanted Magick: Elfdreams of
Parallan Albträume . . .

Benjamin Towe

authorHOUSE®

*AuthorHouse™*
*1663 Liberty Drive*
*Bloomington, IN 47403*
*www.authorhouse.com*
*Phone: 1 (800) 839-8640*



*Published by AuthorHouse 12/18/2017*

*ISBN: 978-1-5462-2034-3 (sc)*
*ISBN: 978-1-5462-2032-9 (hc)*
*ISBN: 978-1-5462-2033-6 (e)*

*Library of Congress Control Number: 2017918804*

*Print information available on the last page.*



*This book is printed on acid-free paper.*

# Contents

Wisps…
Threads…
Threads of Magick…
Threads of fate…
Threads of time…
Threads connecting worlds …
Dreams connecting worlds …
Dreams of Magick…
The Magick of Dreams…
Magick connecting dreams…
Magick connecting worlds…
Dream raiders…
Elf pressure…
Albtraum…
Albträume, elf dreams, nightmares…
Albträume...

Ǿ ∞ Ǿ

To new readers, the foreword of Unwonted Spellweavers details events in the doomed world Sagain, ancient World of the Three Suns, and the underworld realm Vydaelia and provides background for the story. Established readers will recognize material from Thirttene Friends, Deathquest to Parallan, the Orb of Chalar, Chalice of Mystery, Dawn of Magick, Lost Spellweaver, First Wandmaker, Wandmaker's Burden, Emerald Islands, and Mender's Tomb. This tome bridges the Donothor and Elfdreams series and introduces Spellweavers Xenn, Agrarian, Phyrris, Aergin, Purya, and Jodie. Unwonted Spellweavers chronicles events after the time of the Spellweaver Gaelyss, expands on events in the Orb of Chalar, and leads up to events in Deathquest to Parallan and Death of Magick.

To all… I say, "Thanks" and "Happy Reading."

BT

# Foreword

## I. Artifacts and events of Sagain, a World of Magick...

### *i. The first sorcerer of Sagain...*

The bizarre meandering sun drew near worlds and bathed them with its gray light. Magick flourished in the Gray Wanderer's peculiar shadow. The Gray Wanderer bent and oft ignored Nature's laws. Gray stardust fell from the wondrous sun to fortuitous worlds. The smallest particle of gray sand from the Wanderer filtered through even the densest atmosphere to the surface of encountered worlds. The most miniscule piece of the gray sun emitted the telltale gray light and shared the wandering sun's power, energies, and essence. A titanic collision with one of Nature's pawns sent precious fragments of the gray sun speeding away into the void of space. In a twist of fate and Magick, an irregular three-by-five-foot fragment of Grayness neared the simple world Sagain. Cydney Klarje, a shepherd watching his flocks, watched a great ball of fire fall from the sky, strike far to the southeast, and erupt into a massive fireball. Flames and heat roared across the savannah. Death claimed every creature in the propinquity of the cataclysm. Hundreds of square miles lay devastated. Great wind emanated from the impact site, swept across the plain with pyroclastic flow, and approached Cydney. The herder inhaled deeply and prepared for death. A minute fragment of the gray wanderer from deep space preceded wave of destruction by a millisecond and struck Cydney's chin. A larger fragment sailed past and buried into the Copper Mountains to the north. Gray smoke trickled from the impact site in the Copper Mountains. Intense gray light bathed, surrounded, and persistently cloaked Cydney. Mighty wind picked up and carried the horrified shepherd toward the distant Bald Mountains and left him in an area of desolation. Cydney crashed to the ground far from the impact and inexplicably survived. A heart-shaped, cherry-red mark appeared on Cydney's chin where the tiny gray fragment struck him. Consciousness left him, and the herdsman entered a deep sleep. Young Cydney dreamed of his simple home and loving family. Shapeless grayness entered his dreams.

Wisps...
Threads...
Threads of Magick...
Threads of fate...
Threads of time...
Threads connecting worlds ...
Dreams connecting worlds ...
Dreams of Magick...
The Magick of Dreams...
Magick connecting dreams...
Magick connecting worlds...
Dream raiders...
Elf pressure...
Albtraum...
Albträume, elf dreams, nightmares...
*Grayness...*

Ǿ ∞ Ǿ

In a twist of fate and quirk of Magick, Cydney Klarje became the first sorcerer of Sagain and passed his traits and birthmark along certain members of his line. Cydney's descendant Mayard Klarje bore the cherry-red heart-shaped birthmark on his chin. Mayard oft disagreed with the ruling Council of Thynna, the governing body of the most populous conurbation and center of Magick on Sagain. Mayard Klarje wandered and sought the source of Magick. The source of Magick evaded Mayard Klarje, but the wayfaring sorcerer discovered many treasures. Grayness oft entered his dreams and guided him in his self-appointed stewardship of Magick. Dreams gifted the knowledge to facilitate the creation of the great blade Exeter.

### *ii. Origins of the great blade Exeter…*

To the north of Thynna, happenstance led Copper Mountain miners to an odd grayish-red ore. The stone was discovered precisely at a point of impact of a visitor from deep space during the cataclysm that forever changed Sagain and heralded the Dawn of Magick. Gnomish and Dwarfish gem masters, miners, and alchemists extensively studied the irregular rock, which periodically gave off gray auras. Rarely thick red liquid oozed from the odd stone. By all accounts the ore was unique on Sagain. A twist of fate brought the odd piece of grayish red ore into Mayard Klarje's possession. The Burgomaster of Gnometown gifted Mayard the stone in appreciation of the sorcerer's help in apprehending troublesome highwaymen. Mayard carried the Copper Mountain stone for years. Grayness and a female warrior visited his dreams and told him to merge a new discovery with the Copper Maintain stone. Mayard Klarje awakened and found a fist-sized red heart-shaped stone on the foot of his bed. The stone synchronously pulsed with his beating heart. Mayard removed the Copper Mountain stone from his Bag of Holding. True to his dream visitor's word, red fluid oozed from a single sight on the gray-red rock. Mayard placed his lips onto the stone and drank deeply of the slightly bitter crimson liquid. Mayard felt warm, flushed, and suffered a slight headache. The symptoms soon passed. The rich red fluid satisfied his thirst and hunger. Mayard placed the newfound heartstone to the site from which the liquid flowed. Intense purple and gray auras filled the room. The larger Copper Mountain stone absorbed the smaller stone. The auras briefly changed to red and then grayness filled the room. Mayard Klarje uttered the Permanence Spell incantation and touched the site where the stones came together. The spirit of the stones guided Mayard to the swordsmith Roswell Kirkey at the Copper Mountain mines. Roswell forged the great blade Exeter from the merged stones. Exeter appeared as a well-made longsword, with a hilt formed of a reddish black material and a golden blade. The hilt of the weapon retained the reddish color. No runes appeared upon the weapon and no gems adorned the hilt. Exeter's beauty was in her simplicity. Mayard Klarje never held Exeter. His nephew Rhiann traveled in Mayard's guise and took possession of the blade. Exeter's feminine warrior spirit communicated telepathically to young Rhiann, "I must have some secrets.

Suffice it to say, I'm a sister of Grayness. The greatest mages will not understand the Magick that empowers me. My voice will appear in the mind of my wielder, but only when he grasps my hilt. I'm sympathetic and empathetic. I feel both the physical and mental wounds received by the person grasping my hilt. I'll do all I can to save my wielder from falling in battle. I sense enemies within thirty paces and determine the enemy that poses the greatest threat. I'll save my bearer and serve as a companion during dark, cold, lonely, and forsaken times." Rhiann entrusted Exeter to his fabled apprentice Iyaca Vassi, who held it for 6000 years. Iyaca passed it to young truth-seeker Confusious, who became Sagain's renowned Old Wanderer. For the gift of a Haste Spell, the Old Wanderer gave Exeter to a young Light Sorcerer Alisskirin. One-day Alisskirin became Head of the Order of Light Sorcerers. Exeter became a treasure of the Laurels, the citadel of Light Sorcery on Sagain.

### *iii. Origins of the Staves of Sagain…*

Rhiann Klarje bore the cherry-red heart-shaped birthmark and assumed stewardship of Magick with the death of his Uncle Mayard Klarje. In a twist of fate and quirk of Magick, Rhiann discovered the point of impact and the Bloodstone, the source of Magick on Sagain. Rhiann witnessed the formation of the artifacts, the Thirteen Staves. Two irregular fragments had separated from the bleeding gray Bloodstone. The Great Purple Staff Atlas formed from the largest fragment. Symbols appeared on Atlas's shaft.

Ǿ ∞ Ǿ

Atlas filled the cavern with eerie purple light. Four Windward Staves formed from a quartet of smaller, identical slivers of the Bloodstone and aligned facing north, south, east, and west. Runes of N, S, W, and E on their tips differentiated the four otherwise identical staves. Four sets of the same runes formed around the circumference of each staff at its midpoint

Ǿ ∞ Ǿ

The Staff Pleione formed from second largest fragment of the

Bloodstone. Atlas and Pleione merged their powers and created the Pleiades, the Seven Sisters, from a septet of identical smaller fragments. The Pleiades, the Seven Sisters, the seed of the union of Atlas and Pleione, were named Alcyone, Merope, Celaeno, Electra, Maia, Taygeta, and Asterope. Like the great blade Exeter, Atlas, Pleione, the four Windward Staves, and the Seven Sisters shared the essence of the Gray Wanderer. Rhiann Klarje discovered the working of the ninth level Translocation Spell in the Bloodstone's grotto. The Translocation Spell required shypoke eggshells as material component. Rhiann used the power of Translocation to duplicate Sagain's Seven Wonders on other worlds and gather the Thirttene Friends in Green Vale in the World of the Three Suns.

Ǿ ∞ Ǿ

### *iv. Conflict of Light and Dark Sorcery… the Steward of Magick's concerns…*

Unrest and conflict between Orders of Light and Dark Sorcerers in the world of Magick led Rhiann Klarje to divide his treasures. His most loyal friend the Siren Maranna's reliable wings carried Pleione and the Seven Sister Staves, the Pleiades, to his brother Arthur Seigh Klarje at the Laurels, the center of Light Sorcerers. The eight staves nurtured Magick and became the cornerstone of the Laurels. Arthur Seigh Klarje later moved to a small hamlet Koorlost at the behest of his parents. Rhiann Klarje gave Atlas to Arthur at Koorlost, which became the center of Dark Sorcerers. Atlas nurtured young Arthur's minimal Magick. The purple staff became the cornerstone of Dark Sorcery and later filled the hand of the Head of the Dark Order. The great staff's Return Spell sent it back to Koorlost if its bearer fell. Rhiann Klarje retained the Staves of the Four Winds. The Windward Staves begot great and additive power. Rhiann Klarje feared their falling into the wrong hands and separated the four brothers. Rhiann Klarje carried the N, S, E staves of the Four Winds. He entrusted the Staff of the West Wind to his apprentice Iyaca Vassi at their home Harmony House. Iyaca gave the staff to young thinker Confucius. An elderly Confucius gave the staff to Rhiann's descendant Boton Klarje at Low Gap. Boton bore the red, heart-shaped mark of the Klarjes. The Staff of West Wind also bore the moniker Staff of Stone. Boton Klarje earned the title Stonemaster from his use of the six-foot long artifact. Inherent powers of the Staff of the West Wind included the spells Stone Wall, Stone to Mud, Stone to Flesh, Stone Shape, and Petrification, Comprehend Languages, and Detect Magick. The Head of the Order of Light Sorcerers carried Pleione. Seven prominent Light Sorcerers known as Staff-bearers wielded the Seven Sisters. Boton Klarje rose to the Head of the Order of Dark Sorcerers and carried Great Atlas during his tenure. Boton discovered the power of Translocation and carried Atlas to the World of the Three Suns. Controversy rocked his tenure. False rumors, fabricated evidence, and forged documents portrayed the heartbroken, tragic character Boton as the vilest and greediest sorcerer to ever walk Sagain. As his tenure neared its end, Boton felt no one was worthy to carry great Atlas. Boton chose Clysis of Usialonia as his successor and gave the Staff of the West Wind to the relatively weak sorcerer. Boton entrusted Atlas to Maranna's care. The Thirteen Staves of Sagain… Atlas, Pleione, the four Windward Staves, and the Seven Sisters contained a bit of the Gray Sun Andreas.

### *v. Origin of the Elixirs of Mastery of Magick…*

In the chambers of a dead Captain of Koorlost, Light Knights of the Laurels found a parchment, which was written in Old Language. The parchment was titled simply, "The Record of Boton Klarje Jhundi, the Head of the Order of Dark Sorcerers, complied by Confusious the Wanderer in the 580th year of Boton, of Alisskirin of the Laurels, the 731st, and by the ancient Thynnese calendar, by the reckoning of those loyal to the Nameless Enchanter of Thynna, the 9905th. The scholars of the Laurels translated the document in the 3rd year of Gwindor, the 9908th by the ancient Thynnese calendar.

It read,

*"The supreme accomplishment of Dark Sorcery is the creation of the Elixirs of Mastery of Magick. This is the chronicle of Boton Klarje Jhundi. It is taken from his words and records my observations of his deeds.*

*"The greatest Dark Sorcerer of his generation was Boton the Necromancer.*

*Boton's avarice is unsurpassed in the annals of Sagain. Boton rose to the Head of the Order of Dark Sorcerers through thievery and deception. Once he held the purple staff, he sought supremacy over all Sagain. The greedy Head of the Order summoned the demon Uyrg from his dark lair in the Gray Abyss. Boton pleased the demon with bounty usually stolen from the Light Sorcerers. Worse yet, payment was often in flesh. Uyrg is particularly fond of the flesh of maidens and children.*

*"For the price of never-ending fealty, Boton received the dark ichors that coursed through the demon's veins. The ichors were mixed with five material spell components. These were the components of the Spell of Slowing, the components of the Teleportation Spell, the components of the Spell of Wisdom, the components of the Spell of True Seeing, and the Components of the Spell of Limited Wish. Uyrg only gave enough ichors for the creation of fifteen phials of elixirs. The prized and extraordinarily rare material components were mixed with the dark ichors of the demon in a priceless chalice and subjected to Spells of Transforming. The Spell of Slowing components created four Elixirs of Longevity. The components of the Teleportation Spell created three Elixirs of the Stars. The components of the Spell of Wisdom created three Elixirs of Enhancement. The Spell of True Seeing created two Elixirs of the Future. The components of the Limited Wish created three Elixirs of Wishing. Boton in his eagerness to enhance his power consumed one of each elixir.*

*Boton attained longevity. The aging process slowed allowing the Dark Sorcerer to maintain the vigor of youth. The Elixir of the Stars gave him an ability that had never been attained by a Dark Sorcerer. He gained the talent to transfer to a fifth dimension, the Astral Plane. He was capable of casting spells and regulating the flow of Magick in the four dimensions from whence he came. The Elixir of Enhancement enabled Boton to cast spells of higher difficulty and gave him the ability to cast more quickly. He fatigued less with spell casting. This ability to cast spells of greater power while maintaining his vigor gave him a tremendous advantage in conflicts with other spell casters. The Elixir of the Future enabled Boton to see possible courses of the river of time. With any given attempt, he could foresee one version of the future. There were too many possible turns and tributaries to the great river to make any attempt at gazing into the future infallible. The Elixir of True Wishing was the greatest Magick. Sorcerers of all means and alignment sought the power of a Wish greedily. The Elixir granted the power of a single Wish. Immediately after imbibing the first Elixir of True Wishing, Boton attempted to strengthen his position by consuming a second Elixir of True Wishing. He had not cast the first Wish before drinking the second phial. The Magick of the two Elixirs could not coexist. The second Wish Spell was lost.*

*Thus, Boton learned each could only be used once, therefore, the greedy wizard had no personal need of the remaining Elixirs. Boton's gluttony and wickedness endured many generations, but his new powers did not release the Head of the Order of Dark Sorcerers from the fealty commitment. The greedy Boton decided to secure the phials containing the Elixirs of Mastery of Magick to prevent their use by others. He created a simple black box to store the treasures, and he hid away the remaining nine precious phials. Boton cast a Spells of Hiding upon the box holding the nine remaining phials. Detection of Magick Spells would not reveal the presence of the powerful Elixirs. The false bottom of the chest was hidden to even most discerning study. A child's hairpin could trigger the latch opening the bottom of the box. Boton smiled when he realized that most sorcerers did not possess a child's hairpin. The number of phials in the secret compartment of the box had been reduced to seven when Boton was forced to barter for his life during one of his astral adventures. The astral travel carried him to the shadow of a gray sun and he inexplicably lost his powers. He parted with two Elixirs of Longevity. The chest thus contained two Elixirs of the Stars, two Elixirs of Enhancement, and two Elixirs of the Future, and a single Wish Elixir.*

*Boton lived beyond all his peers. He remained youthful in appearance though nearly a thousand years old. His mind remained strong but eventually his body started to fail. Boton's greed led him to secure the Phials of Mastery of Magick to prevent their use by others. The simple little box was entrusted to the care of the Dark Sorcerers. Boton said it should be considered a symbolic treasure without bartering or Magick value. None realized that the simple box contained the phials. The first caretaker was Montague. Montague was a powerful sorceress who did not share the knowledge that Boton had of the Elixirs. The wretched Dark Sorcerer also displaced the great Staff of the Dark Order, feeling such jealousy that he could not transfer the artifact to another. He betrayed Koorlost and all those who loved her. Family and bloodline mattered not to one so consumed by power. He finally chose to use the Wish Spell that he had saved for so long. He thought carefully about the wording of the Wish.*

*He finally chose, "I wish for the return of youth and to retain the wealth, wisdom, and knowledge that I have attained with age."*

*Boton awakened upon the sands of the great arid desert of central Sagain. His mind could recall all of the Spells that he had learned. He tried to stand but could not. He tried to sit up but could not. He glanced at the tiny fingers of his hands. He was an infant alone in the desert. He had no Spell components. He saw the approach of the sand wolf. He heard the deep growl. He was barely a snack for the large beast."*

*By the hand of Confusious* the Wanderer

Those who knew the handwriting of the Old Wanderer felt the document was indeed written by the hand of Confusious. Several copies of the document surfaced in settlements as far reaching as the Samm Hills, Origage, Chapel Hill, White Satin, Vallidale, and Athenia.

Leaders of the Laurels Gwindor and Eyerthrin doubted the veracity of the document, for it spoke of things, which could not be confirmed. The widespread appearance of the chronicle throughout Sagain perpetuated its rumors. Many people accepted the story as factual. Few doubted Confusious. As a result, throughout much of Sagain, Boton was remembered as the vilest sorcerer ever to walk the lands of the world of sorcery.

### *vi. Perpetrators of a false legacy...*

Loyal eight-legged, eight-eyed Arachnis waited over seventy years. Finally, a flash of red light filled the cavern and heralded the return of his Master, the Demonlord Uyrg. His evilness arrived on the block of red stone. The Deceiver and Arachnis bowed humbly and greeted him. Arachnis gave his master a copy of the vellum allegedly written by the wanderer Confusious about the erstwhile Head of the Order of Dark Sorcerers Boton Klarje. The furious Demonlord cursed loudly and repeatedly!

"#@! *#!

"#@! *#!

"#@! *#!

"At least you did *this* well. Even I can't tell it's a forgery," the Demonlord growled.

"Handwriting is one of my skills," the bloated Arachnis bragged.

"Don't flatter yourself. This document gives the wretched weakling Boton his deserved legacy. Cursed sorcerers! Cursed staves! Cursed gray lights!

"#@! *#!

"#@! *#!

"#@! *#!

"Cursed above all others, the winged wench! The Siren's death doesn't satisfy my anger! I wanted her to suffer more! First time I've been thwarted, even for a time! This world will pay dearly!" the Demonlord shrieked.

### *vii. The origin of the Orb of Dark Knowledge...*

The greatest accomplishment of the Light Sorcerers of Sagain was the containment of the Demonlord Uyrg by an alliance of eight Light Sorcerers. Gwindor, Nolvotor, Coalzar, Valzartan, Tanacand, Pravazar Kreuseul, Telmazar, and the Light Sorceress Knarra carried Staffs of Sagain and comprised the alliance of Light Sorcerers. Head of the Order of Light Sorcerers Gwindor carried Pleione, the Staff of the Order of Light Sorcerers. His colleagues carried the Pleiades. Nolvotor carried Celaeno, bequeathed him by Knarra's father Hiram, the son of Lena and Eyerthrin. Knarra carried Alcyone, bequeathed by her mother Lena. Pravazar Kreuseul carried Asterope, which was an heirloom of the prominent Kreuseul family of Athenia. Pravazar Kreuseul's great-grandson Clopidrel stood in line to succeed him as staff bearer. Clopidrel was betrothed to a beautiful sorceress named Meredith Klarje from Athenia. Meredith was custodian of the Chronicle of the Klarjes, which detailed the deeds of the long line of stewards of Magick on Sagain. Telmazar carried Maia. Coalzar carried Taygeta. Valzartan carried Electra. Tanacand carried Merope. The Staff Bearers had worked tirelessly to defend what remained of Sagain's culture. Knarra's attributes made her unique in a world of sorcerers and sorceresses. The color of her long tresses changed with her affect, much like the scales of a prismatic dragon. Knarra had contributed greatly to the preparation of the Sphere of Imprisonment, a crystalline device devised to incarcerate the life force of the Demonlord Uyrg and made in part from scales shed by great Prismatic Dragon Eyerthrin.

If the far-fetched plan succeeded and the alliance imprisoned the demon, Gwindor feared retribution from the forces of the Gray Abyss and an unparalleled outpouring of evil against the world of Sagain. Gwindor's plan included casting Translocation Spells upon his seven co-conspirators. His seven companions activated the spell with individual Limited Wishes. The power of the Limited Wish was intrinsic to Pleione and the Seven Sisters, but mastering the Seventh Level dweomer still required great study by the Staff Bearers. Even given a lifetime of a thousand years, most sorcerers never advanced beyond Second or Third Level spell ability. Limited Wish's Magick had to be channeled to an explicit occurrence. Gwindor and Eyerthrin had modified the great Translocation Spell and mastered sending willing travelers on a one-way journey without accompanying them. In a quirk of Magick, Gwindor and Eyerthrin, in so doing, sacrificed the capacity to bring the travelers back. It was one-way Magick! Eyerthrin used the dweomer to send Taekora to a world called Donothor. Gwindor duplicated Eyerthrin's incantation and gestures for Knarra's Translocation to send the young sorceress to her Aunt Taekora. Gwindor initiated the modified Translocation Spells and used his Limited Wish to delay their activation until each recipient cast his or her Limited Wish. Only then would the great spells take their effect and whisk their recipients to their destinations. Only Knarra's destination was defined, and only she, Taekora, Gwindor, and the late Eyerthrin knew her objective. Casting the time-consuming modified spells exhausted Gwindor's supply of shypoke eggshells, the material component needed for the dweomer. Gwindor planned to stay behind, cast a Permanence Spell upon the Sphere of Imprisonment, and face any consequences of the group's actions. Knarra warned her mentor and grandfather Gwindor that casting such demanding spells placed him in jeopardy because of his advanced age. Nevertheless, the elderly Light Sorcerer had been steadfast in his resolve to carry out the plan.

Mighty Prismatic Dragon Eyerthrin's final thousand points of light and subsequent combustion spell cast in his death throes annihilated nearby enemies. Decimated legions of Light Knights bravely antagonized the Demonlord's legions before retreating to Athenia. Gwindor beleaguered Uyrg's chimera with Pleione. The ancient green she-dragon Jhade bravely flew amongst the legions of the Demonlord and spewed thick poisonous breath upon them. Word reached the Demonlord that his arch nemesis Gwindor and the Tome of Translocation waited at Awl's Peak. The actions of *the Eight's* allies bought them time and lured the Demonlord to Awl's Peak. Pleione and the Seven Sisters augmented their bearers' powers.

The fiend arrived at Awl's Peak in his favorite form, a massive fire demon bearing a flaming whip and massive sword. Magick Mouths announced his every step and paltry Fire glyphs exploded beneath his lower appendages and produced no more than a nuisance. The Light Sorcerers had cast False Aura Spells throughout the passages. The meaningless auras made Detect Magick spells useless. Uyrg broke through the meager defenses and saw Gwindor working alone over a spell book in an isolated cave. The demon advanced and began a furious spell attack. Gwindor feigned injury. The Demonlord cautiously advanced toward his prey to finish destroying his adversary. The seven conspirators broke their Silence and Invisibility Spells and simultaneously cast Hold Monster Spells. The seven spells slowed the great Demonlord. Gwindor threw the Imprisoning Sphere into the air, and the orb hovered over the beast. The eight Light Sorcerers directed Pleione and the Seven Sisters toward the demon. Rays of gray light flowed from each staff and surrounded the fiend. Uyrg snarled, cursed, and vowed vengeance. Pleione and the Pleiades enhanced the additive effects of the simultaneously cast Hold Spells. The unimaginably strong Magick overpowered Uyrg. The tiny palm-sized sphere hovered and rotated over its massive quarry. The beast's great form slowly transformed to a mauve wispy mist and flowed into the hovering sphere. When the gaseous form was fully inside the sphere, the device began to fluoresce a myriad of colors. Gwindor took a small chest. Three symbols, infinity with null on either side, were etched into the wood of the top of the chest. He gently placed the old Tome of Translocation and the few remaining precious shypoke eggshells on the plush velvet lining of the little chest.

Gwindor declared, "We do not have the knowledge or power to destroy the life force of the demon. We cannot know the course of the river of time. Our progeny may discover a means to forever rid the world of Uyrg's evil essence. The future may call for the destruction of this creation. We hope to craft a prison inescapable from within, but from without I've left a fail-safe. Like a poison should have an antidote, Magick should always have a turn around, a fail-safe. Destroying our creation will require the simultaneous force of not less than four staves of Sagain and the wisdom of a Light Sorcerer. You will travel to distant worlds to prevent the unwarranted collecting of the staves of our forefathers. Once you leave Sagain, the symbols on the staves will fade. They'll reappear only in the presence of one of the staves of the orders, Pleione or Atlas. Let us conclude this deed. I wish you all well in your new worlds."

Gwindor's seven co-conspirators secured their staffs across their backs and uttered Limited Wish Spells in a predetermined sequence. Old Gwindor watched and kept his staff Pleione leveled in the direction of the revolving sphere, which rotated in the center of a circle created by the eight Light Sorcerers, who stood shoulder-to-shoulder within an arm's reach of the Sphere of Imprisonment.

Nolvotor said, "It is my wish that the life force and foul spirit of Uyrg be confined to the Sphere of Imprisonment that hovers before the Eight."

He sliced his hand with an ornamental dagger. His blood dripped over the rotating sphere. The surface of the sphere sizzled and gray smoke rose from the orb. The interior of the sphere became smoky. Nolvotor took the staff Celaeno in his left hand, and passed the dagger to Coalzar. A loud thunderclap and a flash of lightning followed and Nolvotor vanished.

Coalzar shouted, "It is my wish that Uyrg may never be freed by one who willingly serves Uyrg. Uyrg can interact only if the holder of the Sphere of Imprisonment sacrifices some of his life's blood." Coalzar opened a wound in his hand and allowed his blood to flow over the sphere. The smoky interior became mauve. He took Taygeta into his left hand and passed the dagger to Valzartan. Coalzar vanished following another thunderclap and flash of lightning.

Valzartan said, "It is my wish that the Sphere of Imprisonment be resistant to forces of Magick." He cut his hand and allowed his blood to cover the small rotating globe. The Sphere of Imprisonment began to radiate heat and took on deep red inner hues. Valzartan took Electra in his left hand and passed the dagger to Tanacand. Thunder and the flash of light again followed. Valzartan disappeared.

Tanacand stated, "It is my wish that Uyrg never again be able to draw the blood of another or cause direct physical harm to another." He sliced his finger and allowed his blood cover the surface of the ball. The surface again sizzled. A rainbow of colors filled the interior. Tanacand took

Merope in his left hand and passed the dagger to the Light Sorceress. He vanished after another thunderclap and flash of lightning.

"It is my wish that the Sphere of Imprisonment be resistant to the forces of Nature," the lovely Light Sorceress Knarra uttered. The Light Sorceress held in her left hand a small grotesque figurine that resembled the gnarled demon. She took the dagger, cut her left hand, and allowed her blood to cover both the orb and the figurine. She crushed the figurine with her bleeding hand. Her flowing tresses became every color of the rainbow. The Light Sorceress then took Alcyone in her left hand and passed the dagger to Pravazar Kreuseul before she also vanished following the thunder and lightning.

"It is my wish that Uyrg never attain physical form in this world," Pravazar said. He cut his hand with the dagger and squeezed a snow-white Phoenix feather. He incanted and drove the Phoenix feather into the smooth surface of the sphere, where it disappeared. The interior became a brilliant white. The rotating globe briefly resembled a tiny sun, which illuminated the cavern with the brightness of midday. Pravazar took Asterope in his left hand and passed the dagger to Telmazar, who served as Gwindor's lieutenant since the death of Eyerthrin. Pravazar vanished following the thunder and lightning. The brightness faded.

"It is my wish that this appendage creates Death Magick within the Sphere of Imprisonment. If the Sphere of Imprisonment is disrupted, Death Magick will destroy the weakened life-force of Uyrg and any being allying with Uyrg at the site of the disruption," Telmazar forcefully stated. Telmazar used the dagger, cut his hand, gripped a jet-black Tuscon feather, and pushed the Tuscon feather through the hard surface of the ever-changing Sphere of Imprisonment. The globe darkened and all illumination left the cave. The Tuscon feather touched the open wound on Telmazar's hand. Telmazar fell dead on the floor before the thunderclap occurred. His staff Maia fell by his side. Lightning flashed and the entire cavern reverberated. Dim light slowly returned. Telmazar's body remained upon the floor of the cavern.

Gwindor stared at the slowly rotating orb. A myriad of smoky colors filled the rotating Sphere of Imprisonment. Telmazar's death shook Gwindor's confidence. Had the full extent of Magick taken effect? There was nothing for it. He had no choice but to proceed.

Gwindor extended his hand and grasped the Sphere of Imprisonment. He uttered the one-word incantation that created the Permanence Spell and completed the Magick. He sighed and began to speak in a monotone, "It is my hope that…"

Gwindor did not finish his thought. He sensed heaviness deep in his chest. His vision dimmed and he called out to his apprentice Eprozar, the youngest of the Light Sorcerers, who'd remained invisible and witnessed the events. Eprozar ran to his mentor. Gwindor fell to his knees. The young sorcerer took the Sphere of Imprisonment from Gwindor.

"Guard well the Sphere of Imprisonment. It should be called the Orb of Dark Knowledge. It must not fall into the hands of the Dark Sorcerers. Guard it *well*," Gwindor gasped.

The words were Gwindor's last. The Sphere of Imprisonment changed to a colorless orb. Eight Limited Wish Spells had confined the life force of Uyrg to the Sphere of Imprisonment, Telmazar and Gwindor perished in the effort. Eprozar ran from the cave. The young Light Sorcerer removed a cherry bomb from his robes, threw it into the cave, and fled down the mountainside. He carried the chest bearing the Tome of Translocation, the Orb of Dark Knowledge, the Staff of the Light Order Pleione, and the Staff Maia. The ground rocked from the force of the explosion of the cherry bomb. Gwindor entrusted the rainbow bush's explosive fruit to the young apprentice to use in case of emergency. The blast collapsed the ceiling of the cave and destroyed all evidence of the activities of the alliance of Light Sorcerers. The rubble became the tomb of Gwindor and Telmazar. Inside the little sphere, the consciousness of Uyrg gloated. Time meant little to the demon. Eprozar carried the orb from the cave and into seclusion. Dreams troubled Eprozar.

### *viii An imperfect imprisonment…*

Uyrg's most loyal servant Arachnis dozed. When Arachnis slept, he felt his master's presence and heard his Master's words. An unwonted and unwanted effect… quirk of Magick… The Light Sorcerers' shell did not stop the Demonlord's dream invasions. The Demonlord's utterances were clear. *"You must go where I have been. Summon up all debts. If they escape me, my enemies can only go to world's where there is Magick. They have discovered the Translocation Tome. There will be a path to follow. Enlist all my servants. Follow the will of the Chalice. Avoid the staves! Seek the enemies out. Follow the line of Dark Sorcerers. Follow the Orb that imprisons me. It will lead to where the rainbow-haired sorceress hides. Gwindor died an old fool. He knew not the full extent of my powers. Their petty incomplete efforts left open a door. Allow the Chalice to remain in the possession of the minion who holds it. Those of greatest avarice will come to hold the cup. The weak-minded will covet the orb that imprisons me. Through the orb, I'll invade their thoughts. Their dreams are open to me. They'll sacrifice their life's blood to seek my guidance. You will always find a willing servant. The weak will not resist the temptation of power."*

The loss of their most powerful leaders and six of the Seven Sisters weakened the Light Order. Only Pleione and Maia remained.

Dreams troubled Light Sorcerers who guarded the Orb of Dark Knowledge. *The Eight* had imprisoned the physical form of Uyrg, but the execution of their plan was imperfect in many ways. In a quirk of Magick, the fiend's consciousness reached from the orb into the dreams of any being capable of Magick. Dreamraiders found the minds of spell casters more easily accessed when the spell caster slept. The Dream Master Uyrg was the ultimate architect of nightmares. Stewardship of the Orb of Dark Knowledge and leadership of the Order of Light Sorcerers fell on the able shoulders of Clopidrel Kreuseul. Dreams troubled him.

### *ix The arrows of Clysis of Usialonia...*

Boton Klarje Jhundi presented the Staff of the West Wind to timid Dark Sorcerer Clysis of Usialonia. Boton's choice of such a weak successor perplexed most of the dark order. For a millennium, Clysis hid in the caves of Mt. Airie and carried the staff of the West Wind, whilst thinking he carried Atlas. Clysis never learned the powers of the great staff. Boton entrusted Atlas to his steadfast friend the Siren Maranna at her home Cragmore. The Light Sorcerer Alisskirin brought down the walls of Koorlost with the Thunderstruck Spell fomented by touching together two opposing artifacts, the Staff of Entry and Staff of Closure. The act cost Alisskirin his life. Once Koorlost was destroyed, Atlas lay at Maranna's home Cragmore. Clysis over time became more adept, led the Order of

Dark Sorcerers for two thousand years, and exceeded his predecessors' cruelty, greed, and selfishness. Clysis was entrusted with guarding the treasures of the order and the instructing the young. Treasures included the Black Box, a seemingly common little chest that contained the hidden Elixirs of Mastery of Magick. Dark Sorcerers gave the Black Box great symbolic significance. The Black Box did not emanate Magick and had no known intrinsic power. Dark Sorcerers sought the *lost* Elixirs of Mastery of Magick and Orb of Dark Knowledge.

Elderly Clysis labored to cheat time and the forces of nature. He sought youth, power, wealth, and now survival. Clysis chose as his apprentice Morlecainen, a young necromancer driven by ambition and lust for treasure, from a pool of promising Dark Sorcerers. Clysis did not fully trust and share all his knowledge with the younger sorcerer; he tolerated Morlecainen because of his abilities in Magick, enthusiasm, and willingness to follow orders.

The Head of the Order of Dark Sorcerers Clysis of Usialonia and the Head of the Order of Light Sorcerers Kreuseul of Athenia were equally matched and always on opposite sides of the fence. Clysis strived to gain an advantage over his adversary.

Nature threatened Sagain. The world's climate changed. The distal twin suns grew larger. Doomsayers clamored about global warming and predicted the end of Sagain. The great and now powerful Clysis turned the pages of many tomes, ancient and new, and hoped to gain knowledge of a means within Magick to either avert the impending natural disaster or to escape the presumably inevitable destruction of Sagain.

Dreams disturbed Clysis. The Dark Sorcerer learned things from his vividly detailed dreams. Dreams directed him to an ancient tome, from which he learned of powerful Death Magick. Attaining this Magick promised an overwhelming advantage. Creation of the Death Magick required the tail feathers of the Tuscon, a bird precariously close to extinction. The Tuscon was a completely black bird of prey. A bite from its beak or slightest scratch from its talons was fatal. Farmers and hunters had diligently hunted the reviled creature and burned its habitat. This had resulted in the extinction of Sagain's Phoenix population. The Phoenix shared the Tuscon's habitats and had been invaluable to sorcerers. The snow-white birds had provided many spell components. Legends of the bird's immortality were unfortunately untrue. If burned, the Phoenix did not rise from its ashes. A dead Phoenix was simply a dead bird. Dreams told Clysis of the final Tuscon. The bird died in the sorcerer's heavily protected hands and grudgingly gave up its life and feathers. Clysis harvested six feathers and fashioned six arrows. He cast True Flight and Permanence Spells upon the arrows. The shafts of the arrows covered the lethal appendages taken from the Tuscon. He completed the construction of the arrows with a Limited Wish Spell. The tail feathers of the last Tuscon of Sagain had given the Dark Sorcerer six unerring arrows laden with Death Magick. The six arrows meant six certain deaths regardless of the power or prominence of the target. There had never been such a potent Death Weapon. Limited Wish, True Flight, and Permanency Spells cast upon the arrows secured their lethality. Casting the powerful spells weakened Clysis. His dreams became more vivid and detailed and urged him to master the Translocation Spell and helped him translate the ancient runes of the Tome detailing the spell. With the help of his dreams and assistant Morlecainen, Clysis constructed a place to house the objects of his dreams and ambitions and create a conduit for their escape. The room was about thirty paces square and had a ceiling the height of eight sorcerers. Clysis and Morlecainen were faced exhaustion, but they had fashioned a possible escape. The Dark Sorcerers called their creation the Room of Sorcery. He and Morlecainen filled the chamber with artifacts and riches.

Headaches and unsettling dreams beleaguered the stewards of the Orb of Dark Knowledge. The Light Sorcerers did not endeavor to empower the device. Their goal was to keep it secure and out of the clutches of self-serving Dark Sorcerers. The Light Sorcerers entrusted the care of the ancient Orb of Dark Knowledge to the Head of the Order of Light Sorcerers Kreuseul. Kreuseul was the most powerful Light Sorcerer of many generations. He came to prominence in a time of great need. Dreams troubled Kreuseul.

Dreams guided Clysis's actions. Old Clysis turned to Morlecainen and said, "My body cannot do what my spirit wishes. Your legs and eyes must carry out my plan. A simple appearing chest lies in the vault of the Light Sorcerer Kreuseul. It is guarded by powerful glyphs. You will recognize the chest by the series of symbols etched upon this parchment. You will see the symbol of infinity in the center and the symbol of null located to either side of it. Do not attempt to open the chest."

Morlecainen asked, "Master, how am I to get this chest? Won't the Arch Light Sorcerer defend it? His Magick is renowned."

The old Necromancer Clysis reached into his large cabinet, removed a small bow and quiver., and said, "Guard well these six irreplaceable missiles."

Morlecainen protested, "Master, I've no skill with the bow."

Clysis answered, "Your lack of skills with the bow will not matter. Go first to the dwelling of Garijane and aim an arrow in his direction. You will not miss your target. There will be such a commotion that attention will be drawn from Kreuseul. Go to Kreuseul's castle. He will guard his domain. Aim in his direction and again you will not miss. Follow the directions that I have etched upon this parchment to gain entry to his great vault. Take his staff and use your bow to eliminate his offspring. The son will try to avenge the father otherwise. Return to me in haste. There will be great repercussions."

Morlecainen accepted his instructions. He studied the parchment and then placed it within his raiment. He then donned a black robe and left the place of abode of Clysis's home, which was perched upon a craggy precipice on Mt. Airie. The Dark Sorcerer made his way to Garijane's austere dwelling and surprised the Light Sorcerer. Morlecainen fired the arrow before Garijane could react. The arrow only pierced his forearm, but he fell dead instantly. Morlecainen resisted the urge to pilfer through the young Light Sorcerer's belongings. His master's words were firmly etched in his thought.

Morlecainen without delay went Kreuseul's luxurious estate. His Invisibility Spell served him well. Many prominent Light Sorcerers streamed out of the estate. As Clysis had predicted, Kreuseul sat alone in his study. The lanky Dark Sorcerer drew his bow, placed the arrow against the bowstring, stretched the string tight, and released the arrow. The arrow found its mark, and the elderly Light Sorcerer fell limply to the floor. Morlecainen studied the room. The room appeared as the parchment from Clysis had indicated. He uttered a Detection of Magick Spell, and symbols of protection betrayed the hidden location of the entrance to the vault. He drew his staff and fired Magick Missiles from the staff toward each of the glowing symbols. The room rocked with the explosions of the glyphs. Clysis had correctly predicted that a series of mechanical devices would appear upon the wall to the west. No door was perceptible. Morlecainen pulled the devices as instructed by the writing of Clysis. Many gears turned. How did old Clysis know such detail about the secrets of the residence of Kreuseul?

Secret doors appeared and opened. The tall necromancer entered the vault. There were so many items. Kreuseul's staff was missing. Had the sorcerer anticipated the attack? Kreuseul had allowed his young son to take the staff to his chamber to practice spells of protection. The son and the staff were missing. Morlecainen surveyed the area. The other object of his search sat upon a piece of red velvet on one of the higher shelves. The uninspiring chest bore the symbols that were sketched upon the parchment. Infinity was flanked on both sides by null. (Ǿ ∞ Ǿ). Morlecainen picked up the chest. its considerable weight surprised him. He hurriedly left the vault and fled the estate.

Morlecainen's dreams told him of the staff Maia's location, and he stole the artifact from an aged Light Sorcerer. That gave the pawns of Arachnis two of the rare staves, the heirloom of the order of Dark Sorcerers carried by Clysis and Maia. Morlecainen learned from Maia. The lone remaining of the Pleiades, Maia resembled the Staff of the West Wind, but she bore seven sets of Symbols and not four. The staff Clysis carried was, after all, the Staff of the West Wind. Long ago, the nefarious Boton deceived young Clysis and it took two millennia for Clysis to fully recognize the deception.

Thus, Morlecainen, acting on the guidance of his mentor Clysis, slew the head of the order of Light Sorcerers, the beloved Clopidrel Kreuseul, and obtained the Translocation Tome, shypoke eggshells, and the Orb of Dark Knowledge through stealth, thievery, deceit, murder, and Magick. He had not found the Staff of Kreuseul, great Pleione.

Morlecainen returned unimpeded to the craggy slopes of Mt. Airie and stood before Clysis.

"Well done my novice," Clysis said.

The climate worsened. The world and therefore the Orb of Dark Knowledge was facing doom.

Dreams pressed Clysis and filled the old sorcerer's fitful attempts at sleep with thoughts of the Orb of Dark Knowledge. Dreams told him of its presence in Kreuseul's vault, the configuration of the head of the Order of Light Sorcerer's dwelling, location of the vault, and means of entering the vault. The Tome of the Translocation Spell rested in the chest with the Orb. His dreams urged him to master the Tome of Translocation and helped him translate the ancient runes of the tome. As head of the order of Dark Sorcerers, Clysis already held the little ornamental chest that unbeknownst to him contained the seven Elixirs of Mastery of Magick. The old sorcerer treasured the artifact and guarded it dearly.

Clysis spent days studying the Tome of Translocation. Hints from his dreams continued and he learned when he slept. Enhancing and modifying this Magick had been arduous, but ultimately Clysis mastered the incantations to augment the Spell of Translocation with Limited Wish. The combined spells had been cast only unlucky seven times. Ancient Prismatic Dragon Eyerthrin used the united dweomers to send his daughter Tackora to another world. Light Sorcerer Gwindor duplicated the effort and sent Knarra along the same course and six other Light Sorcerers to undefined destinations. Clysis was confident. The old sorcerer and his apprentice Morlecainen made their final preparations.

Quirks of fate and Magick placed the young *invisible* son of Clopidrel Kreuseul and Meredith Klarje at the Room of Wizardry just as Morlecainen closed the door. The youth wore his father's Robe of the Order of Light Sorcerers and carried his father's spell book, the staff Pleione, and the chronicle of the Klarje family. The quantity of Magick within the Room of Sorcery obscured him, and he slipped inside.

Clysis crumbled shypoke eggshells, conjured furiously, and completed the complicated gestures and incantation of the Translocation Spell. Clysis uttered the Limited Wish. "It is my wish that the Room of Sorcery and all its living, non-living, and Magick contents be sent to a world away from Sagain that has a familiar, habitable, and unthreatened environment and all living inhabitants of the Room of Sorcery arrive in the new world unharmed by the journey."

The staff Pleione, the chronicle of the Klarje family, and son of Clopidrel Kreuseul and Meredith Klarje joined Clysis, Morlecainen, the Orb of Dark Knowledge, and the artifacts they had gathered. Within the Room of Wizardry, the travelers carried the Orb of Dark Knowledge, the Tome of Translocation, the concealed Elixirs of the Mastery of Magick, and three staves of Sagain; the Staff of the West Wind with old Clysis, Maia of the Seven Sisters with Morlecainen, and the Staff Pleione with Kreuseul's son. Clysis and Morlecainen squirreled away many antiquities within the chamber. The boy wore the robe of the Order of Light Sorcerers and kept many treasures within its hidden pockets.

Three travelers departed Sagain and in the span of a few heartbeats arrived in the wilds of the primitive world. A fleeting bright light appeared in the night sky. The Limited Wish protected Old Clysis through the journey. *"It is my wish that the Room of Sorcery and all its living, non-living, and Magick contents be sent to a world away from Sagain that has a familiar, habitable, and unthreatened environment and all living inhabitants of the Room of Sorcery arrive in the new world unharmed by the journey."* Clysis, Morlecainen, and their stowaway survived the journey. However, when the Room of Sorcery settled at its destination, the old Dark Sorcerer succumbed from the strain of casting the Seventh and Ninth Level Spells. Quirk of Magick…

Undaunted, Morlecainen tentatively opened the door and peered out onto marshy swampland. The young stowaway sorcerer remained invisible and carried the spell book of his father and wore his father's robe. The lad helped himself to some of the large quantity of material spell ingredients in the Room of Wizardry. Innumerable pockets in the Robe of Sagain stored all he wanted. Many sounds and smells saturated the area and aided the Invisibility Spell in keeping him undetected. He slipped past Morlecainen and stepped outside.

Quirks of fate and Magick brought many of Sagain's greatest treasures to the primitive world Donothor. Light Sorceress Knarra of *the Eight* carried the storied staff Alcyone. Young Prismatic Dragon Taekora escaped Sagain with the great sword Exeter, the crowning achievement of an ancient Dwarfish swordsmith Roswell Kirkey. Clysis, Morlecainen, and the stowaway son of the slain Light Sorcerer Kreuseul brought in the Room of Wizardry the Orb of Dark Knowledge, Tome of Translocation, the hidden Elixirs of the Mastery of Magick, Staff of the West Wind, Staff Pleione, robes of Sagain, and Staff Maia of the Seven Sisters. Four staves of Sagain reached the primitive world. Quirk of fate and Magick… unwonted and unwanted…

## x. *Unaccounted for artifacts of Sagain...*

### *Atlas: the staff of the Order of Dark Sorcerers...*

Knowledge of the fate of the legendary purple staff Atlas evaded Clysis, Morlecainen, and the consciousness of the Orb of Dark Knowledge. Boton Klarje entrusted the purple staff Atlas to the Siren Maranna, who kept it at her home Cragmore in a hidden space beneath the floor of her sitting room. Maranna revealed Atlas and Boton Klarje's instructions to the then Head of the Light Order Alisskirin. Alisskirin recognized the artifact and advised it remain in Maranna's stewardship. Maranna placed the staff back within the secret compartment. Alisskirin passed to his forefathers when he brought down the black walls of the Dark Sorcerers' stronghold Koorlost with the Thunderstruck Spell created by touching the Staff of Closure to the Staff of Entry. Thunderstruck destroyed Koorlost, Alisskirin, and the Staves of Polarity. The Siren Maranna sacrificed herself to banish the Fire demon lord. Great Prismatic Dragon Eyerthrin flew rapidly to the siren's home Cragmore, removed artifacts, and stored them within two tiny Bags of Concealment. Eyerthrin took the marvelous never empty pot and supply of Jove's nectar, but the Prismatic Dragon failed to discover the purple staff Atlas.

### *The Windward Staves...*

Three Windward Staves were last known in the hand of the Nameless Enchanter of Thynna Rhiann Klarje, the ancestor of Boton Klarje Jhundi and Meredith Klarje Kreuseul. Legend held Rhiann Klarje carried the three windward staves away from the world. Clysis carried the Staff of the West Wind.

### *The seven sisters, the Pleiades...*

Six of the Seven Sisters departed Sagain in the hands of Light Sorcerers. Alcyone with Knarra, Asterope with Pravazar, Celaeno with Nolvotor, Taygeta with Coalzar, Electra with Valzartan, and Merope with Tanacand. Morlecainen usurped and carried the seventh sister Maia. Improbably,

Pleione, Alcyone, the Staff of the West Wind, and Maia of the Pleiades reached Donothor. Four Staves of Sagain arrived in one obscure world. Did the devoted Arachnis and cunning Deceiver have the means to free their Master?

### *xi. Threads connecting worlds…*

Events in the doomed world Sagain affected the World of Three Suns, Donothor, and the Blue World. Artifacts and natives of Sagain survived and reached other worlds. Observers in faraway galaxies witnessed the supernova explosion that obliterated Sagain. More than stardust remained after the World of Sorcery exploded. An irregular three-by-five-foot gray stone and thin purple staff floated through space. Searching…

### *xii. Twists of fate: Quirks of Magick…*

Wisps…
Threads…
Threads of Magick…
Threads of fate…
Threads of time…
Threads connecting worlds …
Dreams connecting worlds …
Dreams of Magick…
The Magick of Dreams…
Magick connecting dreams…
Magick connecting worlds…
Dream raiders…
Elf pressure…
Albtraum…
Albträume, elf dreams, nightmares…
Albträume...

Ǿ ∞ Ǿ

## II. Ancient Events in the World of the Three Suns

Three very different suns gave light to Parallan, the world of the Drelves. Total darkness never covered the land. The little yellow sun Meries traversed the sky in sixteen hours. When Meries drew high in the sky, the little star bathed the World of the Three Suns with amber light, warmed the world, and imparted beautiful yellow and orange hues to the skies of Parallan. In contrast, the dark sun Orpheus was akin to a large black unmoving spiraling defect in the sky. Giant Orpheus gave little light but controlled the movement of Meries. Andreas, the Gray Wanderer, appeared in the sky irregularly. Oft times Andreas came into view as a gray speck on the horizon. From time to time the wanderer left the skies altogether. Every now and then the gray sun wobbled a bit closer to the World of the Three Suns.

Eight-hour periods of waxing and waning amber light made up one cycle of Meries. The little yellow sun never left the horizon, but every sixty cycles Meries slunk down in the amber sky and lingered at its zenith for a time of fifteen cycles, or 240 hours. These nadirs of Meries's light were called dark periods. During the dark period, scant light that reached the World of the Three Suns derived mostly from great Orpheus with variable contribution from the Gray Wanderer. The times of greatest light were called light periods, the lesser light were amber periods, and the cyclic extended periods of least illumination were called dark periods.

Some peoples used the arbitrary term "day" to describe one eight-hour cycle of bright light and the term "night" to describe the eight-hour amber periods. The terms day and night had little meaning during the 240-hour-long time of decreased illumination of the dark period. Most folk simply used the term dark period. But the time from the beginning of one dark period to the beginning of the next was consistently the equivalent of 75 cycles of Meries, or 1200 hours.

On the odd occasion, the Gray Wanderer drew near Parallan. Approximations of Andreas gave wondrous gifts to the fauna, flora, and folk of the World of the Three Suns. During these unpredictable Approximations, the Gray Wanderer filled the sky, bathed the land with its deep gray light, and augmented forces of Magick in the world.

Many peoples of Parallan celebrated significant rituals of their ilk during dark periods. For instance, the forest dwelling Drelves harvested the tubers of the precious enhancing plant only during the dark period. Vital to the Drelves, the enhancing plant's tubers matured in eight dark periods. Thus, a season of the harvest encompassed eight dark periods, and equaled the time of 600 cycles of Meries; 480 cycles of light and amber periods and the equivalent of 120 cycles of relative darkness. Drelves called the time between harvests a "season of the harvest" or a "year." Drelves usually matured in fifteen to thirty *years* and chose life-mates when they found love. If blessed by good health and bountiful harvests of the disease fighting enhancing root, the forest folk lived to see hundreds of harvests. Teachers oft lived longer, and ultra-rare Spellweavers had uncommonly long lives.

Crossing a wandering monster or a voracious plant ended many lives prematurely in the World of the Three Suns. Encountering a Droll's axe, Kiennite's bow, or shaman's spell shortened one's life very quickly. Drelves were an uncommonly careful people and lost few of their numbers in such ways. Drelves remained within the central forests of Parallan and never infringed on the territories of others. All the same, the forest folk's ancestral enemies the Drolls and Kiennites brought war to the forest people. Drolls loosely organized into clans and Kiennites lived in warrens. A powerful Droll named Moochie of the Korcran Clan fought the Drelves. To some, a thousand of his folk were a thousand Drolls; to others, a thousand Droll; a village might be called Drollen, simply Droll, but not *Drollish. Kiennish* described something related to Moochie's gnarly allies, the Kiennites. But *Drollish described* nothing. *Drollish* was thought superfluous. The big warrior Moochie thought all this foolish, but some of his ilk would fight over the pronunciation of their names. However, to Moochie's way of thinking none of Drollen ilk was as bad as the Kiennites. The Kiennish warren lord Pierce changed his name to Tumuch, because others teased him "too much.". One named Moochie couldn't belittle another's name *too much.* The name had served the big Droll well, and Moochie had smacked many who belittled his moniker.

Teacher Edkim breathed deeply and basked in thick gray light. The wandering sun Andreas emitted the gray light, drew near the land, and now filled the usually amber skies. Edkim had been the spiritual leader of the Drelves and supervised he harvest of the enhancing root tubers at Green Vale for twenty-four years. At this moment he witnessed his first Approximation of the wandering gray sun Andreas. The Teacher waited and hoped that Andreas granted his ilk the gift of a Spellweaver. The ultra-rare purveyors of Magick were born only during these extraordinary times. Now the Teacher waited outside the stately red oak home of Drelvish life-mates Carinne and Glinne. Edkim had presided at the ceremony of lifetime commitment that united the young Drelvish couple several harvesting seasons earlier. Skilled midwives attended Carinne, who was laden with child and confined. Teachers customarily attended births of Drelvlings. The light of the gray sun concentrated on the great tree. In times past, the dense cone of gray light oft heralded the birth of a Spellweaver.

During Approximations, the Gray Sun Andreas hovered like a giant gray ball near the World of the Three Suns and blocked out the light of Meries and the black giant sun Orpheus. The grayness of the Approximation of Andreas produced Parallan's darkest times. Amber gave way to gray. Ordinary gave way to Magick. Anything might happen. For the most part, little amusements occurred. The gray light of Andreas transformed the World of the Three Suns and heightened Magick. Songbirds changed their tunes. Hummingbirds stopped humming and sang phrases. Rocks radiated auras. Elephants flew. Other than the times of Approximations, Magick was limited to the varied spells of Drelvish Spellweavers and the lesser dweomers of shamans of the goblin-like Kiennites. Every Kiennish offspring born during the time of the gray light had the limited powers of a shaman. Kiennish shaman passed their powers down their line. Spellweavers were always born during Approximations, but most Approximations passed without the birth of a Spellweaver. Some Teachers lived their entire lives without witnessing a single time of the gray light. Ten generations of Teachers might pass between births of Spellweavers. Edkim had seen a hundred harvests of the enhancing root. Drelves typically described longevity in terms of harvests of the precious plant's tubers. The tubers matured in eight dark periods, the equivalent of 600 cycles of Meries.

"Teacher, it is time," Glinne's familiar voice called.

Edkim entered the great tree. Grayness bathed the small group gathered in the friendly confines of the great red oak. Two new voices rang through the long *hollowed* and now *hallowed* base of Glinne and Carinne's great red oak home. Gray light concentrated on the brace of robust, healthy sprouts. Auras danced upon every item within the dwelling, and all within sensed a great wave on the usually tranquil sea of Magick. Though most Drelves were unable to cast spells, Magick touched the forest people, and they usually detected its presence. Carinne and Glinne had anticipated one child and chosen the name Gaelyss. Now two babes arrived. The second son was given the name Yannuvia.

Edkim joined the elders and the gathered community in the common area of Alms Glen and began, "The long wait is over. We are given Spellweavers."

"You…you said *Spellweavers*. What…?" the elder Blanchard queried.

"Yes. Spellweavers. Carinne and Glinne have two sons. The gray light shines upon both. Two copies of the ancient spell book appeared," Edkim replied.

"Two copies…two copies of *the Gifts of Andreas to the People of the Forest*! Has this ever happened?" the elder continued.

"Neither in the recorded annals nor the tales we tell by the fires. The most recent copy of the ancient spell book replicates when a new Spellweaver is born. The three Teachers, who preceded me, never saw the book's replication. We have been so long without the embellishment of Magick. The gifts from the Wanderer are called Gaelyss and Yannuvia. The sprouts are very healthy," Edkim replied.

The twin Spellweavers followed different paths. Gaelyss concentrated on his studies whilst adventuresome Yannuvia bent the rules and explored his beloved forest. Gaelyss spent time with four close friends Meryt, Debery, Zack, and Bryce. Yannuvia oft dragged she-Drelve Kirrie, a year younger, along with him. The young Spellweavers were set to accompany other 13-year-old Drelvlings to Meadowsweet and Green Vale for the harvest. Selection was a great honor. Dreams troubled the youthful Spellweavers. On the eve of the harvest trip, Yannuvia went on walkabout and thought lost. Whilst they were in Green Vale, Magick touched Edkim, Zack, Bryce, Meryt, and Debery. Unwonted Magick…

War came to the Drelves whilst Yannuvia was away. The Kiennites' greatest leader General Saligia brought a massive force against Alms Glen and Drelvedom. The great battle cost Drelvedom the iconic Lone Oak,

Tree Herder Old Yellow, beloved Teacher Edkim, Meryt, Zack, Bryce, Debery, charmed wyvern Dallas, and 64 other Drelves. Heroism by Edkim, Morganne of Meadowsweet, Sergeant Major Rumsie, Kirrie, and untold others saved Drelvedom. The Teacher Edkim employed an artifact called the Cold Stone, fomented Cold Magick, and destroyed the Drolls' treasured Fire Horse brigade. The Teacher later seriously wounded General Saligia with a Magick Missile. Casting the spells cost the Teacher Edkim his life. Kiennish warren leader Delano helped grievously wounded Saligia from the field and with the help of a minstrel managed to get the injured liege back home to Aulgmoor. In the Kiennish citadel Aulgmoor, the Mender Fisher saved the General. Saligia swore vengeance and continued his struggle against the Drelves with renewed vigor. Yannuvia returned from his walkabouts changed. The thirteen-year-old Spellweaver went into the wild woods to seek the power hidden behind Alluring Falls and was lost to the Drelves for eight years. Instead of eight years, Yannuvia had sensed the passage of less than a single dark period, about sixteen days. Yet he appeared to have aged sixty years. Yannuvia's close friends, Joulie and Jonna, the daughters of veteran Ranger Banderas, later joined him on his journeys and likewise returned much older than their years. Unwonted and unwanted quirks of Magick…

Deception and difficult choices set brother against brother. Outside forces stirred the pot. Drolls transformed to look like Drelves killed the Spellweavers' mother Carinne and others in an ambush at the Drelvish sanctuary Sylvan Pond. Spellweaver Yannuvia employed Fire Magick and destroyed Kiennish Fort Melphat and smote a legion of Droll and Kiennish warriors. The caretaker of Green Vale, the ancient Tree Shepherd branded Yannuvia as "Fire Wizard." Spellweaver Gaelyss witnessed events that convinced him that his brother was a traitor to Drelvedom. Yannuvia lost several close friends in combat with the Drolls, but developed an association with the enigmatic Mender Fisher. The prodigal Spellweaver lost Kirrie to his brother Gaelyss.

Fisher typified ultra-rare Menders. Given the opportunity, a Mender healed a warrior and then the warrior's enemy. Mender's nature precluded haughty eyes, a lying tongue, hands that shed innocent blood, feet swift to run into mischief, deceitful witness that uttered lies, and sowing discord among brethren. Menders were neither loyal nor disloyal. Menders did not display lust, gluttony, greed, sloth, wrath, envy, and pride. Likewise, Menders did not show signs of chastity, temperance, charity, diligence, patience, kindness, and humility. Menders did not seek adultery, fornication, uncleanness, lasciviousness, idolatry, witchcraft, hatred, variance, emulations, wrath, strife, seditions, heresies, envying, murders, drunkenness, reveling, "and such things." Menders understood mending. Menders *were* Magick.

In the hamlet Lost Sons, Yannuvia gathered with those loyal to him and disenchanted with the course chosen by his brother Gaelyss and Drelvedom's ruling Council of Alms Glen. The mysterious Dream Master and mysterious Good Witch showed the Drelves images of a new home and offered a means of passage. Ranger Beaux brought word of the council's decision ordering the brethren of Lost Sons back to Alms Glen. The Drelves of Lost Sons unanimously rejected the council's demand. Elder Dienas relayed the community's wishes to the Spellweaver Yannuvia. Everyone drank "Seventh Nectar" from a refilling vessel in preparation for their journey. Spellweaver Yannuvia, Mender Fisher, Teacher Morganne, Clouse, Ranger Klunkus, Beaux, Joulie, Jonna, Elder Dienas, Elder Yiuryna, and all other members of the group joined hands. Yannuvia used a red- and-black tipped wand and uttered the command, **"Hairy true man."** The Spellweaver Yannuvia and the folk of Lost Sons arrived on the rocky shore of a great underworld sea in a massive underground expanse. Eerie luminescence filled the area and rendered light roughly equivalent to the Dark Period. The peculiar light came mostly from glowing growths on the distant ceiling and walls of the expanse. The sojourners gathered their humble packs and clustered together. Yannuvia's spells provided enough nourishment to satisfy their hunger for food. Every Drelve longed for a comfortable tree to call his home. Most of the exhausted refugees from Lost Sons quickly fell asleep. The Spellweaver sighed. Oh, for a sleep dweomer… His dull headache lingered. The Spellweaver closed his eyes and enjoyed Morganne's closeness. The orange-haired she-Drelve's slow deep breathing, pleasant delicate scent, and warmness relaxed the Spellweaver. Yannuvia recalled greeting Morganne when he returned from his first walkabout. "*Morganne of Meadowsweet, Teacher of the Drelves, I must say you are pleasant to look upon. I spoke to Sergeant Major Rumsie during the celebration. You underestimated the value of your contribution to* *the defense of the realm. You are a worthy replacement for Edkim.*" Yannuvia could no longer fend off exhaustion and fell asleep.

Once Morganne realized Yannuvia was asleep, she stopped her pretense. She had wanted to remain awake until the Spellweaver slept to practice saying something she had not found the strength to tell him. In a whisper, the she-Drelve tenderly uttered, "I love you, Yannuvia. If you would have me, Spellweaver, I'd give you everything of my being." Relieved to have muttered the words, Morganne then found sleep. Nature's gentle nurse…

Yannuvia's dreams retraced the history of his life. He dreamed of his youth and time with the beloved Teacher Edkim. His mind revisited youthful days playing with his twin brother Gaelyss under the loving supervision of his mother Carinne, sneaking with his childhood friend Kirrie to see the great Lone Oak, and using infamous invisimoss to evade Sergeant Major Rumsie and Drelvish guards. The Spellweaver dreamt of leaving Alms Glen on the eve of his neophyte group's trek to Meadowsweet and Green Vale, meeting water sprites, and journeying to Alluring Falls. What Yannuvia sensed as the passing of a few cycles of Meries appeared to have aged him nigh sixty seasons. Dreams had robbed him of his youth. Presently the Spellweaver dreamed of the Gray Wanderer Andreas filling the amber skies of Parallan. Yannuvia had witnessed the rare Approximation four times. The beauty of Green Vale reentered his memory. The Thirttene Friends…the Tree Shepherd…

Redness filled his dreamy thoughts.

Wisps…
Threads…
Threads of Magick…
Threads of fate…
Threads of time…
Threads connecting worlds …
Dreams connecting worlds …
Dreams of Magick…
The Magick of Dreams…
Magick connecting dreams…
Magick connecting worlds…
Dream raiders…

Elf pressure…
Albtraum…
Albträume, elf dreams, nightmares…

*Grayness…*

The Dreamraider Amica appeared as the Good Witch in Yannuvia's dream. The beautiful matronly female with smooth, lovely fair skin, deep blue eyes, and soft blonde hair that fell gently down the length of her back. She wore a soft white dress made of cottony fabric, which stopped alluringly several inches above her knees and exposed her smooth long legs. Her silky hands ended in long fingers with well-groomed nails. She smiled coyly at the dreaming Spellweaver.

Albträume, elf dreams, nightmares…

The Spellweaver surveyed his realm.

Who could ask for better support?

Klunkus and Beaux to lead his defenses…

Fisher and Clouse to work with healing and horticulture…

The Teacher Morganne's extensive knowledge of the enhancing plants…

A new beginning…

Thirteen changes of seasons passed in the World of the Three Suns whilst the First Wandmaker and his 232 companions traveled in the blue light.

Ǿ ∞ Ǿ

*In the World of the Three Suns…*

The veteran ranger Tomayo reported to the Council of Alms Glen, "The whole of Lost Sons is abandoned. We searched every tree. My rangers found no evidence of Yannuvia, Dienas, Beaux, or Klunkus."

Kirrie added, "I cannot locate the Teacher Morganne. The Teacher's home the Old Orange Spruce is in order in every way, but the Teacher and the gray stone she always carried are missing."

Gaelyss asked, "Have you received word from the north, Sergeant Major Rumsie?"

"The armies of Drolls and Kiennites have not dispersed. the banners of Aulgmoor fly above the encampments and the numbers grow. Some steadily cross the Ornash toward our lands. Every indication points to all-out assault on our lands. I have doubled the guards at the meadow and asked our brethren to send support. The scouts have reported Drolls in the wild woods across the way," Rumsie advised.

Young Ranger Loganne added, "Beaux has not returned. But there was a visitor to the perimeter. The pale healer Fisher appeared and asked me to present the council with this artifact. He called it 'the Keotum Stone' and says it protects from the effects of Magick."

Gaelyss said with alarm, "The Healing Stone has disappeared. Kirrie, what of the stone you carry?"

Kirrie answered, "The stone I used to summon the wyvern Dallas remains in my cloak."

"Then only two stones remain in Alms Glen. Thievery! Doubtlessly the work of my brother and his allies!" Gaelyss muttered angrily.

Elder Blanchard turned to Gaelyss and said, "Spellweaver, it seems we have a war on our hands. Our people are without a Teacher. The burden falls heavily on your shoulders."

Spellweaver Gaelyss sighed and replied, "There is no better choice for Teacher than my life-mate Kirrie. She knows the plants of Green Vale and the teachings of Edkim. We will persevere."

War again came to Alms Glen. In the course of the conflict, Teacher Kirrie was thought lost after an airborne battle with a wyvern rider. The life-mate of Drelvedom's premier bowyer and fletcher BJ Aires, Camille Aires assumed the role of Teacher, and Spellweaver Gaelyss united with Fadra of Meadowsweet. The Dreamraider Amica followed the orders of the puzzling Dream Master and brought unexpected help. Her charges the Leprechaun Oilill, Puca Sean, Kelpie Sidheag, and Cloudmare Shyrra discovered a mortally wounded Kirrie. The Dreamraider led the motley group to a grotto hidden behind Alluring Falls. Kirrie drank from the Cup of Dark Knowledge and survived. Kirrie followed Yannuvia's path and returned to Alms Glen changed and empowered by Fire Magick. General Saligia of Aulgmoor mounted an offensive against the Drelves. Kirrie's comrades played an enormous role in swaying the course of the battle. In the guise of a Hippogriff, the puca Sean carried Kirrie to the Kiennites' Fort New Melphat. Kirrie held a piece of sulfur. Twenty-one phrases came together in her mind. Words welled up from the depths of her consciousness.

*"I give you my blood through which you will receive all you seek. You in turn give to me your all."*

Ǿ ∞ Ǿ

*Sean-hippogriff* labored to support the she-Drelve. Kirrie extended her left arm and uttered twenty-one phrases aloud in the dark language of *Grayness.* Gray auras surrounded her. General Saligia and Cu Seven rode away from the castle at a gallop and narrowly escaped. Kirrie crushed the sulfur and sent a white-hot ball of fire into New Melphat. Tremendous explosions followed. Unsatisfied she smashed another bit of sulfur, uttered the phrases again, and sent an even larger stream of Fire Magick into the structure. Another explosion followed. Anguished screams filled the air. Kirrie attacked a third and then a fourth time. New Melphat lay in molten rubble with no signs of life. Kirrie crushed another piece of sulfur.

The púca pleaded, "Kirrie, no more, please! It's done!"

Kirrie's eyes blazed. She sent a fifth Fire Spell into the rubble.

After each spell, the words filled her mind.

*"I give you my blood through which you will receive all you seek. You in turn give to me your all."*

Ǿ ∞ Ǿ

*"I give you my blood through which you will receive all you seek. You in turn give to me your all."*

Ǿ ∞ Ǿ

*"I give you my blood through which you will receive all you seek. You in turn give to me your all."*

Ǿ ∞ Ǿ

*"I give you my blood through which you will receive all you seek. You in turn give to me your all."*

Ǿ ∞ Ǿ

*"I give you my blood through which you will receive all you seek. You in turn give to me your all."*

Ǿ ∞ Ǿ

Five times the words filled Kirrie's mind.
Then...

*"You and I are one."*

Ǿ ∞ Ǿ

The General's party mounted on stone ponies rapidly retreated toward Aulgmoor. Kirrie's small group did not celebrate victory. Instead, Gaelyss and the Council of Alms Glen feared Kirrie's Fire Magick and ostracized her. Kirrie went to Green Vale to seek comfort among the Thirttene Friends, only to be branded "Fire Wizard" by the ancient caretaker the Tree Shepherd. Kirrie thereafter shared the title with Yannuvia.

A flash of redness surrounded the Amica, Oilill, Kirrie, and Cupid. A moment later the Dreamraider, Leprechaun, she-Drelve, and púca breathed familiar fragrant air. The red sand took them back to the red elm where the Sandman saved the Good Witch. Kirrie's hair had lengthened and grew browner. Oilill's beard was a bit longer but overall the leprechaun appeared no worse for the wear. Cupid felt stiff and sore and had several inches of hair growth. The large red elm, which served as a guest house in Alms Glen, was otherwise vacant. Kirrie peeked through the bark and noted only normal peaceful activity in the common area surrounding the big red tree. Two young mature she-Drelves talked near the tree. Quickly Kirrie learned they were little Betsy, who narrowly escaped the meandering Droll and her twin sister. The twins had matured!

Amica cautioned, "You've probably already noted the changes you've endured from traveling in the red and blue light. I must go now. Eleven changes of seasons have passed since we entered the grotto behind Alluring Falls."

Kirrie muttered, "So Yannuvia and the folk of Lost Sons have been gone thirteen years."

Amica stammered, "Uh, yes…"

Words formed in Kirrie's mind…

*"I give you my blood through which you will receive all you seek. You in turn give to me your all."*

Ǿ ∞ Ǿ

Amica said, "From here, getting these t**ds home is a simple task for me. What are your plans Kirrie?"

The she-Drelve replied, "There's nothing for me in Alms Glen. I may go to Meadowsweet and live amongst the Thirttene Friends at Green Vale. Perhaps I'll encounter Shyrra and search for the four stones that disappeared with the Sandman. It'd at least give me purpose."

Amica replied, "Whatever! We must go!"

The Good Witch grabbed Oilill and Cupid and vanished in an instant. Kirrie remained in the red elm for a while and peered through the thick bark. When opportunity presented, she exited the tree, slipped across the common area, and disappeared into the thick brush.

Eleven changes of seasons after the destruction of the Kiennish forts by the Fire Wizard Kirrie and the odd cherubic merchant, the Teacher Camille Aires discovered the four elemental stones (SSF, SSE, SSA, and SSW) in the foyer of the Old Orange Spruce.

Kirrie arrived in Green Vale. Taller trees and bushes rimmed the roughly circular Green Vale, but a valley filled with short shrubby plants dominated the area. A hill occupied the center of the valley. Bright green plush grassy moss extended several paces from the tree line and formed a border around the valley. At the edge of the green moss, the terrain followed a gentle fifteen-degree incline for thirty paces to the vale's floor. The gently rolling floor of Green Vale extended several hundred paces and circled the central knoll. A grassy upslope extended fifty paces from the floor to the top of the central hill. Many small rivulets coursed through the landscape. On top of the hillock a geyser erupted from the very center of the hill and bathed the trees with waters of many hues. After the geyser erupted for thirty-nine heartbeats, the thunder ceased and left the area quiet. Shrubby plants filled the hillsides and the floor of the Vale. None grew on the central hill. The plants did not grow in rows. Instead the plants were arbitrarily set in the gently rolling terrain. Very few other plants intermingled with the enhancing plants. Red, yellow, and orange colors typified foliage of the lands of the World of the Three Suns. The only exceptions were Green Vale and Emerald Island, where deep green plants dominated the flora.

Tears welled in Kirrie's eyes. She recalled words of encouragement she'd uttered to Gaelyss... *"Gaelyss, you have done so much for our people. Alms Glen survives. Though we suffered the loss of little Deirdre and noble Balewyn, we have the healthiest and most populous settlement in Drelvedom's history. More healthy people inhabit Alms Glen than any time in old Clarke and Blanchard's memory. Your spells protect and nurture us. Your brother is...was my friend. He angrily addressed the council and challenged you. He has...changed."*

Like Yannuvia... Kirrie had changed. Being in Green Vale and near enhancing plants comforted the former Teacher. Soon contingents of Drelves would arrive to harvest mature tubers. She approached the closest waist high plant and sang in low soothing voice. The plant curled its leaves and retracted its barely visible needle-like thorns. Kirrie then tenderly touched the spines of the upper leaves of the plant. The enhancing plant pulled its limbs upward and inward. This changed the plant from a full bush to a thin narrow plant. Kirrie then removed a small spade from her pack and knelt at the base of the plant. The ex-Teacher delicately inserted her spade into the ground, moved the digging instrument around the base of the plant, gently pulled the entire plant from the soil, held it aloft, and exposed its roots. The plant emitted gray auras. Kirrie expertly exposed several thumbnail sized tubers dangling from the uncovered roots. She gently pulled tubers from the roots, but very carefully left one tuber undisturbed. The she-Drelve then gently stroked the roots of the plant and carefully placed the plant back on the soft dark ground. The enhancing plant's roots plunged back into the soil. Kirrie sang again, and the little bush expanded its branches and reopened its red flowers. Kirrie munched on a purplish tuber and then walked up to the crest of the central hillock.

The ostracized erstwhile Teacher stood before the ancient Tree Shepherd in the circle of Thirttene Friends.

Ǿ ∞ Ǿ
**I, II, III, IV, V, VI, VII, VIII, IX, X, XI, XII, XIII**
∞ Ǿ ∞

**The Thirttene Friends**

Ǿ ∞ Ǿ
**I, II, III, IV, V, VI, VII, VIII, IX, X, XI, XII, XIII**
∞ Ǿ ∞

**Ǿ ∞ Ǿ I ∞ Ǿ ∞**

The Apple Tree…

**Ǿ ∞ Ǿ II ∞ Ǿ ∞**

The pear tree…

**Ǿ ∞ Ǿ III ∞ Ǿ ∞**

The snowberry bush…

**Ǿ ∞ Ǿ IV ∞ Ǿ ∞**

The purplanana bush…

**Ǿ ∞ Ǿ V ∞ Ǿ ∞**

The tree Sprite's home, the great green oak…

**Ǿ ∞ Ǿ VI ∞ Ǿ ∞**

The Rainbow luck bush…

**Ǿ ∞ Ǿ VII ∞ Ǿ ∞**

The Tree Shepherd…

**Ǿ ∞ Ǿ VIII ∞ Ǿ ∞**

The Jellybean bush…

**Ǿ ∞ Ǿ IX ∞ Ǿ ∞**

The gem bush…

**Ǿ ∞ Ǿ X ∞ Ǿ ∞**

The silver maple…

**Ǿ ∞ Ǿ XI ∞ Ǿ ∞**

The l'orange tree…

**Ǿ ∞ Ǿ XII ∞ Ǿ ∞**

The Sick Amore…

**Ǿ ∞ Ǿ XIII ∞ Ǿ ∞**

The toot and see scroll tree…

The Thirttene Friends…
The Tree Shepherd sent an icy telepathic, "Fire Wizard!"
Words formed in Kirrie's mind.

*"I give you my blood through which you will receive all you seek. You in turn give to me your all."*

Ǿ ∞ Ǿ

General Saligia's crushing defeat by the Drelves and their odd group of allies ended his dominance of the lands north of the River Ornash. The defeated General lost the support of Woodrow, Wilson, Calvin,

Coolidge, Theodore, Delano, and Roosevelt, leaders of the Seven Warrens of Kiennites. Discord grew among the ranks of the Kiennites. The Droll clans no longer followed his banner. For a time, the Drelves enjoyed a time of relative peace. What General Saligia's brother the High Shaman of Aulgmoor Melphat feared came to pass. Draiths, the attackers from the south, threatened Aulgmoor's domain far more than Drelvish Spellweavers. The Mender Fisher had spoken of the Draiths. One of the pale folk walked among and served the stealthy denizens of the Southern Mountains. Teacher Kirrie on her ill-fated ride upon a hippogriff noted the Droll-sized, bronze-skinned denizens of the south in combat with Drolls and Kiennites. Rangers saw the new folk from the mountains more frequently. For a time, only small numbers of Draiths appeared. Drolls and Kiennites made many unsuccessful sorties against the settlements of the Draiths. The northern allies were invariably beaten back, but oft times damaged the Draith's constructions. The enemies bypassed the dense Drelvish forests around Alms Glen. From those forests, the Drelves witnessed monumental battles on the Ornash Plain. Spellweaver Gaelyss reinforced the Magick protection of the forests around Alms Glen. Rangers watched the skies for the return of the cherub, misty Cloudmare, and Fire Wizard Kirrie. But season after season passed without their return. Camille Aires served diligently as Teacher and oversaw successful harvests of enhancing root tubers in Green Vale.

Alms Glen recovered and flourished under the protection of the Great Defender Gaelyss. Drelves sang by the campfires of the wondrous time when the Gray Wanderer drew near four times in a mere twenty-one seasons of the harvest. Stories told of the beauty of the Lone Oak and the power of mysterious gray stones. No word came of Yannuvia and the folk of Lost Sons.

## III. Events in the Underworld: Vydaelia and Graywood

The First Wandmaker Yannuvia and his followers traveled in blue light from Lost Sons to a massive underground grotto. The *translocated* Drelves made the land around the great underworld sea their home. Luminescent lichen provided light to a plethora of underworld fauna and flora. The marvelous lichen was confined to the area immediately around the great sea. The darkness of the caverns and passageways hindered exploration beyond the sea. The Spellweaver's Continual Light Spells, which he had cast upon staffs and wands, provided limited illumination beyond the great cavern. The intrepid group crossed paths with mysterious Dreamraiders. The transplanted Drelves encountered Carcharians, Duoths, Shellies, Bugwullies, Pollywoddles, Boxjellies, sea lions, Mountain Giants, cave wargs, and sea elves. Yannuvia had drunk from the Cup of Dark Knowledge, sipped the Seventh Nectar, walked in the gray light, and used the Dream Master's wand. Mender's blood had touched him. 13-limbed monsters, perplexing enemies, steadfast friends, and seductive temptresses complicated the Wandmaker's life. The Drelves found both allies and enemies among the Carcharians. Odd Duoths raided their onyum patch. The Central Sphere and its 88 satellites aided the First Wandmaker in creating powerful artifacts. Omega Stones and graparbles perplexed the group. The beautiful sea elf Piara and eight comrades arrived as fugitives from tyrannical Carcharian King Lunniedale. The Dreamraider provided help, but the cost of her help and ultimate motives remained obscure. Yannuvia made many difficult choices. Dreams made him aware of the Wandmaker's burden.

*"Guard well this orb. Fading of the sphere's light means…it's time to repay the debt you've incurred. Whether by you or the hundredth generation removed, yours is a debt that must be repaid…*

*"Placing the Central Sphere in the light of the Gray Wanderer will restore the orb's grayness."*

Over time Yannuvia created several wands. The wandmaker developed a small *Menderish* nodule in his left hand that enlarged with each creation. The red and blue tipped wand which facilitated their travel to the underworld became known as the Master Wand, and it was involved in the creation of all subsequent wands.

Yannuvia recorded each wand in *the Gifts of Andreas to the People of the Forest*, the Spellbook entrusted to all Spellweavers at the time of their nymph hood. Each Spellweaver added new spells and personal experiences to his Spellbook during his life's journey. The notation began with the Old Drelvish numeral I, indicating his being the first Wandmaker. Then the number of the wand in order of its creation was written in script rather than numeral. The wand's name and the unique command to activate its power followed. At the time of the Giant Amebus's attack on Vydaelia, Yannuvia had created 10 wands.

I. (one) Knock Wand with the command "**Cow vine cool ledge**."
II. (two) Wand of Lightning with the command "**Grove veer cleave land.**"
III. (three) Wand of Masonry with the command "**Wood row will son.**"
IV. (four) Wand of Levitation with the command "**Rich herd nicks son.**"
V. (five) Haste Wand, Wand of Speed, with the command "**Jar old ford.**"
VI. (six) Wand of Flight, Wand of Flying with "**Run nailed ray gun.**"
VII. (seven) The United Scepter of the Approximation, an exceptional artifact with command "**Abe Linkin**"
VIII. (eight) Wand of languages with "**yule less says grant**"
IX. (nine) Wand of Healing with "**rut fir ford bee haze**"
X. (ten) Wand of water breathing with "**herb art hoof ear.**"

Sea elf Piara felt a connection to her great-great grandmother and saw images through her ancestor's eyes. The mysterious exiled queen of Doug-less left Vydaelia to follow her intuition and hide her pregnancy, the result of her unwise tryst with the Wandmaker Yannuvia. Her journey cost the life of her four-armed Carcharian guardian Urquhart and resulted in her capture by grayish-green sea elves led by Commandant Inyra. Piara discovered her uncanny resemblance to the Gray Matron, the founder of Greywood, and the octagonal structure that served as her ancestor's resting place. The Good Witch appeared to Piara in a dream and described the inner working of the eight-sided edifice in great detail. The Good Witch had said the twin stone Piara wore afforded protection for entering the tomb and served as a focal point while inside the structure. No one had entered the tomb since the Gray Matron's passing. Piara gained entrance to the tomb and found the Gray Matron's journal and the black rod and stone that provided the building blocks for the structure. The journal described events in her ancestor's life and detailed the birth of Alexandrina and the building of the Mender's Tomb.

Four Xennic Stones surrounded the Mender Lou Nester and Gray Elves Victoria and Edward. A circle of gray stone appeared among the five stones of the stone circle that sat on the hillock in the middle of Gray Vale. A black rod and chunk of black stone appeared in the center of the circle. These were called the rod and stone of Ooranth. While Grayness enveloped the vale, Victoria's time to deliver came and her daughter Alexandrina was born in Gray Vale.

Edward and Victoria used the rod and stone of Ooranth to create building blocks. Though growing weaker, the Mender attended little Alexandrina while her parents worked. The sea elves constructed Lou Nester's tomb. Touching the small stone with the cylindrical rod and saying **"Jams Gar Field"** replicated the block. Running the rod over the newly formed replicate reshaped it. Alexandrina used an exceptional scepter UK and the rod and stone of Ooranth to create Graywood. The gray soil, odd gray trees, and gray light strengthened the folk who lived in Graywood.

The Good Witch told Piara a means of entering the tomb. The twin stone amulet allowed safe passage through the warding Glyphs that guarded the tomb. Piara gained entry to the structure. Graywood resident Agarn accompanied her and did not survive entering the tomb. The eight-sided edifice distorted both space and time. The tomb was bigger on the inside. Walls between the doors bore images of Piara's great-great-great grandmother and another who looked remarkably like the Mender Fisher… only the bloke in the tomb's image was paler. Three walls bore identical doors, which were not visible from the outside. Two sarcophagi made of black stone sat near the wall opposite the three doors. like the walls and doors. A simple black rod and little piece of black stone sat on the sarcophagus on the left. Another Twin Stone rested on a thick tome which sat beside the black rod. The twin stone mirrored the artifact Piara wore around her neck. A small purple bag lay beside the tome. A huge stone called heel stone dominated the area of the tomb opposite the sarcophagi. The heel stone was a single block of sarsen stone. It was sub-rectangular, with a minimum thickness of 2.4 meters. (A meter is 39.37 inchworm lengths.) It rose to tapered top 4.7 meters high. A further 1.3 meters was buried in the ground. Gray soil made up the floor of the tomb where the gray stone circle had formed and then disappeared. When the stone circle disappeared, Piara's means of exiting the tomb went with it. The rest of the floor was the same black stone that formed the walls and sarcophagi. The heel stone sat 77.4 meters from the sarcophagi and was nearly 27 degrees from the vertical. Its overall girth was 7.6 meters. It weighed 35 tons.

The she-Drelve Kirrie appeared to Piara in the tomb. She stood in for the Good Witch, who was suffering the early pangs of childbirth, again the fruits of a tryst with the Wandmaker Yannuvia. Kirrie surreptitiously gripped an Omega Stone. Words formed in Kirrie's mind. She said, "Then listen! Touching the heel stone thirteen times produces the gray circle that allows exit from the tomb to the stone circle on the hillock and also induces the formation of images on the three doors. Be wary of the doors. They open gates to other realms. Opening such gates requires precision. Making a mistake brings consequences. Traveling through gates oft comes at a price."

Piara asked, "What images form on the doors? Other realms? All visions I've seen through my great-great-great grandmother's eyes are of my world. Before I met the newcomers at Vydaelia I had no concept of 'other realms.' Where do the doors lead?"

Kirrie gripped the stone and said, "What lies beyond these doors does not concern you, Piara of Elder Ridge. Stick to your business at hand. You wanted to learn of your ancestry. The opportunity to do so has landed in your lap. If one makes a mistake while attempting to open the doors and chooses the wrong sequence…the door leads to a grotto behind a waterfall. Without a means to exit the traveler wastes away in the grotto. With a means to exit and a focal point one might end up… somewhere and sometime else."

Piara said, "Who are you?"

Kirrie said, "I'm another piece of your Wandmaker's past. Remember well what I've told you."

Kirrie placed a blue tile on the floor and stepped onto it. Blueness flashed through the tomb. But for Agarn's corpse Piara was alone. She picked up the second Twin Stone, black rod, black stone, and tome. She held the tiny bag of little weight. To her surprise, the bag accommodated the rod, stone, amulet, and tome.

There was nothing for it.

Piara went to the heel stone and touched the heel stone 13 times. Images formed on the three doors. An image of a red-bearded giant formed on one door. Another door bore an image of a tall man with a cherry red birthmark on his chin. An image of a female fire demon formed on the third. The gray stone circle reappeared in the center of the tomb! Piara stood in the center of the gray circle and tapped her left foot 13 times. Purplish auras surrounded her. In an instant she stood in the center of the Gray Vale Stone Circle outside the tomb in Gray Vale. Only young sea-elf guard Horton stood near the circle. Piara stepped off the gray circular stone and it disappeared.

Horton marveled, "You are finally back! We had given you up for lost. Commandant Inyra ordered one of us to stand guard."

Piara asked, "How long was I in the tomb?"

Horton replied, "A season of growth."

Piara asked, "How long is a season of growth?"

The young gray-green sea elf guard replied, "Sorry. It's the time required for a seedling to spring from one of our planted stones."

Piara said, "Time! How much time?"

Horton thought hard and replied, "My teachers say it's 832040 minute minuteman heartbeats."

Piara described the inner working of the eight-sided edifice in great detail. She left out Kirrie's visit, but did reveal the items she brought out of the tomb, including the second Twin Stone amulet, the black rod, clump of black stone, and the tome. Inyra listened intently.

The gray-green sea elf Commandant Inyra said, "We've heard stories of the Rod of Ooranth and Stone of Ooranth. They are said to be the artifacts used by the Gray Matron's parents to construct the tomb. The runes on the outside of the old tome are not sea elfish. I cannot decipher them."

Piara said, "I can. The runes say 'Alexandrina's memoirs.' They are written in the language of the Omega Stones."

Sea elf Liani said, "Say again?"

Piara said, "I am fluent in 17,711 languages. I can translate the writing in the tome."

Inyra asked, "Why weren't you injured?"

Piara said, "The amulet I wear provides protection. Marvelous little device! It helped guide me to my ancestor's realm, your Gray Vale, and its identical sister. I found its twin in the tomb."

Inyra asked, "Why were you within the tomb for 832040 heartbeats?"

Piara said, "From my perspective, I was only in the tomb for a very brief time."

Nurse Nila said, "I believe her story about the time. Her pregnancy is no further advanced than when we last saw her."

Inyra asked, "What is the power of the twin amulets?"

Piara said, "I don't know. Yet. I hope studying the tome will shed light on the power of the twin sister amulets. I held both amulets in the tomb, but only wore one."

Inyra said, "We now possess the second amulet. Perhaps you should place both around your neck."

Nila warned, "The visage of the Gray Matron on the tomb's door only wears a single amulet. Is it safe for her to wear both? Remember, she carries a child."

Piara said, "I'll do it."

Piara placed the second Twin Stone Amulet around her neck. Pleasant mauves auras enveloped the stones and a low pitch drone flowed from the artifacts.

Inyra asked, "What do you feel?"

Piara recalled the Dreamraider's words from her dream in Vydaelia:

*"Marvelous little device! It has an identical sister. It'll lead you to its twin. Keep it safe and hold it close. It'll both guide and protect you. Pay heed to the twin speak when the sisters are together. The sisters are the keys to unlocking many doors, dissuading Magick, and saving time."*

Perplexed Piara answered, "Nothing… I thought they'd communicate."

Inyra said, "Maybe I should hold one."

Piara removed the second Twin Stone from her neck and gave it to Inyra.

Liani shouted, "Commandant, we can't afford to lose you! Allow me!"

The Commandant ignored the warning, took the amulet, and placed it around his neck. Now intense gray auras surrounded Piara and Inyra.

The *Two Stones Effect* occurred!

The Twin Stones mimicked the larger Omega Stones and exerted the *Two Stones Effect* on the Commandant and Piara. Piara's *Menderish* nature did not prevent the effect. Inyra and Piara began to speak the unnerving language of the Omega Stones and spoke truthfully.

The *Three Stones Effect* occurred!

Piara and Inyra saw into one another's minds.

Piara said, "I don't understand. There are only two identical stones. This effect required three activated Omega Stones."

Inyra muttered in gibberish speech, "I see your Mind's image of the Omega Stones. These are not Omega Stones. But more than that… I see… everything you have said is true. Your baby's father is… the leader of Vydaelia! Your other child is the spawn of the liege of Doug-less! Piara of Elder Ridge, you do get around!"

Nila quizzically asked, "What are you saying?"

Piara replied, "I understand you. Two Omega Stones empower communication in an old dialect and compel the truth. Three Omega Stones enable the bearers to look into each other's mind. We never discovered the effect of four and five stones, and I never knew of more than five of them together. Now the Twin Stone 'speaks' to me. The Twin Stones mimic ALL effects created by multiple Omega Stones. Nothing special happens with four. Five stones produce a *Protection from Magick* effect. Six and seven do nothing special. Eight Stones effect enables *Continual Light*. I don't know what that means. No added effect from nine, ten, eleven or twelve Omega Stones, but thirteen stones produces *Time Saving Effect*. Time will remain constant when passing between realms. 14, 15, 16, 17, 18, 19, and 20 do nothing more. 21 Omega Stones will irreversibly form into a Xennic Stone. Xennic Stones helped the Gray Matron create UK. 88 revolve in the geodesic dome in Vydaelia."

Inyra said aloud, "It'd be hard to get twenty-one people carrying twenty-one rocks to do anything together. So it's mostly moot."

Piara thought, "You understand me. When we hold the Twin Stones, we need not speak aloud. The Twins Stones produce these effects as a pair, but apparently only if worn by two individuals. I wonder… I am not touching you."

Piara grasped Inyra's arm. The Commandant tensed briefly and then relaxed, and silently responded, "I know what you are doing. I feel no different."

Inyra said aloud, "Release me. I want to check distance between us. The Commandant walked toward the door, exited the cabin, and took a few steps outside into the Graywood common area. When he reached a distance of thirteen paces all discernible effects dissipated save a sense of the second twin stone's location.

He reentered the cabin and said, "You entered the tomb without being harmed, so the Protection from Magick is inherent in each Twin Stone. Time passed differently for you in the tomb, so the Time Saving effect requires both stones. We'll learn other effects by trial and error."

Piara said, "The tomb was brightly lit without an apparent source. Perhaps a single amulet can give light in a dark place."

Inyra asked, "What if you desire darkness?"

Piara said, "I suppose you *think* it off."

Nila muttered, "I haven't understood a word either of you have said."

Inyra insisted, "I want to see the inside of the tomb."

Nila said, "Her delivery time is nigh. Piara should rest and take nourishment."

Piara said, "I feel well. I'm not opposed to entering the tomb again, but it'll be more productive after I have read the tome. Allow me some time. It's several hundred pages of writing."

Inyra said, "I still can't read the writing on the tome."

Piara commented, "It's written in Mender and cursive chaotic script. My Menderish traits help me read languages. Apparently wearing a Twin Stone doesn't avail one the ability to read the language."

Piara studied the tome and learned, "These twin stones are two of triplets."

Ǿ ∞ Ǿ

In Vydaelia Clouse noted a drone from the Amulet he wore. The pink stone vibrated. Mauve auras enveloped the stone. The stone shrank and transformed to purplish gray color. The green guy said aloud, "Two of three sisters are reunited."

Ǿ ∞ Ǿ

The inner tomb's heel stone was identical to another in a distant place called Stonehenge. Touching the heel stone reproduced the gray circle that allowed exit from the tomb to the stone circle on the hillock and also induced the formation of images on the three doors. These images provided mechanisms to open gates to other realms. An image of a red bearded giant forms of one door, which leads to giants' realm. Another door bears an image of a tall man with a cherry red birthmark on his chin. The door leads to a stone circle at a place called Uragh Wood in a simple world. An image of a female fire demon forms on the third. It leads to a circle on a green island in a world of three suns. If one chooses the wrong key... the door leads to a grotto behind a waterfall. Without a means to exit the traveler wastes away in the grotto. With a means to exit and a focal point one might end up... somewhere and sometime else. Sometimes traveling through gates comes at a price.

Sea elf nurse Nila led the sea elf to the infirmary and tended her expertly. Purplish fruits and unguents eased Piara's pain. Nila assisted the birth of Piara's progeny. A beautiful pale green, pointed-eared little girl! She had smooth green skin like her mother. Her little pointed ears mimicked the Wandmaker. A little nodule sat at the base of her tiny sixth left finger, a trait shared with her father. She also had the Wandmaker's nose. Yannuvia's contact with the Mender Fisher led to the arrival of Clouse. The Wandmaker's tryst with Menderish Piara resulted in the birth of beautiful *Clouse-ish* tiny... the only name that came to Piara's mind... ... Alexandrina!

Clouse joined Piara in Graywood and the duo learned from The Gray Matron's journal. The inner tomb's heel stone was identical to the one in a place called Stonehenge, which the Gray Matron had visited after traveling through one of the doors in the tomb. Touching the heel stone thirteen times not only produced the gray circle that allows exit from the tomb to the stone circle on the hillock but also induced the formation of images on the three doors.

On the first door, an image of a red-bearded giant formed.

To open the gate, one places two twin stone amulets in the giant's eye sockets, inserting the stone in the left eye socket first. When the amulets are in place a huge ax appears in the giant's left hand. One touches the blade of the axe twice. The axe disappears and a dagger takes its place. One touches the dagger thrice. The dagger disappears and a gisarme appears. One touches the gisarme five times. The gisarme is replaced by a broad sword. One touches the broad sword eight times. A table made of blue wood appears in the tomb. A small cabinet filled with phials filled with varying colored liquids appears. The liquids are green, purple, uncolored, yellow, red, and green. The green potion is a potion of diminution. Drinking it reduces one's height to ten per cent its original. However, one's mass is not changed and he retains all attributes, including strength. The potions are additive. Drinking a second reduces to one per cent. The purple potions reverse the green. Drinking a purple potion does not increase your base size. It only tastes like grape juice. Uncolored potions are the trinity, the base of other potions. The clear potion has a slightly bitter taste. Yellow potions taste like pinanas, rich elongated yellow fruits. The yellow potion is highly nutritious. The red potion tastes like cherry juice. It enables one to control red giants and comes in handy in this realm. When the potions appear, one drinks in order uncolored, yellow, red, and green. This reduces your height. One then drinks the purple potion and regains his height. You then remove the amulets from the giant figure's eye sockets. The door opens. The potions protect one while passing through the gate. The amulet is superfluous.

That door led to giants' realm in a world of a single sun. The Gray Matron also visited this realm. The door in the tomb opens via a trap door beneath the bed in a room. The room is filled with man or elf-sized furniture and materials. The room has four walls of fifty feet. Bizarre tapestries and drawings cover the walls. Some depict a great sea in an underworld cavern illuminated by fluorescing ceilings. Our realm! Other drawings depict a sky filled by three suns, a dark sun, bright yellow sun, and a faint gray sun that almost filled the sky. Drawings of buildings in Graywood dominate the tapestries. The eight-sided tomb on the hill in Gray Vale dominates one tapestry. Figures of gray-green sea elves, the residents of Graywood, intermingle with the structures. It's a panorama of Gray Vale and its folk. Runes written in the language of the Omega and Twin Stones describe the structures. The Gray Matron placed tomes on book shelves, including the history of Gray Vale and the creation of the scepter UK. Another volume told of her exploration in the World of Three Suns and mentioned places like Ooranth, Alms Glen, Ornash, Mirror

Lake, Alluring Falls, and Aulgmoor. Still another spoke of black-robed monks from a place called Calamitous Forest and spoke of them as allies. The language of the Triplet Stones is similar to a writing called 'old Elfish." Powerful Magick protects the door on both sides. Passing through to get back into the tomb in Gray Vale requires either the Triplet Stones amulet or the sequence of drinking potions in the order, uncolored, yellow, red, green, and lavender.

The door leaving the entry room to the giant's realm is merely locked. Passing beyond the locked is deemed quite hazardous. Drinking a red giant control potion is highly recommended. The Gary Matron's journal says little of the realm beyond the locked door. The Gray Matron did not explore the Red Mountain dungeon.

Regarding the second door in the eight-sided tomb…

Touching the heel stone 13 times creates the figure of a tall man with a cherry red birthmark on his chin. The wayfarer's cowl hides much of his face. Differing runes from an old language on their hand-holds differentiated three otherwise identical staves that hover near the robed figure. The staffs aligned to the north, south, and east. Each of the three staves bore four sets of runes about their circumferences at their midpoints.

Ǿ ∞ Ǿ

The old language is from a world called Sagain. The runes of N, S, and E on ends of the artifacts represent direction. The triumvirates of runes at the staffs' midpoints were alien. The staves represent three of a set called *"The Staves of the Four Winds."*

Opening the door requires three Triplet Stone amulets. They must touch the hand-holds of the three hovering staffs. When this is done, another blue wood table appears. It has a shamrock, sprig of mistletoe and a bit of wet red sand on it. One must take up the shamrock and mistletoe and throw the red sand onto the door. The red sand allows safe passage through the gate.

This door led to a stone circle at a place called Uragh Wood in a simple world of a single sun and moon. The circle at Uragh Wood is identical to the Gray Vale Stone Circle outside the tomb in Gray Vale. When you got to Uragh Circle, you placed a shamrock and a sprig of mistletoe in the center of the circle. You touched the monolith, then one of the little stones. You waited a while and then touched the monolith twice. Then you touched another stone thrice. One touched the monolith five times, followed by touching a third little stone eight times. Next it was back to the monolith to touch it thirteen times. Then it was to the fourth stone twenty-one times. You went the monolith again and touched it thirty-four times. Lastly you went to the final stone and touched it fifty-five times. After eighty-nine heartbeats, you received a signal from the Sandman. The Sandman appeared to the Gray Matron, but sometimes the three staves appeared alone.

The three staffs appeared identical save one thing. At the tip of each staff a single rune appeared. The Sandman aligned the staffs to the north, south, and east. The differing runes signified these directions. He placed the artifacts in the exact center of Uragh Stone Circle and allowed them to touch at their bases. If the Sandman wasn't there, the staves appeared and did it anyway. Each of the three staves bore four sets of runes about their circumferences at their midpoints.

Ǿ ∞ Ǿ

When the three staves touched they emitted an eerie purple aura that persisted for a time. The Sandman counted to 144, and a gray featureless stone appeared at the point where the three staves came together. If he didn't appear, one just waited for the stone to appear. The three staves rose from the ground and moved into the sandman's flowing dark robe or just disappeared if he wasn't there. Red liquid oozed from the gray stone and soaked the soil around the little rock. Sometimes the sandman spoke in riddles, and sometimes he simply counted to 144 and then stared aimlessly toward the west. When he finished counting the stone disappears. He then allowed you to gather the soaked sand. When the Gray matron received the gift of the sand, he said to her, "Remember to thank the Staves of the Four Winds, the Windward Staves, children of the Bloodstone, the Source of Magick."

The Staff of the West Wind, also called the Staff of Stone, was missing. The tall Sandman wore a robe and cowl that hid his face. His most telling features were his fathomless eyes. The Gray Matron learned nothing of the missing staff.

The red sand allowed safe passage back to the circle in Gray Vale. One sprinkled red sand in the center of the circle and reversed the pattern of touching the stones. The Triplet Stone amulets also provided protection.

An image of a female fire demon formed on the third door. It led to a circle on a green island in a World of Three Suns, from which the Vydaelians hail. Touch one of the Triplet Stone amulets to her left hand, then another to her right. Press the third to her lips. The visage changed to a kindly matronly female with smooth skin and flowing hair. Touch an amulet to her right hand, then her left hand and the third to her forehead. The door opened. The table with the phials of liquid appears. One drank potions in the order uncolored, yellow, red, green, and purple. Drinking the potions provided protection. Wearing the amulet also availed some protection.

"You stand on a circle of flat, smooth gray stone near a replica of the heel stone at Stonehenge. A little yellow sun danced around an amber sky. Light ran from a large shadowy spiraling hole overhead and a deep gray speck appeared low in the sky. Miniscule gray rays from the tiny speck enhanced the grayness of the stone. When you step off the circle of gray stone, the stone circle disappears. Lush green foliage including bracken, bilberry, bell heather, and ling heather surrounded the area. A wood white, the prettiest moth in all the Emerald Island, fluttered about. To get back home, you returned to this place. The heel stone's twin served as focal point. You touched the false heel stone thirteen times; went to a point thirteen paces from the stone, and sprinkled a bit of red sand. The gray circle then reappeared under your feet. Next thing you stood in the middle of the Uragh Stone Circle. You get back to Gray Vale by following the same process as the second door."

If one chose poorly and made a mistake in opening the doors, the doors led to a grotto behind a waterfall. Without a means to exit the traveler wasted away in the grotto. With a means to exit and a focal point one might end up… somewhere and sometime else. Traveling through gates came at a price.

The Wandmaker Yannuvia led a force of Vydaelians, Duoths, Carcharians, Graywood sea elves, and sea lions against the Carcharian stronghold Doug-less. The allied force employed a captured trebuchet and Giant Amebus Bombs to initiate the assault. The Wandmaker unleashed a brutal Fire Magick assault. Doug-less was utterly destroyed. Its monarch King Lunniedale escaped. Troglodytes filtered into the wetlands near Graywood after the fall of Doug-less. Commandant Inyra refused them entry to Gray Vale and Graywood proper. Many trogs were given simple tasks to do in the outlying farms. Given direction troglodytes worked hard. The beasts were easily charmed and controlled.

Yannuvia's wand making powers ebbed. Until Grayness returned he only created only one type of wand, a wand of Magick Missiles. These wands were as powerful as arrows and shored up our defenses.

Kirrie informed the Wandmaker, "There are five sibling stones. Any two become Twin Stones and activate their effects. Piara carries one. Another rested in the Mender's Tomb and now hangs around Graywood Commandant Inyra's neck. Clouse wears a third courtesy of the fumbling Mountain Giant and by way of the Carcharian commander Fishtrap. I wear a fourth. Fisher brought the fifth to Lost Sons. It revolves around the Central Sphere and provides a focal point."

Yannuvia said, "The Xennic Stone differs. It's larger and can't be differentiated from its four-score and seven fellows."

Kirrie answered, "The Twin Stones have the ability to change their shapes and appearance. They become invisible if they chose. The giant's amulet was large and pink for a time."

The Rod of Ooranth and Stone of Ooranth appeared to the Mender Lou Nester and Alexandrina's parents in Gray Vale. The origin of the artifacts and their name remained unknown. The command **"Jams Gar Field"** activated the power of the Rod of Ooranth. The Rod and Stone of Ooranth came to Vydaelia, where the artifacts were placed in the first geodesic dome under the shadow of the Central Sphere and 89 stones. Wandmakers accepted stewardship of the artifacts, but no one ever used them. The command **"Jams Gar Field"** no longer activated the wand's power. Consensus held removing the artifact from the Mender's Tomb disrupted the flow of Magick within the black rod. Unwonted effect of Magick…?

From humble beginning rose a great city Vydaelia. The people of Vydaelia serendipitously discovered violet glass shards that gave the means to see their way in the dark caverns beyond the great cavern. Yannuvia's staunch ally Sergeant Major Klunkus discovered the first shards of the opaque purple stone. Yannuvia's followers fashioned the shards into lenses. The wondrous lenses heightened the dimness of the caverns. The Third Wandmaker Carinne gave the lenses the name Lightchangers.

The First Wandmaker's contemporaries had set into motion procedures and made alliances that sustained the community. Gray-green sea elves moved to Vydaelia in numbers and the sea elves' domain in Gray Vale become a sister city of Vydaelia. The annals of Vydaelia detailed its people's history. The chronicle rested in the library in the first geodesic dome that housed the central sphere and the 88 stones that circled it. 32 Wandmakers had followed Yannuvia. Yannuvia's green lookalike Clouse served briefly and then yielded to Carinne, Yannuvia's daughter by his slain life-mate Morganne. Sea elf Piara and her exceptional daughter Alexandrina assisted young Carinne. Magick touched the early Wandmakers. Time dulled the grayness of the 89 stones in the first geodesic dome. Later Wandmakers had limited skills. Vydaelia became evermore dependent upon the life-giving vessels in the second great geodesic dome that housed the seven vessels and indebted to those who supplied the needed raw materials for the nectars produced by the vessels. The Vydaelians changed.

# 1.

# 34th Wandmaker

The black rod fascinated an apprentice to the 33rd Wandmaker Fradee. All wandmakers bore the wandmaker's burden and suffered the telltale dream during their tenure as wandmaker. Young Ubough listened to the descriptions of Fradee's dream. The youth carried the black rod to his chamber and studied its simple form. No runes... no scratches... like others before him, Ubough clutched the wand and muttered phrases to no avail. The rod remained inactive. Ubough tired of the futile exercise and stretched out on his cot. Sleep came. Shapeless grayness entered his dreams.

Wisps...
Threads...
Threads of Magick...
Threads of fate...
Threads of time...
Threads connecting worlds ...
Dreams connecting worlds ...
Dreams of Magick...
The Magick of Dreams...
Magick connecting dreams...
Magick connecting worlds...

*Grayness...*

Words formed in Ubough's mind. "Accept the gift of grayness for your people."

The sleeping Ubough managed, "This is not the Wandmaker's dream."

The intimidating voice replied, "No, my servant. This is your call to Grayness. Your call to be a brother of Magick."

Ubough replied, "In my mind I see words, phrases, thoughts that are new to me and without meaning."

Speaking in a dream…
Interacting with one's dream…
Hearing one's dreams and responding…
Speaking and hearing one's dreams respond…

The voice answered, "You will understand when you awaken."

Ubough asked, "Who are you?"

The shapeless form answered, "You are visited by the grayness of Andreas. You may call me Xenn."

Ubough said, "You are only a dream. You are not real."

The voice answered, "In time, you will understand. Even now, it will become clearer when you awaken. You must carry the Rod of Ooranth to the upper world. Grayness will restore its power and enhance you, Spellweaver Ubough."

Ubough answered, "Now I'm reminded this is but a dream. I'm merely a wandmaker's apprentice. Spellweavers are born to my ancestors the Drelves only in the time of Approximation."

Grayness replied, "You will be reborn when you stand in the gray light. A gift awaits your awakening. Study it well. It'll show you the way to the surface world. Rest well my servant. "

The grayness left his dreams. Ubough's dreams rekindled memories both good and bad. The apprentice awakened. A small phial sat on his bedside table. Runes on the phial caught his eye.

Ǿ ∞ Ǿ

Grayness visited Ubough's dreams and told him to carry the black rod and stone to the surface world. The visitor said there'd be a gift. The enigmatic runes graced many artifacts known to Vydaelia. Ubough removed the blue stopper from the little bottle and sniffed the thick liquid inside. The aroma mimicked Mender's sleep poultice. The pale healers commanded great knowledge of natural and herbal remedies. For instance, sleep poultice contained thirteen herbs and spices. Specifically, valerian root, dream fruit, passionless fruit, booderries, byneberries, melon toning, butter fly, slumber berry, nodding ham, kava kava, lavender, rose petals, and a live cricket. The identity of the ingredients was commonplace knowledge. Only Menders knew the secret of mixing the ingredients and creating the cataplasm. There was nothing for it. Ubough lifted the phial to his lips and quaffed the thick gray liquid in a few gulps. The mixture tasted like smoky molasses and warmed the Wandmaker's apprentice. Details of the route from ruined Doug-less to the upper world through the dangerous giants' realm appeared in his mind.

Ubough discovered an avenue to the upper world via the ruined Carcharian stronghold Doug-less, but the elders of Vydaelia forbade exploration of Doug-less. Ubough slipped through Vydaelia's opened outer curtain gate and traveled along the shore of the great sea to the ruins of Doug-less. He defied the laws of his predecessors and elders of Vydaelia, stepped through the forbidden door in the passageway in the ruins of Doug-less, followed the passage, walked onto the surface, and stood in the amber light of the upper world. Doing so aged him thirty years. Lightchangers dimmed the light of the upper world. Whilst the young renegade Wandmaker's apprentice stood in the yellow-orange-red foliage, the amber light changed to gray. The black rod emitted a low-pitched hum. Ubough held the rod in his left hand. The rod changed to an ashen gray color. Thoughts entered Ubough's mind.

The rod meld to his hand and burned his flesh. Ubough winced. Deep maroon fluid oozed from the now gray rod.

Wisps...
Threads...
Threads of Magick...
Threads of fate...
Threads of time...
Threads connecting worlds ...
Dreams connecting worlds ...

Dreams of Magick…
The Magick of Dreams…
Magick connecting dreams…
Magick connecting worlds…
Dream raiders…
Elf pressure…
Albtraum…
Albträume, elf dreams, nightmares…
Albträume...

Ǿ ∞ Ǿ

A guttural voice filled his mind.

*"I give you my blood through which you will receive all you seek. You in turn give to me your all."*

Ǿ ∞ Ǿ

Quirk of Magick… Ubough now understood the working of the artifact. The rod returned to its dark black color. New commands activated its powers. The command required to duplicate the black stone was now, **Hand rue jack son**. The artifact revealed other powers. **Frank land pierce** triggered the artifact's Death Spell**. Tea ore door rose veldt** triggered True Seeing. Merely holding the artifact equated to a Languages Spell. The grayness around Ubough deepened. The wandering sun Andreas drew near the land and bathed the world with its gray light. The Grayness awakened additional forces in Ubough's mind. Odd thoughts and uninterpretable phrases filled his thoughts.

The wandmaker's apprentice narrowly avoided detection by a roaming giant. The giant walked past the youthful Vydaelian and entered the bush. Shouts erupted. A group of bronze-skinned seven-foot-tall blokes attacked the eleven-foot-tall giant and smote him with weaponless attacks. The powerful warriors did not see young Ubough. He scurried back into the passage and made his way along the dangerous passageways back to ruined Doug-less and then to Vydaelia. His walkabout incurred the wrath of the elders, and he endured a tirade from the Wandmaker Fradee. Ubough retreated to his small quarters in the inner ward of Vydaelia. He lived in a cottage near the 4th dome, which housed the odd chrysalis that had encased the first Wandmaker Yannuvia now for 987 years. Vydaelia had changed in those many years. Ubough read and reread the chronicles and longed to regain the powers of the early Wandmakers. His zeal kept him at odds with the leaders of the community. His most recent escapade had led to unprecedented beratements. Ubough entered his humble chambers and collapsed on his bed. Sleep came quickly. Redness invaded Ubough's dreams.

Wisps…
Threads…
Threads of Magick…
Threads of fate…
Threads of time…
Threads connecting worlds …
Dreams connecting worlds …
Dreams of Magick…
The Magick of Dreams…
Magick connecting dreams…
Magick connecting worlds…
Dream raiders…
Elf pressure…
Albtraum…
Albträume, elf dreams, nightmares…
Albträume...

Ǿ ∞ Ǿ

Redness cleared. A Drelvish female sat upon a wyvern. The visage duplicated a mural on the wall of the second geodesic dome in Vydaelia. The she-Drelve in the mural played an important role in the early history of Vydaelia. In his dream, Ubough looked upon an image from Vydaelia's past. The she-Drelve spoke, "Do you have any a** left? You took a rather nasty rebuking."

Ubough said, "I broke the rules. I had it coming. What does my derriere have to do with anything? I know your face but not your name. Who are you?"

Kirrie said, "I'm another piece of your First Wandmaker's past. Remember well what I'm going to tell you."

Ubough muttered, "The Chronicles of Vydaelia mention Dreamraiders. Everyone knows the Wandmaker's dream. Long ago the Good Witch saved Vydaelia from a triskaidekapod and Giant Amebus. Are you the Good Witch? I'm only the Wandmaker Fradee's assistant, and I've fallen from grace. Why do you invade my dreams?"

Kirrie spoke, "I followed your first Wandmaker's path. We walked together in the light of the three suns and shared many childhood memories, including the Lone Oak, Invisimoss, Sergeant Major Rumsie, cleaning boots, and Tree Herder Old Yellow. Fire Magick touched us. Our people rejected us. The patriarch of Green Vale and caretaker of the Thirttene Friends the Tree Shepherd deems us Fire Wizards. I have killed more Drolls and Carcharians than Yannuvia."

Ubough said, "Show me other images, Dreamraider. I may as well enjoy your visit."

Kirrie answered, "I don't have the ability to change my look once I have appeared. I am Kirrie, a sister of Grayness and only a messenger. Grayness binds you and me. We are brother and sister. You have stood in the Gray Light of Andreas. You drew your first breaths in the surface world in the gray light. You are reborn. Magick touches you, Ubough of Vydaelia. Grayness sends you a gift. When you awaken, you'll understand the meaning of the phrases coursing through your mind. Fare well, Ubough of Vydaelia."

Red lights flashed around the image. The dreaming Wandmaker's assistant watched her eyes. Kirrie's image did not speak again. Blueness surrounded her and she faded from Ubough's mind's eye.

Ubough awakened and found a small quantity of sulfur. Jumbled phrases ran through his mind. The phrases sorted into the incantation of Fire Magick. Ubough held the sulfur. Fire wizard!

Ubough lost his youth, but found Magick. Thereafter when he slept and dreamed, spells appeared in his mind. The light of Magick burned brightly in Ubough. Spellweavers were born during Approximations of Andreas. Ubough's second birth forever changed the Wandmaker's apprentice. Dreams left him stronger. Yannuvia, the founder of Vydaelia and first Wandmaker, was Spellweaverish, Menderish, Drelvish, and Wandmakerish. Ubough was Spellweaverish and Wandmakerish.

The First Wandmaker Yannuvia's "Menderish" side required his entering a pharate state called "confinement." During Yannuvia's prolonged confinement, the light had dimmed in succeeding generations. Wandmakers had become short-lived manufacturers of trinkets. But, in Ubough, the bright light returned. Ubough's creations rivaled those of great Yannuvia. His explorations of the underworld had yielded great treasures usually discovered at locations depicted in his dreams. Grayness gifted the activating commands and uses for the black rod and cube of black stone. Ubough followed the footsteps of Yannuvia, Clouse, Carinne, and 30 others and became 34$^{th}$ Wandmaker of Vydaelia.

Dreams directed Ubough to return to the surface. War between the Giants and their bronze-skinned enemies had filled Ubough's journey with danger. The Wandmaker edged his way along the passageways from one hiding place to another. Ubough carried a little brown pouch, a wondrous Bag of Holding, which was an heirloom from the First Wandmaker. Yannuvia came into possession of the artifact in the storied grotto entered through an exceptional portal behind Alluring Falls. The "Bag of Concealment" surprisingly had little weight. Adding items did not change the bag's weight and shape. Items conformed to the size of the bag's opening when touching the leather-like artifact. The little bag was bigger on the inside and contained many artifacts, including a tome with raised runes on its soft vellum, spell book, two phials filled with green liquid, two phials filled with lavender fluid, a large bluewood table the height and breadth of a Drelve, a cabinet made of similar blue wood, and 13-inchworm-length sided squares of odd blue and red stones. The spell book's cover was velvety soft, and the raised runes were smooth to the touch. Flashes of light emanated from the tome if it was removed from the bag. The runes on the tome began to glow and produce beams of colored light. Appearing in the order of red, orange, yellow, green, blue, indigo, and violet, the beams danced around. One felt dread and uncertainty when holding the spell book. When someone placed both hands around the book's binding and lifted the volume, the nigh weightless thick text shrank to fit comfortably in his hands. The spell book of Dark Magick's title read 'Death by Fire.'" The book reduced its size and entered the bag!

His knowledge of the route abetted him. Thundering footsteps approached from the rear. The Wandmaker crowded into a narrow crevice in the rocky passageway.

Ubough cowered in the crevice. **Several** giants urgently ambled past the 34th Wandmaker of Vydaelia. Some assisted wounded comrades. Pressed back into the rocky crevice, Ubough's mind wandered and revisited his dreams. Time was difficult to measure in the underworld. Menders and Menderish sorts shared ability to measure time and physical parameters. The unvarying beat-to-beat interval of the *minute* minuteman's heart gave a constant increment of time. In the underworld, there was no day or night, no light, amber, and dark period. In Vydaelia an artifact called the Day Glass measured time in increments equal to the light and dark periods on Parallan.

A lumbering giant kicked a loose stone. The stone flew across the corridor and struck Ubough's finely made tunic. The giant's keen senses detected the soft sound. The beast towered thrice Ubough's height, grasped an ugly thick broad blade, turned its hideous head rapidly from side to side, and sniffed the corridor's stale air. Perhaps the stench of the flowing ichors of the giant's wounded comrades covered Ubough's scent. Ubough clutched the black rod. The giant detected him and menacingly advanced. There was nothing for it. Ubough extended the black rod and uttered **"frank land pierce," the** phrase imbedded in his memory but never before spoken. The darkness of the corridor obscured most of the Death Spell's aura. The giant's heart stopped and the hulking creature fell. Ubough moved quickly ahead. Lightchangers augmented his vision and he detected an opening in the opposite side of the twenty paces wide hallway. The corridor was at least the height of four Vydaelians stacked atop one another… a little taller than the giants.

Ubough rushed past the large body of the fallen giant and heard movement ahead. Quickly he dashed into the opening. Overwhelming stench disgusted him. Three giants dashed past him. Ubough was in a twenty-by-twenty pace chamber, which was evidently a storage area for the carcasses of victims of the giants that had not yet graced the big beasts' tables.

The three giants rushed to their fallen comrade. The most adorned of the three quickly turned and rushed to the opening of Ubough's hiding place. The Vydaelian squeezed between the carcass of a cave deer and a partially eaten stone eel. Convinced the grotto was clear of enemies, the massive beast returned to his mates.

Ubough clutched the rod, which was more a lifeline with each passing moment and concentrated. The rod emitted an imperceptible black mauve aura and activated Comprehend Languages. Ubough now understood the giants' guttural language.

"Not a mark on 'im!" said the giant that crouched over the body of the fallen giant.

"I told Gruggle he was too old to fight Draiths. He should have stayed with the females," growled the giant who had checked Ubough's hiding place.

"Fenytek, you know as well as I do that King Krable has pressed everyone into service. In case you didn't notice, we just got our butts kicked out there!" the third giant muttered.

"Topmacks! You blowhard! We might have fared better had you fomented a better plan! They baited us! And we fell for it! You ordered us to charge into three of 'em! Thirty others were just waitin'!" the kneeling giant growled.

"If I wanted your opinion, I would give it to you, Tegrah Tall! Your name belies your deeds. It's only the luck of having tall parents that makes you a half a finger taller than anyone else. You should have been called the teller of tall tales," Fenytek growled.

Tegrah the Tall harrumphed, "I'm glad it's you, Fenytek, and not I, who must inform King Krable of this debacle. With old Gruggle's demise, we've now lost eight on this foray! You jest at my height, but were you not old Krable's spawn, you'd not be in command."

The third giant Topmacks raised a thick furry sixth finger, shushed his quarreling comrades, and said, "We may have been followed!"

The commander Fenytek chided, "You old fool! You are older than this pile of rubbish lying before us! Draiths can't descend into the depths. They can't see in the dark. Their torches can't reach these depths! As far as our 'debacle' goes, I have learned the location of their females and young. Yes, we lost a few comrades, but we learned much in return. So Krable, my father, will laud my efforts. Now, if both of you will grovel before me, I'll forgive your impudence and impotence in battle. I might even give you a bigger ration of ale. You may start begging now."

Topmacks and Tegrah the Tall sighed and then whimpered together.

"I'm sorry, boss," Tegrah the Tall, whined.

"I'm sorry, too, boss," Topmacks chimed in.

"That's more like it," Fenytek gloated. "Now let's get this garbage out of the corridor. We'll put him in storage."

"With the carrion, boss?" Topmacks queried.

"Isn't he carrion? He won't make the mush taste much worse," Fenytek grunted.

Ubough's stomach turned. He pushed further into the disgusting grotto and managed to stay out of sight. The commander Fenytek, taller Tegrah the Tall, and old Topmacks unceremoniously dumped Gruggle's body onto the pile of carrion, turned away, and rushed back into the hallway.

Ubough struggled free from the carnage within the grotto, went to the opening, and listened intently. The three giants were out of sight and sound. He crept into the hallway and moved down a few paces and found another small grotto. It was empty and too small for a giant. The fatigued Wandmaker slumped down against the wall and took some dried ration.

Ubough chewed on dried booderries and sighed. Conflicts raged in the early years. Yannuvia had allied with gray-green sea elves, sea lions, and Duoths to crush Carcharians. Mender's Blood touched and changed the First Wandmaker. Yannuvia was Drelvish, Spellweaverish, Menderish, Wandmakerish, greenish, grayish, older than his stated age, and more complex than anyone who lived before him. The Mender Fisher and Menderish Clouse led Yannuvia into the outer dome and the Wandmaker entered the pharate state in which he remained nigh a millennium later. Time had taken Vydaelia's founders. Sea elves integrated into the complex community. The seven vessels provided nourishment. People became what they ate and drank.

Ubough's thoughts drifted to the chamber of the 89 stones, the domed room where he had spent so much of his time as Wandmaker. His predecessors had adhered rigidly to the elders' guidelines. Elders deemed Ubough a rebel and renegade. Ubough ignored them and followed the suggestions of his dreams. Repeatedly he disregarded the warnings of the council and elders and explored the passageways extending into the darkness away from the lighted sanctuary of Vydaelia. Ubough had received training given all young Wandmakers. This included forays into the upper passages to peer through one-way mirrors into the upper world. Vydaelians wore Lightchangers to protect their sensitive vision. Magick barred passage through the polished mirrors. Young Ubough stared into the amber light and yearned to feel its effects. His dreams directed him to the dangerous route through ruined Doug-less, the only known path to the upper world.

A dream told Ubough to remove the arm-length fingerbreadth thick black rod from its hidden location in the geodesic dome that housed the 89 stones. The artifact remained inactive since Elder Piara had sent it to Vydaelia from Graywood. Ubough's dream provided instructions for removal of the device from the recessed area in the chamber's wall. Wandmaker Fradee conducted a cursory search for the black rod, but given its lack of utility the Vydaelians wasted little energy in searching for it. For a time Ubough kept his possession of the black rod and little block of stone that accompanied it secret. Dreams directed his first trip to the surface and awakened both the Rod of Ooranth and Magick in Ubough. Ubough understood the working of the artifact. The rod returned to its dark black color. Deep red liquid oozed from the rod. Words appeared in Ubough's mind.

*"I give you my blood through which you will receive all you seek. You in turn give to me your all."*

Ǿ ∞ Ǿ

Ubough New commands activated the powers. The command required to duplicate the black stone was now, **Hand rue jack son**. The artifact revealed other powers. **Frank land pierce** triggered the artifact's Death Spell**. Tea ore door rose veldt** triggered True Seeing. Merely holding the artifact equated to a Languages Spell. Dreams hinted at other powers, and Ubough knew he only had scratched the surface of the artifact's secrets. Ubough became the 34$^{th}$ Wandmaker when Fradee passed away. He named young Clarissa, a descendant of Yannuvia, his apprentice. Ubough used the wondrous device to augment his given skills and accomplished deeds far beyond those of his predecessors. The newly installed Wandmaker announced he had "found" the Rod and Stone of Ooranth. His announcement was met with skepticism.

The 34th Wandmaker continued his clandestine forays beyond the outposts established by the forefathers of Vydaelia into the realm above the underworld caverns. Ubough transferred much of the mundane duties of Wandmaker to his very worthy and qualified successor and apprentice Clarissa, who had been designated the 35th.

Clarissa performed duties assigned to apprentice Wandmakers. Most important was preparation of the building blocks for Centurions' weapons, war wands. The first three Wandmakers, Yannuvia, Clouse, and Carinne, Yannuvia's spawn by Morganne of Meadowsweet were prolific producers of exceptional wands. Each stone produced a wand. During the added grayness of an Approximation multiple stones aided in the creation of exceptional devices. One such artifact was the United Scepter of the Approximation (USA), with the command "**Abe Linkin**."

The wands were essential to the successful operation of the underworld city, such as the production of the nutrients specific for each specific class of Vydaelians and the weapons the city guards demanded. Magick of the wands was finite. With time, the devices waned ever so slightly in their power. Denizens of the underworld caverns were often subjected to either servitude or gracing the tables of the underworld city's inhabitants. Subjugated troglodytes carried out much of the city's manual labor.

Repeatedly the council of elders demanded Ubough devote his time to tasks as Wandmaker. But few could argue with the 34th Wandmaker's successes. For the first time in memory, the devices created in the chamber of the 89 stones by Ubough and Clarissa were more powerful than the preceding generation's devices. Ubough ignored the demands of the council and persisted in his explorations. He explored the underworld, the upper world, and…the world of his dreams.

Ubough came to eagerly anticipate sleep. In sleep, he learned new dweomers. His dreams suggested he make further exploration and he followed his dreams' suggestions. Spells came to him. Then the inevitable happened. The dream dreaded by the Wandmakers came to him.

Wisps…
Threads…

Threads of Magick...
Threads of fate...
Threads of time...
Threads connecting worlds...
Dreams connecting worlds...
Dreams of Magick...
The Magick of Dreams...
Magick connecting dreams...
Magick connecting worlds...
Dreamraiders...
Elf pressure...
Albtraum...
Albträume, elf dreams, nightmares...

Ubough stood alone and stared at the slowing rotating central stone. The gray spherical six-foot diameter central sphere dominated the chamber of the gray stones, where 33 Wandmakers had practiced their rare craft. Eighty-eight identical smaller stones revolved around the massive gray stone. The fourscore and eight smaller stones moved at precisely the same speed in counterclockwise orbits in the same plane. Each small stone was 1/88th the size of the large central stone. Some indistinguishable gray rocks shared orbital paths. Nearest the central stone, one small stone revolved in an orbit with twice the diameter of the central stone. Another single stone coursed through an orbit of thrice the diameter of the big stone. Next two stones circled in four times the diameter of the central stone. The pair maintained the same speed and kept a constant separation. Then three stones coursed through five times the diameter of the big rock. Then five stones circled at an orbit of six diameters. Eight stones circled at seven diameters. Thirteen flew around the inner stone at eight diameters. Twenty-one circled at nine diameters. Finally, thirty-four circled at ten diameters. Thus, the outermost of the small stones circled at a constant speed in an orbit of thirty feet radius. Individual stones maintained a constant distance from the central stone and those that shared its orbit. The furthest stones were twenty-seven feet away from the central stone. The big stone maintained a position precisely in the center of the chamber. It sat above the floor so that its center was thirty-four feet above the floor. This allowed the little stones to maintain their orbits without striking the floor.

The eighty-nine stones bore identical symbols.

Ǿ ∞ Ǿ

The symbols were part of the stones. Ubough noted the runes on the stones emitted their customary grayness. Ubough had worked in the chamber of the stones for many seasons. The eighty-nine stones had never changed.

Until now…

The Central Gray Stone ominously left its central location and eerily wobbled downward and approached the lone figure in the chamber. The small stones froze in position. The symbols and grayness faded from the little stones. The Central Stone's grayness also faded as it neared. Though faint, the symbols remained.

Instinct told the Wandmaker to flee, but he felt his feet were fixed to the floor. Ubough could not run away. Chills coursed down his spine. The chamber became hot, and then cold, and the Wandmaker labored to breathe. The six-foot diameter sphere stopped precisely three feet from his face. The faint symbols disappeared and an image formed in the usually smooth gray surface of the slowly rotating sphere. Though he wanted to close his eyes, Ubough could not turn his gaze from the horrific face that filled the surface of the sphere.

A fell voice rose from the image and permeated the air, "The time has come today. You must repay the debt of your forebears. You're indebted for the first wand. The fading of the central stone and activation of this dweomer mean I am vanquished. If we are having this conversation, the implausible has happened. If I have diminished, you will diminish. Your people will suffer and eventually perish. You can restore the Magick of the sphere and the greatness of your people. You must take the treasured Central Stone to the surface world when the gray sun draws nearest. The gray light will restore its power… and your power to create. You cannot restore *me*, but you can continue my *line*! Carry my seed to the light of the gray sun Andreas!"

Why did this befall him?

This night Ubough despised the title Wandmaker and regretted having the power to create the wands carried by the Vydaelians.

The image in the sphere changed…to the face of the Wandmaker Fradee who preceded him. With each passing belabored heartbeat, the current Wandmaker saw the image change to reveal another face of earlier Wandmakers.

All-in-all 33 generations of Wandmakers had preceded Ubough. 33 images passed before Ubough's eyes. He had just seen their faces and looked upon the history of Vydaelia.

Drenched with sweat, Ubough awakened from the dream. The Wandmaker remained in his warm bed. He leapt from his divan, slipped on his yellow robe, and rushed to his workroom, the chamber that contained the stones. As always, the gray central sphere radiated strong gray light. The eighty-eight smaller stones obediently circled the central rock. Ubough slumped onto the workbench.

Bereft of sleep, he would rest no more this night.

For the 34$^{th}$ time, the Master of the Dreamraiders had delivered his message. For the 34$^{th}$ time, it was just a dream.

Long ago, the first Wandmaker had stared into the sphere and saw only the reflection of his anguished face.

The first Wandmaker remained in confinement.

Ubough did not suffer the disturbing dream again. Oddly, his dreams had waned of late.

Young Clarissa was quite adept at the day-to-day tasks of Wandmaker. Ubough defied the elders and again set out to experience the upper world. The Wandmaker hoped returning to the surface might rekindle his dreams. He followed the directions dreams had given him. Then he encountered the giants and had to evade them over and over again and long since left his known routes. He had since wandered in the caverns trying to find his way.

Fatigue…

Sleep…

Nightmares…

But no guidance from his slumber…

Ubough labored to evade the foul giants.

Something cold and slimy slithered across his left hand and brought

Ubough back to the reality of his situation. His rations were short. Even the power of the black rod was limited. Ubough had fashioned some meals from the flora and fauna of the underworld passages he had traversed, but the giants had consumed most everything in this area. The big creatures evidently ate everything. He had seen evidence of this in the hideaway.

Perhaps his journey was as foolhardy as the council had supposed. Perhaps he'd find his way to the surface world and further his Magick. Ubough stretched and risked a deep breath. He inched from his hiding place.

Then…

Pain ever so brief…

Ever so horrific…

Then the darkness and silence of forever…

Ubough never saw the powerful forearm. The Draith scout crushed the 34th Wandmaker's cervical spine.

Dreams came to Clarissa and told her she was the 35th Wandmaker.

# 2.

# New People of the Plain of Ooranth

Many generations of Draiths scratched out an austere existence in the harsh environs of the mountain range south of the Ornash River plain. Zysle had survived many campaigns against the mountain folk's ancestral enemies the giants. He was a master of the open-handed fighting techniques that made Draiths such formidable foes.

The young scout Luzu awakened Zysle.

Zysle asked, "Has the scouting party returned?"

Luzu replied dutifully, "No, Master Zysle, but I thought you'd want to know. Grayness returns. The wandering sun approaches."

Zysle lamented, "I'd hoped not to see it in my time. None of us were around to witness the last one. Matrons should tend and reassure the young. Let's hope the event doesn't last long and the Dark Period returns soon."

Luzu asked, "Does the gray light help the giants, Master?"

Zysle replied, "Giants benefit no more from the Approximation of the gray sun than do we. They cower in the depths of the mountains. Let me know when our scouts return?"

Luzu answered, "Master Zysle, Chief Scout Farinx led his squad into the underground caverns four cycles of Meries ago. They should have been back by now."

Zysle said, "Have more confidence in our scouts. Farinx is a veteran. We need intelligence about the giants' movements."

Luzu responded, "Farinx couldn't find his *** in the dark. He's overrated. I could do better."

Zysle smiled. The old Draith liked seeing confidence and competitiveness in his young charges. Serving as guard and messenger in the corral was about the least popular duty for a young Draith. Luzu preferred to be with the underworld explorers and made no bones about it.

Zysle replied, "I don't expect you to care about Farinx and his troupe individually, but you must care about our common good."

Luzu said, "I want to fight. I've honed my skills and beaten three of Farinx's scouts in challenges. I should be in the thick of it."

Zysle countered, "Have you beaten Farinx?"

Luzu scoffed, "Farinx is Chief Scout. I haven't been given the chance to challenge him."

Zysle answered, "No. His experience makes him too valuable to risk injury. When he was your age, Farinx and I had this same conversation. He was undefeated in the Liege's competitions. You must train, remain steadfastly loyal, and take every opportunity to prove your abilities. Make yourself look good and others look bad. Kick ***! If you do, your time will come."

Luzu bowed politely and said, "Thank you, Master, for your sagacious words."

The young Draith sentry briskly turned and walked away. Old Zysle squinted into the hated gray light. His ilk had never benefited from the closeness of the sun called Andreas by many peoples of the world of the three suns. Magick flourished when the sun drew near, and Magick was not the friend and ally of the Draiths. The Draiths did not share the love of Andreas and yearned for the departure of the wandering gray star. This Approximation of the odd gray sun, like all others, had occurred unpredictably and had been a long time coming. The celestial body nigh filled the sky, blotting out the yellow light of little Meries and the unmoving black sun Orpheus. Draith sages long felt Orpheus controlled Meries much as a child used a returning toy on a string. Those same teachers of the seven-foot tall mountain people felt the Draiths drew strength from the ever-present Orpheus. Though little Meries never dipped below the horizon, the little sun's light waned as it approached the horizon. The black sun never left its position high in the sky and always gave the world of the three suns some light. Parallan's surface never saw the darkness of the subterranean caverns. When the gray wanderer Andreas arrived, the odd light from the sun superseded that of Orpheus and Meries and bathed the land in this cursed light.

Zysle hated the gray light.

Zysle had endured many campaigns against ancestral enemies of his people, the giants and ogres who dwelled beneath the mountain range many called the Impenetrable Peaks. The old Draith knew the darkness of the caverns. Giants and ogres had infravision, the ability to see in the dark. Zysle's teachers and forebears attributed their enemies' ability to the cursed, bizarre, and wretched forces of Magick that influenced the world. At times such as the present, when the gray sun drew near, those forces of Magick rose to a crescendo and made the Draiths' enemies ever more brazen and inexplicably more powerful. Nonetheless, a few well-placed blows from the powerful open-handed attacks by Draith scouts typically sent the larger giants and ogres scurrying cowardly back into the caverns and darkness. The beloved mountains were the ancestral home of the Draiths. The reclusive ilk preferred the inaccessibility of their domain. The Draith word for the mountain range translated roughly as "sanctuary." Always few in number the Draiths had never challenged the peoples who occupied the lands beyond the mountains and seldom contacted them. Zysle's forebears had strayed out onto the great plain of Ooranth that stretched out beyond the mountains. The reddish-yellow grasses stretched out beautifully in the light of the amber sky. The veteran scout Cuurth fell in conflict with legions of northlanders, Drolls and Kiennites. The battle ended when a spell caster aboard a Hippogriff arrived. The small party of Draiths retreated, but an enemy's thrown spear found Cuurth.

But now Andreas choked out most of the beautiful amber light.

Farinx returned with only three scouts. His other squad members fell against the giants. Young Luzu summoned Zysle and other leaders of the commune to the Draith leader Droger's large grotto.

When all had gathered, the veteran Farinx reported, "Traveling the catacombs became ever more challenging because of the element of darkness. Fortuitously patches of luminescent lichen were scattered about the wall and allowed our lighting devices to blend in. Still we had to rely on smell, hearing, and stealth. Individual giants posed little problem. A few chops to their knees brought them down to our level and neck blows finished them. Giants defend their homes tenaciously! Larger groups posed greater challenges. After several battles reduced our number to four, we switched tactics and explored as far as we could. Our light sources faded. Once removed from the cavern walls the lichen slowly fades. Giants searched for us. Just as our light sources failed, we came across another denizen of the inner mountain. He wasn't as ugly as a Kiennite or Droll. Reminded me a bit of the forest people, but for his grayish-green coloration. The smaller pale creature evaded three giants and was attempting to steal away into the darkness. He wore these odd eye covers and moved about in the darkness. We watched him placing things in this little bag. He stuck objects much larger than the opening to the bag inside the sack. Objects got smaller when he touched them to the sack, and the bag's shape did not change when he put large objects into it. One forearm blow ended his life."

Droger interrupted, "Magick!"

Farinx continued, "Yes, my liege. The small brown bag is made from the hide of some small animal. The bag of holding conceals its contents and weighs little. I peeked inside the bag and saw other items. It contains small squares of odd blue and red stone. I did not reach into the bag."

Luzu quipped, "Are you afraid, brave Farinx?"

Farinx glowered at Luzu and said, "I'll see you in the arena anytime, spawn!"

Droger growled, "Enough insolence! Wisdom, not fear, predicated Master Scout Farinx's action!"

Voices of approval echoed the leader's opinion. Young Luzu gulped.

Zysle interjected, "We're Draiths! Stay calm! Discipline! Control your actions! Continue Farinx."

Droger said, "Generations of our ilk lived without facing the ****** Grayness! Now it's with us! **** Magick! Best left to Kiennite scum and insignificant forest people! Cursed gray light! Magick lurking in the realm of our enemies vexes me, but I want nothing to do with that sack of ****!"

Farinx moved a torch toward the little bag.

Zysle stood and suggested, "My liege, the bloke who carried the Magick sack no longer draws breath. Where did he come from and why was he walking among the giants? I share your contempt for the gray light and all it renders, but we should study the contents of this bag."

Droger growled, "I'll leave the studying to you, Zysle. Just get that sack away from me!"

Zysle took the finely made bag and retired to his austere chambers. The old Draith's curiosity pushed him to learn more about the items taken from the doomed, light-green, vaguely Kiennish-appearing creature, the denizen of the deep caverns whom the scouts had stumbled upon. The bag was nigh weightless and about 12 inchworm lengths long. Odd sounds came from the bag. He peeked inside. A block of black stone and rod about a forearm's length (to a Draith), which was made of the same shiny black stone of unparalleled smoothness, were among the loot. A crystal ball caught his eye. The little orb was about the size of a blue blooter eye, but it was perfectly round. Smoky fumes wafted about inside it. The glassy surface bore no scratches. Zysle flipped it in his hand. It felt oddly comforting. The old Draith had no way of further identifying the Reflecting Orb, a marvelous device that returned spells to their senders. Flattened tiles of bright red and blue stone caught his eye. Zysle removed the blue stone, and it expanded to half his body's length on a side. Holding the odd stone unnerved him. The old Draith touched the bag to the side of the blue tile and the stone shrank and reentered the little bag. Removing and replacing the blue stone did not alter the bag's weight. In contrast, the purplish black wand felt good in his hand. The device emitted slight droning sounds. Fatigue gripped the old Draith. Zysle placed the rod on the table by the head of his bed.

Zysle opted to further examine the bag when rested. The long-widowed Zysle retired to the solitude of his austere bed. Dreams came to Zysle.

Wisps...
Threads...
Threads of Magick...
Threads of fate...
Threads of time...
Threads connecting worlds ...
Dreams connecting worlds ...
Dreams of Magick...
The Magick of Dreams...
Magick connecting dreams...
Magick connecting worlds...
Dream raiders...

Elf pressure…
Albtraum…
Albträume, elf dreams, nightmares…

Redness filled Zysle's dream.

Out of the red mists a face entered his dream. Horrific and vaguely female, the creature had fiery red eyes, unsightly wings, and long muscular arms ending in long curved talons, which were covered in dark ichors. The strangely attractive creature pursed her lips, blew the sleeping Draith a kiss, and simply hissed, "Pleasant dreams, old fellow! How do you like these?"

The she-beast revealed long curvaceous legs.

"Who…what are you? Why do you invade my sleep?" Zysle asked.

Hearing one's dreams and responding…
Speaking and hearing one's dreams respond…

"My, you're a simple ****!" the voice clamored.

"Rudeness! Why am I talking to you when I am sleeping? You are a sorceress, aren't you? Though I cannot challenge you, I call you a coward! Face me when I can fight!" Zysle responded defiantly.

"Calm down! Calm down! Calm down, you son-of-a *****! I'll kick your *** anytime, anywhere! But that's not my purpose in being in your dreams. Is this picture easier for your simple mind?" the she-beast asked vehemently.

She changed to the precise image of Zysle's long dead mate Loratideen. Every detail was accurate all the way to the individual strands of her hair.

As he slept, Zysle perspired heavily and moaned plaintively.

"You defile the memory of my mate. She fell to a giant's club. My scouts are my life now. If you seek to influence me, find a way to advance their efforts," his sleeping mind replied.

"You opine over your lost love. Pure ***** heat, that's all she felt for you. Suffer as much as you will, *******!" she uttered disdainfully.

"Draiths are governed by commitment, not passion, harlot! Face me and say such things!" Zysle growled.

"You tempt me, old timer. I'll give you that. At least you have some fight left in you. Our paths will not lead to battle, but I'll do as you want and help your scouts. You're not ready for everything that's in the little bag. I'm taking the red and blue stone tiles and Fire Magick tome. But I'm leaving the black rod and stone of Ooranth. From one comes many. Tap the stone with the rod and say 'G**orge dub you bush**.' You may keep the little glass orb that you fancied. It will save you from Magick. Just don't drop and break it! I'll also leave you a personal present. You'll find my gift when you awaken," the image answered in Loratideen's voice. Quirk of Magick... the black rod's command changed along with ownership. Intentional omission... the Dreamraider omitted many features of the powerful artifact.

Blueness surrounded her muscular form. She faded away. A flash of brilliant blue light followed. Zysle the Draith wandered deeper into sleep.

Zysle awakened and discovered a crossbow, several black bolts, odd purplish black rod, and block of purplish black stone resting on his bed. The contents of the Magick bag were spread out in the room. The red and blue tiles were noticeably missing. Zysle gripped the well-made crossbow and inspected the bolts, which were fashioned from the same black stone. The old Draith's prowess was in the open-handed combat favored by his ilk, but the crossbow felt comfortable in his hand. Zysle tentatively picked up the black rod. Grayness briefly surrounded and alarmed the Old Draith, and he released the black rod.

Unwonted and unwanted effect of Magick...

The fallen Ubough understood the working of the artifact. Magick touched him. In Ubough's hand, the command required to duplicate the black stone was, **Hand rue jack son**. **Frank land pierce** triggered the artifact's Death Spell**. Tea ore door rose veldt** triggered True Seeing. Merely holding the artifact equated to a Languages Spell.

The Draiths' massive leader Droger had led them to many victories over the giants and ogres. Droger's alchemists found luminescent stone and fashioned crude lights that enabled Draiths to pursue their great enemies into the expansive caverns beneath the world's surface. Droger's forces delivered a terrible blow to the giants and killed the giant king Rumpel. Droger's victories had unexpected consequences. The Draiths homes became more secure, and the previously paltry numbers of Draiths increased. Population growth resulted in the need to find more territory. The limited resources of the mountains could no longer sustain the Draiths.

Droger looked to the plain of the River Ornash and sent more scouts to investigate surrounding areas. Talk spread among the people of Droger's ambitious plans to move beyond the mountains. Zysle and others had searched the plain before the mountain and found a prime location. Droger commissioned the construction of a fortress on the plain in the shadow of the mountains. Construction was oft interrupted by attacks from wolf-faced Drolls and gnarly Kiennites. The attacks were invariably repelled by the Draiths with minimal casualties, but the wooden construction suffered at the hands of the attackers. Lack of progress frustrated the Draith leader.

Many elders had opposed Zysle's study of the black stone and the cylindrical bar. Undaunted and buoyed by instructions from his dreams old Zysle persisted. The hardest stone and the heaviest blows delivered by weapons did not scratch the surface of the stone. Dropping it from the thousand-foot precipice of Nederwald did not damage the cubic stone. When all efforts had failed to tarnish the stone, Zysle in frustration struck the black cube with the cylindrical rod. Nothing happened. Then he remembered the Dream Visitor's suggestion. shrugged his shoulders, muttered "G**orge dub you bush**," and struck the black stone with the rod. The stone briefly shimmered and silently grew larger and then split into two equal parts, each the size of the original. Zysle muttered, "I'll be ******!" Zysle heard no sound from the contact. Dark maroon liquid oozed from the Rod of Ooranth. His eyes beheld an eerie green aura. Words appeared in Zysle's mind.

*"I give you my blood through which you will receive all you seek. You in turn give to me your all."*

Ǿ ∞ Ǿ

Zysle's deep green eyes changed to gray. The old Draith wiped the red liquid from the artifact with his fingers. The arthritic pain gifted by time and hard work left his hand. Zysle tasted the deep red liquid. A brief surge of the vigor of youth passed through his body. Muttering **"Gorge dub you Bush"** and striking each of the daughter stones reproduced the same effect. Curiously, Zysle aligned two stones. The surfaces meld together and produced a single stone equal in size to the two parts. Zysle struck the larger stone with the cylindrical rod. Placed end-to-end and at angles, the stones meld together and created shapes. After hundreds of separations, the original stone remained unchanged. Many usages did not alter the cylindrical rod. Zysle referred to the stone and rod as **Stone of Ooranth** and **Rod of Ooranth**, the Stonemaker. Zysle reported his results to Droger, but omitted telling of his dreams and the voices in his head. Droger was suspicious of all things Magick. The Draith King eliminated those things that irked him. The battle-scarred king soon saw the utility of the tenacious daughter stones.

Droger assigned scouts the duty of guarding Zysle and arranging the fruits of his efforts. The Draiths began construction of an edifice and permanent home made of the replenishing stone created by the black rod. Walls of the fortress slowly took shape. Droger chose to call the fortress Ooranth and renamed the plain the Plain of Ooranth.

Curiosity brought others of the world of the three suns to the plain to look upon the growing fortress. The ever-vigilant Draith scouts quickly dispatched the interlopers. The meandering Drolls considered the plain of Ooranth part of their domain. Droll chieftains sent more and larger patrols, and skirmishes became more commonplace. Between conflicts, the Draiths quickened the pace of construction. Within a few dark periods, the walls took shape.

Zysle slowly gained expertise with the wondrous black rod. The discovered the means to create hinged and jointed stones by carefully stroking the edges of stones with the rod and either tangentially touching them or forcing them together.

The citadel Ooranth grew.

Droger lived to see the completion of the outer curtain and the donjon or central tower of the citadel. Zysle was given long life. None of the Draith elders and teachers understood the gift, but most assumed Zysle's working with the strange rod imparted longevity. Draith elders looked upon this with mixed feelings. Some pondered whether Magick had in some way spoiled Zysle and labeled him Alchemist.

Ultimately, the Draith alchemist remained a true Draith in all other ways, but eventually the inexorable march of time took its toll on Zysle. The Draith council met in the council room of the new tower of Ooranth. Finding a replacement for Zysle was the primary task before them. Most Draiths found any connotation of Magick distasteful. The debate was long, but finally a youth named Xerin was chosen.

Tentatively, young Xerin approached old Zysle where the elder Draith labored.

"I am instructed to serve you, Master," Xerin said.

Zysle muttered **"Gorge dub you Bush",** struck a small black stone with the rod, and produced two identical stones. He did not acknowledge the youth.

Awkwardly, the youth continued, "Master, do you require any assistance?"

Zysle turned his gray-green eyes toward the youth and finally asked, "Is this something that you want to do?"

"It is my privilege to do the will of my elders and people. What I want is not important. Your question confuses me, Master. Should not any Draith accomplish whatever he can for the betterment of our people? Our teachers say we should strive for excellence and accept nothing less than being the best at any task. The new arena is filled every amber period. Competition grows fierce, even among the older groups. I look forward to my days as a scout. Perhaps it will be me that breaks the stone of Ooranth with my hand," Xerin answered.

Zysle's facial expression did not change. Draiths seldom showed emotion. The rigors of life in the mountains and the constant wars with giants and ogres had hardened the Draith people. Emotions and feelings were driven deeply into their consciousness. Zysle found the youth's answer acceptable.

"The elders and the council reveal their fear of Magick and the shadow of the gray sun. My eyes have changed to gray. This enhances their fear. I can now see movements in the dark," Zysle responded flatly.

The old Draith saw the youth look reluctantly into his eyes. Xerin awkwardly said, "Master, your eyes are gray. I …we're told it's because of your great age."

"Many Draiths are old, but only I have gray eyes. My past training serves me well and helps me maintain control. I am still Draith. I simply have taken the tool, spent many dark periods studying it, and like all my brethren, endeavored to serve my fellows. Consistency is the rule of our people. It should be the rule of the world. I trust you know the story of how the device came into our possession." Zysle responded.

"Master, I only know the devices were taken from a fallen ally of the giants. Our scouts bravely entered the darkness and took the stones from the underworlder," Xerin acknowledged.

"We know not what lurks beneath the world. This rod may only be the tip of their powers. Still, I think they would have sought its return long ago had they the knowledge of its location. Are the small greenish-gray underworlders allies of the giants? We don't know the allegiances of the creators of this device. The scouts who killed the underworlder and gained the rod and stone had no time to investigate the area for others of his ilk. I understand the ways of our people. I don't understand Magick. Something tells me the underworlders seek the device. All my instinct tells me it's very important that those touched by Magick not regain this artifact. It has powers still unknown to me. Thus, I watch," Zysle coolly answered.

"Thus, I will also," the youth responded.

Old Zysle passed the black rod of Ooranth to Xerin. Xerin struck the stone of Ooranth with the rod and said, **"Gorge dub you bush."** Maroon liquid oozed from the rod. Zysle gave the youth the little bag of holding.

The two sat in the amber light. Words formed in Xerin's mind. "Your command is **"Mill lard fill mar."** Xerin gripped the black rod, muttered **"Mill lard fill mar,"** and struck the stone of Ooranth. The stone divided into daughter stones equal in size to the original. More phrases entered Xerin's mind.

*"I give you my blood through which you will receive all you seek. You in turn give to me your all."*

Ǿ ∞ Ǿ

Old Zysle smiled and presented the small crystal orb and said, "Guard well this little orb. It may save you from Magick one day."

Thereafter dreams troubled Xerin.

# 3.

# Tiffanne

To the north, beyond the great plain of the Ornash River, in the dense central forest by the red meadow where the iconic Lone Oak once stood, Drelves sat in council. Veteran Ranger Birney reported, "Large numbers of Drolls mass north of the River Ornash. They have been sending parties to the south, but few return. Our scouts report the people of the south, the Draiths, continue construction of a black-walled citadel."

After reporting to the Council of Alms Glen, Rangers Birney and Mikkal returned to patrolling the perimeter of the erstwhile Red Meadow, the home of the long lost Lone Oak. Mikkal's mind was with his life-mate Tiffanne, who was laden with their first child and currently on pilgrimage to Sylvan Pond. Long had Drelvedom suffered the lack of a Spellweaver.

Tiffanne leaned against a willing rambling bramble bush in the shady forest by Sylvan Pond. The bramble bush moved its exposed roots against the gravid she-Drelve's lower back. The effleurage effectively eased tension in the expectant mom's tight muscles. Tiffanne had come to the Drelves' second-most secret sanctuary to learn from the elders about the ample flora and fauna in the fertile region. Matrons took Drelvlings to Sylvan Pond and taught them important trades and instructed them on many aspects of Drelvish society. The gathering at Sylvan Pond coincided with the harvest of the enhancing root tubers at Green Vale. 13-year-old Drelvlings travelled with the Teacher to Meadowsweet and the Green Vale to harvest the enhancing plant tubers. Being chosen was a great honor. For the 11$^{th}$ time the current Teacher Boyd led the most promising thirteen-year-old

Drelvlings to Meadowsweet and on the hidden lush green valley of the Thirttene Friends, rainbow geyser, and exceptional enhancing plants. Elder Evelynn led the trek to beautiful Sylvan Pond. The plush area abounded with fruits of the forest. Unlike Green Vale but very much like the rest of the world of the three suns' forests, the area was filled with plants of every hue of orange, yellow, and red. Alms Glen was about a quarter period's run from Sylvan Pond. The Drelvish matrons began the important process of teaching the youths about the herbs, vegetables, fruits, and other medicinal plants found around the pond. The path to Sylvan Pond began at the extreme northeast corner of the great meadow where the Lone Oak had stood for millennia, followed the woods toward Meadowsweet, crossed through hazardous areas of wild woods, and diverged from the route to Meadowsweet. The trail meandered through the plush forests and went deeply into Drelvish lands. Guards kept constant vigil at the intersection where the paths separated from the thoroughfare to Meadowsweet. As the path continued, fewer guards were posted. The forests protected the Drelves. Only guards that accompanied groups from their homes stood with them in the secure area around Sylvan Pond.

Tiffanne was heavy with her first child. Pregnancy furthered her beauty. Her life-mate Mikkal served as a ranger in the forests near Alms Glen. Mikkal oft patrolled the fringes of the Drelves' realm with his friend Birney. The she-Drelve worked yeoman-like and left the work area only at the insistence of the matron Evelynn. The bright orange rambling bramble bush bunched its plush leaves and pulled in its thorns and created a pillow for Tiffanne. Tiffanne eased further onto the orange mossy ground and leaned into the tame bramble bush. Legend held the Great Defender Gaelyss charmed the bush centuries ago and added a Permanence spell to assure plant remained loyal to Alms Glen. Magick of the Permanence Spell imparted unnaturally long life on the bramble bush. The plant had to this point outlived the Spellweaver by five hundred years. Since Gaelyss's death, the Drelves had been without a Spellweaver. The ultra-rare purveyors of Magick were born only during the unpredictable Approximations of the gray sun Andreas. The last Approximation occurred 89 years ago. Few Drelves remembered the event.

Tiffanne leaned back and stared into the skies. The three suns were so different. Orpheus and Meries never left the skies and prevented total darkness. The massive slowly spinning Orpheus cast unvarying dim light, never changed its position in the sky, and controlled little Meries much as a child controlled a returning toy on a string. The little yellow sun Meries moved rapidly, habitually traversed an ellipsoidal path in the sky in sixteen hours, and bathed Parallan with waxing and waning of amber light. Brightest light occurred when Meries reached its zenith and dimmest illumination coincided with the little sun's nadir. After sixty cycles, Meries inexplicably tarried for fifteen cycles at its nadir, withheld its amber rays, and created dark periods. Meries' movements created predictable cycles of amber, light, and dark periods. Amber and light periods lasted eight hours. A cycle of one light and amber period was a day. The time from the beginning of one dark period to the next was seventy-five days. During the 240 hour long dark period, Orpheus provided the light. The enhancing root tubers matured in eight dark periods, or 600 days. Drelves termed eight dark periods a year and measured longevity in terms of years. Kiennites measured longevity in terms of dark periods. "He's 500" meant a Kiennite had seen 500 dark periods. The third sun the Gray Wanderer Andreas rarely drew near Parallan, almost filled the sky, and bathed the World of the Three Suns with its marvelous gray light. These events were called Approximations. 89 years had passed since the last Approximation. Now the gray sun occupied a midpoint in the sky. More often the gray sun left the skies of the diverse world of diverse peoples to the unmoving black celestial giant Orpheus and the dancing bright yellow sun Meries, which regularly rose and dipped in the sky. Meries never sank below the horizon. The regularly appearing dark periods coincided with the nadir of the little yellow sun in the skies. Little Meries gave the mostly amber character to the skies of the world of the three suns. Most variability of the amber light was the result of the position of the bright little sun. Tiffanne thought of the campfires and the songs of the elders. The elderly she-Drelve Sara Jane Rumsie told colorful stories of Approximations.

Tiffanne's eyelids grew heavy and she snuggled into the soft moss and beckoning leaves of the orange rambling bramble bush. The mom-to-be smiled and dozed. Her mind returned to her nymph hood in Grove Town, her family's move to Alms Glen, meeting her beloved Mikkal, and their blissful ceremony of lifetime commitment. Her mother Stella made

Tiffanne's soft orange dress. The inexperienced Teacher Boyd presided over the ceremony. The elderly she-Drelve Sara Jane Rumsie played her lute and the elder Forbin played tunes on his toot-and-see scroll. Tiffanne basked in the warm memories recreated by the dream. Redness surrounded the images of Mikkal, Boyd, her mother, and Alms Glen.

Wisps...
Threads...
Threads of Magick...
Threads of fate...
Threads of time...
Threads connecting worlds ...
Dreams connecting worlds ...
Dreams of Magick...
The Magick of Dreams...
Magick connecting dreams...
Magick connecting worlds...
Dream raiders...
Elf pressure...
Albtraum...
Albträume, elf dreams, nightmares...

A face appeared in the simple little she-Drelve's dreaming mind. Kindly and beautiful, the matronly female had smooth, lovely white skin and deep blue eyes. Soft blonde hair fell gently down the length of her back. She was as tall as a Droll, which made her twice Tiffanne's height. She wore a long flowing robe made of cottony fabric that exposed smooth hands with well-groomed nails.

She spoke barely above a whisper, saying, "You have labored long, my little one. I won't long disturb your needed rest. You child arrives soon. If he's special, you should give him the name Xenn. Grayness leaves you a gift. Rest well."

Blueness surrounded the lovely matron and she faded from the dream. Tiffanne's dreams returned to her beloved Mikkal. When she awakened, the expectant mom discovered a well-made green robe lying on the ground.

The robe was emblazoned with the name Xenn written in old Drelvish and three symbols.

Ǿ ∞ Ǿ

Tiffanne studied the odd garment. The three symbols on the little green robe also graced stones considered heirlooms of Alms Glen. The Teachers presented odd gray stones after each harvest. Teachers called the artifacts the Elemental Stones of Summoning and Keotum Stone. The triumvirate of runes appeared on the stones when Andreas drew near. The little robe's green material clashed with the fauna and flora of the World of Three Suns. Greenness appeared only in unripe fruit of the rare tetra-berry bush, Green Vale, legendary Emerald Isle, and rarely envious folks. Drelvish garb blended into their orange-yellow-red surroundings and complemented the forest folk's natural chameleon-like ability. The little green robe stood out against the trees, mosses, and grasses. Tiffanne playfully inserted her index finger into the garment's tiny left sleeve. The green robe instantly enlarged, covered her protuberant tummy, and perfectly fit her. Tiffanne marveled at the softness of the lightweight material and reluctantly removed the robe. The odd garment shrank to its former size. The amber light faded.

Was a storm brewing? Tiffanne looked to the cloudless sky. The Gray Wanderer Andreas appeared as large as Orpheus and sent gray beams of light toward Parallan. The mom-to-be heard shouts of jubilation all around.

The Drelvish matron Evelynn ran toward Tiffanne and gleefully shouted, "Raise your voice, child! The Approximation! The Gray Wanderer Andreas draws near! We must break for Alms Glen and make ready!"

A tinge in Tiffanne's lower tummy and the vigorous kicking of her unborn Drelvling prevented her sharing Evelynn's jubilation. The group made the four-hour return trip to Alms Glen. Tiffanne's labor pains intensified and her time drew near. Experienced Drelvish midwives rushed to Tiffanne's red elm home.

Mikkal and Birney talked often of future plans and the commitment of parenthood. Mikkal had worried about his life mate Tiffanne's trek to Sylvan Pond. His friend reassured him about the trove of experience surrounding Tiffanne. The friends continued what had been a mundane tour of duty. Then… a flash of red light and a groan in the bushes at the fringe of the forest.

# 4.

# The Flight of the Sorcerer

Shypokes had soft scales and, sadly, were long extinct. The little dragons had minimal ability of Magick. About all they could do was change color and warm their eggs. Many scholars debated whether the little creatures were truly dragons. The animals and their eggshells were powerful spell components and had always been sought for this reason. Their scales were soft, not as soft as Prismatic dragon scales, but soft. Shypokes purred and sang little songs to attract mates. The songs of the last shypokes were said to be hauntingly sad. The shypoke was little more than half a cubit long. That's about two hands length. Only fossilized eggshells remained on Sagain, but the shells maintained their potency. The distinctive, pleasant aroma of crushed shypoke eggshells mimicked the scent of basil and allspice. The powdered eggshells were a bit irritating to the eyes and nasal passages and induced tearing and sneezing. Obtaining the rare spell material component of the Translocation Spell required great effort and a lot of luck. The Head of the Order of Dark Sorcerers Boton Klarje-Jhundi rationed his shypoke eggshells carefully.

Casting the Translocation Spell again meant his taking considerable risk, but every passing day brought more concern about his *benefactor* and frustration over the prosperity of the Light Sorcerers. On the positive side, the Dark Sorcerers' stronghold Koorlost grew stronger by the day, and the *benefactor* remained true to his word, so far as Boton knew. True, reports came of unexplained occurrences in the north and mostly against isolated settlements loyal to the Laurels. Evidence found at these attacks suggested the head of the order of Dark Sorcery fomented them.

Documents were "found" that told of the creation of powerful artifacts of Magick and iniquitous alliances. These alleged deeds brought demands of retribution to the leaders of the Laurels. Boton's reputation as greedy, callous, and powerful grew exponentially with each malfeasance. Truth be known… Lord Boton had not fomented the deeds. Each report of growing unrest and the burgeoning armies of the Laurels pleased the dark sorcerer's *benefactor.*

Back in Koorlost, Boton felt as comfortable with the Translocation Spell as he could. But questions kept popping into his mind.

Doubts… he felt more doubt with every spell he cast. Quiet moments found him questioning even his most loyal followers. Words often filled his mind.

*"I give you my blood through which you will receive all you seek. You in turn give to me your all."*

Ǿ ∞ Ǿ

What if his subordinates Bijna or Ross tried to learn the spell? What if they found the nine Elixirs of the Mastery of Magick?

Maybe *the benefactor* was just what he said he was, a gift giver. Boton eased some of his doubt by carrying the staff of the Dark Order Atlas and placing the chest with the remaining elixirs in his vestments. The Staff of the West Wind would protect Koorlost. *Was that even important? Why did it matter? What was that noise? Doubts…questions…*

"Am I watched?" Boton murmured. He glanced at the smiling hologram of his slain life-mate Cherie. "Were you only here," he sighed.

Why did his servant Malik insist on bringing him warm milk? True, Malik had always done that, but…doubts… questions…

Perhaps it was better he cast the spell from where he couldn't be monitored as closely. Did he see something in the corner of his eye? *Was* he being watched? The *Visitor*-benefactor no longer accessed his conscious thoughts. Did his fellows seek his power? Sneaking about…doubts… questions… quirks of Magick!

Wanting to hide his efforts from the prying eyes of the Light Sorcerers and even those of his order that might be contemplating a coup should he falter, Boton used his new power of astral projection and cast the

Translocation Spell from the astral plane. Fantastic lights shimmered around Boton as he gestured, crushed the fragments of the shypoke eggshell, uttered the precise phrases detailed by the tome, and cast the spell.

Foreboding grayness suddenly replaced the multicolored beautiful auras, surrounded, and somehow weakened him.

*To the north in the laurels, the stalwart ally of the Light Sorcerers, the prismatic dragon Eyerthrin felt a third great wave on the sea of Magick. Mere astral projection could not hide Ninth Level Magick. Eyerthrin had never sensed greater power from Koorlost. The power of the spell had to be Ninth Level. In the context of the recent attacks on the villages, it was particularly foreboding.*

Boton moved through grayness. The sorcerer felt as he did when, as a boy, he took an ill-advised draw on an oldster's pipe and filled his lungs with smoke of strong pipe weed. Thoughts of impending doom streamed through his mind. The Head of the Dark Order felt progressively weaker, stumbled, and fell to the ground. It hurt more than before. Astral Projection had not helped!

Was he paralyzed?

Dark yellow light bathed him. Reluctantly he took a shallow breath, tentatively tested the air, and quickly followed with a deep inspiration. The air was clear. Alien plants surrounded him. His eyes detected reds, yellows, oranges, but nothing green. He lay on red moss and stared upward. An eerie gray moon almost filled the sky. Perhaps he was lying on a moon spinning around a bizarre world! No, the massive body that filled the sky above him emitted the gray light. It was a sun. The grayness was strangely familiar. There was another…small and yellow like the twins that warmed Sagain and a third, very dark, large, and distant. A cone of gray light flowed from the hovering celestial body, focused, and concentrated on the Dark Sorcerer.

For the first time in his long life, his mind was devoid of Magick. He strained to recall even the simplest spell. His mind was clear. The ever-present runes inscribed on the Staff Atlas faded. He barely detected the symbols of null and infinity. Then they were gone. At the moment, the great Staff Atlas seemed little more than a well-made walking stick, and he, Boton, only an aged man. Still he clutched Atlas, the Staff of the Order.

Perhaps he had made a mistake in carrying Atlas instead of the Staff of the West Wind, but Boton had felt insecure in leaving Atlas with Bijna. Now his mind was clear of the envious and paranoid thoughts. Why should he mistrust the ever-loyal Bijna? Foolhardy! He had jeopardized the nine elixirs and risked Atlas! Where was Atlas's power? A flicker of gray light extended from Atlas to the hovering giant sun. The gray sun drew even nearer as he lay prostrate and terrified on the red grass.

The first ninth level spell he'd cast in the Astral Plane had failed miserably. He'd Translocated to a bizarre world and left himself helpless!

Drelvish Ranger Birney sat on the lower limb of a great red oak at the edge of the wide meadow that bordered the dense forest that surrounded Alms Glen, the center of Drelvedom. His friend and fellow Ranger Mikkal stared across the meadow. Soon the duo planned to leave their perch and take the 6765 Yardley paces walk around the meadow as part of their guard shift. Birney munched on trail mix. Booderries and red tetraberries were his favorites. Mikkal's thoughts remained with his life-mate Tiffanne. She was in good hands at Sylvan Pond, but he'd welcome her return. Her time of delivery of their firstborn was nigh. The Light Period had yielded to the amber period. The Gray Wanderer drew closer. Elders thought an Approximation was imminent.

Birney stood quickly and said, "Mikkal, there's a disturbance in the edge of the forest about a hundred paces to our right. I saw a flash of light and heard a muffled cry. The Keotum Stone emits gray light! Something is afoot."

Mikkal and Birney scurried down the red oak and rushed toward the commotion with weapons drawn. A tall person was lying in the red moss and clutching a staff. The gray light grew denser.

*Boton heard soft footsteps. Two creatures approached. The figures were shorter than he and of frail stature. One was a bit taller and seemed to be in charge. These creatures were similar yet also differed from the Fracer and Nylles, the swamp elves he encountered in his first Translocation. Boton's mother had read stories of mythical creatures called dwarves and elves. Even the Old Ones did not number such beings. He assumed the creatures only the stuff of Faerie Tales. Both approaching creatures carried weapons, well-made short swords and long bows slung across their backs. The Dark Sorcerer felt the tip of the sword of the smaller of the two at his throat.*

Mikkal urged, "Robes! He may be a Spellweaver of sorts! Watch him closely, Birney!"

Birney placed the tip of his short sword at the stranger's neck.

The tall male muttered some unintelligible phrases.

*When Boton tried to speak, the creature pressed the blade further and actually nicked the skin of the sorcerer's neck.*

Mikkal said, "He is trying to put us under a spell! Stop him, Birney!"

Birney pressed the tip of the sword and drew a bit of blood. The tall stranger became quiet.

*Boton was unable to conjure and recalled no spells! His eyes adjusted slowly to the dim light.*

Mikkal said, "Who are you, sorcerer?"

*The taller of the two creatures spoke again, but Boton could not understand. The sorcerer shook his head negatively to communicate his lack of understanding. Aided by his usual trick of applying amber to his hand before he traveled, Boton continued to grasp the staff Atlas, which had an intrinsic Languages Spell. Why was it not working? The gray light from the hovering celestial body continued to focus on Atlas.*

Mikkal reached into his pack and removed a gray stone in the shape of an oblate spheroid. The Drelve extended the stone toward the tall stranger. The stranger touched the Keotum Stone and activated one of the artifact's many powers, Comprehend Languages. The gray rock changed from cold hard lifeless stone to warm soft flesh. Mikkal pulled back the stone and it resumed its previous appearance.

*The taller elfish creature extended and allowed Boton to touch a gray stone. The stone, smooth and warm to the touch, energized The Dark Sorcerer. With his touch, the taller creature pulled the stone back and it returned to a hard rock. The Comprehend Languages Spell popped into his head, and Boton spoke fluently with them. He felt his strength begin to return as he touched the stone, but the character pulled the rock further away.*

"You are a strange one, traveler. Do you serve Aulgmoor, Ooranth, or the forest?" Mikkal asked.

"I can answer you more freely if you remove the blade from my throat," Boton gasped.

*Why did the creature mention the name of the black stone of which Koorlost was built? Ooranth?*

"You will not move your hands! You appeared before our eyes! You are a Spellweaver. You are not Drelvish. Who are you?" Mikkal demanded.

"Mikkal, we should take him to the elders," Birney said urgently. "He must be a spy."

"Birney, he doesn't look like a Draith. He's not big enough to be a Droll. Could be a big Kiennite though," the leader Mikkal mused. "Kiennites can sometimes cast spells, Birney. Guard him well while I bind his hands. A Spellweaver must move his hands to cast spells."

"You've never seen a Spellweaver. None of us have. Magick has long since deserted us," Birney answered.

"That's not entirely true. The Keotum Stone told us of his arrival. It tells me now that he is a threat. Maybe that's just my intuition. The gray light certainly focuses upon him. And I'm not going to lead him to Alms Glen. My life-mate is heavy with child. The Approximation nears. This scoundrel foments trouble," Mikkal replied.

Mikkal deftly bound the stranger and fumbled through Boton's black robe and discovered many of the sorcerer's pockets. Dark Sorcerers did not share have the robe making skills of the Light Sorcerers, but Boton had constructed several secret compartments. Boton felt smugly that his prizes would be safe, but his robe had never been subjected to the searching skills of the Drelves. His simple leather Bag of Concealment went unnoticed.

But the sorcerer gasped when Mikkal pulled a small ornate box from one of the pouches. In his zeal and covetousness Boton had wanted the elixirs against his person and not within his rucksack.

"Well, well, well. What have we here?" Mikkal said. Arcane runes covered the little box. The Drelve inspected the box but did not try to open it.

"Those writings are not of this world, Mikkal. He is not of this world. I sense evil about him. He's dangerous. Perhaps I should slay him now," Birney offered.

"There is Magick about this box. The Keotum Stone detects and may protect us from it. I sense a trap. What's in the box, conjurer?" Mikkal asked. The Ranger held the palm sized gray stone near the ornate container and the stone pulsated a deeper gray, dispelled the Aura Spell, and disarmed the Warding Glyph.

"It's just…ornamental," Boton answered.

*Why? Why? Why did he bring the Elixirs of the Mastery of Magick with him? Because he didn't want Bijna or anyone else drinking them, that's why! But it was a poor reason. He should have trusted his council. They had ever been loyal. Curse his paranoia! Curse his "benefactor." He should have anticipated the unexpected and unwanted side effects of the elixirs. The angry voice of his captor brought Boton back to the reality of the moment.*

"Just ornamental! Right. That's why it was hidden, and protected by Magick. False *and* real Magick traps. What now? You devious one. There's…yes, a needle trap. I'm sure it's poisoned." Mikkal chided. "If the chest's not important, I'll just smash it."

Boton did not answer. His mind searched for words. Some spells required only a verbal component, but the head of the order of Dark Sorcerers could muster none!

Mikkal raised the box. His fingers nimbly removed the needle-like trap, which fell harmlessly to the ground. Mikkal carefully picked up the device. Boton hoped he would scratch himself just a bit. That's all a Tuscon feather required to produce an excruciating death!

"It's a modified bird's feather. I don't recognize the blackness of the quill, and I know every living creature in these forests. I'm growing quickly weary of you, traveler," Mikkal stated. The Ranger discarded the quill, and it scratched the truck of a small everred tree. The Drelves concentrated on their captor. They failed to notice the everred tree's leaves wilted and died.

The Tuscon quill lay to the side of the pathway, a deadly needle in a stack of dead underbrush.

Boton shouted, "No. The chest is valuable, but only to me. It belonged to my mother. You do have mother's, don't you?"

The Sorcerer cringed as he recalled the expense of obtaining the Tuscon feather. Two red diamonds! The Tuscon was a completely black bird of prey. A bite from its beak or the slightest scratch from its talons were excruciating painful and uniformly fatal. The reviled species' extinction was sought throughout the lands of Sagain. Farmers and hunters had diligently hunted the creature and burned its habitat. The bird's numbers had diminished and finding it was a challenge. Boton and others of his orders had mixed emotions about the shrinking habitat of the Tuscon. The vile birds shared the habitat of the snow-white Phoenix. The Light Sorcerers treasured the Phoenix for its feathers and down and used them in many spells. Legend held that a dead Phoenix rose from its ashes. Thinking of this misconception, Boton's beleaguered mind forced a wry smile. A dead Phoenix was simply a dead bird! Boton learned of the Phoenix during his time at Maranna's. The birds had bequeathed him powerful Spells of Healing, which saved his but not his beloved Cherie's life.

Memories, spells, and conscience returned. Gray light now bathed the sorcerer and reversed the effects of Astral Travel. Grayness also changed the ambient light. A nick to his throat brought him back to the reality of his predicament.

Birney pressed his sword's tip against Boton's neck. The Keotum Stone empowered the Delves to Detect Magick and afforded protection from most Magick. The tall sorcerer did not know whether the power came from the stone or was innate. Drelves apparently had abilities to detect things Magick. Boton regretted the failure of the Glyph of Warding upon the chest containing the phials. Did none of his Magick work in the irritating light of the gray sun?

Mikkal eased open the lid of the little box and found nine identical pewter phials. He placed the gray stone near them and arcane runes appeared on all; the differing runes identified five different liquors within the phials.

Mikkal smiled and said, "You carry something of value, traveler."

"Let's kill him now," Birney urged.

"He may hold more secrets, my friend. What are these potions, Sorcerer? What is the power of your staff? Where is your spell book, transgressor? Answer me quickly or I'll have my companion relieve you of your head!" Mikkal muttered.

Boton noted Mikkal's anger and impatience. His strength returned, but Birney's blade at his throat prevented any sudden movement or speech. Thinking only of survival he silently thought "Let me escape. I hope to never return to this domain!" Then the gray light faded from Boton. He felt immense relief. There was still the matter of a sword at his throat.

The traveler thought quickly, "The phials! If you will spare me, I'll tell you of their Magick."

*Mikkal seemed dubious. Perhaps the Drelve detected the lie. An individual could benefit from only one each of the five unique elixirs. Boton Klarje-Jhundi was already enhanced. Drinking more of them would not benefit him. Still he carried them...why? Bijna...trust...had he only left them at Koorlost, along with instructions! If Boton fell, Bijna might have again rallied Koorlost. Now Atlas was also beyond the reach of Bijna Torva, the most loyal person he had known. Boton felt shame. How could he have been so stupid?*

Traveling in the Astral Plane and lying in the gray light had taken his Magick, but the gray light reawakened his conscience. The head of the order of Dark Sorcerers of Sagain again had full power, but without the paranoid delusions. The elixirs were formulated with demon's blood and now tainted him. He was more powerful but tainted nonetheless. He again felt twinges of strength. Would the paranoia return with everything else? Mind games...Demon's blood...Had he become demon seed? Magick...

First, he had to get out of his predicament. He must survive and get back to Koorlost, even if it meant sacrificing some of the elixirs.

Boton continued, "What can you learn by killing me? You see the light fades from me and concentrates to our left. There! Toward the forest! I'll allow each of you to choose one of the elixirs from the chest. I swear, upon all that is important to me, that each individual can partake of but one of the Elixirs of the Mastery of Magick."

Mikkal held the little chest. Birney did not lift the sword from the interloper's throat, but looked to the left.

"He...he's right. Mikkal. There is a cone of gray light! I've never seen Andreas so near! Mikkal, it's your tree that's illuminated! We can't tarry!" the younger Drelve shouted.

"Calm down, my young friend. Sorcerer, you have arrived at a time of celebration for our people. You seem inconsequential anyway. I can't read these runes. I suppose smashing the phial will accomplish nothing. I choose the phial with the heart shaped rune and unbroken line," Mikkal said.

"I...I choose the same," Birney stammered.

The young Drelve removed the sword from Boton's neck and allowed him to stand. Mikkal and Birney took the two phials from the chest. Mikkal closed the chest.

Boton said, "You've chosen well. Both are Elixirs of Long Life. Drinking the liquor activates the Magick. Nothing more is required. Every drop must be taken. May I leave?"

"I sense you say the truth. I'll allow you to leave. The Magick of the forest notes your essence. Our Spellweavers will know if you return, and you will be instantly obliterated. There will be no saving you, should you return! Suffering and death! Do you understand this?" Mikkal sternly replied.

"Yes. Just give me three steps! Give me three steps, mister. You'll never see me no more!" Boton answered. The Drelve was not a good liar. Boton recalled the young hunters saying they had never seen a *Spellweaver* earlier in the encounter.

Mikkal returned the small chest to Boton and said, "I hope you heed my words. The spell that brought you here will doom you if you cast it again. You can't do much harm with a worthless staff and no spell book. Be gone!"

*The elfish creatures spared Boton's life. Relieved, he concentrated on the focal point in Koorlost, said, "Cherie!" and disappeared. The focal point, Return Spell, Atlas, luck, all four, or just a quirk returned him to the old wanderer Confucius's chamber in Koorlost. The old wanderer Confusious continued to munch on the biscuit he had started as Boton left. "Three minutes," the old man muttered and never looked up from his scone. Boton briefly acknowledged him and teleported to the solar. He summoned Bijna and entrusted Atlas again to the Watcher of the Tower. He also informed Bijna of the Elixirs of the Mastery of Magick. The phials were entrusted to the care of Montague, the oldest daughter of Grudlethich, the older sorceress who had survived the attack on the Caravan of Heartache by the wyrm of the Laurels. Montague professed to Boton she had chosen a young ambitious Dark Sorcerer named Clysis as her future life-mate. If Montague and Grudlethich were happy, that was all that mattered to Lord Boton. Boton expressed his congratulations. He pressed Atlas into Bijna's reluctant hands and took the Staff of the West Wind. "Were there any consequences from my absence?" Boton anxiously queried.*

*"Lord Boton. You were only away from the solar for three minutes. Did the Old Wanderer tell a bad joke?" Ross questioned.*

Birney looked quizzically at Mikkal and said, "I don't understand. We have no Spellweavers. I could have killed him while he was defenseless."

Mikkal answered his young companion, "It's the time of the Approximation, Birney. Strange and wondrous things happen. Many things we can't understand. Yes, I was bluffing! The stranger could not have known that we are without the power of Spellweavers. I did not sense he was evil, and I don't think he is a threat to us now. I can't explain it. I know we hold treasures in these phials. The gray light made him speak the truth. Now the gray light shines upon my dwelling! We must go!"

"What of the phials?" Birney asked as he followed Mikkal into the forest.

"We will give them to the Teacher. Boyd will guard them. He always has done what is in the greatest interest of our people. I'll seek him out when we return," Mikkal answered.

The Drelves quickly traversed the pathway. They encountered more of their kind patrolling the fringes of their domain. Mikkal reached his home, a stately red oak tree. The Gray Sun steadily approached and concentrated dense grayness upon the tree where Tiffanne was confined. The Gray Sun steadily approached and concentrated dense grayness upon the tree where Tiffanne was confined. Mikkal rushed to the side of his life-mate Tiffanne and witnessed the birth of his son.

The Teacher Boyd returned from Meadowsweet and excitedly acknowledged the birth, "A Spellweaver arrives with the gray light! The first since the Great Protector Gaelyss! We are blessed! What name have you chosen for him?"

Tiffanne replied, "Teacher, his name is Xenn."

The Elixirs of Longevity became heirlooms of the Drelvish people. Along with the gray stones, the Keotum Stones and Elemental Stones of Summoning, the elixirs passed through generations. The birth of the first Spellweaver in many generations was the treasure attained by the Drelves.

Not all dwellers of the World of the Three Suns relished the grayness of the Approximation. While the Drelves in Alms Glen reveled in the news of the birth of the Spellweaver Agrarian, others of Parallan fumed in the grayness. Old Zysle sat with his protégé Xerin and talked of the future of the Draiths. The southerners had withstood another attack on their citadel city Ooranth. The black-walled citadel expanded with each passing cycle of Meries, thanks to the malleable black stones produced by Zysle's efforts with the Rod and Stone of Ooranth.

# 5.

# Xenn's Early Life

Teacher Boyd spent long hours in the foyer of the Old Orange Spruce, the Teacher of the Drelves' ancestral home. The young Teacher read and reread the thick volumes of the Annals of Drelvedom. Little Xenn was the first Spellweaver born to the Drelves in 20 Approximations of Andreas and 991 seasons of the harvest. The ancient Spellbook had replicated at the time of Xenn's birth. The book contained the cumulative knowledge of Drelvish Spellweavers, with the Great Defender Gaelyss's entries being the last. Teachers were stewards of Drelvedom's heirlooms. The Old Orange Spruce was home to the Annals of Drelvedom, the collection of Spell books, the four Elemental Stones, and the two little phials recently attained by Birney and Mikkal from the odd visitor. Boyd hoped to gain knowledge of the Teacher's role in nurturing and supporting Spellweaver. No Teacher had done so for nigh a millennium. Boyd tapped the knowledge of Sara Jane Rumsie and Forbin. The duo had actually walked with the Great Defender Gaelyss and briefly met his renegade brother Yannuvia. Now Sara Jane and Forbin shared the dark brown hair of age. The silver-gray of youth had long left their locks. Both had seen over a thousand seasons of the harvest. Spellweavers oft and Teachers occasionally attained such longevity, but having two such treasures from one generation reach the milestone was unusual. Old Clarke Maceda, a contemporary and ally of Yannuvia was 1200 years old when he fell to a Droll's ax on the ridge overlooking the River Ornash. Early in their lives Sara Jane and Forbin were exposed to great outpourings of Magick and several Approximations of Andreas, but no one really knew the secret to their long lives. Gaelyss lived over 500 seasons of the harvest and drew his last breath 500 years ago.

Mikkal and Tiffanne nurtured their son Xenn. His grandmother Stella taught him as well. Ranger Birney had a special relationship with the Drelvling. Elder Evelynn shared her extensive knowledge of the diverse flora and told of flesh-eating plants, unfriendly walkabouts, exploding peashooters, grab grass, walkabout bushes, orange Triffids, pyrocanthas, Tree Herders, venous fly traps, tetra-berry bushes, booderry bushes, milk trees, and walkabout bushes. When the elusive walkabout plants sensed an examiner nearby, they uprooted and walked about. Displacer plants were tricky also. The actual plant was either a pace to the left, right, front, or rear of where it appeared to be, and its auburn thorns were quite hostile. Peashooters fired projectiles from their stems that stung intruders. But most of the flora was friendly. The contrary plants served the purpose of educating the unwary of the intricacies of the forests. Orange triffids helped the youths in their horticultural studies. Xenn began classes with nymphs of the same age. Xenn learned of creatures such as wyverns, Baxcats, lee cats, Leicats, griffons, griffins, griphins, gryphons, hamadryads, humming birds, pi rannas, leprechauns, Manticores, medusas, dragons of various colors, nagas, troglodytes, Pegasi of various colors, satyrs, dryads, Minotaurs, pixies, sasquatch, trolls, wyrms, wyverns, sirens, huldra, chimeras, sphinxes, banshee, boogie men, bogeymen, brownies, centaurs, hippogriffs, Dobies, Efreet, fauns, fawns, foans, sprites, adherers, shape changers, doppelgangers, and other fanciful ilk.

At the beginning of the Xenn's seventh year, the Teacher Boyd called him to the Old Orange Spruce.

"It is time," The Teacher began, "The time has come for you to receive your Spellbook."

Boyd presented a text. The book bore runes written in the Old Drelvish language of the Annals and was titled *The Gifts of Andreas to the People of the Forest.* The Teacher placed the book in Xenn's hands. When he placed the book in the Spellweaver's hands, the book's leathery cover changed. Odd additional runes appeared on the covers of the tome. Xenn stared at the book he held.

*The Gifts of Andreas to the People of the Forest*
ΛΑΡΛΣ
Α&Ω

"What? What does it say, Teacher?" Xenn asked.

Boyd honestly answered, "Since I became Teacher, I have safeguarded the old editions of the tome in the Old Orange Spruce, but I haven't placed a Spellbook in the hands of a Spellweaver. The writing is new to me. This volume of the Spellbook appeared at your birth. It's to be presented to you at age 7. Don't *you* understand the runes?"

Little Xenn replied, "No, Teacher. I don't know what it means. Will you teach me the spells of the tome?"

Boyd replied, "I am not a Spellweaver and cannot interpret the tome. I can only assist you in the general knowledge of our ilk and the World of the Three Suns. You must study the tome. It will become your legacy. Your spell book is unique. I can only recommend that you study the text thoroughly."

Xenn studied the tome. Simple spells came quickly. The tome included the Great Protector Gaelyss's protective Magick. It also contained Yannuvia's Fire Spells.

The most promising thirteen-year-old Drelvlings were chosen to make the trip to Meadowsweet and the Green Vale with the Teacher to harvest the enhancing plant tubers. It was a mixed honor, for the trip was dangerous. The Council of Alms Glen had heated debate regarding Xenn's making the pilgrimage. Boyd asserted that the Annals of Drelvedom documented that every Spellweaver participated in the harvest at age 13 with the exception of the Lost Spellweaver Yannuvia. Tradition held the experience was important. Birney argued that Droll activity had increased along the Meadow of Lament. Elder Evelynn, Xenn's mother Tiffanne, and his Grandmother Stella opposed his going to Meadowsweet. Aged Sara Jane Rumsie and Forbin relayed wondrous things happened when Spellweaver Gaelyss went to Green Vale. Boyd confirmed Gaelyss's record in the annals. When all was said and done, Xenn made the journey.

Birney and Mikkal chose veteran Rangers to make the journey and took extra precautions along the way. The trip to Meadowsweet was uneventful, and the folk of Drelvedom's second largest conurbation prepared a feast to welcome the young Spellweaver. Xenn particularly enjoyed the stories of the veteran Meadowsweet Ranger Narce. The group spent a restful period in guest trees and sent out at the next morning. The Dark Period began as they trekked toward the hidden Green Vale.

Birney and Mikkal led the large group along the path that exited Meadowsweet to a dead end. A massive cluster of red oaks blocked the way, towered over the path, and blocked out the receding rays of the suns. Boyd moved to the front and spoke ancient phrases in a whispered voice. The great trees responded to the ancient message, moved apart, and revealed the Green Vale. Red and orange foliage changed to deep green. Taller trees and bushes rimmed the entire roughly circular area, but a valley filled with short shrubby plants made up the greatest part of Green Vale. A hill in the center of the valley obscured the far side of the circular vale. Bright green plush grass covered a rim that extended several paces. At the edge of the green moss, the terrain inclined gently at about fifteen degrees for thirty paces and reached the floor. The floor of Green Vale extended several hundred paces, rose gently in several areas, and circled the central knoll. A grassy upslope began where the floor ended and extended fifty or so paces to the top of the central hill. Many small rivulets coursed through the landscape. A gentle breeze crisscrossed the warm valley. The odd sky overhead had some blueness intermingled with the ever-present amber light, but now the gray light emanating from the advancing Andreas dominated the sky and merged with grayness of clouds.

Shrubby enhancing plants filled the hillsides and the floor of the Vale. The enhancing plants did not grow in rows. Instead the plants were arbitrarily set in the gently rolling terrain. None grew on the central hill. Very few other plants intermingled with the enhancing plants. Instead of enhancing plants, a myriad of bizarre plants covered the top of the central knoll.

Enhancing plants were about waist high to the average Drelve. The bushes bore bristles of green leaves and bright red flowers.

Boyd led the party of Drelves into the Vale. Once they entered, the great red trees closed the opening behind them. Birney remained at the now hidden entryway.

An inquisitive neophyte Deppie approached one of the nearest bushes, reached out, and touched the bright red flower.

"Ouch!" Deppie shouted. "It bit me!"

Boyd chastised Deppie and said, "Some plants have teeth, but enhancing plants do not. They have feelings and deserve our respect. You must approach the plant in such a way that it knows you appreciate its meaning and value. The *Thirttene Friends* stand together on the central hillock. Like the enhancing plant, the Thirttene are special and unique. They *are* Magick. Even when we are without a Spellweaver, we are not without the Thirttene. Their gifts have saved us many times. But we must reserve their fruits for times of need. We are now given a Spellweaver. Now the time has come to harvest the root. Gather around the shrubs. I'll show you the proper way to approach the plants. We always harvest the tubers in the dark period when they have greatest potency. The Approximation grants even greater potency to the tubers."

Boyd went to the first plant on the downward sloping terrain and sang in a low soothing voice. The plant curled its leaves and retracted its barely visible needle-like thorns. The Drelve then tenderly touched the spine of the upper leaves of the plant. The enhancing plant pulled its limbs upward and inward. This in effect changed the plant from a full bush to a thin narrow plant. Boyd then removed a small spade from his pack and knelt at the base of the plant. The Teacher delicately inserted the spade into the ground, moved the digging instrument around the base of the plant, gently pulled the entire plant from the soil, held it aloft, and exposed the roots. The entire plant emitted a gray aura. Boyd expertly exposed several thumbnail sized tubers dangling from the uncovered roots. He gently pulled the tubers from the roots, but very carefully left one of the tubers undisturbed. He then gently stroked the roots of the plant and carefully placed the plant back on the soft dark ground. The enhancing plant's roots plunged back into the soil. The Teacher sang again, and the little bush expanded its branches and reopened its red flowers.

The Teacher said, "Disturb only the plants with flowers. That's the sign that their roots bear mature tubers. Once we have harvested, I'll tell you more of the Thirttene."

The Drelves went about thc task laboriously. Deppie had difficulty in getting past the thorns. The neophyte was a bit clumsy in stroking the spines of the leaves. Boyd applied unguent to the wounds left by the thorns. Xenn learned the process quickly. The central hillock and its circle of green trees kept the young Spellweaver's attention. Xenn detected a subtle movement amongst the trees. *Was someone standing on the grassy knoll?* He stared at the area in question. Nothing…

Boyd called the neophytes together and directed them to follow him to the hilltop. Warm sweet air, a fair breeze, and pleasant light greeted them and created the overall sensation of a warm eve either just before or after a cooling rain. Blue-gray clouds gathered above them. A few raindrops drizzled downward from the low-lying clouds. Thunder rumbled faintly in the distance. When they approached the central hillock, the group defined the dimensions of the mossy grassy knoll. The radius of the perfectly circular knoll was one hundred and sixty-nine feet. A circle of thirteen exceptional trees of various shapes and sizes occupied the top of the knoll. Many of the trees bore fruits. Like the enhancing plants, the trees at the top of the hill were mostly green.

The same plush green moss covered the ground of the hillock. Xenn and his comrades shook off the trepidation of walking on the strange green colored moss and enjoyed the feel of the mossy floor. Drelves were wary of unusual grass. Most stories they'd heard of odd grasses warned of danger. Shocking grass shocked, grab grass grabbed, and centipede grass uprooted in sprigs of one hundred and walked around. The mossy ground of Green Vale was plush and comfortable.

Thunder rumbled. A geyser erupted from the pool at the very center of the knoll and bathed the trees on the hilltop with waters of many hues. The geyser erupted for thirty-nine heartbeats. Then the thunder ceased. Boyd introduced the youths to the *Thirttene Friends*. The *Thirttene Friends* circled the geyser pool in the center of the hillock. The geyser pool had a diameter of thirteen paces. Iridescent lights flickered in the clear sparkling waters of the pool. The overall diameter of the top of the hillock was about thirteen times the diameter of the gently effervescing geyser pool.

Boyd said, "It's nice to be among friends."

Xenn said, "Teacher, I saw someone on the hill earlier."

Boyd replied, "Yes, the shy dryad that lives in the great green oak usually hides from us. Behold, the Apple Tree, the Pear Tree, the Snowberry bush with one hundred and sixty-nine white berries, the purplanana tree with thirteen elongated purple fruits about six inchworms' lengths long and several intricate webs intertwined in its branches with little black spiders nestled in their webs, the large green forty-foot tall oak that bore no fruit and provided the dryad a home, the Rainbow Luck Tree or cherry bomb bush with small cherry-sized fruits of red, green, blue, black, white, and chromatic (multiple colors) variety and 13 thirteen fruits of each variety, and the Tree Shepherd, the steward of Green Vale, that now projects an image fourteen-feet-tall and fruitless. The shy Dryad sits on the Tree Shepherd's branches. Next, the jellybean bush bears one hundred and sixty-nine speckled berries. the little shrubby gem bush with clusters of thirteen gems of thirteen colors, the Silver Maple with thirteen green leaves and innumerable leaves of silver, the thirty-nine-foot tall l'orange tree that bears thirteen huge orange fruits and deep blue-green and ice-covered leaves, the Sick Amore that bears thirteen bittersweet heart-shaped fruits akin to a love potion, and finally the thirteen feet tall "toot-and-see scroll tree with thirteen branches, a trunk with a diameter of thirteen inches, leaves divided by thirteen veins, and thirteen fruits."

"There will be many lessons about the *Thirttene Friends*. The Tree Shepherd is most often silent, and the dryad is staying in the tree. We've had a successful harvest. We'll return to Meadowsweet and celebrate our success."

The Tree Shepherd sent a telepathic message to Xenn, "Do not follow the paths of the Fire Wizard. Remain a friend of the forest, Spellweaver."

Xenn returned the thought, "I've barely scratched the surface of the spell book. I have no command of Fire Magick."

The Tree Shepherd added, "Then don't study the fire spells, lest you become 'Fire Wizard', young Spellweaver."

Xenn felt Boyd's hand on his shoulder. The Teacher said, "Spellweaver, we must not tarry. Getting back to Meadowsweet and the safety of the great trees is foremost on my mind."

Birney and Mikkal helped gather the harvesters and the group made their way out of Green Vale. Birney hailed them just beyond the entry to the Vale and said, "Wait! Stay hidden!"

Narce from Meadowsweet appeared from the underbrush. The veteran warned, "A large group of Drolls and Kiennites have broken through the forests between here and Meadowsweet. A scouting party is hot on my trail. It won't be safe to return by the usual route."

Mikkal said, "Our forest friends should slow their progress. They can't fight through this underbrush."

Narce struggled to catch his breath and added, "A treehugger is helping them through the woods. Treehuggers impede the motility of our forest allies. They don't do much damage and are mostly all talk, but tree huggers have long arms and can tenaciously hold onto a tree. Treehuggers will cling to a tree till death takes either them or the tree."

Birney asked, "Strange creatures! Does Meadowsweet need my sword and bow?"

Narce answered, "No. The hamlet is safe for now. Great numbers of Orange Triffids, walkabout bushes, and rambling bramble bushes have formed a perimeter around the village. Shrinking violets are interspersed among the larger bushes. The little blighters single out treehuggers. The enemies are bogged down in the forest. Many triffids and walkabout bushes have sacrificed themselves on our behalf. Treehuggers hastened the demise of many of our allies. Our scouts hazarded getting near the Drolls' camp and learned their goal is to find a way to reach the lower gap in the Peaks of Division and surreptitiously attack the black citadel. They are rather blocked off from Meadowsweet by our friends of the forest and quite near giving up on the task. However, large numbers block the usual path back to Alms Glen, and many scouting parties head this way. Neither heading for Meadowsweet nor hunkering down at this location is a good option. Both actions pose too much danger to the Spellweaver."

Birney asked, "What is the alternative?"

Narce said, "It's a long way around and exposes us a bit, but I know a path that approaches the River Ornash headwaters and allows slipping along the growth at the river's edge."

Mikkal said, "Narce, there's too much open ground. We'll be exposed. A party this size will easily be noticed by the Drolls. Even a blind Droll will know we're in the area. Their sense of smell alone will clue them into us. How does that protect my son, the Spellweaver?"

Narce said, "You are correct. We will be exposed. A small number of us, three or so, might go unnoticed or else outrun any stragglers. I and one other can carry the Spellweaver toward the Ornash. The Drolls won't expect us going behind them. The main body of their force is well within the borders of the central forest. You can nigh smell the stench from here."

Mikkal said, "Your tracking skills are unsurpassed, Narce. I fear dividing our number. You said Drolls are very near. What of the Teacher and harvesters? What do you suggest?"

Narce said, "Birney, do you know the old route from Green Vale to Sylvan Pond?"

Birney replied, "I traveled it as a Drelvling. Quite an adventure. It's seldom used. The circuitous path leads to Sylvan Pond. It's a half-period run to Alms Glen from Sylvan Pond, and the way has been secure since the treachery that claimed the mother of the Great Defender Gaelyss long ago. It'll be hard to lead a large party quietly through those thick woods, even with our skills and friends of the forest helping us."

Narce said, "It won't be easy. But the deeper you go into the woods, the less likely the Drolls will follow. Six of my colleagues from Meadowsweet hide a short distance from where we stand. They will accompany you and create a diversion if the Drolls get close. Your party can move through the forest slowly. With any luck, the group should evade the Drolls and make Sylvan Pond."

Birney said, "Too risky on both accounts!"

Xenn volunteered, "I have some Magick."

Teacher Boyd interjected, "Spellweaver, your skills need refinement. I'd rather risk the harvest than your safety."

Xenn objected, "The harvest is too important to our people. I should stay with the Teacher and harvest. Is it not my decision to make?"

Mikkal said, "My son…uh, Spellweaver, Drelvish tradition holds the Spellweaver is the highest rank among us. By custom… you are in command. But please don't insist."

Narce said, "Many Drolls are hacking through the brush and moving in this direction. Failure to break through to Meadowsweet has worked them into a frenzy. With the treehugger's help, they may well find their way to this location. We can't just hunker down and tarry among the plants. Already I smell the smoke of their fires."

Mikkal said, "Then I'll accompany you and Xenn. Birney, try to get everyone to Sylvan Pond and on the Alms Glen."

Birney protested, "Shouldn't I go with Xenn and Narce and prevent Tiffanne losing both life-mate and son?"

Mikkal replied, "My friend, you are in no less peril, and you bear the responsibility for twenty of our folks. Tell my life-mate… tell her I was obliged to stay with my son."

Narce said, "Axes! They are near!"

Birney gave a salutatory nod and gathered the terrified youths, Teacher Boyd, and other harvesters. The veteran led them into the underbrush. Six scouts from Meadowsweet flanked the harvesting party by a few feet on both sides and the rear. Mikkal, Narce, and Xenn headed in the opposite direction.

Narce whispered, "Our path takes us to the shores of Mirror Lake and dangerously close to the forbidden Alluring Falls. We must guard our ears in the vicinity of the falls. We'll follow the base of Mirror Mountain till we reach the foothills of the Peaks of Division. We'll pass the headwaters of the River Ornash and the Kiennish fortress in the gap. This is the main route followed by the Drolls and Kiennites into the central forests. Once we pass the gap keep we'll find great coverage from the forest. If we follow the foothills we'll reach the wild woods and Meadow of Lament. Our scouts tell us most of the Drolls' force is concentrated in the area near Meadowsweet. Our path is long and dangerous, but our fellows may face greater risk."

Mikkal said, "There's nothing for it. Let's get started."

Friendly plants helped the trio along the way. Legends of the enchanted falls kept superstitious Drolls away from the area. Narce's knowledge of the area facilitated fast travel. The beauty of Mirror Mountain reflecting in the lake with the same name soon filled their vision. Soon the thunderous roar of the falls obscured sounds of the forest. The three Drelves walked through plush underbrush and away from Alluring Falls. Gradually the sound of the waterfall diminished. The weary Drelves enjoyed peace and quiet. Soon the trio reached the beckoning crystal clear waters of a small brook and enthusiastically washed mud from their hands and hair. The Spellweaver removed his clothes and hung them on a sunflower bush. The unusual yellow plant's warm leaves started drying the Spellweaver's raiment. Young Xenn eased his tired body into the cool waters. Small fishes playfully wriggled around his toes. After the refreshing bath Xenn rejoined Mikkal and Narce and the three Drelves enjoyed a bit of trail mix. Narce guided them along the stream, which joined a second stream and then a third. The confluence of the three streams became the mighty

River Ornash, which eventually reached the great western sea where the legendary Emerald Isle beckoned adventurers. The headwaters of the River Ornash sat near the thoroughfare that led to the Kiennish stronghold Aulgmoor. Soon the Drelves reached the road. They had to wait while three heavily laden wagons rolled past. A hundred Drolls and several Kiennites accompanied the wagons. Narce adroitly led them across the road. Their path paralleled the steadily enlarging river. Narce's scouts had correctly noted almost all Drolls were concentrated in the forest area around Meadowsweet. Almost all of them…

Narce saw all but one of the Drolls and dragged Xenn into the underbrush… right to the large Droll who was relieving himself.

The seven-foot tall wolf-faced warrior growled, "Well, well, well! What have we here?"

Narce threw himself between the massive Droll and Xenn. The Droll hit Narce with his axe, and the veteran Ranger fell silently to the ground. Mikkal shouted and belted the Droll with his short sword. The Droll howled. His comrades crashed through the underbrush and now Mikkal stood before six Drolls. Xenn backed toward the water's edge and watched in horror as his father valiantly battled the six Drolls. Mikkal's sword felled one enemy, but the others overwhelmed him and shouted victorious howls. Mikkal lay beside Narce.

The large Droll who smote Narce said, "We have a young one, boys. Scarcely a sprig of brown in his hair. Let's take him back to camp for some fun."

Xenn extended his hands and muttered an Entangle Spell. Nearby vines wrapped around the big Droll's legs and brought him to the ground.

Another Droll shouted, "Dewrong! That's Magick! He's a Spellweaver! We'll be rewarded well! Bind and gag him quickly lest he places spells on us!"

Xenn managed a Command Spell, saying "Stop." The second Droll stopped moving, but his fellows rapidly gagged and bound the young Spellweaver. Dewrong angrily ripped the vines from his massive body.

The big Droll growled. "I'm going to enjoy tearing you up, Spellweaver. Your ilk has tormented my ancestors. Stole the heirloom that controlled the Firehorses! Destroyed the Firehorse brigade! Know Dewrong Korcran will be your end."

A Droll shook his unmoving comrade and said, "Dewrong, Tummus isn't moving and does not speak."

Dewrong said, "He seldom says much of import, Norgle. It was a simple spell. Smack him! He'll probably wake up. I'm more interested in getting our prize back to camp."

Norgle slapped Tummus. The force of the blow knocked the Droll down and aroused him. Tummus jumped up and said, "What'd you do that for, Norgle. Dewrong, Farong, Fluggle! You've captured the Spellweaver! May I tear off a few of his fingers?"

Dewrong said, "Patience, Tummus. There'll be plenty of time for it. He'll sing like a bird and tell all about Drelvedom's defenses. Let's make ready. Farong and Fluggle, carry his sorry a**!"

Farong said, "Boss, it won't take both of us to carry his scrawny a**!"

Dewrong Korcran said sternly, "Listen to me, you t**ds! Keep that a******'s mouth covered and his hands secure. I don't want spells thrown against us."

Fluggle timidly answered, "You got it, Boss!"

Norgle asked, "What about Zagnar?"

Dewrong said, "What about him? He got bested by a Drelve! He's just carrion. Do you want to carry him back to camp, Norgle?"

Tummus, Farong, Fluggle, and Dewrong shared a laugh. Norgle growled under his breath. Only Xenn saw the movement in the dark waters of the Ornash. Farong and Fluggle threw their axes over their backs and picked up the struggling Spellweaver. A dark form silently moved across the water.

Norgle screamed, "It's the river spirit! I knew we were too close to the river!"

Dewrong said, "Fool. It's just some sort of black horse. Soon it'll be food for the Hippogriffs."

Fluggle dropped Xenn and said, "I'm not so sure Boss! It was walking on the water!"

Dewrong said, "Enough quibbling! Draw your axes! Horse stew sounds good to me!"

The kelpie appeared a strong and powerful horse that stood on the water. Its dark black hide was smooth, black, shimmering, and cold as death, and looked smooth like a seal. The kelpie's nostrils flared and dripped and her dark eyes glared lifelessly at the five Drolls on the shore. The ominous water horse visage jumped over the Drolls and blocked the path leading away from the river. The black large and powerful horse now stood before Dewrong, Tummus, Fluggle, Norgle, and Farong. Water dripped constantly from its mane. The horse's nostrils created illusions of grandeur and fashioned overwhelming urges to touch the Kelpie's nose. The World of the Three Suns never saw the darkness of night, and the Kelpie presented darkness beyond any night. The sight of the dark wet horse perplexed the wolf-faced warriors. Then the Kelpie waylaid them. Flying hooves kicked and tore into the Drolls.

The water horse boldly delivered a powerful kick that sent Farong falling backward. She then jumped into the air and landed squarely on top of Fluggle. Dewrong hit the water horse with his axe, but the weapon adhered to the kelpie's sticky skin. Two powerful forelegs crushed every bone in Dewrong's chest and he fell lifelessly to the ground. The dark horse bit, kicked, stamped, and pummeled Tummus and Norgle. Soon all five Drolls joined their colleague Zagnar, who fell to Mikkal's blade. Then the Kelpie ravenously consumed her victims. The water horse turned and looked back toward Xenn. She paused for a moment and then bounded back toward the water's edge, jumped over the underbrush, and stood over Xenn. The dark horse visage shimmered and the creature changed to the visage of a young fair maiden. The maiden removed Xenn's gag and loosened his bindings. She flatly stated, "Sorry, I was famished. I can't live on fruits of the forest."

Xenn went to his father's body. The young Spellweaver sobbed. The maiden said, "There is nothing you can do for him. Breath has left his body. These woods teem with the wolf-faced warriors. I can't defeat them all. I've a friend who can carry you to Alms Glen."

Xenn fought through his tears and said, "You know Alms Glen. You don't look like a friend of the forest. I owe you my life. Why do you spare me?"

The maiden said, "Call me Sidheag. Just say… I'm beholding to some of your ilk. My friend arrives."

A misty gunmetal gray equine silently coasted to a landing near the fallen Drolls. The ghostly mare was much larger than a typical workhorse and appeared a wisp of cloud shaped like a beautiful charger. The beast's three huge eyes sparkled like red diamonds, the rarest of Nature's jewels, and unlike anything Xenn had witnessed in his young life. The central third eye was blind. The creature had no wings and was pleasant to gaze upon.

Xenn commented, "Is it a mare? What manner of creature is this?"

Sidheag answered, ***"She's*** a Cloudmare, one of the Old Ones. Yes, she's a mare. That's because there *are* only mares. Thus, the name Cloudmares! They are foaled by the wind."

Xenn said, "She flies without wings. I've read of creatures like you in the Annals of Drelvedom. A water horse and Cloudmare helped save Drelvedom from General Saligia."

The Cloudmare sent a telepathic message, "You read about *us*, young one. I am Shyrra. I see your thoughts. You grieve the loss of your father. I'll bear you and his remains to Alms Glen. Then I'll carry your comrade to his family in Meadowsweet. Anyone who sees me will not remember. My Forget Spell will assure it. I'll spare your memory, but you must tell no one about Sidheag and me. That's all we ask in return."

Xenn sobbed. Sidheag used ropes taken from the Drolls to bind Mikkal's corpse to the Cloudmare. Shyrra carried Xenn to Alms Glen and left him near the Old Orange Spruce. Then she returned to the river's edge where Sidheag still dutifully guarded Narce's body. Shyrra bore Narce to Meadowsweet. Sidheag returned to the River Ornash and Shyrra flew away.

# 6.

# Xenn and Fire Magick

**Ranger Birney** used all his skills to help Teacher Boyd and the harvesters evade Drolls in the forest between Green Vale and Sylvan Pond. Denizens of the forest came to the Drelves' aid. Rambling bramble bushes, shrinking violets, orange triffids, climbing red ivies, creeping willows, and other mobile bushes moved out and attacked Drolls. Shrinking violets minimized, sneaked into the enemies' ranks, removed arrows from quivers, loosened scabbards and pant ties, tied shoelaces together, crawled up enemies and scratched their eyes with little branches, and irritated enemies' noses with pungent sulfurous oils. Droll and Kiennish warriors found empty quivers, fallen swords, and dropped trousers. Wolf-faced warriors tripped over their shoes, found mote in their eyes, and experienced the olfactory sensation of a large mooler passing gas after eating onyums and garlic beans. The plants got Birney's party out of a few tight spots. Nevertheless, thrice Drolls neared the harvesters. First, a large walkabout bush stepped between the Drelves and their pursuers, grabbed the Droll in front, and held him within its branches. The Drolls' treehugger ally turned the table and grabbed the walkabout bush. The treehugger held the bush whilst Drolls hacked the walkabout to bits. Secondly, the Rangers from Meadowsweet to the west of the main party gave up their position and drew the Drolls away from the party. Three Drolls drowned in quickmud while pursuing the Rangers. Thirdly, a triffid moved between the Drelves and Drolls and attacked the Drolls. The treehugger again grabbed the triffid. However, Ranger Cyndi from Meadowsweet had a clear shot and dropped the treeherder with an arrow. The triffid clobbered two Drolls into oblivion. Other walkabouts surrounded the Drolls and smote three others. The remaining Drolls retreated back toward the ruined forest near Meadowsweet. Birney and the harvesters quickened their pace and made the trek to beautiful Sylvan Pond. The plush area abounded with fruits of the forest. Unlike Green Vale but very much like the rest of the forests, the area was filled with plants of every hue of orange, yellow, and red. Alms Glen was about a quarter period's run from Sylvan Pond. The path to Sylvan Pond began at the extreme northeast corner of the great meadow where the Lone Oak had stood for millennia and now deemed the Meadow of Lament, followed the woods toward Meadowsweet, crossed through hazardous areas of wild woods, and diverged from the route to Meadowsweet. The trail meandered through the plush forests and went deeply into Drelvish lands. Guards kept constant vigil at the intersection where the paths separated from the thoroughfare to Meadowsweet. As the path continued, fewer guards were posted. The forests protected the Drelves. Only guards that accompanied groups from their homes stood with them in the secure area around Sylvan Pond. The group followed the path to Alms Glen and remarkably arrived without sustaining casualties. Alms Glen welcomed their return, but everyone's thoughts went to the safety of the young Spellweaver.

Then Xenn appeared outside the Old Orange Spruce unharmed with his father Mikkal's body. Xenn reported the ambush by Drolls and the battle rendered him unconscious. He awakened outside the Old Orange Spruce and conjectured a Samaritan delivered him to Alms Glen. Xenn informed the Council of Narce's death. Elder Forbin played a lament for Mikkal and Narce on his lute. Birney accompanied him on a "toot-and-see-scroll." The community entered a time of mourning.

The Drolls abandoned their assault on the woods abruptly. Scouts reported the enemies withdrew to the fortress in the gap. Drolls kept watch on the River Ornash from a distance. For a time at least, the Drelvish territories were safer. Birney requested and received permission to change his duties to allow him to guard Xenn. The veteran Ranger seldom missed being by Xenn's side when the Spellweaver left Alms Glen. Tiffanne occupied herself with assisting Elder Evelynn and teaching Drelvlings of the wealth of the forest. Xenn spent three Dark Periods with his mother and stirred little outside the family tree. Xenn retired to his large lower branch bedroom and snuggled into the soft mossy bedding. Finding sleep had been difficult. Xenn stared at the spell book lying by his bed. He had not opened it since his father Mikkal's death. His Magick had done nothing to help. Young Xenn struggled with his feelings of worthlessness. Tiffanne brought an enhancing root tea mixed with passionless fruit and dream fruit. Either the tea or his mother's hug worked, and Xenn found sleep. He dreamed of excursions with his father to the fringes of the Meadow of Lament to the site where Mikkal and Birney had obtained the treasured elixirs from the odd traveler. The Spellweaver dreamed of his trip to Meadowsweet as a neophyte and the odd exchange with the Tree Shepherd. Time spent with the Teacher Boyd passed through his dreaming mind. Then redness filled his dream.

Wisps…
Threads…
Threads of Magick…
Threads of fate…
Threads of time…
Threads connecting worlds …
Dreams connecting worlds …
Dreams of Magick…
The Magick of Dreams…
Magick connecting dreams…
Magick connecting worlds…
Dream raiders…
Elf pressure…
Albtraum…
Albträume, elf dreams, nightmares…

The redness cleared. A young orange skinned male stood with his back to Xenn. The visitor to Xenn's dream wore a green robe identical to the artifact Xenn's mother had found in Sylvan Pond.

Xenn spoke, "What trickery is this?"

The visitor turned and Xenn looked upon himself.

Xenn said, "Leave my sleep! Rest has eluded me."

The visitor to his dream answered, "All in good time! Tell me… why do you not wear your robe?"

Xenn said, "Obviously, it's green. I'd stand out in the forest like a sore thumb!"

The Dream visitor replied, "You stand out anyway. It's a Robe of Sagain, you dumb ****** ******! Only a handful survive. It's just hanging in your closet! S**t fire! You don't know its value. A Light Sorceress seamstress constructed the robe from silk of Sagain, the feathers of the snow-white Phoenix, one of the three shypoke scales remaining in the Laurels, and the scales of a prismatic dragon. Moreover, the seamstress risked death as she tenuously placed a jet-black Tuscon feather within the fabric of the device. Once placed in the robe, the Magick of the robe harnessed the malevolent force within the jet-black feather and instead instilled a protection against Death Magick upon the wearer of the cloak. The robe is patterned like the ancient robe of the Order of Light Sorcerers. The properties of silk of Sagain included the facility to adapt to the size of each wearer of the garment. The Light Sorcerers cherished the spiders that created the silk. The tiny arachnids required two centuries to produce the silk needed to create the robe. The silk had been used to create little black dresses which had adorned many young women during their ceremonies of commitment. Even more rare were the adamantine spiders that created the slender cords that the sorceress used to bind the silk and other materials. The robe has many hidden pockets. It'd give great advantage in a conflict with another Spellcaster, and it hangs in your ****** closet!"

Xenn timidly said, "It's green!"

The visitor replied, "Amazing! It contains a prismatic dragon scale within its folds! It can be any color you want! Its last wearer wanted green!"

Xenn said plaintively, "Leave my dream! I recently saw my father fall. I found sleep, only to have you interrupt my dreams."

The visitor said, "Oh, boo hoo hoo, you wimp! Grow up! You are a Spellweaver! You have access to Fire Magick!"

Xenn said, "I have no command of Fire Magick."

The ersatz Xenn added, "Too bad! You might have saved your father had you been sorcerer enough to master the spells in your tome."

Xenn asked, "Such cruelty! Who are you?"

The image shimmered and changed to a young male a bit taller and stouter build than Xenn. The green robe expanded to accommodate his added height and weight. He was reddish and greenish at the same time and had pointed ears and vaguely Drelvish features. Little red sparks flickered from his eyes. The visitor spoke, "I ponder my mother's interest in you, wimp. I grew tired of mimicking you. My name is Jar Dee Ans. I prefer Dee. You may call me Fire Master, Rat Master, or simply Master. I'm here at another's behest to grant you gifts, though I don't understand why. Words and phrases will appear in your mind. When you awaken, you will understand them. You'll also find ample supply of the yellow granules you'll need to foment the power of fire. I'll leave you to your nap, Mama's boy. Grow up! Maybe you'll save someone dear to you one day. Personally, I doubt it. You are a t**d to my eyes."

Blueness surrounded the young male and he faded from sight. Xenn returned to restless sleep. When Xenn awakened he found a small chest filled with sulfur granules. He removed a few granules and the chest refilled. Twenty-one phrases milled around like ripples in the tissues of the Spellweaver's mind and then organized in orderly fashion. The phrases represented an incantation of a spell. His thoughts became clear. Words appeared in the young Spellweaver's mind:

*"I give you my blood through which you will receive all you seek. You in turn give to me your all."*

Inexplicable surges of strength raced through Xenn.

Xenn picked up his spell book. Odd additional runes appeared the book's leathery cover.

*The Gifts of Andreas to the People of the Forest*
ΛΑΡΛΣ
Α&Ω

Xenn opened the book and turned to the pages written in the hand of the Fire Wizard Yannuvia. He now understood the incantations of the mighty fire spells. Most fire spells required sulfur as a material component. The previously incomprehensible words now read as easily as the first Drelvling books he'd read. Xenn took the green robe from his closet. He put the robe on. Its color changed to subdued orange. The robe fit perfectly and did not reduce his mobility and dexterity. Xenn placed spell components in the robes large pocket. The weight of the robe did not increase. He filled pocket after pocket. After this time Xenn wore the robe wherever he went.

Xenn exited his tree. There was little activity in the Alms Glen common area. He walked toward the fire pit in the center of the common area. Drelvlings had piled wood in the pit at the end of the Amber Period for the fire matrons needed to prepare the next period's meal. At an early age, Drelves became adept at using seven methods of fire starting, including hand drill, two-person friction drill, fire plough, pump fire drill, bow drill, fire piston, and flint and steel. Xenn gripped a granule of sulfur and muttered a six-phrase incantation the Lost Spellweaver Yannuvia had called Firestarter. He directed his fingers toward the unlit tinder. A rivulet of redness flowed from the tips of his fingers to the stack of wood. Flames erupted on the wood. The flames quickly roared. Xenn thought quickly, remembered the incantation of Affect Magick and Normal Fires, and reduced the flames. Elder Evelynn arrived with her bow drill, shrugged her shoulders, and placed her pots on the fire pit. Evelynn complimented Xenn on his robe.

In Green Vale, the Tree Shepherd muttered silently, "Fire Wizard."

Xenn had lived with his parents. The words of the dream visitor burned in the young Spellweaver's mind. "mama's boy… "wimp", ****** ******." Xenn didn't understand the visitor's lewd, suggestive references to his mother. During rest periods young Xenn heard Tiffanne's sobs in the silence of the inner tree. Xenn had honored Tiffanne from the time he could toddle and mutter his first words. The visitor's innuendo perplexed him. Most young Drelves remained in their parents' tree until after their thirteenth year, but now Xenn questioned his staying longer. Over his mother's objections the youth chose to move from the red oak where he had come into the world in the gray light and where his father Mikkal and Mother Tiffanne had been so happy.

The Spellweaver Xenn moved to the stately ancient red oak that had been home to many Spellweavers, including the Great Defender Gaelyss. The great tree had been vacated since Gaelyss's passing. Xenn spent many periods confined to his tree immersed in study of the Spellbook. The young Spellweaver concentrated on Fire Magick. Dreams troubled Xenn. Images of his father's death at the hands of the Drolls repeatedly appeared in his slumber. Ranger Birney, his mother Tiffanne, Teacher Boyd, Elder

Evelynn, elderly Sara Jane Rumsie, Elder Forbin, and his grandmother Stella urged the youth to get involved in community activities. Xenn stayed mostly confined to his tree. During the third Dark period after the harvest, Xenn read until he fell asleep. The reviled dream of his father and Narce's deaths recurred. The dreaming Spellweaver welcomed the appearance of the redness. The rude young visitor would be an improvement.

Wisps…
Threads…
Threads of Magick…
Threads of fate…
Threads of time…
Threads connecting worlds …
Dreams connecting worlds …
Dreams of Magick…
The Magick of Dreams…
Magick connecting dreams…
Magick connecting worlds…
Dream raiders…
Elf pressure…
Albtraum…
Albträume, elf dreams, nightmares…

Redness cleared and revealed a face, but not the arrogant young male who had antagonized him in an earlier dream. Instead the young Spellweaver looked upon a pleasant feminine visage. Kindly and beautiful, the matronly female had smooth, lovely white skin and deep blue eyes. Soft blonde hair fell gently down the length of her back. She was as tall as a Droll, which made her about twice Xenn's height. She wore a long flowing robe made of cottony fabric that exposed smooth hands with well-groomed nails.

She spoke barely above a whisper, saying, "You have studied long, Spellweaver. I won't long disturb your needed rest. You are no longer a child. You have great skills."

Xenn responded, "Who are you? You are not Drelvish. You are so beautiful. Your voice…it soothes my aching heart."

The matron replied, "*Who I am* is not important. Think of me as a Good Witch. I visited your lovely mother just before your birth and left you a gift."

Xenn ashamedly said, "I'm afraid I've not appreciated the value of your gift. The robe remains unused. I have been chastised for it."

The Good Witch smiled demurely and said, "Tact is not one of my son's best attributes. He has a rather large learning curve. I'm here in his stead. I've appeared to your forebears. I have another gift for you."

Xenn queried, "Why?"

The Good Witch again smiled and said, "We are brother and sister… in Grayness. We'll talk soon."

Blueness surrounded the visage and she faded from Xenn's dream. The Spellweaver languished through another dream about his father and Narce and the Drolls. Then a bit of dreamless sleep came to the Spellweaver.

Xenn opened his eyes, stretched, and sat up on the side of his bed. He was taken aback! He was not alone. The woman in his dreams sat on the soft chair in his room. The Good Witch sat comfortably on the settee in his foyer. The beautiful, mature female had smooth, lovely white skin and deep blue eyes. Soft blonde hair fell gently down the length of her back. She was as tall as a Droll, which made her time and a half as tall as the Teacher. Now she wore a short white dress made of cottony fabric, which stopped alluringly several inches above her knees and exposed her smooth long legs. Her silky hands ended in long fingers with well-groomed nails. She said, "Hello, Spellweaver."

Xenn pinched his leg to assure he was awake and said, "At least I know what 'soon' means to you. How'd you get in the tree. It bars entry to all outside Drelvedom."

The Good Witch said, "I've been here before. But that's not important now. I don't have much time, and we have work to do."

Xenn looked about his chamber. A table made of bluewood sat in the center of the room. Blue and green were unusual colors in the World of the Three Suns. Small capped phials filled with clear, yellow, red, and green liquid, and an animal-hide container filled with smoky water sat on the table.

The Good Witch said, "The glorious gift of the Flame Spell requires only your knowledge, a bit of sulfur, and a gesture to direct the dweomer's effects. You have mastered the twenty-one phrases. You must validate your commitment to Grayness."

Xenn said, "I'm committed to Drelvedom and the forest."

The Good Witch said, "You must also be committed to Grayness. You'll be rewarded and better equipped to defend Drelvedom… and avoid experiences like witnessing the death of your father."

Xenn asked, "How do I do confirm my commitment? "

The Good Witch answered, "You must drink from the Cup of Dark Knowledge. The esyuphee hide sack contains the smoking water of Fire Lake, a great source of Fire Magick. When the yellow sun Meries reaches its nadir and the dark period begins, a chalice will appear on the table. When the chalice appears on the table, pour some of the smoking water into it."

Xenn asked, "How much?"

The Good Witch answered, "The cup will let you know when you've added enough. Then you must pour four potions into the chalice and mix them with the water. The order of the potions must be **U**ncolored, **Y**ellow, **R**ed, and **G**reen. The Cup of Dark Knowledge always demands an item of Magick. The waters of Fire Lake will suffice. Drinking this mixture will enhance your power."

Then Purple auras filled the inside of the Spellweaver's tree. A beautiful gem-laced cup appeared on the bluewood table. The ornate twelve-inch-tall cup's base was six inches in diameter and stem six inches long. Its bowl held little more than half an average tankard of ale. A faint mauve glow surrounded the chalice. A large upward pointing triangle dominated the bowl. Flowing runes covered most of the bowl of the deep red cup. Pristine stones of all colors lined the rim and also adorned the sides of the cup.

The Good Witch said, "The Cup of Dark Knowledge is infused with my Master's spirit. It hungers for Magick items and draws power from everything it consumes. It goes wherever and whenever it wants. It enjoyed coming to you. Every use makes it stronger."

Xenn decanted smoky fluid from the purple esyuphee hide sack into the cup and then one after the other poured uncolored, yellow, red, and green potions into the chalice. Auras filled the room with each addition. Xenn eased the ornate vessel to his pale orange lips and gently sipped the smoky warm effervescing liquid. Goose bumps covered his carroty skin and he felt chilled to the bone. He tipped the cup and quaffed the remainder of the liquid. Words appeared in his mind.

*"I give you my blood through which you will receive all you seek. You in turn give to me your all."*

Inexplicable surges of strength raced through Xenn.

The Chalice and bluewood table disappeared. The Good Witch said, 'Search your thoughts. It's there."

Xenn concentrated and then said, "Phyrris."

A small flame erupted on the tip of his left index finger. The Spellweaver shook his finger vigorously and yelped. The flames brought no pain.

The Good Witch laughed and said, "The simple Fire Spell demands no sulfur, merely the command."

Xenn said, "Yes… the command… 'Phyrris' is the Old Drelvish word for 'fire.'"

The Good Witch said, "The Fire Spell can be a light in dark times."

Xenn pondered, "Had I known this Magick by the River Ornash, I might have saved my father and Narce. I thank Grayness for the gift of the spell."

The Good Witch smiled and said, "Perfect the spell. Your learning just begins, Spellweaver."

She placed a blue tile on the floor of the treehouse and stepped on the tile. The Good Witch disappeared in a flash of blueness. Xenn ventured out of the tree and used his new-found spell to help Evelynn and others with fire-starting and did so without tapping into his supply of sulfur. Ranger Birney noted the young Spellweaver's emergence into the community and returned to the wide meadow that bordered the dense forest around Alms Glen. Birney received accolades for getting the Teacher Boyd and the harvesters back safely through Droll-infested forest. News of Mikkal and Narce's deaths soured his success. Birney concentrated on protecting Xenn and comforting Tiffanne. Xenn's withdrawal to his tree and Tiffanne's busily helping the matrons made Birney's efforts superfluous. The Ranger assumed his duties as Sergeant of the Guard. Something had spooked the Drolls and the force assailing the forest had retreated shortly after Birney's party returned from Green Vale. Xenn had related some details of his father and Narce's deaths, but the youngster had suffered some element of shock and had sketchy recall, scarcely knowing how he and Mikkal's remains got back to Alms Glen. The Cloudmare Shyrra for her own reasons had asked Xenn not to reveal the activities of herself and her Dark Water Horse companion, Bottom line was little activity in the meadow. The solitude and inactivity of the guard duty fueled Birney's grief. Birney felt the loss of Mikkal more with every shift. The shock and anger the Ranger felt immediately upon learning of Mikkal's death turned to anger and then sadness and withdrawal. Birney spent long hours just sitting in the upper branches of a great red oak and staring at the site the ionic Lone Oak had stood. Drolls felled the Lone Oak and his best friend. Birney kept the Keotum Stone in his pack and held a toot-and-see scroll. Young Rangers assisted him, but oft times the veteran sent them away and opted to sit for extended shifts. Xenn noted Birney's absence from gatherings in the common area. The second Dark Period since the harvest began. Elder Evelynn and her charges prepared a bountiful feast of the forest compliment by enhancing root tuber jam and tea. Xenn entertained Drelvlings with his Fire Spell, Fairie Fire, and Dancing Lights Spells. Elder Forbin and Sara Jane Rumsie played campfire songs. Sara Jane relayed stories of the early days of the Great Defender Gaelyss and described the beauty of the Lone Oak. When the festivities ended, Xenn left the common area and followed the well-trodden path toward the Meadow of Lament, the erstwhile Lone Oak Meadow or Red Meadow. The Council of Alms Glen insisted Rangers walk with the Spellweaver, though no one had seen a Droll in over fifty cycles of Meries. Xenn reached the red oak where Birney stood guard, beckoned to the veteran, and scurried up the tree. Birney stared glass-eyed across the expanse. The lesser light of the Dark Period still allowed full view of the expanse. A small group of Purple Moolers munched on grass on the far side of the meadow. Red deer, orange rabbits, yellow grouse, wood ducks, and flying squirrels moved around the meadow. Predators seldom came near the meadow. The presence of the fauna furthered the idea that Drolls and Kiennites for the moment were away.

Xenn politely asked, "How goes the watch?"

Birney said, "Quiet."

Xenn sat for a moment and followed, "We missed you in the common area, Birney. Your voice compliments Forbin's lute so well."

Birney said, "Spellweaver, you should remain within alms Glen.

Wandering about places you at risk. I appreciate your visiting me, but I am content to continue my watch."

Xenn replied, "Sergeant Birney, I don't take a step outside my tree without a Ranger companion. I gather it's on your orders. Nary a Droll has shown his face since we returned from, I'm sorry. We all miss my father."

Birney said, "He was my greatest friend. His life taken needlessly by Drolls. We shared so many adventures, including the encounter with the wizard, who mysteriously appeared on the night you were born. My eyes tell me no Drolls are nearby, but my bow longs to exact revenge. I'd volunteer to travel beyond the River Ornash, find the enemies, and kill many. My need for vengeance consumes me."

Xenn said, "Birney, the Drolls who killed my father and Narce are dead. They met terrible fates."

Birney quizzically looked at Xenn and asked, "I thought you had little memory of the events surrounding Mikkal's death. What have you recalled?"

Xenn looked about. The brace of Drelves were alone in the tree. Birney had sent the other Rangers to Alms Glen to tallow their participation in the festivities. The guard who accompanied Xenn waited at the base of the tree. Seeing his father's best friend's grief outweighed the Cloudmare's request for anonymity. Xenn said, "I was doomed. My father and Narce lay dead. My puny spells did little more than infuriate the Drolls. They restrained me and made ready to carry me to my end. Then a river spirit fell upon them. A Dark Horse. The creature defeated and devoured the Drolls. Later a misty mare joined us. The Cloudmare carried me to Alms Glen with my father's body. She spoke telepathically and swore me to secrecy. I don't know why. I'll ask the same of you. I just felt you had to know."

Birney marveled, "The stuff of legend! Drolls fear the water. The Annals of Drelvedom tell of such creatures. They fought with our forebears against the greatest Kiennite General Saligia. What you've told me explains the Drolls' retreating. These creatures robbed me of my chance to exact revenge against the Droll that killed Mikkal, but there are many more Drolls. A fortress sits in the Gap in the Peaks of Division. The fortress teems with the wolf-faced killers and their Kiennish allies. I'm ready to risk the wrath of the Council of Alms Glen to go the Gap and slay Drolls."

Xenn said, "You'd be following the path of the Lost Spellweaver Yannuvia."

Birney made a little smirk and wryly said, "As do you, my young Fire Wizard."

Xenn said, "I have studied the Fire Magick in my Spellbook. I am not a Fire Wizard."

Birney kept his gaze fixed on the wide meadow and commented, "Fire Magick has not been kind to those it empowers, Xenn. History tells us it seduced the Spellweaver Yannuvia and Teacher Kirrie."

Xenn said, "History also tells us Yannuvia and Kirrie contributed to the defense of Alms Glen and likely kept the forces of General Saligia of Aulgmoor from overrunning us. Sara Jane Rumsie and Forbin give first-hand accounts that confirm the Fire Wizards' contributions."

Birney said, "Sara Jane and Forbin are treasures. I have greatest respect for them, but both are steadfastly loyal to the Council of Alms Glen and the memory of the Great Defender Gaelyss. Drolls killed Yannuvia's mother Carinne at Sylvan Pond. Perhaps his actions were justified."

Xenn said, "Carinne was also the Great Defender's mother."

Birney flatly said, "Gaelyss did more to defend Alms Glen than any other Spellweaver. Yannuvia and Kirrie took the fight to the enemies. I favor their tactics."

Xenn said, "Sergeant Birney, the Council disdains offensive action and orders our Rangers to avoid the lands north of the River Ornash. From what I've seen, the Council may be right."

Birney said, "The water spirit did not harm you, Spellweaver. You were brought home safely. Now you should return to the common area. I'll watch the meadow and road to the north."

Xenn said, "You aren't going to attack the Drolls, are you, Sergeant Birney?"

Birney said, "I've but one bow and blade, Spellweaver. What could I do?"

Xenn said, "Well, I'll be getting back. I hope your watch goes well."

Birney replied, "Seek rest Spellweaver. Soon the time of the harvest returns. Perhaps the enemies will return then."

Xenn descended the tree and found a young Rangers named Tippy, Cannou, and Tyler2. Tyler2 was the second born of twins. His brother was

Tyler1. The trio had arrived to relieve Birney, but the Sergeant refused relief and ordered them to walk Xenn back to Alms Glen. Xenn entertained his guards with playful Magick.

Alms Glen and Meadowsweet enjoyed eight Dark Periods without outside attacks. Ranger scouts noted Drolls near the gap and rarely parties approached the River Ornash. Teacher Boyd again readied for the harvest, chose the most promising neophytes, and invited the Spellweaver to accompany the harvesters. Xenn obliged. The group of neophytes included Tyler3, the younger brother of the twin Rangers, and Narce's younger brother Dayle. When Xenn decided to go along, Sergeant Birney transferred his responsibilities at the Meadow of Lament and led the group. The trip was uneventful. Meadowsweet welcomed Xenn. Narce's absence clouded the gathering. After a period's rest, Boyd and Birney led the group to Green Vale. Boyd went about instructing the youths on the proper harvesting technique, and most mastered it quickly. Xenn walked up to the top of the hillock in Green Vale. The dryad peeked out from the branches of the Tree Shepherd. The Tree Shepherd sent a telepathic message, "You study Fire Magick. You are not a friend of the forest, Fire Wizard."

Xenn returned the thought, "I only study the spells to gain knowledge to defend my people."

The Tree Shepherd sent the silent message, "Fire wizards are not welcome in my vale. You cannot resist the lure of power."

Xenn walked away and rejoined Boyd and the hardworking youths and participated in the harvest. The skies opened up and refreshed the harvesters. Rolling thunder heralded the eruption of the geyser amongst the Thirttene Friends on the hillock. The dryad played in the spraying rainbow waters. Tyler3 started toward the hillock, and the shy tree spirit fled into her great oak home. When the harvest was concluded, Teacher Boyd gathered the neophytes and talked with them about Green Vale and the Thirttene Friends. Birney said little on the trek back to Meadowsweet, and following a rest period, even little on the journey back to Alms Glen.

Elder Evelynn greeted them on their return. Birney immediately went to the Ranger post at the fringe of the Meadow of Lament. Scouts provided their latest intelligence. Small numbers of Draiths had scouted the meadow and followed the road north toward the gap. Drelvish scouts had followed at a distance and witnessed a chance encounter between the Draiths and a Droll scouting party. The Drolls outnumbered the southerners five to one, but the fight ended badly for the wolf-faced warriors. Draiths fought without weapons, surpassed the Drolls in dexterity and speed, and matched them in strength and constitution. The Draiths returned to the meadow, walked to the western edge of the field near the Drelves' outpost and inspected the woods, including Wall of Thorns Spell remnants left over from the Great Defender Gaelyss. The seven-foot tall bronze-skinned warriors stared upward into the trees and made eye contact with Ranger Tippy. The brief stare down led nowhere. The southerners abruptly left the meadow and returned toward the site of Lost Sons and the destroyed Kiennish fortress that had stood on the site. Cannou and Tyler2 followed them and watched them pass through the southern gap in the Peaks of Division. The route led to the ever-growing black-walled citadel the Draiths called Ooranth.

Birney listened intently and dispatched Tippy and a contingent of Rangers to watch the Gap to the north which led to Aulgmoor. In the cycles of Meries that followed the skirmish between the Drolls and Draiths, the Droll clans and Kiennish warrens augmented the garrison at the Gap Keep. Two Kiennish shamans accompanied a large force of Drolls to the River Ornash. The Kiennites supervised the construction of a bridge at Rorke's Drift, a narrow expanse in the River Ornash near its headwaters. The Kiennites used rudimentary spells to reinforce the bridge. Drolls crossed over the bridge and built a guard tower. Kiennites brought a Hippogriff to the watch tower and placated the beast with its favorite food, horse meat. Kiennish warren leaders grudgingly gave up some stout stone ponies to feed the beast. Drolls on the wall walk of the watch tower kept eyes constantly on the River Ornash. Ranger Tippy returned and reported to the Council of Alms Glen.

Elder Evelynn said, "Why'd Drolls and Kiennites employ a Hippogriff? Horses are important to both their societies. Hippogriffs prefer horse meat to anything else."

Veteran Ranger Garland surmised, "They built a watch tower on the wrong side of the river. The Draiths won't have to cross the river to attack them. Strange tactics."

Sara Jane Rumsie added, "Such tactics imply they fear the River Ornash more than the Draiths."

Xenn looked to Birney, but the Sergeant maintained his stoic gaze and silence.

Elder Evelynn asked, "Sergeant Birney, what are your thoughts?"

Birney icily answered, "We should destroy it."

Elder Evelynn replied, "Sergeant Birney, we can't risk an open assault against such a force of Drolls and Kiennites."

Birney platonically replied, "You asked my opinion. The Drolls again establish numbers on this side of the River Ornash. The next step is another assault on Meadowsweet or the Meadow of Lament. Watchful waiting has never served us well."

Sara Jane Rumsie said, "I've the greatest respect for you, Sergeant Birney. My father the Sergeant Major was oft torn between the Spellweavers Gaelyss and Yannuvia, but he always followed the wishes of the Council of Alms Glen. The Great Defender Gaelyss long kept us guarded."

Birney added, "It was Yannuvia's Magick that destroyed the fortress that sat on our doorstep, and Kirrie's spells that removed later threats. If the Council will excuse me, I must return to my duties at the meadow's edge."

Birney stood and left the common area. Elder Evelynn soon after adjourned the meeting but beckoned Xenn to remain.

Evelynn said, "I've seen little of you, Spellweaver. I'm told you spend long hours studying your spell book. Have you yet mastered the Wall of Thorns Spell? Gaelyss's use of the dweomer shored up our defenses."

Xenn answered, "I have not yet mastered the spell. In fact, Elder, I'd hope to get in some studying before the next light period. If you will excuse me."

Evelynn nodded. Xenn returned to his tree and passed through the thick bark. A Drelvish matron was sitting on his overstuffed chair.

Xenn said, "Who are you? How'd you enter my tree?"

The she-Drelve answered, "Relax, Spellweaver, I've seen the inside of this red oak many times, though they're not my favorite memories. I could tell you many stories about the Great Defender Gaelyss."

Xenn said defiantly, "I won't have you speak ill of the Great Defender in my presence and his former home. Everyone knows he had the pick of any tree in Alms Glen, save the Old Orange Spruce, but he remained in his humble red oak. Granted, it's grown a lot over the centuries."

She said, "I'm not here to bad-mouth his *meager-ship*. Well, I can't resist throwing in a comment or two. I'm here to talk to you. I've checked your spellbook. The pages of Fire Magick are getting a lot of wear, Spellweaver. The Tree Shepherd wouldn't approve, but I do."

Xenn said, "You should not touch *the Gifts of Andreas to the People of the Forest!* "

Lettering on its cover identified the ancient spell book.

*The Gifts of Andreas to the People of the Forest*
ΛΑΡΛΣ
Α&Ω

The she-Drelve glibly replied, "Don't be upset. I safe-guarded the ****** thing and the archives for years." She stood, walked over to the wide bed, and patted it firmly. She continued, "Still comfortable! I shared this bed with the Great Defender. He, in turn, shared it many times over with others, including a ***** from Meadowsweet named Fadra."

Xenn said, "The Annals detail the acts of Spellweaver Gaelyss and his life-mate and Teacher Kirrie, and his second life-mate Fadra. The Great Defender thought Kirrie was dead and took his second life-mate Fadra, who lived with him over a hundred changes of seasons. All Drelvlings learn of Kirrie's deeds... and misdeeds. Kirrie returned touched by Fire Magick. The Tree Shepherd labeled her Fire Wizard, and the Council of Alms Glen banished her. You are not Kirrie. These things happened so long ago, and you remain young."

The Kirrie-person answered, "I saved their a**** and they banished me. Magick is left on the Council's doorstep and they do little with it. The Elemental Stones sit on their laurels in the Old Orange Spruce. Camille Aires found the stones 13 years after the disappearance of the Lost Spellweaver Yannuvia and the folk of Lost Sons. Drelves have done little with them in a millennium."

Xenn said, "The Annals record the deeds of Camille Aires, the life-mate of the great bowyer and fletcher BJ Aires. Only Byrum Goodale approached BJ's expertise. Camille recorded efforts of the Great Defender, BJ, Sergeant Major Rumsie, and others to use the four rocks. BJ used the Air Stone to improve the flight of his arrows. Something to do with the fletching. During Approximations of Andreas the Elemental Stones glow and reveal runes on their surfaces. Elders and the Council break them out during celebrations. The Great Defender studied them. Given his frustration and futility, I haven't wasted time of them."

Kirrie said, "I remain Drelvish and thus anti-Kiennish and anti-Droll. The Drolls and Kiennites always remain a threat to our people. They will return. Their numbers grow by the cycle of Meries. Your father's friend Birney is right. It'd be best to destroy their fort."

Xenn replied, "That'd go against the will of the Council of Alms Glen."

She said, "Some things stay the same. The Council has always been timid."

Xenn asked, "Who are you? I'm awake. You aren't a Dreamraider."

She laughed, "I've already told you, I'm Kirrie. Are you sure we aren't dreaming, Spellweaver? Stay sharp! Keep practicing! One day we may truly be brother and sister of Grayness. I have a little gift for you."

Redness briefly filled Xenn's sitting room. The redness dissipated and revealed a small bluewood table before the Kirrie-person. On the table, a minuscule vat sat over a tiny flame that flickered a myriad of colors. The transparent vat was not much larger than a tavern mug. Little rivulets of gray smoke rose from the tiny vat and produced light similar to the rays of the gray sun.

The Kirrie-person said, "Behold the Seventh Vessel."

Unseen hands poured small quantities of liquids in the order lavender, uncolored, yellow, red, and green. The fluid in the vessel effervesced with the addition of the liquids. After the green liquid was added, unseen hands dropped ripened enhancing root tubers into the mixture. White, then yellow, red, green, and finally gray smoke briefly rose from the little vessel. When the gray smoke cleared, the fluid within the Seventh Vessel was perfectly clear.

She picked up the Seventh Vessel and said, "This is the Seventh Nectar. Drink it. Trust me, it'll quench your thirst, and enlighten you, and make you stronger… perhaps strong enough to avenge your father and truly protect your people. Fire Magick burns within you. The Seventh Nectar will brighten the flame. You know I speak the truth."

The Spellweaver took the simple cup, turned it to his lips, and drank the Seventh Nectar. Xenn felt a force ripping at the very fabric of his essence.

The Spellweaver briefly disappeared and sensed cold…nothingness? Xenn reappeared, and then changed in color in the order translucent, brilliant yellow, red, green, snow-white, gray, and finally to an ever so faintly green tinged yellow-orange color.

Kirrie said, "Excellent! Note your new energies. You will gain more by touching the Elemental Stone of Fire."

Xenn said, "The Elemental Stones rest in the Old Orange Spruce. The Teachers keep them covered with an ancient plot of invisimoss. I've touched the stones many times. No one has found power from them."

Kirrie said, "When you touched the Summoning Stone of Fire, the Elemental Fire Stone, you had neither drunk from the Cup of Dark Knowledge nor tasted the Seventh Nectar from the Seventh Vessel. Fire Magick touches you. Grayness blesses you. Holding the Elemental Stone of Fire (SSF) will etch new powers in your essence."

Xenn said, "I'm welcomed by Teacher Boyd to enter the Old Orange Spruce at any time to study the Annals. My Knock Spell gives me entry. Each Teacher has a unique song to sing to gain access."

Kirrie said, "Silly! I know! I was Teacher before I became an exile. This is my song."

Kirrie sang.

Xenn asked, "Beautiful lyrics! You *are* Kirrie!"

Kirrie said, "I'm glad you noticed."

Xenn glanced at his hands and said, "Why am I greenish?"

She answered, "Part of the plan, Spellweaver. Go touch the SSF. I've got to be going."

The matron placed a blue tile on the floor and stepped onto it. Blueness flashed through the treehouse and the she-Drelve, Seventh Vessel, bluewood table, and blue tile disappeared. Words appeared in Xenn's mind.

*"I give you my blood through which you will receive all you seek. You in turn give to me your all."*

Xenn pondered the ever so slight hint of green ness in his orange-yellow skin. The Spellweaver noted now his spell book was open on the bedside table. He glanced at the page. A new spell was inscribed on the page. It was written in a different handwriting. Xenn read the incantation and the phrases stuck in his mind. The Drelvish hero Bryce then uttered these same phrases of old Drelvish tongue. Thirty-four shimmering images of the little Drelve formed on the field of battle. Performing indistinguishably, every image drew its longbow, notched an arrow, and made ready to fire. When a Kiennish shaman named Knickknack growled, extended his gnarly left hand, and muttered, "Be gone!" a violet violet ray of Magick streaked toward the images of Bryce. The Magick Missile sailed through the thirteenth image from the west. The image vanished. In its place, additional images formed and 55 images of the Drelve appeared. The knowledge of the Mirror Images Spell died with Bryce on the Meadow of Lament. Bryce was not a Spellweaver, so his spell was not inscribed in the spell book. The incantation now appeared in the spell book and Xenn's mind.

Xenn yawned. His bed beckoned. The Spellweaver anticipated a visit to his dreams. Instead he enjoyed a period of uninterrupted sleep. The Spellweaver awakened and made his way to the Old Orange Spruce. When he reached the ancient tree, he muttered the incantation of his Knock Spell, passed through the thick yellow-orange bark, and entered the foyer. He called out to the Teacher Boyd, but as he anticipated the young Teacher was busily instructing the youth. He descended the stairs to the storage area that housed the many Spellbooks and antiquities treasured by Drelvedom. He went to a corner of the room and bent down and removed the invisimoss from the group of Elemental Stones.

Kirrie used the Summoning Stone of Fire (SSF) to summon the wyvern Dallas during the Battle of Lone Oak Meadow. The artifact had been an heirloom of the Korcran family of Drolls. The artifact differed from the Fire Stone possessed by the Lost Spellweaver Yannuvia. The Summoning Stone of Fire (SSF) looked like a rock and was precisely the same size and shape of the Summoning Stone of Water (SSW). The Summoning Stone of Fire (SSF) bore the image of a proud Fire Horse. Runes appeared on the stone's smooth surface.

Ǿ ∞ Ǿ

The Water Stone (SSW) appeared an ovoid watery shape, a prolate spheroid. The curious artifact was like water, or soft clear gelatin Runes and an ever so faint image of a water horse appeared on the surface of the artifact. The ovoid blue Water Stone looked more like a glob of water and felt wet. The precise image of the water horse was faintly visible on the surface of the watery material.

∞ Ǿ ∞

The Air Stone (SSA) had the appearance of a rainbow bent into fattened cigar shape. The weightless Air Stone (SSA) looked like a rolled-up rainbow. Its density was similar to the misty equine Cloudmare Shyrra. the scintillating colors. Runes appeared on its beautiful surface. The Air Stone or Wind Stone was sometimes called the Summoning Stone of Air (SSA).

∞ Ǿ ∞

Earth Stone (SSE) shared the oblate spheroid shape of the Fire Stone (SSF), Air Stone (SSA), and Water Stone (SSW), but it looked like a clump of red clay. Three runes glowed brightly on its surface.

Ǿ ∞ Ǿ

The Earth Stone hummed and emitted faint gray light. The Earth Stone (SSE) appeared a smooth clod of dirt, an ovoid jar of clay.

Runes appeared on all four oblate spheroids.

Xenn grasped the Summoning Stone of Fire. His ever-so-slightly green tinged orange-yellow skink briefly faded to gray. The room filled with grayness. Briefly the SSF disappeared from his hand. Xenn felt powerful. The SSF reappeared. Words appeared in Xenn's thoughts.

*"I give you my blood through which you will receive all you seek. You in turn give to me your all."*

Xenn placed the SSF with its fellows. The Spellweaver placed the invisimoss in his pack and ascended the stairs. Boyd had not returned. Fatigue gripped the young Spellweaver. Xenn exited the Old Orange Spruce and returned to his own tree.

In Green Vale the Tree Shepherd muttered, "Fire Wizard."

# 7.

# Birney's Dream: Omega Stone

Ranger Birney did not sleep. The veteran lay on his simple cot in the small red elm that was his home and recalled his great friend Mikkal and the many hours he'd spent with Mikkal and Tiffanne. Tiffanne had nigh chosen Birney as her life-mate, but Birney never revealed his feelings to her. Thus, she turned to Mikkal and their love blossomed. Ever the true friend, Birney stood by Mikkal as his best-Drelve at the ceremony of life-time commitment that united the happy couple. Birney had stood toe-to-toe with Drolls twice his size and Kiennish shaman, who fired blistering Magick against him. He'd accompanied the Teacher to Green Vale and stood among the Thirttene Friends whilst the enhancing root tubers were harvested and resisted the advances of the flirtatious Dryad. He'd battled noir skats, wailers, Baxcats, Leicats, and most predators that invaded the forests around Alms Glen. With Mikkal he'd bested the strange tall sorcerer that fell from the skies and bequeathed the brace of potions to gain his freedom. He'd felt the joy of seeing Xenn enter the world and the exhilaration of standing in the gray light of the Approximation. Now, the veteran Ranger struggled with his feelings. Looking into Tiffanne's eyes furthered Birney's angst. Since Mikkal fell, Birney had spent much time with the young Spellweaver Xenn, stood guard by his tree, and served many extra watches in the great trees bordering the wide Meadow of Lament. Nothing quelled his anger. The Ranger closed his eyes. Sleep was long in coming. Finally, he dreamed, but his dreams afforded him no relief from his torment. Mikkal's face appeared over and over again as Birney's sleeping mind rehashed memories from nymph hood forward. Redness filled his slumber and actually brought relief.

Wisps…
Threads…
Threads of Magick…
Threads of fate…
Threads of time…
Threads connecting worlds …
Dreams connecting worlds …
Dreams of Magick…
The Magick of Dreams…
Magick connecting dreams…
Magick connecting worlds…
Dream raiders…
Elf pressure…
Albtraum…
Albträume, elf dreams, nightmares…

Ǿ ∞ Ǿ

Slowly an image appeared in the veteran Ranger's mind. The face of a beautiful female appeared. The very tall and alluring female in his dream had smooth reddened skin, fiery red eyes, and wore a blazing red dress. Long green hair fell provocatively across her back and chest and produced a disheveled look. The female walked proudly back and forth across a field of green grab grass with purplish flowers. Dangerous red grab grass grew in marshy lands. The blades of the thick grass tenaciously held to any poor creature that stumbled upon it, and the grab grass's victim usually starved or fell to a predator. Emerald green grab grass tantalizingly grasped and released the female's powerful lower legs. The female's strong hands ended in digits with long sharp talons. Tiny sparks of blue flame burst from her talons as she rubbed them together. The sleeping Drelvish Ranger beheld her beauty, *felt* her hot breath, and welcomed relief from the torment of the dreams of his dead friend. Vibrant black and red flower petals showered the beautiful female. She pursed her lips, emitted small bursts of hot breath, and burned petals that neared her. She rolled the digits of her left hand, created a small ball of deep green flame, and playfully tossed it up and down. She gently inhaled and then slowly exhaled gray smoke, which enveloped the little ball of flame. Smiling wryly, the female allowed the smoke-enshrouded green fireball to rest in her palm. The smoke condensed, cleared, and transformed the green ball to a small gray crescent-shaped stone.

"Does this temper your grief, Ranger!" the svelte female hissed. She raised her skirt tantalizingly to mid-thigh and revealed long smooth legs. Little flames arced from the fabric.

Birney tensed.

"Are you mute?" the she-beast continued.

Still Birney remained silent.

"Has a noir skat got your tongue? Talk to me," the female continued.

"The annals of Drelvedom tell of invaders of my forebears' dreams. Why do you visit me, Dreamraider? Magick does not touch me," Birney managed to come back with.

"You may call me Amica. I like the name. I might be your worst nightmare…or…your most pleasant dream," the she-beast seductively answered.

Birney was bewildered.

Speaking in a dream…

Interacting with one's dream…

Hearing one's dreams and responding…

Speaking and hearing one's dreams respond…

Birney said, "Leave me to my grief. Save your little rocks for sorcerers. The annals also speak of stones of various sorts. The Teachers relay the stories to us as Drelvlings. We bear a stone larger than the one you hold in your hand while on duty. Mikkal…" The words lodged in the sleeping Ranger's throat.

The female said, "Your friend. It pains you to speak his name. Know the Drolls mocked him as he died and planned to torture his son, your Spellweaver."

Birney argued, "You can't know details of his death. Xenn barely recalls the events."

The image shimmered and transformed to a strong and powerful horse. Its hide was dark black and its mane dripped constantly. Its hide was smooth, black, shimmering, and cold as death, and looked smooth like a seal. The ersatz kelpie's nostrils flared and dripped and her dark eyes glared lifelessly at Birney. The horse's nostrils created illusions of grandeur and fashioned overwhelming urges to touch the Kelpie's nose. The Kelpie visage presented darkness beyond any night. The dark horse visage shimmered and the creature changed to the visage of a young fair maiden. The image shimmered and returned to the fiery female demonic visage. She queried, "Xenn betrayed his rescuers, the water horse and Cloudmare. Your thoughts tell me he confided in you. The Cloudmare spared him from the effects of her intrinsic Forget Spell. No one remembers a Cloudmare unless the Cloudmare chooses to allow it. But I know well the details of your friend's death. He suffered."

Birney asked, "You gave a masterful performance. I don't want your rock. Magick Stones spelled the end of the legendary Teacher Edkim and contributed to the seduction of the Lost Spellweaver Yannuvia and Teacher Kirrie. Your dark horse friend robbed me of the chance to avenge my friend."

The Dreamraider answered, "Had the Kelpie not intervened, your Spellweaver would have died over the Droll's firepits. Had Edkim not used the Cold Stone against the Firehorse Brigade at the Battle of Lone Oak Meadow and Kirrie used Fire Magick against the Kiennish fortresses, Alms Glen would have long ago fallen."

Birney said, "The Annals of Drelvedom record those deeds. Still, I'm suspicious of devices of Magick. I'm not Spellweaver. I'm a fighter. For all I know the odd rock will do me in."

Amica said, "You can be careful and tentative or you can take steps to avenge your friend and safeguard your people. I'll tell you what I know of Omega Stones. All are unique and touched by grayness. Graparbles form in the tissues of some touched by grayness. At the time of death, these tidbits of grayness leave the fallen bodies. Thirteen graparbles merge to form an Omega Stone. This stone comes from a place called Vydaelia. Thirteen Vydaelians gave up the ghost in order to form this Omega Stone. It doesn't have much value of itself. Omega Stones are indistinguishable outwardly. Grasping activates the stones. Gripping the roughly kidney-shaped artifact only brings warmth from the stone and results in a series of runes, starting with a single rune. This single rune appears on its surface during the

Approximation of Andreas. Each stone gives its bearer a false impression. Without the presence of another stone and unless Magick touches the bearer, the only effect is this false feeling. Those touched by Magick may gain new power…maybe. An Omega Stone seeks its fellows. When two or more stones are in proximity, the bearers gain the ability to communicate in the chaotic evil language of the abyss and become aware of other stones and who carries them. Sometimes other artifacts detect the presence of Omega Stones and the gray light of Andreas always activates their runes. When three stones come together, the bearers see into one another's thoughts. The mind reading effect supersedes spell-reflecting abilities and Magick resistance. So, two Omega Stones empower communication in an old dialect and compel the truth. Three Omega Stones enable the bearers to look into their colleagues' minds. Vydaelians possessed five Omega Stones and never discovered additional effect of four stones. Artifacts called Sibling Stones mimic ALL effects created by multiple Omega Stones. Nothing special happens with four. Five stones produce a *Protection from Magick* effect. Six and seven do nothing special. Eight Stones effect enables *Continual Light*. I don't know what that means. No added effect from nine, ten, eleven or twelve Omega Stones, but thirteen stones produces *Time Saving Effect*. Time will remain constant when passing between realms. 14, 15, 16, 17, 18, 19, and 20 do nothing more. 21 Omega Stones will irreversibly form into a Xennic Stone. Omega Stones are smaller than the Keotum Stone, which is 1.6180339887498948482 larger and heavier than an Omega Stone. Your Keotum Stone is unique. The Cold Stone and Fire Stone mentioned in your Annals of Drelvedom are Xennic Stones. The four Elemental Stones are the same size as Xennic Stones, but that's where the similarities end."

Birney commented, "Boring! Magick rocks don't interest me! I'll stick to my sword and bow. You should be talking to Spellweaver Xenn. How do you know so much of the Annals of Drelvedom?"

The Dreamraider said, "I've a good friend, who safeguarded your heritage. She's told me a lot of Drelvish history… and I witnessed a good bit of it. You are a warrior. I'm counting on you to convince your Spellweaver to act against the Drolls. The Omega Stone is gambit for your reluctant Spellweaver, but I also have gifts for you."

She produced a mooler hide sack and removed perfectly round light brown balls with white specks. You'll be interested in these."

Birney said, "They look like the balls our youths sport with in the meadows. Dreaming of such things means nothing. When I awaken, you and they will be gone. I look forward to that."

She said, "These are dried Duoth droppings."

Birney muttered, "Droppings! I know not and care not what a Duoth is! How dare you bring excrement into my home… uh, dream."

The Dreamraider laughed and said, "Duoths produce unwonted excrement. Many folks think their stool doesn't stink. Duoth excrement *really* doesn't stink and has many unique characteristics. Most creatures don't produce such droppings. There's great power in Duoth Dropping Soup. Long ago a Mender created healing potions and unguents from Duoth droppings. Duoth Dropping Soup has many of the same properties. If dried long enough, Duoth scybala make explosive sling bolts."

Birney sardonically replied, "Weaponized excrement! Are you jesting?"

The Dreamraider answered, "Dried Duoth Droppings will explode on impact. They must be thoroughly dried first. Duoth droppings are perfectly round. They are brown with white stuff on them. Do you know what that white stuff on Duoth poop is, Birney?"

"Uh, no, I do not," Birney quickly replied.

"That's Duoth poop, too," The Dreamraider answered and laughed again.

Birney said, "Please leave my dream."

The Dreamraider said, "In good time. These Duoth bombs are quite useful. They will produce a large hole in the Drolls' fortress. The Omega Stone has potential value to your people. The Spellweaver will appreciate its value. Use it as gambit. By the way, you may call me Amica."

Birney said, "Knowing your name doesn't change anything, Amica. Xenn has always followed the path suggested by the Council of Alms Glen. He won't stray from that path."

Amica replied, "Don't be so sure, noble warrior. Xenn saw his father's throat ripped out by Drolls. Fire Magick touches him. I'll leave you to your sleep, but heed well my words. The Council of Alms Glen has sometimes followed a path detrimental to your people. Were it not for the actions of the Fire Wizards Yannuvia and Kirrie, the Drolls and Kiennites would have razed this spot where your tree home stands long ago. They may yet do so, Ranger Birney."

Blueness surrounded the image and the visage disappeared from Birney's dream. The Ranger entered deep sleep.

# 8.

# Xenn and Birney's Risky Path

A tapping on his door awakened Ranger Sergeant Birney.

Birney sat up on the edge of his rustic bed. Meries' yellow light sneaked through the willing bark of his red oak home and reflected from several items lying on the little table near his bed. A gray crescent shaped stone and six perfectly round brown and white objects about the size of blue blooter eggs had appeared during his rest period. Birney walked to the table. Another tap on his tree stopped him.

Birney said, "Who's there?"

Xenn answered, "Xenn."

Birney replied, "Enter Spellweaver. You are always welcome in my home."

Xenn passed through the tree's bark and stood with Birney. Birney relayed his dream to the Spellweaver. Birney said, "These appeared while I slept. I was just going to check them."

Xenn said, "Just a moment."

The Spellweaver muttered a lyrical incantation and directed his hands toward the items. All developed an aura of Grayness. The Spellweaver uttered a guttural incantation and again pointed toward the devices. The Spellweaver said, "Well, the stone radiates Magick. The round objects are hard to define. None of the items present an immediate threat. I sense no auras of evil. Are these eggs?"

Birney said, "In my dream, the visitor who identified herself as Kirrie, said these were the excrement of some creature called a Duoth."

Xenn said, "It has no odor. I'm glad I didn't touch it."

Birney said, “She said it was weaponized.”

Xenn said, “I’m not the best student of the bestiary. But I can’t recall Duoth.”

Birney said, “Nor can I. She said the stone would have value to you and called it an Omega Stone. Quite honestly, Spellweaver, she intimated that I should use the device to tempt you to go along with an assault on the Drolls and Kiennites. Should we touch it?”

Xenn replied, “Thank you for being up front with me, Ranger Birney. You were my father’s closest friend. I value your friendship, too. There’s nothing for it. I’m going to hold the Omega Stone.”

Xenn picked up and held the Omega Stone. The stone warmed in his hand.

A single rune appeared on the rock and persisted for thirteen heartbeats.

**Ω**

Then the single letter faded, and three runes appeared on the surface of the rock, which briefly emitted gray light.

Ǿ ∞ Ǿ

The runes faded after 21 heartbeats and the single rune reappeared. The pattern repeated three times.

Words appeared in Xenn’s mind.

*“I give you my blood through which you will receive all you seek. You in turn give to me your all.”*

New phrases appeared in Xenn’s thoughts. Initially a word jumble, the phrases organized into an incantation.

Birney said, “Well, Spellweaver, what does it do?”

Xenn replied, “Slow Spell. Requires a bit of treacle. But… The Dreamraider told you the stones impart a false message. Seems pretty worthless unless we find another one.”

Birney said, “It’s just as well. I wasn’t about to use it to try to persuade you to go with me and attack the Drolls and Kiennites. Six round pieces of **** won’t make a difference.”

Xenn replied, “I don’t require persuading. Why do you think I came to visit you? Too long the Drolls and Kiennites have taunted us. Let's make ready."

Birney asked, "Are you sure, Spellweaver?"

Xenn said, "Drolls wantonly killed my father and Narce before my eyes. I'd be dead too were it not for the River Spirit. I'm ready, if you are."

Birney said, "I've been ready. I have a pack made up. Almost went alone a few days ago. What about the Duoth droppings?"

Xenn said, "We'll bring them along."

Birney agreed, "Good idea."

Xenn said, "Birney, do you have some molasses?"

Birney grabbed a small earthen jar and passed it to the Spellweaver. Xenn placed it in his pack and said, "Might come in handy with the new spell."

Birney knew all the paths in and around Alms Glen. Getting past the sentries in the trees was not a problem for the veteran. The brace of Drelves maneuvered along the forest edge to the road heading north toward the gap in the Peaks of Division and the large fortress constructed by the Drolls and Kiennites. Xenn followed the veteran's steps. Birney retraced the route he followed in leading the Teacher Boyd and the harvesters back from Green Vale whilst Narce and Mikkal's fateful trek led the young Spellweaver in another roundabout route to Alms Glen. The forest opened before them and closed after they passed. The light period gave way to the amber period, but the light still exposed them in the open. The path to Sylvan Pond began at the extreme northeast corner of the great meadow where the Lone Oak had stood for millennia, followed the woods toward Meadowsweet, crossed through hazardous areas of wild woods, and diverged from the route to Meadowsweet. The trail meandered through the plush forests and went deeply into Drelvish lands. Guards kept constant vigil at the intersection where the paths separated from the thoroughfare to Meadowsweet. As the path continued, fewer guards were posted. The forest protected the Drelves. Only guards that accompanied groups from their homes stood with them in the secure area around Sylvan Pond. The veteran she-Drelve Narana had stood guard at the intersection of the roads to Meadowsweet and Sylvan Pond many times. Birney and Xenn traveled unnoticed until they reached the intersection of the routes to Meadowsweet and Sylvan Lake and fell under Narana's watch. The she-Drelve hailed them from her perch in the lower branches of a red elm.

Narana said, "Sergeant Birney, why do you travel with the Spellweaver so far from Alms Glen? These routes are hardly secure."

Birney answered, "We've encountered no enemies. The Spellweaver requires material components for his spells. We must gather them near Mirror Lake and the headwaters of the River Ornash."

Narana replied, "Sergeant Birney, shouldn't others gather the materials?"

Xenn said, "Brave Ranger, I must gather certain materials myself to preserve their potency. I'm in good hands."

Narana said, "I shan't question you, Spellweaver. I have not seen any incursions by Drolls and Kiennites for some time. There are few guards posted beyond this point. Since…I'm sorry, Birney and Spellweaver Xenn, the deaths of Mikkal and Narce, the elders have restricted travel between the communities. Only heavily guarded troupes travel between Alms Glen and Meadowsweet. If you stay near the path to Sylvan Pond, you should be safe. Scouts say the Drolls are very active near their tower on this side of the River Ornash. They keep fires going and watch both sides of the river. Kiennish shaman fire spells randomly into the water. They have not advanced south in numbers since they attacked the Spellweaver, Mikkal, and Narce, but small parties are always foraging for game and fruits of the forest. Be careful, Spellweaver. We came close to losing you."

Xenn said, "Thank you, Narana. Watch your back."

Xenn and Birney veered toward Sylvan Pond. Birney took gray berries, popped the skin on some of the thumbnail-sized fruits, and rubbed the pungent juice on Xenn and then himself to hide their scent. Once past the final Drelvish guard posts, they returned to the general direction of the Drolls' tower. Twice the Drelves encountered Droll patrols. They followed the second patrol back to the recently constructed tower near the River Ornash. The brace of Drelves followed the noisy wolf-faced warriors without fear of being heard. Drolls oft sniffed the air, but grayberries grew commonly in the wood and the smell did not alarm the Drolls. The forest began to thin as they neared the river Ornash. Hiding became a greater challenge and then nigh impossible. Xenn and Birney hunkered down behind one of the last great red oaks standing in view of the tower. The massive tree's trunk bore the scars of Drolls' axes, but the warriors evidently tired of the process of chopping the tree down or else chose to leave a bit of shade. Numerous Drolls moved about the thinned forest. Most hewed small trees for firewood. Xenn stopped and removed an old clump of dark orange moss. The Spellweaver muttered phrases and *Enlarged* the moss. The young Spellweaver then threw the sheet of invisimoss over his shoulder, placed his arm around Birney, and stood close.

"I can still see you," Birney exclaimed.

"Of course, you can. You're inside the moss," Xenn explained.

"Oh. The moss does feel good. It's soft and warm," Birney said as she awkwardly snuggled closer to Xenn.

The Drelves sneaked between remaining trees. The light period continued. They avoided passing near Drolls working at various tasks. Drolls they passed turned up their noses and sniffed the air. Gray berries gave the scent of a skulunk passing a distance away. Skulunks were not Magick. They just smelled bad. Xenn and Birney stopped at the base of a large everyellow tree. The pair rested and munched on some delicious trail mix. The lingering odor of the gray berries depressed their appetites a bit, but the trail mix still was good. After a respite, they continued onward and nearer the River Ornash.

"Quick, get off the trail. Someone's coming!" Birney whispered. The little Drelves slunk to the side of the path and sat beneath a bramble bush.

A huge Droll walked near them, stopped for a moment, sniffed, and looked all around. Invisimoss shielded them from the keen eyes of the sentries, and the gray berries disguised their essence form the guards' keen noses. Drolls had destroyed the forest near the tower and laid bare the land. There was nowhere to hide. Sentries on the wall walk at the top of the thirty-foot-tall tower had a clear new of the area around. The tower sat about fifty Yardley paces from the River Ornash. Drolls constantly watched the river. A Kiennite wearing an ornate robe walked back and forth across the bridge near the tower and fired bolts of purplish energy into the water. Huge fires burned on both sides of the river.

Xenn said, "Magick Missile Spells."

Birney observed, "Fishing? Guess they are too lazy to use poles."

Xenn whispered, "We are out of sight and smell. There's so much noise with all the chopping and fires, they won't hear us."

Birney asked, "Are we going to use the odd round balls?"

Xenn said, "Yes. How far can you throw one of them?"

Birney said, "Not as far as I can hit the enemies with my bow. I'm in easy range of the tower from where we stand, but there are too many to take out with arrows. In fact, even if your spells destroy the tower, there are so many Drolls about that I don't think we can succeed. We ought to fall back, Spellweaver. In my greed for vengeance, I have placed you at risk."

Xenn said, "No one is guaranteed his next breath. Let's proceed."

Birney sighed.

Xenn said, "I'll use the Slow Spell I learned. All I have to do is squeeze the little Omega Stone and use some treacle. I'll have a Fire Spell ready. Let's move forward and see what these Duoth Bombs do."

Birney again hesitated, but Xenn insisted. The duo inched across the cleared area, dodged Drolls moving about, and approached the tower. Once a large Droll stopped near them and accused a colleague of relieving himself of gas. The Drolls had a laugh, and went about their tasks. Xenn and Birney moved forward. Soon they stood about fifty paces from the tower. Birney said, "I can hit the tower from here. Let me have the Duoth Bombs."

Xenn said, "I'm going to hit the Kiennish shaman on the bridge with a Magick Missile, then I'll use the Slow Spell on the Drolls around us. If the tower doesn't fall from the bombs, I'll start using Fire Magick."

Birney said, "There's nothing for it."

The veteran ranger stepped out of the invisimoss.

Drolls saw him and shouted.

Xenn pointed at the Kiennite on the bridge and sent an unerring Magick Missile into him. The shaman wailed and fell into the River Ornash. Birney hurled a Duoth Bomb. The Round ball hit the tower and exploded. Three Drolls fell from the allure, timber in the wall shattered, and the tower shook. Xenn gripped the Omega stone with his left hand. It warmed in his hand. The Spellweaver muttered the phrases he'd found in his mind, rubbed a bit of treacle between his right second and third fingers, and turned around and directed his fingers toward various groups of Drolls. Pink auras surrounded the Drolls. The wolf-faced warriors started moving very *quickly* toward the pair of Drelves.

Birney threw a second Duoth bomb into the tower and another

explosion ripped into the wall. Several timbers fell, and Drolls running down the wall stairs lost their balance and fell.

Birney wailed, "You've placed a *Haste Spell* on them, Spellweaver! They are closing on us fast!"

Xenn panicked and released the Omega Stone. The stone indeed bequeathed him the power of a spell, but it was actually a Haste Spell. Birney abandoned his attacks on the tower, threw a third bomb on the bridge, and blew the timbers apart. Terrified Drolls fell into the water. Their colleagues on the far side of the River Ornash hustled to ready boats to cross the river. Birney threw the three remaining bombs in three directions into large groups of Drolls near the Drelves. Each bomb exploded and sent wolf-faced enemies into the air. By the time Birney threw the fifth Duoth bomb, Xenn had completed a Fire Spell. The Fireball exploded on the tower and immolated all Drolls on the tower. Xenn then dropped a charging Droll with a Magick Missile.

Birney shouted, "Let's get out of here, Spellweaver!"

Xenn screamed, "Don't see an exit strategy!"

Birney drew his bow and fired arrows in rapid succession at rapidly charging Drolls. Xenn resorted to Flaming Hands Spells. The flames left his outstretched hands and fanned out over 90 degrees. He turned and cast three spells in succession and differing directions and cleared the area immediately around them, but several Drolls closed from the remaining direction and were getting precariously close.

Xenn shouted, "Drop to the ground."

Birney fell flat.

Xenn sent another Flaming Hands Spell in the fourth direction and smote many Drolls. Now the area around them was devoid of enemies. Many Drolls moaned and cried from pain. Boats were in the water. Xenn sent another Fire Spell toward the water's edge and obliterated three boats that reached the shore.

Birney pleaded, "Now's our chance, Spellweaver! Let's retreat to the large tree!"

Xenn ignored his pleas and sent another Fire Spell into the group of Drolls that were originally away from the tower and had now gotten about a hundred paces from the Drelves. Sixty Drolls fell. Now no enemies were standing on this side of the river. Xenn walked toward the River Ornash, muttered, "For my father!" and sent a massive Fire Spell into the Drolls gathered on the far side of the River. Screams and wails filled the air. Enemies started running toward the mountains. Xenn sent another fire spell across the river and destroyed a barracks. He then sent two more meaningless bursts of Fire Magick into the already deceased enemies.

Birney pleaded again for retreat. Little sparks flickered from Xenn's finger tips and eyes. Birney threw his arms around the Spellweaver. Xenn struggled briefly. Finally, the stalwart Ranger dragged the Spellweaver toward the sparse trees.

Words appeared in Xenn's mind.

*"I give you my blood through which you will receive all you seek. You in turn give to me your all."*

In Green Vale, the Tree Shepherd muttered, "Fire Wizard!"

Birney feared the glassy coldness he saw in Xenn's eyes. Xenn folded the invisimoss and placed it in his pack. A short distance from the carnage the Spellweaver stopped Birney. He gripped the Omega Stone and uttered the phrases in his mind, and directed pink areas toward a rambling bramble bush. The rambling bramble bush rambled very quickly across their path. Xenn said, "I'm sorry we wasted your treacle. The devious artifact led me to believe it empowered me with a Slow Spell. Now I know reversing the incantation and using the treacle produces Slow Spell. The Haste Spell requires only gripping the Omega Stone and uttering the incantation. Quirky."

Birney panted, "Misspeaking the spell almost got us killed."

Xenn distantly replied, "What doesn't kill us merely makes us stronger."

Xenn stepped into the middle of the road the Drolls created.

Birney cautioned, "Spellweaver, please stay off the road."

Xenn emotionlessly answered, "We've nothing to fear. I'm the meanest *** ** * ***** on the road."

Birney said, "Just the same Spellweaver, I'd rather err on the side of caution. I'm more comfortable in the forest."

Xenn said, "I want to find more enemies."

Birney answered, "Predators and scavengers are going to the battle site. We can evade them in the woods."

Xenn relented and followed Birney into the forest. The pair made the journey back to Birney's tree without incident. Both collapsed and quickly fell asleep. Grayness entered Xenn's dreams.

Wisps…
Threads…
Threads of Magick…
Threads of fate…
Threads of time…
Threads connecting worlds …
Dreams connecting worlds …
Dreams of Magick…
The Magick of Dreams…
Magick connecting dreams…
Magick connecting worlds…
Dream raiders…
Elf pressure…
Albtraum…
Albträume, elf dreams, nightmares…

Ǿ ∞ Ǿ

Shapeless grayness filled the Spellweaver's slumber. Words appeared in his mind.

*"I give you my blood through which you will receive all you seek. You in turn give to me your all."*

# 9.

# Misleading the Council of Alms Glen

Tapping at the tree's bark awakened the duo. Young Ranger Toolum excitedly relayed that the elders called an emergency meeting of the Council of Alms Glen. Toolum, Xenn, and Birney walked to the common area. Alms Glen was abuzz.

Elder Evelynn said, "Spellweaver, thank Andreas you are safe. Scouts report a great battle near the River Ornash. The Drolls' tower and bridge are destroyed. Their bodies litter the field. We suspected the southerners, the Draiths, but they don't employ Magick. Forbin and Sara Jane Rumsic reported the explosions brought back memories of the destruction of the Kiennish forts during the time of the Great Defender Gaelyss."

Xenn's mother Tiffanne said, "Destruction of the Drolls' outpost makes Alms Glen more secure. We are indebted to those who fomented the deed."

A chorus of "Hear! Hear!" rang out in the meeting.

Elder Evelynn looked to Xenn and asked, "Spellweaver, were you involved?"

Xenn answered, "I'd say it was the work of a Fire Wizard, and I agree with my mother."

Teacher Boyd said, "The route to the harvest will be more secure. Our path has always been avoidance of offensive action and dependence upon the forest for protection. At critical times in our history, Magick has benefitted Drelvedom. It would seem this is another of those times. I do have one concern. The ancient square of invisimoss has disappeared from the Old Orange Spruce. Sergeant Birney, have you heard anyone speak of it?"

Birney said dispassionately, "I'll look into it, Teacher."

Xenn took the large chunk of invisimoss that had covered him and Birney from his pack and tossed it toward the Teacher. Xenn said, "I found this in the woods, Teacher. It's my gift to Drelvedom."

Boyd opened the large section of the deep red moss and marveled, "This is so much larger than the artifact used by the Lost Spellweaver to view the Lone Oak. It's one of my favorite stories from the Annals of Drelvedom. Invisimoss is so rare. Thank you for your gift, Spellweaver."

Xenn said smugly, "It's the least I could do for the Council."

Boyd returned, "Sergeant Birney, the old swatch of moss still has great sentimental value. Will you investigate its disappearance?"

Birney merely said, "I'll look into it, Teacher."

Boyd and Evelynn stared at Birney.

Evelynn said, "Sergeant Birney, we have little information about the Drolls' fate. We don't know who killed them. Please increase the guard at the meadow's edge."

Birney answered, "Elder, what matters is that the Drolls are dead. The manner of their demise does not concern me. I shall increase the guard and stand with them."

Xenn stood and said, "I'll stand with Sergeant Birney. Teacher Boyd, Elder Evelynn, and members of the Council… I have checked. No purveyors of Magick remain in the area."

Evelynn said, "You are here."

Xenn said, "I am here. Drelvedom's enemies have retreated to the Peaks of Division. With any luck, their ranks will be so weakened that the southerners, the Draiths, will overrun them."

Birney and Xenn walked to the perimeter. Neither spoke.

# 10.

# Nyssa from Fox Vale

The Drelves enjoyed several peaceful changes of seasons. Teacher Boyd led successful harvesting trips to Green Vale. The Drolls did not rebuild the tower near the Ornash and remained largely around the Gap Keep in the Peaks of Division. Kiennites ever strengthened the fortress. Only rarely Droll scouting parties crossed the River Ornash. Sergeant Birney maintained Drelvedom's vigilance and Xenn strengthened the defenses. In Xenn's thirtieth year he joined Boyd for the trek to Meadowsweet and Green Vale. Drelves from outlying communities joined in the harvest as always. Xenn's eye was drawn to young Nyssa from Fox Vale. Over several harvests their love blossomed, and Teacher Boyd performed a ceremony of life-time commitment. Nyssa and Xenn shared the tree that the Great Defender Gaelyss had used as his home. Xenn shared everything with his beloved Nyssa, including the enigmatic Omega Stone. Previously he had only revealed the artifact to Sergeant Birney. Xenn and Birney discovered the stone's deceptiveness the hard way. When Xenn gripped the stone, an incantation appeared in his mind. What he thought would result in slowing his opponents actually sped them up. The Dreamraider Amica left the Omega Stone with Sergeant Birney after invading his dreams. She relayed some history of the artifacts in general, but imparted no specific knowledge of the particular stone she left in Birney's tree house. After the first near disastrous casting of the Haste Spell on the Drolls, Xenn profited from the Omega Stone by learning the incantations for Slow and Haste Spells. The Spellweaver just preferred using them without using the odd artifact. Xenn revealed the Omega Stone to Nyssa whilst Birney visited the couple. Xenn gripped the stone. Words formed in his mind.

*"I give you my blood through which you will receive all you seek. You in turn give to me your all."*

The stone warmed in his hand.

A single rune appeared on the rock and persisted for thirteen heartbeats.

**Ω**

Then the single letter faded, and three runes appeared on the surface of the rock, which briefly emitted gray light.

Ǿ ∞ Ǿ

The runes faded after 21 heartbeats and the single rune reappeared. The pattern repeated three times.

Words appeared in Xenn's mind.

*"I give you my blood through which you will receive all you seek. You in turn give to me your all."*

Nyssa asked, "What do you feel?"

Xenn said, "Same as before. Slow Spell, but I know the incantation is reversed. I now command both Slow and Haste, but I must conjure and use material components. The Haste Spell from the Stone only requires gripping the stone and uttering the incantation, but I'm leery of its effects."

Nyssa said, "Let me hold it. See what it tells me."

Xenn replied, "You are not Spellweaverish. It might be dangerous."

Nyssa argued, "You have said it's not evil. Let me try."

Birney interrupted, "Let me try it first."

Xenn hesitated and then said, "Ok, but drop it if you feel pain."

Birney took the gray crescent shaped stone and gripped it. The Single rune appeared and the pattern repeated. Birney laughed and muttered a series of nonsensical phrases. The veteran Ranger jubilantly said, "It works! I'm empowered by Magick!"

Xenn said, "What do you mean?"

Birney said, "Don't tease me! I know you see it, or more appropriately, don't see it! I'm invisible!"

Nyssa laughed. Xenn fought doing the same and said, "No, Birney, you are not invisible. We see you."

Birney reiterated, "I'm invisible! I can't see myself. How can you see me?"

Xenn said, "It's a delusion. Give me the rock."

Birney gave Xenn the Omega Stone. The Spellweaver did not grip the artifact. Birney disappointedly said, "Could you really see me?"

Nyssa smiled and answered, "Yes, every browning hair."

Birney declared, "I really thought I was invisible. Did I at least get the incantation right, Spellweaver?"

Xenn said, "Not a single phrase. Invisibility is not hard to master, but it's difficult to use. Invisible people can't see one another."

Nyssa said, "My turn."

Xenn said, "It fooled Birney, but he's no worse for the wear. I suppose we can try."

Nyssa took the Omega Stone. The little rock warmed and softened in her small hand. It's series of runes appeared. Nyssa uttered phrases and pointed her finger at Birney. Birney shrugged. Nyssa said, "Oh no! I've *Held* him and don't know how to release him. I should have never tried to touch Magick!"

Birney said, "Nyssa, I can move. I felt nothing."

Nyssa quickly gave the stone to Xenn and said, "It gave me the impression I could make someone stop moving. *Hold Person*... I..."

Xenn said, "It fooled you. What else did you feel?"

Nyssa said, "I felt... safe. But I always do with you two fellows."

The three Drelves shared a laugh. They spent periods studying the Omega Stone. They held it two at a time and all three together. The artifact yielded no more secrets. Xenn concluded the artifact, typical of its kind, fed misinformation. Xenn carried the stone to the Old Orange Spruce. The Teacher Boyd was again busily instructing neophytes about the upcoming harvest trip to Green Vale. Xenn again used Knock to enter the old tree and descended the stairs. The Four Elemental Stones sat on a small table in the corner of the room in plain view. When Xenn came within thirteen paces of the group of stones, the Omega Stone warmed, emitted grayness, and revealed its single rune. The sequence did not follow. The bookcase holding the many archived Spellbooks sat a goodly twenty paces away of the far side of the wall. Xenn's spell book was safely tucked in an ambry in his little tree. Out of curiosity Xenn moved to within thirteen paces of the spell books. The stone warmed and revealed its gray auras and single rune. Xenn walked to the quartet of Elemental Stones and brought the Omega Stone near them. No new effects occurred. The Spellweaver reluctantly touched the Omega Stone to each of the artifacts. Only the grayness and the surface runes appeared. Xenn placed the Omega Stone in his pack, ascended the stairs, and left the Old Orange Spruce.

Xenn and Birney accompanied the Teacher Boyd and the neophytes to Meadowsweet and Green Vale and participated in a bountiful harvest. The Tree Shepherd remained silent and the Dryad did not appear. The harvesters made the journey uneventfully. Nyssa accompanied Elder Evelynn and he group that went to Sylvan Pond. Nyssa was expert at herbology and caring for the Drelves' forest friends. The groups rejoined at the intersection of the roads leading to Meadowsweet and Sylvan Pond. The return trip went well.

Birney was awarded the rank Sergeant Major and assumed the command of all Drelvedom's Rangers. Teacher Boyd developed great experience and received accolades for his work. Many felt Boyd among the greatest Teachers and compared him to Edkim. Xenn and Nyssa remained childless. Both worked tirelessly to further Drelvedom. Approximations came. No Spellweavers arrived with the gray light.

Time changed Birney and Nyssa's hair from silver and orange to brown. Xenn, typically of Spellweavers, aged imperceptivity to a given generation of his people. In his hundred and eleventh year, Birney passed command of the Rangers to young Timper. Nyssa and Xenn shared a hundred and seven years. After her passing, Xenn never took another life-mate.

Centuries passed. Generations of Drelves walked with the Spellweaver Xenn.

# 11.

# Ambush: Old Xenn

**X**enn slumped into plush orange moss that surrounded a great everred tree and stared across a clearing about a hundred paces wide. The aging Spellweaver dabbed beads of reddish perspiration from his brow and welcomed the end of the long dark period. The surface of the World of the Three Suns never experienced the blackness of the subterranean caves. The dark period occurred when Meries lingered at its nadir. Now the little yellow sun skipped across the sky and brightened the world. The Drelve's chameleon-like ability blended his deceptively frail figure into the red-orange forest surroundings. Xenn's party returned from harvesting the precious enhancing root tubers at Green Vale, the unique closely guarded green milieu where the plants grew. Now in his 987$^{th}$ year, Xenn accompanied Drelves' Teachers and helped harvest mature tubers from the roots of the life-enhancing plants. The old Teacher Batali served 144 years but died five dark periods earlier, and his erstwhile apprentice Pryam completed his first harvest as Teacher. The old Spellweaver Xenn had seen many close calls and a few tragedies. Gnarly goblin-like Kiennites and huge wolf-faced Drolls, the oft-allied ancestral adversaries of the Drelves had never discovered the hidden vale and its treasures. In the distal past Drolls nefariously used bizarre Magick, transformed to Drelves, and attacked the hidden Drelvish haven Sylvan Pond. Drelves sang at the campfires of those lost at Sylvan Pond, including Carinne, the mother of the only twin Spellweavers in the annals of Drelvedom, and Laurenne, beloved life-mate of an elder Moblee.

Drolls relied on cunning, strength, instinct, and numbers. Many

Drelves admired their enemies' strong features, canine faces, and long flowing manes and considered Drolls rustically handsome. Xenn hated and equated the large bipedal Drolls to cur-faced mongrels. Centuries had not tempered the Spellweaver's anger over the Drolls' murder of his father Mikkal. People saw things differently. Eye of the beholder…Fortunately, Xenn's party had not encountered one of those multi-eyed beasts. The legendary eye of the beholder floated ominously in the air, cruised the caverns and denser forests of the World of the Three Suns, and assailed victims. The beholder's varyingly-sized eyes fomented diverse attacks.

Drelves harvested enhancing root tubers every eighth dark period. Teachers expertly taught thirteen-year-old Drelvlings to carefully harvest the mature tubers without shocking the parent plant. The bright light warmed Old Xenn and eased a bit of the pain in his joints. The Spellweaver remembered his mother Tiffanne and many friends, including his greatest friend and ally the Ranger Birney. Seeing friends and loved ones pass away was one of the disadvantages of living 987 years. Xenn had taken a life-mate and shared a hundred seasons of the harvest with his beloved Nyssa. Spellweavers enjoyed uncommonly long lives, but the enjoyment waned with the passing of Nyssa. The couple had remained childless. Xenn had seen Approximations at intervals of 13, 21, 144, 8, 233, 1, 3, 144, 1, 89, 13, 13, 144, 55, 8, 21, 13, and 8 years. 18 Approximations passed without the birth of another Spellweaver. 55 years had now past since Andreas last drew near. The Drelvish people longed to bask in the gray light.

Xenn's party had a close call immediately after exiting Green Vale. Over time, Drolls had overcome their fears of the dark River Spirit, Xenn's Magick, and legends of enchanted areas in the central forests. More adventurous and malicious Kiennites likely spurred on the large party of Drolls. The enemies nigh stumbled on the secluded Green Vale. Experienced Drelvish scouts named Alo and Wera saw through illusory spells cast by nefarious Kiennish shamans, discovered the invaders, discouraged the wolf-faced Drolls with well-aimed arrows, and then warned Xenn, the young Teacher Pryam, and the root gatherers. Every Kiennish whelp born during an Approximation had some modest powers of Magick, mostly illusory. Tree Sprites, Dryads, Drelves, and Tree Herders usually saw through the illusory spells. Thanks to the astute scouts Alo and Wera, the outnumbered Drelves beat a hasty retreat into the thick red and orange underbrush. Red oak trees and reinforcements from Meadowsweet kept the Drolls and Kiennites from discovering Green Vale. Unique green plants grew in Green Vale and differed from the reds, oranges, and yellows of the forests of the World of the Three Suns.

Draiths grew ever stronger in the south and strengthened their black-walled conurbation Ooranth, to the Drolls and Kiennites' chagrin. The seven-foot-tall, bronze-skinned Draiths expressed little interest in the affairs of Drelves and preferred to stay clear of the depths of the forest. Draiths came from the great mountain ranges to the south and were ancestral enemies of the races of giants that lived in the mountains. Drelves witnessed monumental battles between the armies of the Drolls and Kiennites and the Draiths. The Kiennites lacked a leader with the power and charisma of their greatest General Saligia, adversary of the Great Defender Gaelyss and legends of Drelvedom including Sergeant Major Rumsie, fletcher and bowyer BJ Aires, Camille Aires, Teacher Edkim, Tree herders Old Yellow, Big Red, and Orange Julian, legendary Ranger Banderas, aged Ranger Clarke Maceda, and others. The annals of Drelvedom recognized all contributors to Drelves' history, though the songs by the campfires weren't always kind in their remembrance. The annals told of the Lost Spellweaver Yannuvia and Kirrie, erstwhile Teacher and life mate of the Great Defender. Yannuvia and Kirrie carried the designation "Fire Wizard." Xenn's Magick had kept the Drolls and Kiennites at bay for centuries, and the aged Spellweaver had narrowly avoided the stigmata that led to the exiles of Yannuvia and Kirrie. Unfortunately, the Spellweaver did not enjoy a good relationship with the Tree Shepherd in Green Vale. The shepherd of the Thirttene Friends lumped Xenn in the group of Fire Wizards. Fire Magick… unwanted Magick in the Tree Shepherd's way of thinking.

The Annals of Drelvedom told of Drelves named Klunkus, Beaux, Dienas, Yiuryna, the unwonted Mender Fisher, unpredictable Dreamraider Good Witch, and the Dreamraider's odd companions, strange sojourners of questionable motive, the merchant Cupid, Kelpie Sidheag, puca Cupid, and Cloudmare Shyrra. The Dreamraider's odd alliance helped the defenders of Alms Glen stave off the assault of Saligia's greatest force, which included wyvern riders and terrible beasts such as Xorn. Only the Teacher Edkim's use of an artifact of cold Magick to destroy a hundred firehorses and their Droll riders in the campaign that cost the Lone Oak was greater legend.

Xenn had not witnessed such monumental battles during his long life. The Annals did not credit Xenn with his greatest victory over the Drolls. Xenn and the Ranger Sergeant Birney hid their roles in anonymity. The Annals merely recorded the destruction of a Droll outpost and death of a thousand Drolls at the hands of unknown purveyors of Magick. Teachers taught the most likely fomenters were the crew that destroyed the Kiennish forts during the time of the Great Defender Gaelyss. Time dulled the Drolls' memories of the carnage, and again each harvest of the enhancing root placed the harvesters at risk and brought on skirmishes with Drolls and Kiennites. Drelvish scouts spying on Droll and Kiennite camps heard harrowing tales of disappearances in the River Ornash. Many rumors circulated about the return of the Fire Wizards, Yannuvia and Kirrie, or the nefarious Dreamraiders, who fomented mischief and drove the wedge that alienated the twin Spellweavers Gaelyss and Yannuvia. Xenn furthered the Great Defender's defenses around Alms Glen. The site of the abandoned hamlet Lost Sons remained barren. The Kiennites never rebuilt the destroyed fortresses that had stood to the north and south of the red meadow and fell to the fire spells of Fire Wizard Kirrie and her companions so long ago. The red meadow never regained the splendor it enjoyed during the Lone Oak era, and it never saw another great battle after the fall of Saligia of Aulgmoor.

Xenn breathed deeply. Hours of running had spent the old Spellweaver's physical strength. Spellweavers' greatest ally, the wandering sun Andreas toggled a bit closer in the sky. Was an unpredictable and infrequent Approximation imminent? Sometimes Andreas teased! The gray sun's rays had immeasurable effect unless the bizarre sun approached the land. Scattered beams of grayness filtered through the thick red and orange leaves above him, reached the Drelve's face, gave him a bit of energy, and drew his eyes to the sky. Xenn basked in the growing gray light for a moment. His joints still hurt. Age challenged the rejuvenating powers of Andreas. Xenn closed his eyes. Perhaps a moment's sleep… Not to be…

Alo's alarmed voice split the air, "Drolls! We are discovered! To the trees! Make ready!"

Xenn stood and looked around the stately red oak. Several Drelves deftly scurried up orange elms and red oaks. Five Drelvish archers stood shoulder-to-shoulder and aimed well-made bows toward the small meadow. Large menacing wolf-faced figures emerged from the thick woods to the west.

Alo cried, "Fire!"

Drelves' arrows sped toward the advancing Drolls. An arrow struck one of the seven-foot tall creatures in the middle of his throat and felled him. The remaining arrows hit and barely slowed the advancing enemies. The archers fired two more volleys, turned, and fled to the cover of the underbrush. Their comrades positioned in the lower limbs of the trees.

Xenn dipped his index finger in treacle, directed his left hand toward the charging Drolls, uttered several phrases, and sent a flash of brilliance across the clearing. The Slow Spell retarded the enemies' movement and enabled Alo and his archers to reach the underbrush. Drelvish archers fired from red oaks toward their slowly moving adversaries and struck down two additional Drolls.

Alo drew his short sword and faced the unenviable task of battling the axe-wielding Drolls hand-to-hand.

Xenn again muttered phrases, sent a mauve ray toward the nearest Droll, struck the beast with an unerring Magick Missile Spell, and slew the wolf-faced enemy. The spell caught the attention of three Drolls nearest the victim of the Magick Missile. The three Drolls made a lethal mistake and paused. Drelvish archers dropped them where they stood.

The young Teacher Pryam, erstwhile neophytes, and accompanying elders carried the precious, harvested enhancing root tubers into the forest and gathered at a point beyond Alo's brave stand. Drelves who had not harvested the enhancing root tubers were called neophytes. A Drelve who had seen a thousand Dark Periods and not harvested was still a neophyte. Old Clarke Maceda, a contemporary of the Great Defender Gaelyss and his twin brother the Lost Spellweaver Yannuvia, saw 1106 changes of season and never participated in a harvest. Old Clarke joked about the oldest neophyte in the history of Drelvedom. He was likely correct.

The Drolls stood confused. Five were dead. Then a large Droll wearing the hides of rare mountain sheep and carrying a huge two-handed sword burst into the clearing with another dozen Droll warriors carrying large spears and axes. Two scrawny, goblin-like creatures followed the hulking

Drolls. Xenn and Alo's party now faced a Droll chieftain, two Kiennites, and twenty-five Drolls, albeit Xenn's earlier Slow Spell afflicted half the enemies, Drolls fanned out to attack the Drelves' positions.

The Droll chieftain growled and shook his crude two-handed sword. Several Drolls dropped their axes and hurled spears toward the trees. The sheer force of the spears' impact shook the trees and dropped two Drelves to the ground. The Drelves scurried back up the trees. The Kiennites drew odd crossbows. The creature to the chieftain's left fired a bolt into the trees. The crossbow bolt exploded on impact and jarred the young archer Cerro from his perch. Rangers ran onto the field and retrieved the unconscious Drelve. The second Kiennite fired his bolt toward Alo. The bolt followed an eerily accurate course. Alo adroitly moved his shield and stopped the missile in the nick of time. The Kiennites cursed and reloaded.

The hulking tribal chieftain angrily growled commands. Drolls closed in on the outnumbered Drelves' positions in the trees and underbrush. All the while Drelvish archers assailed the Drolls and occasionally scored a mortal center shot. Xenn cast a very brief incantation that created thirteen identical images of himself. A second spell produced a translucent shield before each of the thirteen images. Trusting his fate to the Mirror Image and Shield Spells, Xenn stepped from behind the red oak, shouted loudly, and then again conjured. Seeing thirteen Drelvish Spellweavers simultaneously conjuring spooked the Drolls. The wolf-faced enemies stopped and stepped backward.

One of the Kiennites shrilly shouted, "Fools! It's trickery. There's but one of him. Strike down the images and he'll fall."

Three Drolls hurled spears toward the *thirteen Xenns*. The three spears passed through images of the Spellweaver. Once attacked an image faded. Magick shields did not impede mundane weapons from passing through illusory Spellweavers. Seeing three fewer images of the Spellweaver encouraged the Drolls. Xenn's mirror images shuffled constantly. The second Kiennite aimed his crossbow and fired. The bolt uncannily crossed the meadow, moved around two Drolls, discovered the true Xenn, and bore down on the Spellweaver. The missile thumped harmlessly against Xenn's Magick shield. The ten remaining images of the Spellweaver shimmered, shuffled, and briefly faded from view. The images reappeared, and the Drolls now saw twenty-one Xenns.

"Idiots! Don't attack him with Magick! Remember the lessons of Lone Oak meadow!" the Droll chieftain grumbled. He glibly continued, "You're going to suffer before you die, Spellweaver!"

Drelves sang of the storied Mirror Images Spell, and Drolls and Kiennites cursed the dweomer. When the wandering gray sun Andreas was near, Magick touched mundane plants, animals, minerals, dirt, fire, and water. Only spell casters commanded spells. Only ultra-rare Drelvish Spellweavers possessed the ability to cast spells. Except… long ago… during a visit to Green Vale during an Approximation in the time of the twin Spellweavers Gaelyss and Yannuvia, four Drelvlings Bryce, Meryt, Debery, and Zack and beloved Teacher Edkim gained the ability of a spell. Unwonted gift of grayness… Bryce used Mirror Images in the Battle of Lone Oak Meadow and greatly contributed to the Drelves' victory over the combined forces of the Kiennish General Saligia, the greatest and most nefarious leader of the Kiennish folk. Bryce's images multiplied when Kiennish shaman attacked them with Magick. An Arrow of Slaying ultimately overcame the little Drelve's spell.

The Kiennite's crossbow bolt pinpointed Xenn but did not give lasting advantage for the enemies. Xenn's twenty-one indistinguishable images shuffled constantly. The enemies turned from Alo's group and charged the old Spellweaver's mirror images.

Xenn grudgingly reached into his purple mooler hide rucksack and removed a rare piece of sulfur. Twenty-one images of the old Drelve crushed the sulfur, performed complicated hand gestures, and muttered arcane phrases. Twenty-one reddish rays moved toward the Drolls and Kiennites. Only one was *real* Magick. Xenn centered the spell twenty paces in front of the Chieftain and Kiennites. The fireball exploded, consumed fifteen Drolls, and engulfed the Chieftain and two Kiennites. Secondary explosions erupted from one Kiennite's quiver and slew the unfortunate bowman. Flames covered the second Kiennite and consumed his bow and quiver, but five undamaged bolts fell to the scorched ground. The gnarly Kiennite survived the flames, broke from the fray, and ran away. The Droll chieftain pulled thick hides over his burly frame and yelped in pain.

Quirk of Magick… the fireball spell spared seven Drolls. The septet closed on Xenn's images. The Drelvish Spellweaver's Slow Spell affected six of the seven. The screams and wails of their comrades consumed by the fireball waned. The Drolls stopped ten paces away and stood bewildered before Xenn's images. The wounded chieftain furiously bellowed commands. The seven Drolls feared their commander more than Xenn and again charged toward the images of the Spellweaver. Even those slowed by Magick closed the short distance quickly. Xenn's images perfectly mimicked his movements. The Droll that moved with normal speed struck and dispelled three images. Eighteen *Xenns* remained. The seven large creatures' close proximity to Xenn prevented further attacks by the Drelvish archers perched in the trees. Alo and five comrades brandished short swords and bravely charged toward the Drolls. Xenn pulled a dagger from his belt and stabbed the normally moving Droll twice. The small blade only infuriated the Droll. Alo and his rangers moved quickly and engaged three Drolls. The remaining four Drolls concentrated on Xenn's eighteen images. The Drolls eliminated five images. The Droll chieftain growled thunderously and charged toward Xenn.

Alo and his comrades evaded the Drolls' great axes. Drelves' garb facilitated blending into the forest but did not provide the protection of armor. Direct hits from the Drolls' axes were usually lethal. Xenn dodged the Drolls, sprinkled a bit of quicksilver on the ground, and uttered several phrases. The Haste Spell quickened the Drelves' attacks. Xenn possessed an artifact called an Omega Stone. The device purportedly gave the power of Haste without having to use material component, but Xenn declined using the finicky and deceitful device if he possessed quicksilver. Xenn revealed the Omega Stone only to his old friend Birney and life-mate Nyssa. At baseline Drelves enjoyed better dexterity and now quadrupled the speed of the six *slowed* enemies. One Droll continued to move at half the Drelves' pace. While Xenn was gesturing to finish the Haste Spell, the four Drolls attacked and dispelled four images. Nine *Xenns* remained. Was it just luck that the wolf-faced warriors missed the *real* Xenn? The hallowed spell book, *the Gifts of Andreas to the People of the Forest* always gave the same answer, "It's Magick!" … or quirks of Magick… sometimes unwonted… sometimes unwanted…

A *slow* Droll narrowly missed Xenn and eliminated another image. The Droll moving at normal speed also slashed through a pseudo-Xenn. The Drolls' chieftain approached. Xenn moved rapidly to the left, separated from Alo and his comrades, and drew the chieftain to his remaining seven images. The chieftain ordered four Drolls to pursue Xenn. Three Drolls battled Alo and five other Drelves. Drelves loathed hand-to-hand combat with the larger Drolls. Xenn's Magick *slowed* the Drolls and *hasted* the Drelves. Alo and his fellows quickly felled one Droll and reduced the odds to six to two. The chieftain and the other four Drolls battled the seven deadly Xenns. The *hasted* Spellweaver Xenn scurried a hundred paces to the fringes of the clearing. The frustrated chieftain and his minions followed. Xenn fired a Magick Missile toward the bigger, stronger, and angry chieftain. The spell had no effect. Magick afforded the old Droll protection. The quick thinking Xenn fired a second and third Magick Missile into the charging Drolls to the left and right of the chieftain. Both Drolls fell. The chieftain and two *slow* Drolls reached Xenn.

Xenn avoided the chieftain's massive two-handed sword, but the Drolls arrived and eliminated two images. Xenn was left with himself, four images and three angry Drolls. The chieftain's smoldering garb added to the stench of burning foliage and flesh. Alo's group mowed down another Droll, but the *slow* Drolls wounded two Drelves. The four Drelves quickly killed the remaining opponent, and Alo and three unwounded comrades rushed across the clearing to support Xenn.

The Drolls' axes hewed through another image and further reduced Xenn's advantage. The Droll's axe struck the image of the Spellweaver, the image wavered briefly, and one less Xenn was on the field. Only four Xenns remained. The chieftain narrowly missed the Spellweaver again.

"I can smell you, scumbag! I'm going to get you soon!" the chieftain growled.

Fatigued and down to four images against three Drolls, Xenn simply parried. He ran side to side. Magick constantly shuffled his images, increased the speed of his tired legs, and slowed two of his three larger opponents. The Drolls faced a situation akin to the child's game "hide the thimble." Magick made the images indistinguishable. Alo and his scouts approached and shouted battle cries.

Furiously, the chieftain ripped his axe through Xenn's two left-most images and eliminated them. Alo reached the Droll to the chieftain's right and engaged the creature. The other three Drelves attacked the Droll to the chieftain's left.

Xenn dropped to his knees, avoided the massive sword, pointed his left index finger at the chieftain, and shouted, "Surrender!" in Droll dialect. The Command Spell failed. The Spellweaver rolled to the ground. The chieftain hurled his sword aside and pulled from his belt a barbed cat o' nine tails made of mooler hide and tetra bush thorns. The angry Droll snapped the whip through the three remaining images before him, dissipated all but the actual Spellweaver, and trapped Xenn within the coils of the device. The barbs of the cat o' nine tails dug into the Spellweaver's flesh.

The chieftain pulled Xenn toward his hulking frame and chided, "I'm going to rip off your head and eat your heart!"

The coils restricted Xenn's movement. Unable to gesture effectively, his mind searched for a spell with only a verbal component. Magick Missile and Command had been ineffective against the experienced Droll chieftain. In his moment of despair, Xenn looked into the face of his massive opponent. The chieftain's wolf-like facial features and powerful frame made him oddly alluring.

What to do?

Against the cat o' nine tails…

The powerful chieftain held Xenn within his barbed whip and pulled the Spellweaver toward his waiting clenched left hand. Xenn fought to remain conscious, barked the Magick Missile command, and directed the power of the spell toward the handle of the whip in the Droll's right hand. The force of the spell cut the mooler hide coils of the rope. Xenn dropped unceremoniously to the ground.

"Cursed warlock!" the chieftain growled.

The huge Droll futilely swung his left fist, missed Xenn's head, lurched forward, and struggled to maintain his balance. The angry chieftain tried to stomp the Spellweaver, but Xenn rolled aside. The thorns of the cat o' nine tails dug into his flesh.

Alo delivered a fatal blow to his opponent. Three other Drelves bested the remaining Droll warrior. The now-outnumbered chieftain howled, abruptly threw off his cumbersome robes, and ran toward the woods from whence the marauders had come.

Alo quickly went to Xenn and helped the Spellweaver remove the tangled coils of the barbed whip from his body.

Xenn breathlessly commanded, "Don't mind me! Check on the

wounded and make safe Teacher Pryam, the young, and harvested enhancing root."

Alo removed the whip and said, "You have again saved us, Spellweaver. I shan't leave you bound. The Drolls might return."

The old Spellweaver stood on wobbly legs, brushed off his clothing, and urged, "We must tend the wounded, seek a place of refuge, and regain our strength and energies. Secure remnants of the chieftain's robe and Kiennites' weaponry. They attacked us with exceptional missiles. But make haste."

"Thanks to your spell, making *haste* will be easy!" Alo conceded.

Drelves scurried down from trees and scanned the battlefield. The enemies wounded five Drelves but killed none. In the time of the twin Spellweavers, Drolls and Kiennites brazenly attacked parties moving to and from Green Vale, and assaulted Sylvan Pond, and killed Drelves, she-Drelves, and Drelvlings indiscriminately. Xenn's father Mikkal fell battling Drolls. Attacks had rarely occurred in recent generations. Drolls and Kiennites were more occupied with battles with the Draiths, who gained prominence and ever enlarged their citadel Ooranth. The plain upon which the black-walled city sat became known as the plain of Ooranth. Inexplicably and alarmingly, attacks on Drelves were increasing in frequency. Recently the heir apparent to the Teacher's role had been killed in one such attack.

Alo and Xenn hurried to Pryam and the young Drelves. The youthful Teacher Pryam and young Drelves clutched sacks containing the precious enhancing plant root tubers. Necessity pressed Pryam into his role at an early age. The Teacher was most often an elderly and experienced Drelve, but Pryam's predecessor Batali had fallen ill suddenly and his presumed successor Symon fell to a Droll's axe. During the time of the twin Spellweavers, a she-Drelve named Morganne served as Teacher at the age of eighteen years. The legendary hero of the battle of Lone Oak meadow and then Teacher Edkim chose Morganne as his successor, and Magick bequeathed her with the old Teacher's memories. The Teacher Morganne's legacy included songs of her bravery at the battle of Lone Oak and disappearance with the Spellweaver Yannuvia and folk of Lost Sons. The annals were quite vague about events of this time period. Time clouded the facts surrounding the story. The she-Drelve Kirrie, the life-mate of the

Great Protector Gaelyss succeeded Morganne as Teacher and wrote very little in the annals. Kirrie followed Yannuvia's path and shared his "fire wizard" legacy. She had disappeared after the great battle that resulted in General Saligia of Aulgmoor's final defeat. Teacher Boyd served the Drelves during Xenn's early years. The first Teacher Dirt was a prolific writer. If someone respected you as a writer, he said your name was Dirt. Pryam was a good student of the old texts.

Youth betrayed and fear overcame Pryam. In a trembling voice the young Teacher said, "I am not of much account. I did nothing."

Xenn quickly interrupted, "Right now, I am not of much account. You protected and kept safe the youths and harvest. You did your job, Teacher."

Alo added, "Using the blade is not your role."

Pryam observed, "Should we attend the dead enemies?"

Alo urged, "No time! We must seek the safety of the forest. The sounds and smells of battle arouse the beasts. Already the scavengers of the forest gather. Predators will find us," Alo urged.

Xenn agreed, "Unfortunately I've used my strength. I can't *heal* our wounded until I rest. Let's make for Alms Glen!"

Drelvish scouts hurriedly searched the scorched clearing and recovered five Kiennish crossbow bolts, the Droll chieftain's discarded hides, and a crude amulet made of odd mirror like scales within the thick smoldering fur. A simple necklace made of thick mooler hide fibers suspended the amulet. The veteran Alo advised against studying the weapons and armaments in the field and suggested the group proceed to Alms Glen. The Drelves gathered their wounded and hustled away from the smoldering field.

The harvesters reached Alms Glen in about six hours. The elders Tull, Brie, and Molinna greeted them, matrons quickly attended Cerro and his wounded comrades, and other Drelves brought nourishment. Initially the Spellweaver Xenn refused treatment. The thorns on the Droll's whip inflicted many small wounds. Tull insisted the Spellweaver apply enhancing root balms to his injuries. Old Tull was highly respected. His knowledge of the Annals of Drelvedom and herbology was comparable to even the greatest Teachers. He had worked in Green Vale at the harvests and assisted in Meadowsweet many times. Elder Brie sent for the bowyer Brynne Aires, who descended from BJ Aires, one of the heroes of the battle of Lone Oak meadow. BJ Aires and Byrum Goodale were the most renowned Drelvish bowyers and fletchers. Some of BJ's bows and arrows survived centuries of use. Drelvish self-bows were treasured family heirlooms and young Drelves trained diligently in archery. BJ Aires's life-mate Camille Aires served as Teacher of the Drelves and discovered the four elemental stones 13 years after the disappearance of the Lost Spellweaver Yannuvia. BJ and Camille's daughter Caroline served the Rangers for many changes of seasons and led many pilgrimages to Green Vale. The Aires family passed the roles of bowyer and fletcher along their line. Brynne was now twenty years old and had mastered many of her ancestors' techniques. Brynne soon arrived and joined the recuperating Spellweaver and his beleaguered party.

Once Brynne arrived, Xenn spoke to the group, "Fire Magick should have consumed the mooler hide. The Droll's garb had some means of fire protection."

The elder Brie asked, "We know little of destructive Magick. The Great Protector Gaelyss concentrated on healing and defensive spells. Spellweaver, how could Drolls defend against Fire Magick?"

Xenn rubbed his aching left forearm and replied, "I am not a student of history. The Fire Spell incantation appears in *the Gifts of Andreas to the People of the Forest.* Teacher Pryam, you'd answer better than I."

Pryam timidly replied, "I'll try, Spellweaver. The Teachers Kirrie, Morganne, and Camille Aires chronicled in the Annals of Drelvedom deeds of the twin Spellweavers, the Fire Wizard Yannuvia and the Great Protector Gaelyss. The Spellweaver Yannuvia disappeared repeatedly for extended periods and inexplicably aged. The Great Protector Gaelyss and Sergeant Major Rumsie discovered Yannuvia's alliance with Saligia of Aulgmoor and vanquished the Fire Wizard on what we call the Knoll of Shame, which overlooks the Ornash River. Ultimately Yannuvia, the Teacher Morganne, other traitors against Drelvedom, the elders and people of Lost Sons, and other folks vanished. The incantation for the Fireball Spell appeared in spell book of the Great Protector Gaelyss. Gaelyss refused to study and never mastered the spell. Unwanted Magick… The Spellweaver assumed his brother Yannuvia bequeathed Fire Magick to the people and feared his twin's intent. Gaelyss received unwonted warnings about his brother. In his spell book Gaelyss wrote of an encounter with a *supposed* Tree Sprite matron in Green Vale.

The Tree Sprite matron confided, '*I'm not an enemy. I'm simply a messenger sent to give you a warning. You were spared the effect of the Temporal Stasis. I must warn you of your brother Yannuvia. It is you, Gaelyss, who should lead the Drelves. Your brother treks down a dangerous path. He'll return one day and profess loyalty to your people. You shouldn't believe him. He'll stress striking against your enemies and use Magick to bring them down with spells of fire. He will have changed'*.

Gaelyss also wrote that the Dryad in Green Vale denied fomenting the deed.

"The Great Protector's first life-mate the Teacher Kirrie informed elders of the incantation's appearance in the spell book after Yannuvia and his comrades disappeared. Later Kirrie disappeared and was thought dead. Gaelyss chose Fadra of Meadowsweet as his life mate. Kirrie returned. She had traveled the same path as Yannuvia. Let me review for the newer members of the community. Teachers serve as stewards of the ancient spell book *the Gifts of Andreas to the People of the Forest.* Excepting Yannuvia, every Spellweaver in the history of Drelvedom's spell book rests in the Old Orange Spruce library. The Old Orange Spruce is the ancestral home of the Teachers in Alms Glen. When Approximations of Andreas result in births of Spellweavers, the most recent copy of the ancient spell book replicates. The Teacher presents the new Spellweaver with his copy at age 7, the end of nymph-hood. Spellweavers add dweomers to the book as they live. When Andreas draws near, new spells appear in Spellweavers' minds, usually as the sorcerers' dreams. According to the Annals of Drelvedom, Spellweavers learn new spells in *unwonted ways.* Magick touches all Drelves during Approximations. In our history, non-Spellweavers rarely gain the power of Magick. The Spellweaver Gaelyss recorded in his memoirs the words of the Tree Sprite in Green Vale:

*"I wish every Drelve touched by the waters of the Geyser of the Thirttene Friends this day also be touched by Magick and given the power of casting a spell!"*

"The Teacher Edkim, and 13-year-old Drelves Meryt, Bryce, Debery, and Zack learned spells. The heroes of Lone Oak meadow stood within the multihued waters of the geyser of the Thirttene Friends during the

Approximation. The Spellweaver's life-mate Kirrie attained the power of a Summoning Spell through this gray stone, the Summoning Stone of Fire (SSF)."

The young Teacher Pryam produced a smooth spherical gray stone. Three runes appeared on the artifact.

Ǿ ∞ Ǿ

The runes on the stone emitted gray light that mimicked the light of the Gray Sun Andreas.

Pryam continued, "Only four elemental stones and the Keotum Stone remain in Alms Glen. At the time of the disappearance of the Fire Wizard Yannuvia, the Mender Fisher presented a guard with the Keotum Stone, which affords protection from Magick, detects Magick, senses threats, and facilitates communication. The Teacher Camille Aires discovered the Elemental Stones 13 years after the disappearance of Spellweaver Yannuvia and the folk of Lost Sons and 11 years after the erstwhile Teacher Kirrie and an odd cherubic merchant destroyed two Kiennish forts and then disappeared. Though the stones are called Xennic Stones, our forebears possessed them long before the Spellweaver Xenn's time. We have little knowledge of the powers of the four stones. The Keotum Stone had proven invaluable and is carried by the sergeant of the watch."

Xenn interrupted, "My mother Tiffanne told me she chose my name after a dream, not in reference to the stones. My name has served me well. Teacher, do the Annals speak of the significance of the name Xennic?"

Pryam stammered, "I…I thought you'd know more about the stones and derivation of your name. My forebear Kirrie wrote that the Lost Spellweaver Yannuvia first used the term Xennic. The lost Spellweaver said, *'I'm told…Xennic Stones is merely a name for them.'* The Teacher Kirrie wrote of other stones. The General of Aulgmoor gave the Drelves a Healing Stone in an effort to form an alliance. The elders and the Great Protector Gaelyss surmised the Kiennite didn't realize the significance of the artifact. Gaelyss kept the Healing Stone for a time, but the stone disappeared with Yannuvia and the folk of Lost Sons. Kirrie used the Summoning Stone to call for and control the wyvern Dallas that bore her and the Teacher Edkim into battle. Every Drelve knows the story of the beloved Teacher Edkim and the Cold Stone. Edkim used the artifact to fell a brigade of firehorses and their riders at the battle of Lone Oak meadow. The Cold Stone also disappeared with Yannuvia. After Edkim died, his successor Morganne received his memories through the Magick of another stone deemed the Stone of Knowledge. Alas, this artifact was also lost to us. The Fire Wizard Yannuvia used a Firestone to demolish the Kiennish outpost called Fort Melphat. The lost Spellweaver also possessed a stone that empowered him with Silence. He never revealed the origins of these stones. At one time, the twin Spellweavers held the Stone of Knowledge, Silence Stone, Cold Stone, Firestone, Summoning Stone, and *Healing Stone.* The stones appeared as simple rocks."

Valtyrna, a young Drelve from Meadowsweet, asked, "Teacher, the stones emit a pleasant grayness. The gray stones are not simple rocks."

Pryam continued, "Spellweaver Xenn, will you please take *the Gifts of Andreas to the People of the Forest* thirteen steps toward the forest edge."

Xenn lifted the spell book. The runes etched on the surface of the tome emitted a persistent gray glow.

LARLS
A& **Ω**

The Spellweaver carried the storied Spell Book thirteen paces away from the Xennic Stones. The runes on the spell book, Keotum Stone, and Summoning Stones faded.

"From where does the heirloom *the Gifts of Andreas to the Forest* come," Valtyrna asked.

"My inexperience betrays me. I…I don't…the Annals of Drelvedom tell us it's the gift of the Gray Sun. They didn't say…" Pryam stammered.

The she-Drelve Elisabeth Jane Rumsie had seen well over a thousand seasons of the harvest. She descended from Drelvedom's greatest strategist and commander Sergeant Major Rumsie and his daughter Sara Jane Rumsie. The Rumsies ever served Alms Glen. Elisabeth Jane was the only living Drelve that witnessed the birth of the Spellweaver Xenn. She joked that her goal in life was to live longer than Clarke Maceda, an elderly Drelve who supported the renegade Spellweaver Yannuvia and his Lost Sons followers. In her 1233rd year, Elisabeth Jane had done so. Elisabeth

Jane said, "Teacher Pryam, no one knows the tome's origins. The twin Spellweavers debated it."

Pryam placed the Keotum Stone by the old tome. A set of three runes briefly appeared on the little stone, and then faded.

Ǿ ∞ Ǿ

Pryam continued, "The runes appear on the stone."

The leaders of Alms Glen studied the materials gathered from the attackers. Brynne Aires' study of her ancestor BJ's work aided them. One Kiennite had carried crossbow bolts enhanced by a variety of a Find the Path Spell. Accuracy and the fact they had survived the Fireball blast were the exceptional characteristics of the bolts. The second Kiennite's bolts were destroyed. The secondary explosions, which followed the Fireball Spell, suggested the goblin-like enemy had carried Firebolts. Fire Magick enhanced the crossbow bolts. The presence of the rare Firebolts implied the Kiennite who had carried them was of import and this generation of Kiennites was blessed with a spell caster. Most Kiennite spell casters employed only illusory Magick and had limited power. No legend told of a Kiennite casting an area spell. For the most point their ability of destructive Magick was limited to enhancing items and Magick Missiles.

Like all Drelvish Spellweavers, Xenn was born during one of the rare and unpredictable Approximations of the gray sun Andreas. In addition to rarity and unpredictability, few Approximations resulted in the birth of a Spellweaver. Xenn had practiced his skills and born the responsibility well. Spell books recorded the verbal components and the somatic gestures needed to cast spells. Somatic gestures might be simple or complex. Although rare, the material components needed to cast most spells were well known. Some spells required only a verbal component. Verbal, somatic, and material components thus defined spells. But only a Spellweaver could create the Magick that tied the components together.

Unless...

At the times of the Approximation of the gray sun, when the gray light of the sun bathed the world of the three suns, Magick flourished. Most such Magick was merely playful. Flowers changed color; birds warbled a different song; trees might uproot and walk about; elephants might fly. But even then, only Spellweavers touched the sea of Magick and cast spells. The enhancing abilities and the illusory Magick of the Kiennite shaman paled in comparison the powers of the rare Drelvish Spellweavers.

Xenn and the young warriors' wounds healed quickly under the expert care of the healers of Alms Glen. The forest yielded many beneficial herbs and remedies for maladies. Xenn, Pryam, and the learned elder Tull studied the garb worn by the Droll chieftain. The Keotum Stone confirmed Magick enhanced the cloak. Xenn used Detect Magick Spells and found faint auras. The roughly hewn garment was made largely of fire otter hides and explained the chieftain's surviving the Fireball Spell. Fire otters had innate resistance to flame. The chieftain's amulet was a white rock into which several mirror-like scales were imbedded. Pryam consulted old tomes passed down through generations of Teachers and surmised the amulet was created by a Kiennite enhancer and likely repayment for favors granted the Kiennites by the Droll. No one recognized the scales. For whatever reason, the amulet absorbed Magick Missiles. Xenn suggested testing the amulet's power by having someone wear it and face a Magick Missile. No one volunteered.

Another Approximation passed without the birth if a Spellweaver. Xenn and Alo used their skills to further protect the area around the Green Vale from the probing parties of Drolls and Kiennites. Aura and Magick Mouth Spells scared the simple and superstitious enemies. As time passed, scouts reported seeing fewer enemies. Seeing too few of the dreaded enemies was almost as disconcerting as seeing too many and left one wandering what the enemies were up to! Frequency of Droll attacks had always varied, but the Drelves pondered why there was so little activity in the fringes of their domain. After an extended debate, the elders Brie, Utha, and Molinna dispatched Alo, Wera, Cerro, and a scouting party to the realm of the Drolls. Scouting parties were always exploring the reaches of the lands surrounding Alms Glen and the central forests of the World of the Three Suns. Drelves oft times went on such forays simply to enjoy their surroundings or check up on their enemies' activities. The forest dwellers chameleon-like abilities helped them blend into their surroundings and facilitated their tasks.

Alo's group found several inexplicably deserted Droll villages on the fringes of their domain. He extended the mission and discovered large numbers of Drolls amassing north of the Ornash River. Many Kiennites intermingled with the wolf-faced Drolls. The old enemies often united to make troubles for other peoples of their world.

Alo returned to Alms Glen with this intelligence and summoned the council.

The Elder Tull listened intently to Alo's report and then said, "I've seen many harvests of the enhancing root and along with them the comings and goings of many generations of Drolls. Drolls constantly threaten us outside the forest but seldom aggress into our domain. It's more usual for them to quarrel among themselves than to amass. History tells us of Drolls following General Saligia of Aulgmoor, but Saligia was exceptionally charismatic… at least to Drolls and Kiennites. The Annals speak of his arcane alliances. Saligia's actions divided Drelvedom. The Great Defender Gaelyss remained convinced that his brother Yannuvia betrayed Drelvedom. Gaelyss still wrote of this at the end of his days. For centuries Drolls and Kiennites assailed the developing stronghold of the mysterious folk from the south. Our scouts noted no less than 39 assaults of the edifice called Ooranth by the Drolls and Kiennites. Each time the Draiths drove the attackers back north of the River Ornash. Then the Draiths changed construction methods and used black stone to form the walls. Its origins escape us. Castle Ooranth now dominates the plain given the same name. The Draiths have never aggressed against us. They avoid the forest. Aulgmoor has not attacked the Draiths since a party of the southerners crossed the Ornash and brought ruin to the Kiennite stronghold a century past. Most of us think the Draiths are responsible for the times of relative peace our last three generations have enjoyed. Sure… we've seen the odd attack on our pilgrimages and one must maintain his guard outside the forest. It's been a long while since we've seen attacks like that against Spellweaver Xenn's party. These Drolls you saw… are you sure they weren't simply engaged in some vulgar celebration?"

Alo responded, "They created bridges made of logs and gathered many steeds, hoofed and winged. I'm sure it's their intent to move southward across the River Ornash to the great plain before the impassible mountains. Their leaders wore full battle regalia. They mean to make war."

Another Elder named Windley added, "My grandfather told of wars between the giants who inhabit those mountains and the Drolls. Other ilks are said to inhabit those mountains. Stories passed down allege these mountain peoples nigh annihilated themselves through conflict. But this was generations past."

Elder Utha added, "When has a giant been reported? Our scouts seldom go beyond the Ornash. Young Burl led a party to the plain of Ooranth to survey the area some time ago. The council deemed this necessary because of the decreased activity of the Drolls and Kiennites."

Alo responded, "Hopefully we have intelligence. Burl was just found alone and injured near the fringe of the forest."

A short time later Alo returned with a haggard young Drelve. Burl seemed much older than when the Spellweaver last saw him.

Burl addressed the council; "I regret to report the loss of my comrades. There is great activity on the plain. The Draith citadel grows ever larger. The Draiths are imposing creatures. Not as big as giants, but every bit as bulky as Drolls. Their features were rustically handsome. Close to the height of two Drelves and the weight of six of us, their skin is like polished brass and enables them to blend into the orange and yellow grasses of the plain of Ooranth. Strong hardened faces…evidently the results of generations of battling with the giants and other creatures of the great mountains. They bore few weapons, but most of the activity we observed involved their construction of an edifice. They were using blocks of black stone and the logs of everred trees."

"If one chooses to live on the open plain, he would need protection," Elder Tull surmised.

"I don't see why anyone would want to live anywhere other than within a tree or hillock. The forest protects us. It would seem these new beings don't share this benefit," Pryam added. "Please continue."

Burl nodded and proceeded, "The Draiths build a much more substantial structure than the dwellings the Kiennites and the crude abodes of the Drolls. The outer wall was thick and in places it was the height of ten of us. Towers rise within the structure."

Alo interjected, "Poor defensive strategy. A fixed fortress will be overwhelmed by the hordes of Drolls and Kiennites. Kiennites have built many fortresses."

Elder Utha added, "The Fire Wizard Kirrie and her cherubic comrade destroyed the last two fortresses many centuries ago. A few giants could breech any wall I've seen. And above all else, they are building when the gray sun is away. I'd at least want some vestige of Magick to help me. If one is enclosed..."

The teacher Pryam agreed, "The first thing my teacher imparted to me, and I tell my youths that running is a perfectly reasonable option."

The elder Elisabeth Jane Rumsie said, "A point well taken. It saddens me to think of the many everred trees that are destroyed simply to build a barrier. I agree with Alo's observations. The flame of a Kiennite's arrow or a Droll's torch will bring down such a wall. The great axes of the giants will smash boulders."

Elder Tull pondered, "If they are building on the plain, do these folks invoke Magick to strengthen their walls? If they detected your party, the plains dwellers must be skilled observers."

Burl replied, "We observed from a distance. The blocks adhere... oddly. I saw no evidence of Magick. History tells us the mountain folk disdain Magick and retreat from the grayness of Andreas. Twas not the new folk who discovered us. Whilst we watched them, a Droll scout stumbled upon us. I take responsibility for our losses. We were too intent upon observing the activities on the plain, and the Drolls and Kiennites rained arrows onto our position. My comrades fell. I managed to end the life of the first Droll, who reached our position, but others neared, and I made ready to die. Then the plains dwellers saw the commotion and charged toward the red bushes where we had attempted to hide. The Drolls turned and ran, but the plains dwellers ran like the wind and overcame them. The battle was brief. The Drolls fell quickly before their foes. Unnoticed, I managed to crawl into the underbrush and escape. I suppose some of the Drolls may have escaped as well but I was intent upon my own escape. I managed to return. The Draiths are powerful stealthy, and quick."

"We should learn more about them," Alo observed.

"The Drolls and Kiennites grudgingly yield the realm of the forests to us. The everred trees, our Spellweavers, friends in the forest, and the Magick of the woods create barriers against them. Otherwise they would claim and ruin these domains. Drolls and Kiennites won't willingly surrender the plain. Rest assured they will return to avenge their fallen scouts," Elder Tull answered.

Xenn had quietly listened to the discussions. The Spellweaver said, "The Draiths account for the mustering of the Drolls and Kiennites. I had feared they were readying an assault against the forests around Alms Glen. Burl's information is valuable. We must monitor the movements of the Drolls and Kiennites and not let our guard down. Andreas is but a dot in the distant sky. I'll improve the defenses about Alms Glen."

The elder Elisabeth Jane Rumsie answered, "Thank you, Spellweaver. We are forever indebted to you. We shall remain vigilant. Alo, I ask that you follow the movements of the Droll and Kiennish armies. Burl, you must remain in Alms Glen and recover. You can help the teacher Pryam with the training of the youth. Xenn, I've never dictated your course of action. Serve, as you judge best."

Elisabeth Jane adjourned the meeting and the Drelves went about their assigned tasks. Alo and others followed the Drolls across the plain of Ooranth. Xenn accompanied the party to observe the actions of the enemies and ascertain what he could of the new folk. Following the massive movements of the Drolls and Kiennites required no subtlety. The force disrupted the environment. As Alo and Xenn had surmised, the massive force meandered toward the great mountains and onto the plain of Ooranth. The small group of Drelves, protected by Xenn's Magick and the cover of the trees and their natural chameleon-like abilities, observed the movements.

A particularly nasty chieftain named Pharkle assumed leadership of the Drolls. The Kiennish contingent followed a shaman named Micilex. Micilex was not a powerful illusionist and knew very little Magick. However, he was skilled at casting minor dweomers, which relieved irritating skin rashes and itching. This made him popular amongst the Kiennites whose orange-tinged skin was quite sensitive to plants and insects.

The combined forces of Pharkle and Micilex reached the plain of Ooranth. The Drelves watched from red oaks and orange spruce trees on a hillock that provided a clear view of black-walled Ooranth. The stately trees had survived the ravaging of the forests. Draiths left a few trees standing. In Kiennish General Saligia's day, his armies devastated the woods to the west of the Meadow of Lament and left nothing standing. Drolls constructed a tower near the River Ornash and laid waste the land. Recovery was long in both cases. Draiths sent fighters out to battle the advancing Drolls. The battle was ferocious. The defenders took a great toll on the enemy, but eventually the Drolls' superior numbers and the long-range bows of the Kiennish archers drove the defenders back to their fortress. The Kiennish archers fired flame arrows into the black fortress, but the walls were impervious to the flames. From their perches in the trees upon the hillock Alo, Xenn, and their comrades saw several groups of the newcomers break from the fortress and retreat into the scrubby trees at the base of the mountains, about three hundred paces from the outer curtain of the fortress. Drolls and Kiennites reached the outer curtain of the fortress but neither breached the wall nor found a gate. Heavy blows from the Drolls' hefty axes made nary a scratch in the wall. Drolls brought a trebuchet into the fray. General Saligia had employed the war machines against the Drelves. Massive boulders fired into the black wall simply bounced off the black stone. Trebuchet rounds that cleared the wall were repurposed by the defenders and dropped onto Drolls near the wall. Defenders emerged from the woods and fell onto Drolls near the wall. Comrades inside the fortress came through the indiscernible door and rejoined the fray. Soon the defenders gained the upper hand. Kiennites abandoned the trebuchet and fled toward the River Ornash. The Drolls battled on futilely. Soon the Draiths overwhelmed their wolf-faced foes. Unlike Kiennites, Drolls fought with Pharkle till the last fell. Xenn and Alo returned to Alms Glen and reported the battle to the elders.

***19*** Approximations at intervals of 13, 21, 144, 8, 233, 1, 3, 144, 1, 89, 13, 13, 144, 55, 8, 21, 13, 8, and 55 years passed without the birth of another Spellweaver. Two seasons after Pharkle and Micilex's crushing defeat by the Draiths, for the 20th time in old Xenn's long life, the Gray Wanderer drew near Alms Glen and the World of the Three Suns. Alms Glen was abuzz. The gray light brought with it a Spellweaver. The little bloke was named Agrarian.

***In the underground realm, in Vydaelia, stirring occurred in the fourth dome. The central sphere's light intensified. The 99th Wandmaker Criss Cringal rushed to the fourth dome.***

# 12.

# Finding the Xennic Stone

Xenn had seen nigh a thousand harvests of the Enhancing Root. Now elderly even by the standards of Spellweavers, the Drelve felt every one of those seasons. This date, his Magick again enabled his frail forest people to prevail against their ancestral enemies, the Drolls. Fortunately, unlike an attack four harvests earlier, the goblin-like Kiennites, who also rarely numbered spell casters, had not accompanied the Droll patrol and the Drolls lacked special weapons and armor.

Xenn had come into the World of the Three Suns during an Approximation of Andreas, the dark star also called the Gray Wanderer. Unlike the unvarying growth season of the Enhancing Plant, which matured its tubers at a constant rate, the gray star drew near the world at totally erratic irregular intervals. The average Drelve might see one or two approximations if blessed with a long life, or the gray wanderer might come close to the land within a few harvests. No one could predict the pattern of the unwonted sun. When Andreas drew near, Magick flourished and the peoples of the forest celebrated. Drelves had endured a nigh a millennium of changes of seasons and 19 Approximations since Xenn's birth without seeing another Spellweaver's birth, but the Gray Sun drew near two seasons ago and the infant Spellweaver Agrarian toddled around Alms Glen.

Presently, only the light of the unmoving giant black sun Orpheus and yellow light of the little yellow sun Meries bathed the land. Meries kept to a strict interval and its varying position in the skies determined the extent of the brightness of the amber light that covered the world. Meries never left the sky but at intervals dipped into the horizon and the land entered what were called dark periods.

Gripped by fatigue, Xenn slumped to his knees into the thick reddish moss by the babbling brook. He bent forward and drank deeply of the refreshing water. His thirst was more easily quenched. Overcoming mental fatigue caused by the exertion of spell casting required time. Xenn was the only Spellweaver capable of noteworthy Magick. Little Agrarian could do little more than change the color of flowers or make water flow upward. Xenn was tired from more than exertion. He was old, very old. The Spellweaver's greatest worry was the fate of his people after he was gone. Though wonderfully skilled as archers and expert at the ways of the forests, the Drelves lacked the physical capabilities to battle the stronger Drolls straight up. Xenn's six companions had fought well in the just-ended battle. Unfortunately, the Drelves suffered losses. Two comrades fell before the heavy axes of their larger opponents, but Xenn's party had repelled the Drolls and prevented their approach to the sanctuary at Alms Glen. The Spellweaver used three Magick Missiles and a Sleep Spell and prevented further death and injury. Xenn had been struck on the left shoulder by one of the enemies and young Mius had applied a very good field dressing. The pain in his wounded shoulder made the oldster forget his throbbing, arthritic knees.

Xenn eased back against the rocky bank of the creek and enjoyed the soothing moss. Amber light broke through the canopy of red and yellow leaves. The beauty of the forest never ceased to amaze and refresh him! The frailty of this beauty and the vulnerability of his people concerned the Spellweaver. Had Xenn not accompanied them, all the Drelves in this party would have died and the Drolls would be nearing Alms Glen by now. But not this time…

Mius's voice interrupted his thoughts. The young Drelve implored, "Master Xenn, how is your wound? Should we not return to Alms Glen?"

"Yes, straight away. Make ready," Xenn answered.

The Spellweaver stood, watched the young Drelve move toward the rest of the party, and sighed. Xenn glanced into the water. The scales of little fishes glinted in the amber rays. Xenn envied the carefree creatures as he watched them swim. Responsibilities beckoned, and the old Drelve turned to the path.

Something caught his eye.

Grayness…

Gray light rose from the depths of the brook.

Xenn knelt down and reached into the shallow water. The little fishes scurried aside. His probing fingers reached the source of the light. Xenn gingerly pulled a gray stone from the water and held the little rock in his hand, A beam of grayness left the rock and bathed his body. The rock's surface briefly changed from a cold gray stone to warm soft flesh. Runes appeared on the surface of the stone.

Ǿ ∞ Ǿ

The stone became cold again. Old Xenn felt stronger. The fatigue of his spell casting left him and the old Spellweaver briefly regained the lost energies of youth. The light was familiar. Xenn had felt it during the Approximations of the Gray Wanderer. The runes also appeared on the Keotum Stone, an heirloom of Drelvedom. The four Elemental Stones. (SSF, SSW, SSE, and SSA) bore similar markings.

Ǿ ∞ Ǿ<br>∞ Ǿ∞<br>Ǿ ∞ Ǿ<br>∞ Ǿ∞

Eleven changes of seasons after the destruction of the Kiennish forts by the Fire Wizard Kirrie and the odd cherubic merchant, the Teacher Camille Aires discovered the four elemental stones (SSF, SSE, SSA, and SSW) in the foyer of the Old Orange Spruce. Xenn secretly carried a single Omega Stone, which gave the false impression of empowering a Slow Spell whilst actually hasting the spell's recipients.

Teacher and later Fire Wizard Kirrie used the Summoning Stone of Fire (SSF) to summon the wyvern Dallas during the Battle of Lone Oak Meadow. The artifact had been an heirloom of the Korcran family of Drolls. The artifact differed from the Fire Stone possessed by the Lost Spellweaver Yannuvia. The Summoning Stone of Fire (SSF) looked like a rock and was precisely the same size and shape of the Summoning Stone of Water (SSW). The Summoning Stone of Fire (SSF) bore the image of a proud Fire Horse. Runes appeared on the stone's smooth surface.

Ǿ ∞ Ǿ

The Water Stone (SSW) appeared an ovoid watery shape, a prolate spheroid. The curious artifact was like water, or soft clear gelatin Runes and an ever so faint image of a water horse appeared on the surface of the artifact.

∞ Ǿ ∞

The Air Stone (SSA) had the appearance of a rainbow bent into fattened cigar shape. Its density was similar to the misty equine. the scintillating colors. The object had no weight. Runes appeared on its beautiful surface.

∞ Ǿ ∞

The Air Stone or Wind Stone was sometimes called the Summoning Stone of Air (SSA)

Earth Stone (SSE) shared the oblate spheroid shape of the Fire Stone (SSF), Air Stone (SSA), and Water Stone (SSW), but it looked like a clump of red clay. Three runes glowed brightly on its surface.

Ǿ ∞ Ǿ

The Earth Stone hummed and emitted faint gray light.

Xenn had extensively studied the Elemental Stones and learned little of their natures. Mius returned with his five comrades. Xenn placed the newly-found stone in his pack and the group returned to Alms Glen.

Once they returned Xenn shared his discovery with the elders.

"Let us see the rock," Pryam requested.

Xenn extended the stone to the Teacher and Pryam accepted the rock. The stone briefly emitted gray light and changed to warm flesh. Pryam looked at Xenn's wound.

"Please allow me to touch your shoulder," the elder requested.

Xenn obliged.

Pryam touched the wound and uttered an incantation, which Xenn recognized as a Healing Spell. Xenn's shoulder felt warm and the deep gash closed.

"I've been a Spellweaver for a thousand harvests and never mastered that spell. How did you do so?" Xenn marveled.

Pryam responded, "I've never known Magick. Nor do I know how I managed the spell. The stone granted me the power to heal your wound. This is a wondrous artifact."

Pryam returned the stone to Xenn. Xenn announced, "I feel refreshed by the rock, but it tells me nothing new. Mius, please take the stone."

Young Mius accepted the gray rock. The light again intensified. Mius slowly turned and studied the trees and his companions. He reported, "I can sense things Magick. I lack the power to cast spells. Perhaps the relic should remain with you, elder Pryam."

Pryam accepted the rock, but shook his head negatively. The Teacher said, "I also sense things Magick, but I find no knowledge of Magick within my mind. The power of the healing spell has not returned. I'll return the stone to you, Spellweaver."

"The gray stone restored my energies, but gave me no additional advantage. I cannot explain the spell you received, Pyram, but I am grateful. I feel we should rest and study this further," Xenn responded.

After many periods of study, the Spellweaver and the elders of the Drelves determined the gray stone endowed the power to detect Magick and gave beings without Spellweaver abilities some tangential connection with Magick. For the lack of better term… Xenn's new stone *created* Magick. Pyram gave the stone the name Xennic Stone in honor of its discoverer. During the next Approximation of the Gray Wanderer Andreas, the stone's light intensified and the fragment sent beams to the heavens toward the gray star. Grays rays in turn came from the great sun to the stone.

# 13.

# The Xennic Stone of Magick Creation Xenn, Pryam, and Agrarian

Xenn walked to the Old Orange Spruce. The old Spellweaver tapped on the ancient tree's bark and called to the young Teacher Pryam. Pryam answered and beckoned the Spellweaver to enter. Xenn was relieved that he didn't have to use his Knock Spell. Casting the spell was second nature, but the old Spellweaver felt fatigue now with any exertion. Xenn walked through the tree's thick bark. Pryam sat in the foyer in a small chair and beckoned the old Spellweaver to the comfortable overstuffed chair. Xenn sank into the chair.

Pryam asked, "What is the purpose for your visit, Spellweaver?"

Xenn said, "It's the young Spellweaver's seventh birthday. I want to watch the presentation of his spell book. I also have tasks for him. Please fetch the Elemental Stones. I don't think I'm up to climbing down the stairs."

Young Pryam never questioned the Spellweaver. He descended the stairs and returned with the four exceptional stones. When Pryam came within thirteen paces of Xenn, the four stones emitted grayness. The recently discovered stone greeted the Elemental stones with flashes of grayness that filled the interior of the Old Orange Spruce with gray light quite akin to an Approximation of the Wandering Sun Andreas. The new stone sent concentrated beams of gray light to the four stones. Runes appeared on all the stones.

Pryam said, “I’ve witnessed the gray light only twice Spellweaver, but I feel like I’m witnessing it again, though I know Meries sits at its peak and the Light Period begins outside.”

Xenn answered, “I’ve walked in the grayness of Andreas 20 times in my long life Pryam, and I agree. When I arrived, I felt every one of my 991 years. My energies had ebbed such that casting a simple spell was challenging. My strength returns. The new stone acts like a miniscule version of Andreas in the presence of the Elemental Stones.”

The four elemental stones (SSF, SSE, SSA, and SSW) eerily levitated off the table and moved to positions in the middle of the room. The four stones created a square thirteen feet on a side. The stones hovered 34 inchworm lengths above the floor. The Xennic Stone, so-named by Pryam, left Xenn’s hand and positioned precisely at the center of the square.

Xenn said, “When does the little Spellweaver arrive for his presentation and schooling?”

Pryam answered, “At any moment, Spellweaver. He is a delight and learns so quickly. I hear a knock now.”

Pryam walked to the inner wall and touched the bark. Little Agrarian and his mother Gyada entered. Gyada curtsied to Xenn and said, “Spellweaver Xenn, I was not aware that you’d be instructing Agrarian and he’d see the heirlooms. The elemental stones look lovelier every time I see them. I am honored.”

Xenn said, “Teacher Pryam is quite capable. I’m here to give a bit of guidance, and I’d like to get to know your son better. He is a handsome Nymph.”

Gyada said, “Thank you, Spellweaver. I’ll leave him in your care. The Elders Brie, Utha, Molinna, and Windley have asked us to prepare a special feast. Guests are coming from Meadowsweet and Fox Vale. We’re honoring Elisabeth Jane Rumsie. She has passed Clarke Maceda’s age this past Dark Period. I’ll come by for Agrarian as always.”

Gyada said her goodbyes and walked through the tree.

Xenn, Pryam, and Agrarian gathered in the library of the Old Orange Spruce. Pryam produced the ancient stones. The Enhancing Stone moved to a central position, and the four elemental stones positioned at four corners of a square around the enhancing stone. Little Agrarian walked around the hovering stones and stared at each. The stones hovered at his eye level. The brilliant colors of the Air Stone fascinated the child. He also gently touched the Water Stone and smiled at the Firehorse on the surface of the Fire Stone. The child paused at the relatively plain Earth Stone. Without speaking the child walked into the square area and approached the stone hovering in the center. He reached out his little left hand and touched the stone. The stone shrank to fit into his little hand. The child's orangish skin changed to gray. The little Drelvling stood in the center of the square and looked at Xenn.

Xenn said, "It feels good, doesn't it? Warm all over! Which do you like best, Agrarian?"

Little Agrarian said, "I like them all, Spellweaver Xenn. Which is your favorite?"

Xenn said, "Just call me 'Xenn', little one. You are my equal. I'm partial to fire, but my direction was rather chosen for me. I didn't have the center stone to help me."

Agrarian said, "The Enhancing Stone. It's named for you. Xennic, but isn't Xennic Stones a general term for magic stones… Xenn?"

Xenn said, "Teacher Pryam honors me with the name. My mother chose my name after a dream. So, I don't know whether the stones are named after me, or I'm named after the stones."

Agrarian said, "It doesn't really matter, Xenn. It's Magick."

Xenn said, "You are surely wise beyond your years, Agrarian. What does the stone in your hand tell you?"

Agrarian said, "Only to choose one, Xenn."

Pryam watched intently. Little Agrarian walked to the Fire Stone. The Summoning Stone of Fire (SSF) looked like a rock. The Summoning Stone of Fire (SSF) bore the image of a proud Fire Horse. Runes appeared on the stone's smooth surface.

Ǿ ∞ Ǿ

Agrarian walked to the Water Stone. The Water Stone (SSW) appeared an ovoid watery shape, a prolate spheroid. The curious artifact was like water, or soft clear gelatin. Runes and an ever so faint image of a water horse appeared on the surface of the artifact.

∞ Ǿ ∞

The little Spellweaver went to the Air Stone (SSA), which had the appearance of a rainbow with scintillating colors bent into fattened cigar shape. The object had no weight. Runes appeared on its beautiful surface.

∞ Ǿ ∞

The Air Stone or Wind Stone was sometimes called the Summoning Stone of Air (SSA)

Then Agrarian went to the Earth Stone. The Earth Stone (SSE) shared the oblate spheroid shape of the Fire Stone (SSF), Air Stone (SSA), and Water Stone (SSW), but it looked like a clump of red clay. Three runes glowed brightly on its surface.

Ǿ ∞ Ǿ

The Earth Stone hummed and emitted faint gray light. Agrarian grasped the Earth Stone in his right hand. The stone first shrank to fit his little hand. Then the artifact and the stone in the child's left hand both disappeared. Agrarian's color changed from frag to muddy red, back to red, and then back to his usual pale orange. Both stones reappeared. Agrarian released them, and both floated back into position.

Agrarian left the square and stood by Xenn.

Xenn said, "A quirk of Magick! Earth! A noble choice for a true friend of the forest. I'm honored to stand with you Spellweaver Agrarian. Your name… Agrarian… derives from the Old Drelvish word for dirt or soil. Earth is another word for dirt."

Agrarian said, "I'm honored to stand with you, Spellweaver Xenn. I see spells in my mind. Dig, Rock-to-Mud, and Entangle incantations. The Enhancing Stone will impart a single spell per lifetime to a non-Spellweaver, Detects Magick, Enchant an Item, Permanence, and enhances the particular powers of the Elemental Stones. Most powers of the Enhancing Stone are activated only in the presence of the Elemental Stones."

Pryam stood in awe and said, "I have witnessed something denied all Teachers who walked before me. This shall become a rite of passage of

Drelvedom, just as the delivery of the hallowed Spellbook, every Spellweaver shall partake in the ceremony of the Elemental Stones. Agrarian, Earth Wizard, here is your Spell Book. It replicated the day you arrived and this is the seventh anniversary of your birth."

The Teacher placed the book in Agrarian's hands. When he placed the book in the Spellweaver's hands, the book's leathery cover changed. Odd additional runes appeared on the covers of the tome. Agrarian stared at the book he held.

*The Gifts of Andreas to the People of the Forest*
LARLS
A& **Ω**

Agrarian said, "Thank you, Teacher Pryam, and thank you, Spellweaver Xenn."

Xenn said, "I have one more task for you, Agrarian."

The old Spellweaver took the Omega Stone from his pack. The little artifact had been buzzing throughout the affair. Xenn said, "Grip the stone. It will tell you something. It won't be true."

Agrarian dutifully took the Omega Stone. The stone warmed in his hand.

A single rune appeared on the rock and persisted for thirteen heartbeats.

**Ω**

Then the single letter faded, and three runes appeared on the surface of the rock, which briefly emitted gray light.

Ǿ ∞ Ǿ

The runes faded after 21 heartbeats and the single rune reappeared. The pattern repeated three times.

Words appeared in Agrarian's mind.

*"I give you my blood through which you will receive all you seek. You in turn give to me your all."*

New phrases appeared in Xenn's thoughts. Initially a word jumble, the phrases organized into an incantation.

Xenn asked, "What does it tell you?"

Agrarian said, "A new spell! It's a healing spell. Do you want me to recite the incantation?"

Xenn said, "No. Recite it backwards. If you use the order of phrases given by the stone, you will *harm* the individual you touch. Reversing the phrases will produce the *healing* spell. Also, don't use the stone to cast the healing spell. However, the harm spell might come in handy. I've clandestinely carried this stone for centuries. It now joins the Elemental Stones and Enhancing Stone in the Teacher's care. Master well your Knock Spell. It's a means of entry to the Old Orange Spruce if the Teacher is away."

Pryam said, "If I am here, you are always welcome Spellweavers."

Pryam gathered the six stones, descended the stairs, and placed them back on a table in the corner and covered them with a large piece of Invisimoss.

Xenn said, "I have another gift for you, Agrarian."

Agrarian said, "Spellweaver Xenn, you have already given me so much."

Xenn slipped his robe off his shoulders and extended it to Agrarian. Xenn said, "My mother Tiffanne discovered this robe after a dream. A visitor to my dreams said the robe was not of our world. Someone called a Light Sorceress seamstress constructed the robe from foreign materials; silk of Sagain, the feathers of the snow-white Phoenix, one of the three shypoke scales remaining in the Laurels, and the scales of a prismatic dragon. Moreover, the seamstress risked death as she tenuously placed a jet-black Tuscon feather within the fabric of the device. Once placed in the robe, the Magick of the robe harnessed the malevolent force within the jet-black feather and instead instilled a protection against Death Magick upon the wearer of the cloak. The robe patterned like the ancient robe of the Order of Light Sorcerers. silk of Sagain allows the robe to adapt to the size of each wearer. The tiny spiders that created the silk required two centuries to produce enough to create the robe. The silk had been used to create little black dresses which had adorned many young women during their ceremonies of commitment. Even more rare were the adamantine spiders that created the slender cords that the sorceress used to bind the silk and other materials. The robe has many hidden pockets. It'd give great advantage in a conflict with another Spellcaster and has served me well. When I wear it, I'm neither hot nor cold? It has an endless supply of pockets for storing materials. Placing items in the pockets does not increase the weight of the robe."

Agrarian said, "Spellweaver Xenn, I cannot accept your robe. Everyone in Alms Glen identifies you with it. I'm not sure I've ever seen you without it."

Xenn smiled and said, "It's quite useful. Its pockets function as bags of holding. I have picnic tables and several staffs in them. Just think of what you need, put your hand in a pocket, and what you seek will be there for the taking."

Agrarian said, "Your generosity overwhelms me, Spellweaver Xenn, but you are taller, and no disrespect intended, a bit rounder than I am. The robe won't fit me."

Xenn smiled again and said, "Accept my gift and try it on."

Agrarian reluctantly took the robe from Xenn. It had little weight and its color changed from subdued orange to green. Agrarian was taken aback and said, "Again, no disrespect intended Spellweaver Xenn, but it's green now. I'll stand out in the forests like a sore thumb."

Xenn said, "I said exactly the same thing a thousand or so years ago. Try it on. Think of the color you'd want it to be."

Agrarian said, "I like the rainbows I see after a rain."

Agrarian slipped the robe over his shoulders. It shrank to fit him perfectly. Its coloration mimicked a Parallan rainbow... orange, red, yellow, with streaks of purple and gray. Agrarian beamed and said, "It fits perfectly and feels wonderful. I love the colors. Spellweaver, I see all its contents in my mind. Do you mean for me to keep the components in the myriad of pockets?"

Xenn answered, "I do."

Agrarian pulled the remarkably soft fabric around him. The young Spellweaver said again, "Thank you, Spellweaver Xenn."

Xenn said, "Just Xenn, Spellweaver Agrarian."

Pryam returned. Xenn, Pryam, and Agrarian enjoyed enhancing root tuber tea and booderry muffins. Soon Agrarian's mother Gyada and father Flaey arrived and Agrarian left with them. Old Xenn tarried for a while with the young Teacher and reminisced about the Omega Stone and his adventures over the years.

# 14.

# Last Journeys to Green Vale

Agrarian turned 9. He progressed well in his studies. At 13, the young Spellweaver would make the trip to Meadowsweet and Green Vale. Xenn had not participated in the harvest for many seasons. The Tree Shepherd had refused to communicate with the Drelves during the harvests, and the Tree Sprite did not appear. Xenn chose to stay away, but the Tree Shepherd did not change his attitude to the harvesters. Over the objections of the elders and Pryam, the Old Spellweaver insisted on traveling to Green Vale to speak with the ancient patriarch of Green Vale. Alms Glen had not been attacked in generations. As a result, Xenn had not used Fire Magick. His Magick had been constructive. The old Spellweaver exited his tree and went to the common area. The most trusted and knowledgeable elder Tull stood by the firepit.

Tull said, "Spellweaver, I must ask you to reconsider this trip to Green Vale. You are too important to Drelvedom."

Xenn said, "I appreciate your concern Elder Tull, but young Agrarian holds the future of Drelvedom. My race is almost run. I have unfinished business with the Tree Shepherd."

Tull said, "Spellweaver Xenn, I have personally stood with you in Green Vale scores of times. The Tree Shepherd remained silent. The Lady of the Trees has not revealed herself to the last three generations of harvesters. One more trip won't change it."

Xenn replied, "It's something I must do."

Old Tull said, "I thought you'd not change your mind. At least wear this robe."

Tull expended the folded Robe of Sagain that Xenn had given to Agrarian.

Xenn said, "Elder, I presented the robe to the young Spellweaver. I want him to have it."

Tull replied, "I talked with Agrarian. He insists on your wearing the robe. He is Spellweaver. You are Spellweaver. I am but a messenger."

Xenn said, "I notice your shillelagh and pack and must assume you intend to go along."

Tull said, "I trained Batali. Pryam is young. I will assist him."

Xenn said, "Then, old friend, we will have a memorable trip and harvest. The Drolls have not shown their ugly faces in many seasons. Alo and Wera are as good at leading through the wood as any Rangers I've seen. Let's be off. The Dark Period arrives soon."

Xenn placed the robe over his shoulders. The robe of Sagain expanded to perfectly fit him. Xenn checked the pockets. Young Agrarian had stocked the robe well with material components, and Pryam had placed the Xennic (Enhancing) Stone in one of the robe's pockets. Xenn and Tull met Pryam and the neophytes at the departure point. Elders had ordered more security. Veteran Alo stood ready to lead the group. Agrarian's father Flaey stood with Alo. Gyada led a large group to Sylvan Pond. Young Agrarian remained in Alms Glen to be tutored by Elders Utha, Windley, Brie, and Elisabeth Jane Rumsie. The groups set out at the beginning of the Amber Period. The travel to the crossroads was uneventful. Gyada's group broke off toward Sylvan Pond. The others headed to Meadowsweet. Xenn was greeted with great fanfare. Drelvlings relished his return and the gifts he oft presented them. At the end of the next cycle of Meries, the Dark Period began, and the harvesters headed to Meadowsweet and Green Vale. Alo and Flacy kept the way secure. In Green Vale, Xenn and Tull walked up to the hillock. Xenn touched each of the Thirttene Friends and lingered at the Tree Shepherd. The geyser erupted and sprayed the Spellweaver with its rainbow waters. The Tree Shepherd remained silent. Tull left Xenn at the top of the hill and helped Pryam with the harvest. Several very promising neophytes came along, including descendants of Sergeant Major Rumsie, Sergeant Major Birney, Meryt and Bryce heroes of Lone Oak Meadow, and legendary bowyer BJ Aires. Xenn remained on the hillock until the harvest ended. Pryam called to him. The old Spellweaver touched the ancient bark of the Tree Shepherd and then turned and walked away. Xenn said nothing on the trek back to Meadowsweet. After a rest period, the party headed back toward Alms Glen.

Alo and Flaey led the way. They reached the intersection of the path to Sylvan Pond. The party neared the wide meadow. Alo stopped and raised his left hand.

Tull asked, "What's the problem, Alo?"

Alo said, "Something's not right. I know every tree in the forest. This area has been disrupted… and those trees were not…"

The ranger did not finish his statement. Three Kiennites emerged from their illusory trees and fired arrows toward the Drelves. Two arrows struck Alo and the noble warrior fell. The third arrow whizzed by Xenn and Tull. Three shamans sent spells toward the group. Xenn's robe absorbed the spells. The large tree ahead of them shimmered and the Big Droll Chieftain stood in its place.

Xenn said, "Tree Spells! The Kiennish shaman assumed the appearance of small trees and placed illusory Magick on the big Droll!"

Drolls shouted and emerged from the underbrush. The Chieftain shouted, "Do you recognize me, a******? It's time to die!"

Xenn fired Magick Missiles toward the three Kiennish shamans. Xenn's spells disrupted their spell attempts. Pryam stood between the young harvesters and the Drolls. Tull wielded his shillelagh well. The Elder clobbered the first Droll to reach him. Xenn hit the same Droll with a Magick Missile and the big wolf-faced warrior fell. Xenn carried the Enhancing Stone. He crushed sulfur, muttered the incantation of his Fire Spell, and concentrated on the area where the Droll chieftain uttered commands. Before he finished the incantation, Xenn gripped the Enhancing Stone. Red flames streamed from Xenn's hand and squarely hit the big Droll. The ray exploded into a fireball that heated the entire area. The flames came within ten paces of Xenn and Tull. Tull pummeled the felled Droll with his shillelagh. Flaey dropped two Kiennish archers with well-placed arrowshots. The big Droll fell to his knees, and his warriors near him fell to Xenn's spell.

The Chieftain growled, "**** you, Spellweaver!"

The chieftain struggled to his feet and charged toward Xenn. Every Drelvish bowstring hummed. Arrow after arrow dug into the big Droll. Ten, twenty, thirty, forty hits… Xenn hit him with three Magick Missiles. The chieftain fell about three feet from Xenn. When he fell, his ax hit the Spellweaver's shin and opened a shallow wound. Flaey and other Rangers defeated four Drolls at the cost of the life of a Ranger named Colby from Grove Town.

Smoke filled the air. Eighteen Drolls and six Kiennites were dead. So were brave Alo and Colby.

Tull shouted, "Teacher Pryam, gather the harvesters. Let's quickly make for Alms Glen. More enemies may be near."

There was no answer.

A young harvester said, "Elder Tull, he …Pryam stood between us and the archers. Three arrows hit him before he… fell."

Xenn muttered, "No."

Tull and Flaey gathered the group. Rangers carried Alo, Colby, and Pryam. The encumbered party made Alms Glen without further attack.

Several Drelves and Xenn had suffered minor wounds. Elders Brie, Utha, Windley, Elisabeth Jane Rumsie, and Tull expertly tended the wounds. The Elders called an emergency meeting of the Council of Alms Glen.

Brie said, "We have talked. Pryam fell at such a young age. There is but one logical choice to replace him. Tull, will you accept the role as Teacher of the Drelves."

Xenn quickly stood and said, "Yes, he will."

Tull nodded meekly.

All of Alms Glen sang laments for Pryam, Alo, and Colby.

Xenn and Agrarian labored to shore up the defenses of the realm.

Old Xenn did what he could to protect the forest and his people. He spent many hours tutoring young Agrarian. The aged Drelve recorded his knowledge of Magick in *The Gifts of Andreas to the People of the Forest.* He entrusted the volume and the care of the gray stone to Teacher Tull.

With Pryam's untimely death, the stewardship of the Xennic (Enhancing) Stone, Four Elemental Stones, Keotum Stone, Omega Stone, elixirs of longevity, and collection of spell books fell to his successor Tull. Tull lead the harvest to Green Vale the next year. Xenn was too weak to make the trip. Agrarian was 10. Although resistant to the inexorable march of time, the Spellweaver Xenn eventually grew weaker and passed to his forefathers when Agrarian was 11 years old.

# 15.

## Agrarian's Early Adventures

Agrarian's nymph hood was near idyllic and spent in learning and play. Older Drelves engaged him in mock battles. He learned fencing quickly and developed prowess with the bow. Agrarian grew from a nymph to a strong Drelvling, a term used to describe the young until they reached adulthood. Teacher Pryam, Elder Tull, Spellweaver Xenn, and his mother Gyada nurtured and taught the little Spellweaver. Pryam presented Agrarian with his copy of *The Gifts of Andreas to the People of the Forest* on the little Spellweaver's seventh birthday. Agrarian became the first Spellweaver to participate in the ritual of the Stones. The young Spellweaver bonded to the Earth Stone. (SSE). Spellweaver Xenn allowed the youth to hold an Omega Stone. The artifact deceptively presented the youth with a new spell. Xenn instructed Agrarian to reverse the incantation and avoid using the stone to cast the spell. Agrarian had the use of a Healing Spell at age 7. The spell was quite valuable in helping injured Drelves. Teacher Pryam fell to a Kiennite's arrow when Agrarian was 9. Old Tull assumed the role of Teacher of the Drelves. Elderly Xenn died when Agrarian was 11 and did not live to see Agrarian's trip to Green Vale. Xenn saw his 1001$^{st}$ year and then passed. His last word was "Nyssa." The Annals of Drelvedom and his archived Spellbook contained many tender references to the Spellweaver's life-mate, whose death preceded his own by 900 years. Elder Elisabeth Jane Rumsie joined her ancestors shortly after Xenn. The spiritual leadership of the Drelves fell on the capable shoulders of the oldster Tull. Tull had long helped the Teachers with instruction of the youths and was versed in the harvesting of the enhancing root. The Teacher Tull brought Agrarian under his tutelage and taught the youth the ways of the forest and histories of its people. All Drelvlings attended Tull's lessons, but Agrarian understood them best. No Drelve including Tull could teach Magick. The unwonted ability was innate to Spellweavers.

Agrarian became the first Spellweaver born to the people of the forest in twenty Approximations and followed Xenn by nigh a millennium. With Xenn's death, heavy responsibility fell on the 11-year old's shoulders. Agrarian learned quickly. Spells came easily to the young sorcerer.

His father Flaey was well versed in languages and numbers and taught his son practical things that the Teacher Tull only touched on. His mother Gyada gave him grace, caring, and surprising strength. But Agrarian's greatest tutor was Tull. The old Drelve relished his role as Teacher and poured his soul and essence into educating the youngster.

The defenses around Alms Glen were masterfully constructed and integrated with the natural defenses of the forest. Long ago the Great Defender Gaelyss, Sergeant Major Rumsie, and renowned bowyer and fletcher BJ Aires coordinated defenses against Drolls and Kiennites. Xenn augmented Magick barriers and took a more offensive role against the Drolls and Kiennites. Even as a small nymph, Agrarian aided the defenses against the enemies by casting Faerie Fire, Magick Mouths, Auras, and other harmless warning spells. One of his Magick Mouth's mimicked a Draith's voice ordering an attack. Even the hardiest Kiennite fled upon hearing a command ordering a hundred Draith scouts to attack. Most Kiennites wouldn't hang around to determine it was only a Magick Mouth! Nonetheless the voracious enemies drew nearer and skirmishes occurred. Agrarian used his Healing Spell to assist wounded Rangers. The Drelves positioned archers in the tallest everreds and their arrows brought down Kiennish and Droll warriors that wandered too near the sanctuary. The Drelves were adept at fading into the forests and evading the pursuit of the outsiders. The outsiders often met their doom in natural defenses such as sinking sand and carnivorous plants.

The young Spellweaver Agrarian had seen nine seasons of the Enhancing Root when he learned of the first loss of his kindred. Agrarian was playing with his best friend when they heard the clamor as the defenders returned to the sanctuary. The youths learned of the carnage of battle for the first time. The scouts shielded the young from the graphic details of the injuries, but parents relayed the story of the battle and told the Drelvlings that Alo, Colby, and Teacher Pryam had been killed while returning from Meadowsweet.

A Droll and Kiennite raiding party had gained access to the trails. A vindictive Droll chieftain and three Kiennish shaman lead the assault. The shaman used Illusory Magick and Tree Spells to hide their presence. The shamans had mastered a spell that allowed them to assume the appearance of a small tree. Alo was struck down early in the battle, and Pryam fell whilst shielding the youthful harvesters. Other Drelves had come to the aid of their stricken comrades and the Drolls fell upon them. The Drelves excelled in archery and swordsmanship, but the massive Drolls fought fiercely and injured three Drelves. Old Xenn fought off injury and brought fearsome Magick down on the aggressors. Ultimately the Drelves prevailed and killed the interlopers. The memory of these losses was strongly etched in Agrarian's mind.

Under the guidance of the Teacher Tull, the Drelves tightened the reins on their youths and instructed the Drelvlings to remain in the friendly confines of the secure areas of the forest. The Teacher stressed the importance of safety upon the youngsters, but Agrarian was driven to the woods. His passion to learn was unfathomed. The young Spellweaver studied herbs, wandering plants, soils, and all manner of material components. He helped the elders and matrons in concocting teas, unguents, and potions.

A dream came to the young Spellweaver Agrarian in his twelfth year, shortly after the death of old Xenn. The young Drelve had finished a particularly busy day and sank into the soft down of the bed within his home tree. The bedding had never felt so good. Sleep came quickly. His mind retraced the events of his recent days. He dreamed of the beautiful meadows around Alms Glen and the flora and fauna common there. Redness entered his dream.

Wisps…
Threads…
Threads of Magick…
Threads of fate…
Threads of time…
Threads connecting worlds …

Dreams connecting worlds …
Dreams of Magick…
The Magick of Dreams…
Magick connecting dreams…
Magick connecting worlds…
Dream raiders…
Elf pressure…
Albtraum…
Albträume, elf dreams, nightmares…
Albträume...

Then a face of a beautiful female appeared. She was not Drelvish. Agrarian had never seen a female other than a Drelve. The alluring female was very tall and had creamy skin, soft blue eyes, and a pleasant voice as she spoke to the sleeping youth. She wore a blazing red dress. Coal black hair fell gracefully down her back and chest. The female walked gracefully back and forth across a field of clover as she spoke. The clover was green with purplish flowers. Agrarian had never seen green clover; all the clover in the forests of the world of the three suns was orange and red. Blue flower petals showered around the beautiful female.

The figure softly murmured, "Now you are the Spellweaver of the Drelves. Soon you'll make the pilgrimage to Green Vale. You are so strong, advanced, and dedicated. You *are* the one. Your power is unlimited. I can help you fulfill your potential. You can have everything. That includes me. Seek the treasures of the forest. Come to me. Don't you desire me?"

Agrarian stirred uncomfortably. His mind asked, "What do you mean? No person can own another. My love and commitment are to the forest and my people. I don't seek self-enhancement. I don't understand 'desire.'"

"You are too young. You will come to know of what I speak. Come into the forest, Agrarian. Come to me," the figure purred.

Agrarian said, "The Annals and Spellweaver Xenn told me of invaders of our dreams. You have seduced other Spellweavers. You shan't seduce me."

She purred, "Perhaps in time, little one."

Blueness surrounded the image and she then slowly disappeared from the youth's subconsciousness.

Agrarian slept fitfully the rest of the night. When he awakened after the rest period, he noted something he had never experienced - a headache. He left the tree and looked into the clearing where his mother Gyada and several other female Drelves prepared the first meal after the rest period. He studied them. The Drelve females were pretty. The dream perplexed his young mind. He had only known the gentle affection of his mother. The Spellweaver couldn't get the face from the dream out of his thoughts.

What did she mean?

Where was she?

Who was she?

He had no answers. Should he ask Tull the Teacher? Would the Teacher think him foolish?

Agrarian loved the woods and wanted to explore more of it anyway. He slipped away and made short forays into the forests where he made many friends among the trees and animals. The Teacher and his parents chastised him for his indiscretions.

Redness entered his dreams his dreams again during his thirteenth year.

Wisps…
Threads…
Threads of Magick…
Threads of fate…
Threads of time…
Threads connecting worlds …
Dreams connecting worlds …
Dreams of Magick…
The Magick of Dreams…
Magick connecting dreams…
Magick connecting worlds…
Dream raiders…
Elf pressure…
Albtraum…
Albträume, elf dreams, nightmares…
Albträume...

"You are older now. Have you considered my words? Have you

witnessed the power that Magick can give you? You have seen the ravage of your people and beloved forest. You can stop this. You can caress me. Aren't you interested?" she cooed.

This night his dream mate wore a deep blue shiny gown. Her hair was again as black as the fur of a noir skat. The noir skat was a reclusive creature that roamed the fringes of the forest. In a world without darkness the noir skat's coloration placed it at a disadvantage. The beast's innate ability of displacement negated that disadvantage. Some called the noir skat a displacer beast. Tull told of the fierceness of the feline in his lectures.

Why was thinking about a predator when he looked upon such a beauty?

It was a dream, after all.

Or was it?

The voice appeared again, "Do you prefer this?"

She waved her hands and the dress changed to gray. Her hair became deep green. The green color was foreign, but the hair appeared natural on the shoulders of the female. The grayness of the dress was pleasing- the color mimicked the light of Andreas.

Agrarian was asleep, yet he resisted speaking.

Blueness surrounded her and she again left his dreams. The young Spellweaver awakened in a pool of sweat. The sweat of the Spellweaver like his tears was sparkling, iridescent, and multicolored. Drelves and particularly Spellweavers rarely perspired. A season's age had not given any more insight into the meaning of the dreams. He continued to sneak into the woods alone and searched for green clover and the tall black-haired, no, green-haired female.

She appeared in his dreams on three other occasions. Her hair was red, orange, and blonde. Her garments changed, but the message remained the same, filled with temptation and suggestion.

Agrarian learned more spells and scoured the woods for material components for them.

During his thirteenth season, the gray sun again drew near the land. There was great anticipation among the Drelves and particularly old Tull, but no Spellweavers were born. Agrarian grew stronger and slept well during the closeness of the gray sun. He had not faced the field of battle.

Agrarian went to the woods to further his strength. Studying the plants and animals gave the youth pleasure, and learning new things was the rule and not the exception with each foray into the red and orange forest. Agrarian found signs of activity near one of the meandering streams. There were none of the signs of the wanton destruction that one would see from the Drolls or Kiennites excursions into the forests and this area was too deep for them to reach without detection by the Drelve scouts. He suspected more tomfoolery than danger, but evidence of other folk piqued his curiosity. He noted the darkening of the amber light and realized the dark period was nigh. Tull would be furious if he found the youth absent from the confines of the hamlet. Agrarian rushed home and fell into his comfortable bed. Almost a season had passed since his last dream.

This rest period the dream returned.

Redness entered his dreams.

Wisps…

Threads…

Threads of Magick…

Threads of fate…

Threads of time…

Threads connecting worlds …

Dreams connecting worlds …

Dreams of Magick…

The Magick of Dreams…

Magick connecting dreams…

Magick connecting worlds…

Dream raiders…

Elf pressure…

Albtraum…

Albträume, elf dreams, nightmares…

Albträume...

"You will like this," the voice bragged.

The svelte female stood on a field of redbonnet flowers. Her long tresses were all the colors of the rainbow. Her dress was gray.

"I can change it for you. I can be happy. It will be bright as the yellowest rays of the little sun. I can be angry. It will be blazing red. I can be sad. It will be blue. I can be mysterious. It will be green. I can be scared. You can protect me, as you could protect your people. It will be as white as snow. You might not know what snow is. It can be any color you want. I am yours. You can have everything. Think about it, the power to protect your people," the female said alluringly.

As she spoke her hair changed from rainbow hued to yellow, red, blue, green, and pure white. She then playfully changed the color rapidly in succession.

"You still don't answer. In your pack, you will find a gift. It is a gift of my master. It is a token of friendship. You will find the stone most helpful. The Four Elemental Stones will trigger its power. You will never be without the gray sun again. Remember, young Spellweaver, the Teacher can only tell you the things that have happened. You can change things that *are* to happen. Remember this," she cooed.

Blueness surrounded her and she faded from the dream.

It couldn't have been real. jumped from his bed and rushed to his pack. He found a smooth gray stone. It had little weight and barely filled his hand. The stone felt good in his hand. As he touched the smooth rock, it changed to the feel of warm soft skin and mimicked the gentle touch of his mother.

Agrarian gripped the stone. It warmed and softened in his hand. Telltale runes appeared on its surface.

Ǿ ∞ Ǿ

Agrarian had participated in the ceremony of the Stones with Teacher Pryam and Spellweaver Xenn. He had held the unique Keotum Stone the guard captains carried on their patrols. The other stones rested in the Old Orange Spruce. Curiosity and thirst for knowledge inspired the young Spellweaver to test the new stone in the presence of the four elemental stones and the enhancing stone. Agrarian rushed to the Old Orange Spruce. He respectfully tapped on the tree's bark Tull's voice answered from within the great tree, "Enter, Spellweaver Agrarian."

Agrarian passed effortlessly through the thick bark and stood within the great tree's foyer. It was much bigger on the inside.

Tull said, "What is the purpose of your visit, Spellweaver Agrarian? How may I assist you?"

Agrarian replied, "Teacher, I've had a dream. After the dream, I discovered a stone in my chamber. It looks and feels like the stone great Xenn demonstrated. I'd like to expose the stone to the four elemental stones and the enhancing stone."

Tull said, "I'll assist you."

Tull and Agrarian descended the stairs to the Old Orange Spruce library and storage room. Tull removed the invisimoss from the collection of stones. The Summoning Stone of Fire (SSF) looked like a rock. The Summoning Stone of Fire (SSF) bore the image of a proud Fire Horse. Runes appeared on the stone's smooth surface.

Ǿ ∞ Ǿ

The Water Stone (SSW) appeared an ovoid watery shape, a prolate spheroid. The curious artifact was like water, or soft clear gelatin. Runes and an ever so faint image of a water horse appeared on the surface of the artifact.

∞ Ǿ ∞

The Air Stone (SSA), which had the appearance of a rainbow with scintillating colors bent into fattened cigar shape. The object had no weight. Runes appeared on its beautiful surface.

∞ Ǿ ∞

The Air Stone or Wind Stone was sometimes called the Summoning Stone of Air (SSA)

The Earth Stone (SSE) shared the oblate spheroid shape of the Fire Stone (SSF), Air Stone (SSA), and Water Stone (SSW), but it looked like a clump of red clay. Three runes glowed brightly on its surface.

Ǿ ∞ Ǿ

Gray auras spread from the Enhancing or Xennic Stone to the new stone that Agrarian carried. Drops of dark red liquid appeared on the surface of the new stone. Were it orange instead of red, the liquid would have likened to Drelves' blood. 13 drops of red fluid dripped to the floor.

When the thirteenth drop struck the floor a flash of grayness filled the room.

A tall figure wearing a robe and cowl appeared and towered over the Drelves. Fathomless eyes peered out from beneath the cowl, which covered most of his face. The tall figure before them pulled back his dark cowl and stared at the brace of Drelves in the confines of the massive Old Orange Spruce. Long auburn hair flowed down his back and deep blue eyes peered from beneath his long brows. A heart-shaped, cherry-red birthmark sat on his chin.

Agrarian stammered, "Who… who are you? Why are you here?"

The figure coolly said, "You will not recall my face after this encounter. To the point of my being here… you *called* me."

Agrarian asked, "How… what do you mean, we called you?"

The tall figure answered, "The four elemental stones and the ichor of the Bloodstone fragment summoned me to this place. The power of the Windward Staves brought me. Let me first say to you, young Wizard. Magick touches you. Its touch is not always gentle and the power it bestows has consumed many a sorcerer. Be wary, particularly should the gray sun draw near. In those times Magick's touch mimics the Grasping Hand dweomer. Use your powers carefully. My vision extends far beyond Uragh Wood. Every step you take, every move you make, I'll be watching you. The visitor calmly said, 'I thank the Staves of the Four Winds, the Windward Staves, children of the Bloodstone, the Source of Magick. Release the Bloodstone fragment.'"

The robed figure moved his hands slowly from side to side. Three staffs appeared and hovered by his left flank. The three staffs bore four sets of runes about their circumferences at their midpoints and appeared identical save one thing. The hand holds of the staffs bore single and different runes. The visitor sang and began to tap his left foot. The forebodingly sad song in the language of the mound dwellers (the Tuatha Dé Danaan) of Emerald Isle told of faraway and famous places. Agrarian and Tull watched. The staffs aligned perpendicularly. Determining direction in the World of the Three Suns was ever more difficult from within the big tree, but truth be known the staves aligned to the north, south, and east. The artifacts hovered over the elemental stones. The elemental stones aligned as they did during the ceremony of the stones. The Enhancing (Xennic Stone) sent rays of grayness to the four elemental stones and the new stone. The Enhancing Stone eerily moved toward and touched the new stone. Runes appeared on the stones and red fluid flowed again from the new stone.

Ǿ ∞ Ǿ

The three staves touched at their bases and emitted an eerie purple aura. Agrarian's new stone migrated to the point where the three staves came together. The three staves returned to the visitor's side, and then disappeared. The new gray stone hovered over the center of the square created by the four elemental stones. Red liquid oozed from the leaden rock and soaked into *floor.* After 144 taps of the visitor's foot, the flow of liquid stopped. The enigmatic figure walked to the center of the square and placed both hands on *the stone* and continued to sing. However, his words diverged to more arcane phrases. The visitor lifted his hands from the stone, which hovered before him. Tiny electrical arcs flowed from his fingers to the new stone. Faint unnerving popping and crackling noises filled the large hollowed out red elm.

The robed figure concluded his incantation and spoke, "I thank the Staves of the Four Winds, the Windward Staves, children of the Bloodstone, the Source of Magick."

A thirteen-foot diameter circle of Grayness appeared on the ground around him and the new stone. The rock maintained its deep gray color. The Gray Stone emitted the grayness of Andreas whilst the gray sun was away. The figure said, "You should refer to this precious artifact as a Bloodstone. Magick flourishes in the thirteen-foot diameter circle. Guard well these treasures. You bear great responsibility, young Wizard. Heed the words of the learned Tree Shepherd. Avoid the temptation of Fire Magick. You are now a guardian of Magick. A guardian of Grayness."

Agrarian asked timidly, "Are you a Dreamraider? What is your name? The Teacher and I are awake. Your staffs are beautiful. Where did they go? Where is your home, Sorcerer?"

The visitor spoke, "Some call me the Sandman. I prefer to be nameless. Nameless faces are more easily forgotten. My home is where I stand at the moment, but I prefer the solitude of an isolated wood in a blue world. The staffs are three of four brothers, the Staves of the Four Winds. They are the sons of Atlas and Pleione. I carry *three brothers.* The three brothers appear identical, save the single runes on their hand holds. The runes signify 'E', 'S', and 'N'. The staves find east, south, and north respectively. The fourth brother is the Staff of the West Wind, also called the Staff of Stone. The Staff of the West Wind bears a rune from an Old Language of the letter "W" that was carved into its handhold. If one holds the Staff of the West Wind, he'll always know which direction is west. Other bearers hold Atlas, Pleione, and the Staff of the West Wind. I separated the six artifacts long ago. Atlas and the Staves of the Four Winds falling into the wrong hands would create a force difficult to counter and upset the balance of power."

Agrarian asked, "Are you a spirit?

The Sandman's tone did not change as he replied, "I am quite mortal, and my powers are limited. Again, the Four Elemental Stones and the Bleeding Stone summoned me, and the power of the Windward Staves brought me here. Without shypoke eggshells, I depend on the staves to bear me."

Tull queried, "Shypoke eggshells?"

The Sandman answered, "A beast long extinct! I must go!"

He turned to Agrarian and quietly said, "The Enhancing Stone activates the power of the Elemental Stones. Magick may touch anyone who bears the stone. The Bleeding Stone serves as a source of Magick. Used in conjunction with the Elemental Stones, it creates a circle of Magick. In this circle, the Enhancing Stone will facilitate creation of Magick. I can't tell you anything more specific. Use the power of the stones wisely. Keep them safe."

Agrarian said, "Can you carry me to the blue world?"

The Sandman smiled and answered, "I can travel with others only when I use the Translocation Spell, and that requires shypoke eggshells. I don't share the Dream Raiders' innate ability to Translocate and lack shypoke eggshells to perform the spell and carry you. The power of the Windward Staves brought me. When the staves empower me, I cannot bear another traveler. Don't ask me to explain. It's one of many unwonted effects and quirks of Magick. I must now leave you and return to the blue world. The four elemental stones revert to their powers of summoning, control, and enhancing forces of Nature. It's best the four stones remain in the World of the Three Suns. The gray light of the wandering sun will further enhance the artifacts."

The mysterious traveler then interlocked his fingers and murmured several lyrical phrases. Three ornate staffs positioned by his side. Runes appeared on the staffs and reappeared on the four elemental stones, the Enhancing (Xennic Stone), and Bleeding Stone.

The Sandman said, "I thank the Staves of the Four Winds, the Windward Staves, children of the Bloodstone, the Source of Magick."

Then he and the three staves vanished. Tull and Agrarian sat in silence for a time. Agrarian kept the Omega Stone in one of his robe's many pockets. Tull collected the Four Elemental Stones, Xennic (Enhancing) Stone, and Bleeding Stone and placed the six artifacts under the large plot of invisimoss. Agrarian placed a Magick Mouth Spell on the invisimoss to warm of anyone disturbing the stones.

# 16.

## Agrarian in Green Vale

Tull followed the traditions of his predecessors and chose the most promising thirteen-year-old neophytes for the trip to Green Vale. Spellweaver Agrarian had turned thirteen and awaited his first trip. Agrarian nervously made ready. The young Spellweaver's multipocketed robe made choosing his gear an easier task. While he prepared, Agrarian heard a polite knock at his tree. His father Flaey's voice beckoned, "May I enter?"

Agrarian replied, "Certainly, father. I thought you'd have your own preparations to make."

Flaey answered, "I'm prepared. I've been to Meadowsweet and Green Vale many times. I mainly need my weapons, the Keotum Stone, and trail mix. Your mother Gyada and I are quite proud of you, as a son and Spellweaver. On the eve of your trip to Meadowsweet, I have a gift for you. This was given me before my neophyte trip." Flaey reached deep into his raiment. He extended his hand to Agrarian, opened his palm, and revealed a simple rounded gray stone. It was barely more than a pebble.

Agrarian said, "Father, I appreciate everything you and mother do for me and treasure any gifts, but isn't this a simple pebble? The gray color is pleasant and mimics the Keotum Stone."

Flaey said, "This is a Rock of Andreas. It has passed down from my family for generations. Legend tells that it is a fragment of the Gray Wanderer, cast off during a long distant Approximation. Radiance and gray light spreads out from it only during an Approximation of Andreas. Tradition holds its more valuable than the brightest jewel. Sacrificing the stone for the good of the forest produces Magick as powerful as a

Permanent Wish Spell. So, I'm told. At any rate, we want you to have it as an heirloom."

Agrarian accepted the little rock. Placing it in proximity of the Bleeding Stone, Enhancing Stone, and Omega Stone produced no effects. Detecting Magick yielded deep auras but no specific powers for the little rock.

Agrarian carried the Bleeding Stone, Enhancing Stone, Omega Stone. and spell components in his pockets. He placed his hallowed Spellbook in a pocket alone. The heirloom robe was yellow-orange now.

Agrarian's father Flaey was an accomplished Ranger and often led parties to Green Vale and Meadowsweet. Flaey expertly led the group to Meadowsweet, where the elders welcomed Agrarian. Drelvlings touched his robe, but old Xenn's treats were not there. One little nymph named Missy was particularly distraught. Agrarian asked her why she cried, and the child relayed she enjoyed the candied enhancing root tubers and jelly bellies the Old Spellweaver had carried. Agrarian removed the Bleeding Stone from one of his many pockets. The Spellweaver gripped the stone. Runes appeared on its surface.

Ǿ ∞ Ǿ

Grayness surrounded the small group. Red liquid oozed from the malleable stone in Agrarian's hand. A circle of Magick thirteen feet in diameter now surrounded him. Agrarian produced trail mix and gently heated it with a flame spell. Cocoa beans in the trail mix melted and coated the nuts and grains in the trail mix.

Agrarian said, "I thank the Staves of the Four Winds, the Windward Staves, children of the Bloodstone, the Source of Magick."

When the mix cooled, Agrarian divided it among the young Drelves. He assured the little she-Drelve Missy he'd continue Xenn's practice of carrying treats. The matrons of Meadowsweet prepared a feast of the forest for the travelers. During the next amber period, the last before the dark period began, Drelves from other hamlets arrived. Old Teacher Tull was pleased with the turnout. Agrarian was led to a guest tree that in the past had housed the Spellweavers Gaelyss, Yannuvia, and Xenn. Agrarian dropped onto the guest tree's comfortable griffin down bed and reflected on the eventful day. His mind wandered. The down in his bedding came from a creature with the body of a lion and head and wings of an eagle. Folks gave the beast many names. Griffin, griffon, gryphon, alce, keythong, gryphen, griffen, gryphen, and opinicus…

After a very comfortable rest, Agrarian awakened and exited the tree. The common area of Meadowsweet bustled with activity. More Drelves arrived to participate in the harvest of the Enhancing root tubers. The Drelvish hamlets Warren Town, Boomslang, Redberry Fields, Grovetown, Churchill Downs, Fox Vale, Vale Road, and Shad Cove sent participants to Meadowsweet. Some had encountered Drolls and Kiennites. Travelers risked becoming snacks for noir skats, meow-meow skats, wailers, displacers, Baxcats, Leicats, invisibears, shape changers, and honey bears. The Grovetown group narrowly escaped detection. The Fox Vale lot ran into a hungry wailer, but a quick-thinking elder placed ear plugs in their ears to shut out the orange cat's disabling screams. The fuzzy, warm ear plugs were oft used to clean wax from Drelves' ears. The little blokes expanded to fill the ear canals and block out sound. When the wailer attacked, the Rangers were ready and bonked the ravenous feline on the head. The cat beat a hasty retreat and the group made their way forward.

Tull relished his first opportunity to lead the harvest. Agrarian's father Flaey assumed the lead and followed the path to a dead end. A massive cluster of red oaks blocked the way, towered over the path, and blocked out the receding rays of the suns. Tull moved to the front and spoke ancient phrases in a whispered voice. The great trees responded to the ancient message, moved apart, and revealed the Green Vale. Neophytes marveled at the greenness. Red and orange foliage changed to deep green. Warm sweet air, a fair breeze, and pleasant light greeted them. Blue-gray clouds gathered above them in the darkening amber sky. The overall sensation likened to a warm eve either just before or after a cooling rain. Thunder rumbled faintly in the distance. A hill in the center of the valley obscured the far side of the circular vale. The radius of the perfectly circular knoll was one hundred and sixty-nine arm lengths. A circle of thirteen trees of various shapes and sizes occupied the top of the knoll. Many of the trees bore fruits. Like the Enhancing Plants, the trees at the top of the hill were mostly green. The young Drelves had heard stories of shocking grass, grab grass, and centipede grass. These grasses shocked, held on tightly and wouldn't let go of one's shoe, or uprooted in sprigs of one hundred and walked around. Agrarian and his comrades shook off their trepidation of walking on the strange green-colored moss and enjoyed the feel of the plush, comfortable mossy ground of Green Vale. Taller trees and bushes rimmed the area, but a valley filled with short shrubby plants made up the greatest part of Green Vale. Bright green moss and plush grass covered a rim that extended several paces. At the edge of the green moss, the terrain had a gentle incline of about fifteen degrees and length of thirty paces. The floor then leveled and extended several hundred paces. The area rose gently in several areas. The floor of the vale circled the central knoll. A grassy upslope that extended fifty or so paces led to the top of the central knoll. Enhancing Plants filled the hillsides and the floor of the Vale. Very few other plants were entangled with the plants. They saw no Enhancing Plants on the crest of the knoll.

Enhancing plants were about waist high to the average Drelve. The bushes bore bristles of green leaves and bright red flowers. A gentle breeze that moved from left to right and then from right to left crisscrossed the warm valley. Oddly the sky overhead had some blueness intermingled with the ever-present amber light.

Tull led the party of Drelves into the Vale. Once they entered, the great red trees closed the opening behind them. Enhancing Plants did not grow in rows. Instead the plants were randomly arranged in the gently rolling terrain. Many small rivulets coursed through the landscape. The greenness made the area alien to the young Drelves. Agrarian and his young friends had heard older Drelves speak of harvesting the Enhancing Root, but actually being in the green area was very strange. The inquisitive Drelvling Russell approached one of the nearest bushes, reached out, and touched the bright red flower. "Ouch!" Russell shouted. "It bit me!"

"Plants do not have teeth!" his colleague Miller muttered.

Teacher Tull said, "Well, some do. However, these do not. But they have feelings and deserve our respect." Tull said and chastised young Russell. "You must approach the plant in such a way that it knows you appreciate its meaning and value."

"Teacher, what are the plants in the center? They are so strange? They bear fruits," Miller asked.

"They are the *thirttene friends*," the Teacher answered.

"Aren't all plants our friends?" Russell asked.

Tull repeated words many Teachers had said before him. The

Drelvlings read about the Thirttene Friends in their texts. Veterans of harvests described them in detail, but nothing compared to looking upon the majesty of the circle of exceptional trees standing on the hillock in Green Vale. Old Tull said, "Yes. But these are special, much as is the Enhancing Plant. The thirttene are unique. They are Magick. Even when we are without a Spellweaver, we are not without the thirttene. The power they have given us has saved us many times. But we must reserve their fruits for times of need. We are now given a Spellweaver," the Teacher answered. "But now the time has come to harvest the root. Follow me to the scrubs. I'll show you the proper way to approach the plants. We must harvest the tubers while the light is dim. That's when they have greatest potency."

The Teacher Tull went to the first plant on the downward sloping terrain. The old Drelve sang in a low soothing voice. The plant curled its leaves and pulled in its barely visible needle-like thorns. The old Drelve then tenderly touched the spine of the upper leaves of the plant. The Enhancing Plant pulled its limbs upward and inward. This in effect changed the plant from a full bush to a thin narrow plant. Tull then removed a small spade from his pack and knelt to the base of the plant. He delicately inserted the spade into the ground and moved the digging instrument around the base of the plant. He gently pulled the entire plant from the soil, held it aloft, and exposed its roots to the graying light. The gray light from Andreas concentrated on the roots. The entire plant emitted a gray aura. Tull expertly exposed several thumbnail sized tubers dangling from the uncovered roots. He gently pulled the tubers from the roots, but very carefully left one of the tubers undisturbed. He then gently stroked the roots of the plant and carefully placed the plant back on the soft dark ground. The Enhancing Plant's roots plunged back into the soil. Tull sang again, and the little bush expanded its branches and reopened its red flowers.

"That's how it's done," the Teacher said matter-of-factly. "Disturb only the plants with flowers. That's the sign that the roots bear mature tubers. Once we have harvested, I'll tell you more of the Thirttene Friends."

The Drelves went about the task laboriously. Russell and Miller had difficulty in getting past the thorns. As a vocalist, Miller left much to be desired, and Russell was a bit clumsy in stroking the spines of the leaves. Tull applied unguent to the wounds left by the thorns. The older Drelves quite capably harvested the tubers, and Agrarian learned the process quickly. The central hillock and its circle of green trees kept the young Spellweaver's attention.

Tull called the youths together and directed them to follow him to the hilltop. Flaey trekked ahead of them to the area of the trees. The youths watched closely. A geyser erupted from the very center of the hill and bathed the trees on the top of the hill with waters of many hues. After the geyser erupted for thirty-nine heartbeats, the thunder ceased and the area was quiet. The diameter of the geyser pool in the center of the flattened top of the hillock was thirteen paces. The Drelves reached and looked upon the geyser pool. Iridescent lights flickered in the sparkling clear waters of the geyser pool. The overall diameter of the top of the hillock was about thirteen times the diameter of the geyser. The liquid in the basin bubbled gently. Russell and Miller braced, but the geyser did not erupt.

The *thirttene friends* were spaced in a circle around the geyser. The thirteen trees differed dramatically. The one closest them was about the height of three Drelves. (Thirteen feet). It bore red luscious unfamiliar fruits. One hundred and sixty-nine fruits grew on the tree. The fruits were not uniform. The tree had green leaves. Green seemed normal for this area. The tree had blooms similar to the common bluerose plants, but these blooms were light pink. The second tree was also thirteen feet high; it bore few fruits; the fruits were rounded at their end and smaller toward the stem. The tree had blooms similar to the first tree; in some distant past, both must have been related to the bluerose and other rose plants. Russell counted thirteen fruits. The third tree was more like a bush; one hundred and sixty-nine white berries covered it. The fourth tree had elongated purple fruits that were about a hand long. The bush had several intricate webs intertwined in its branches. There were thirteen fruits on the tree. The fifth tree was large oak forty feet tall. But it wasn't red! There was faint Magick associated with the tree. As far as they could tell, this large tree bore no fruit. The sixth tree was thirteen feet tall and covered by small cherry sized fruits; the little fruits were red, green, blue, black, white, and chromatic (multiple colors). There were thirteen fruits of each variety. The seventh tree was fourteen feet tall, had a thick truck, and bore no fruit. The eighth tree was more of a bush and was covered with one hundred and sixty-nine speckled berries. The ninth tree was a little bush that was covered with gems of thirteen colors. The tenth tree was a silver maple- its leaves were made of silver! The tree had been written of in the old tomes. In this area, the silver maple was the only tree without green leaves. The eleventh tree was very large and bore huge orange fruits. The l'orange tree was thirteen arm lengths tall and bore thirteen of the large fruits. Its leaves were deep blue green. Even though the temperature of the Green Vale was comfortable, thin slivers of ice covered the leaves of the l'orange tree. At least the orange color of the fruits was more familiar. The twelfth tree was a Sick Amore. It bore heart-shaped fruits. The Sick Amore was legendary as well. Ingestion of its fruit was the equivalent of imbibing a love potion. The fruit was sometimes poisoned; it was often bittersweet. After the fruit was gone, the taster longed for more. One who consumed the fruit might become intoxicated and lose reason. Not surprisingly, there were thirteen fruits on the Sick Amore tree. The thirteenth tree was thirteen feet tall; it had thirteen branches; its trunk had a diameter of thirteen inches; thirteen veins divided its leaves. It bore thirteen fruits; the fruits were shaped like small silver scroll tubes. The odd fruits were thirteen inches long. Close inspection revealed that the little scrolls had clear lenses at either end. There were other holes spaced along the slender tube. If one peered through the end of the flute-like structures, the lenses enlarged and magnified objects viewed in the distance. The fluted tube was a looking glass! If one flipped the lenses to the side, blew air through the end of the device, and covered the other holes along the length of the devices, he played different notes. Rangers on patrol at the edge of the woods surrounding Alms Glen always carried a toot-and-see-scroll. The invaluable devices enabled the rangers to scan the far side of the wide filed where the Lonc Oak had once stood in ancient times. The Sergeant of the guard usually carried the Keotum Stone. The artifact had enabled Sergeant Major Birney and Mikkal, the father of the great Spellweaver Xenn to subdue an encroacher on Drelvedom. Flaey now carried the Keotum Stone in his pack. Agrarian stared into the effervescing rainbow waters of the geyser.

Suddenly Russell shouted, "There's someone in the Green Oak!"

Tull chastised the youth, "Silence! You must respect the *Thirttene Friends*."

Tull faced the thick-trunked seventh tree, bowed, and said, "Tree

Shepherd, the youth meant no disrespect. Please pardon his disruption of the tranquility of the circle."

Agrarian reflexively bowed as well and asked, "Teacher Tull, does the Tree Shepherd speak to you?"

Tull answered, "Spellweaver, the Tree Shepherd has not communicated in a long while. The patriarch of Green Vale disdains Fire Magick, and Fire Magick has touched our Spellweavers Yannuvia, Xenn, and Teacher Kirrie. Spellweaver Xenn did not stand on this hillock for seven centuries until he stood before the Tree Shepherd during his last visit, but the Tree Shepherd remained silent."

Agrarian bent down and took a bit of rich earth from the edge of the geyser pool. He allowed the soil to fall through his fingers and said, "This is most fertile earth."

Words appeared in Agrarian's mind, "Yes, young Spellweaver, it's soil from the Hanging Gardens of Sagain. A little piece of my world! It nurtures our roots."

Young Agrarian was taken aback and said out loud, "It's fabulous dirt."

Tull, Russell, Miller, Flaey, and the rest of the party looked toward Agrarian. Agrarian said aloud, "Your voice reminds me of a pleasant breeze. Are you the Tree Shepherd?"

The Tree Shepherd telepathically replied, "Yes, Young Spellweaver, but you need not speak aloud. I hear your thoughts. Earth. You have chosen well. Brother of the Soil. Guardian of Grayness. Guardian of Magick. You are a friend of the forest."

Agrarian thought silently, "Do you mind that my Teacher and friends hear the words I say to you?"

The Tree Shepherd sent the message, "So long as there is not a follower of Fire Magick among them. I have trouble scanning the thoughts of those not touched by Magick. You are the only Spellweaver in the group, and the first since the irascible Xenn. My shy friend feared showing herself."

Agrarian said aloud, "The group before you are only concerned with gathering the enhancing root tubers. All you see are friends of the forest."

The Tree Shepherd communicated, "Then you may ask the Lady of the Trees to partake of the fruit of my friends."

Agrarian answered aloud, "How might I do that?"

The Tree Shepherd sent the message, "Approach her tree, the great green oak to your left and ask her to come out and play."

The Spellweaver moved back to the fifth of the Thirttene Friends, the great green oak. Agrarian gently rubbed the great oak and said, "Please come out to play."

Russell and Miller bought back chuckles. Then a small blue-haired nymph walked quickly through the great oak's bark.

After sleepily rubbing her dark purple eyes, the diminutive forest creature gently stroked Agrarian's long silver hair, winked at him, and asked, "Why are you rubbing my tree? Who are you, pretty thing?"

Agrarian asked, "Are you a dryad?"

The diminutive feminine creature warbled chaotically, "Silly! I'm not a matron! Dryads are huge, nigh as big as Drelvlings, four feet tall! I'm a simple sprite! I'm just three feet tall. I've been sleeping in my tree having the best dream. I was drinking the juice of byneberries. I've never seen you, young…ooh! Spellweaver! You are a Spellweaver! You are posing a riddle! Is it a game? I'll play. I've not seen a Spellweaver since… oops! My friend the Tree Shepherd doesn't like me talking about him. He was a lot like one of the others. Hey, you are like another I knew. The one who accused me of casting spells on him! His name was Gaelyss! Do you think I'm casting spells on you, Spellweaver? Oh, a new Teacher, but not a new Drelve! I've seen you in Green Vale many times. You've brought neophytes. I suppose they'll want to sample *my* fruits. Don't you have any pretty ones? These guys are rather homely. Well, all except this one. The Spellweaver is very pretty."

Now Russell and Miller laughed. Tull sternly chastised them.

Agrarian said, "We'd be honored to share the fruits on your trees."

The Tree Sprite coyly said to Agrarian, "You *are* pretty, Spellweaver. Maybe you'd like to come into my tree for a while. I have byneberry wine and passion fruit. Very tasty! But it's not the sweetest thing I'm offering, if you know what I mean. Tree Shepherd, may I have this pretty Spellweaver?"

Tull kindly said, "He'd best stay with us, Lady of the Trees."

The svelte little tree sprite replied seductively "I won't keep him long, Teacher."

Old Tull complimentarily said, "Oh, I suspect your beauty would forever detain him, my Lady."

The tree sprite blushed, but her bright green skin turned purple instead of red. The tree sprite's blue hair and purple eyes contrasted with her bright green skin. The greenness returned after her blushing ended. Though totally out of place in most of the World of the Three Suns, the little creature appeared perfectly at home in the Green Vale. As tall as thirty-six inchworms stacked end-to-end, the three-foot-tall sprite was about two-thirds the height of Russell, who was an average sized Drelve.

Playing on the sprite's vanity, the Teacher Tull said politely and redundantly, "Thank you for allowing our eyes to behold your beauty, Lady of the Trees. It's been too long. We can't all be as beautiful as you. Please bear with us, and we thank you for allowing our glances."

The tree sprite accepted the compliments and offered, "You may try some of *my* wondrous fruits."

Tull interjected, "Ahem. We'll accept the fruits of the trees, Lady of the Trees."

"But they are so few," Agrarian objected.

Tull replied, "We're given a great honor. It's been over a century since the Tree Shepherd and Sprite offered the gift of the fruits of the Thirttene Friends. *The Lady* has given us permission, Agrarian. Magick and the Gray Wanderer Andreas replenish the fruits and sustain the Green Vale. The Magick that sustains the Thirttene will replace a fruit as you take it. You must never take the entire crop. And show respect as you take the fruit."

The young Drelves took a fruit from the Apple and Pear Tree. New fruits replaced those taken by the Drelves. The Tree Sprite snuggled up to Agrarian and gave him a gentle kiss on the cheek, clutched his left hand, and purred, "Pretty Spellweaver. Nice robe, too." She then mischievously stood on tip-toe and planted a lingering kiss on Agrarian's lips. When the buss ended, Agrarian grabbed her, pulled her to him, and kissed her again.

Agrarian turned to Tull and asked, "Should I step into her tree? She gave us the fruit, and I don't want to disrespect her… and she is pretty… and her kiss felt nice… and she smells so good… and I'll just…"

Tull held the young Spellweaver's robe firmly and said, "Charm Spell, Spellweaver. She's hard to resist. You'd best stay with me. We have finished the harvest and must return to Meadowsweet."

Agrarian reluctantly released the tree sprite's hand and asked, "What's your name?'

Teacher Tull said, "Spellweaver, she'll likely not reveal her name. Secretive woodland creatures hold their identities close."

The lovely little fairy answered, "Alexis. Lexie Glitch. I'm the Lady of the Trees."

Tull said, "Amazing! Have you *charmed* her? Charming dweomers shouldn't affect Tree Sprites, Water Sprites, and Dryads!"

She quipped, "I'm not charmed. I just like the pretty Spellweaver. He's the prettiest visitor to Green Vale since the Green Guy came long ago. The Green Guy reflected my Charm Spell and charmed me and tricked me out of my name, but I didn't mind. I got to kiss him. But you are a better kisser, pretty Spellweaver. The inside of my tree is very cozy, and I am the best hostess! Please visit me, Spellweaver. We could be great friends."

The tree sprite walked over to the tree shepherd, whispered something, returned to the fifth of the Thirttene Friends, and passed through the odd dark brown bark.

The Tree Shepherd sent a message to Agrarian, "I echo my little friend's feelings, Spellweaver. Lexie doesn't like admitting her age, but she is a tree sprite matron. She's just short for a Dryad. Her Charm Spell is hard to resist. I'm impressed you resisted. I nigh uprooted and went into her tree. You have high moral fiber, my young comrade. Please visit again, brother of the land, friend of the forest, Guardian of Grayness, and Guardian of Magick."

Agrarian acknowledged the invitation, turned away, and walked down the hillock. Tull gathered the harvesters and the group uneventfully returned to Meadowsweet. After a period's rest, Flaey and Tull led the group back to Alms Glen. The bountiful harvest provided elders and matrons enough enhancing root tubers to well stock their stores. Agrarian returned to his tree and relished the memories of the trip.

Seasons of the harvest passed. Each year Agrarian accompanied Tull's party to Green Vale. The Spellweaver spent most of his time in the Vale talking with the Tree Shepherd and enjoying the company of Lexie Glitch, the tree sprite. Agrarian studied his spell book. He used the Bleeding Stone and Enhancing Stone to strengthen his defensive spells. Agrarian's Wall of Thorns, Entangle, Plant Growth, Snare, and Hallucinatory Terrain

Spells surpassed even those of the Great Defender Gaelyss. Agrarian mastered the Tree Spell. He enjoyed interacting with Drelvlings and fooling them by assuming the form of a small tree. He kept sweets and fruits in his robe and drew smiles from little Drelves wherever he went. Against the advice of the council of Alms Glen, Agrarian often trekked to the outer communities, the Drelvish hamlets Warren Town, Boomslang, Redberry Fields, Grovetown, Churchill Downs, Fox Vale, Vale Road, and Shad Cove and used his Magick to strengthen their defenses. Flaey was promoted to Sergeant Major and Gyada led the groups to Sylvan Pond. Both the Spellweaver's parents lived well into their 120's. Old Tull aged imperceptivity. His hair was entirely brown when Pryam's death pressed him into service. Approximations occurred at 13, 8, 5, 8, 3, 21, 13, 1, 5,3,5, and 1-year intervals after Agrarian's birth. No Spellweavers arrived with the gray light.

In the south and central area of the world of the three suns, the mysterious people known as Draiths proliferated. The muscular bronze-skinned seven-foot-tall warriors had constructed a fortress made of strange black stone on the plain before the great Southern Mountain range. The bastion grew into a conurbation. Word came from Drelvish spies that the Draiths named their stronghold Ooranth, and passed the same moniker to the black stone and the plain upon which the growing city sat. Patrols from Ooranth reached the fringes of the Drelves' domain. Animosity persisted between Draiths and Drolls. The Draiths repeatedly threw back assaults from the Drolls and Kiennites. Drelvish sentries reported skirmishes with Drolls and Kiennites. Draiths rarely entered the red meadow and inspected the road northward to Aulgmoor and the Drolls' lands, usually in response to transgressions by the Drolls and Kiennites. The bronze-skinned warriors avoided the thick forests around Alms Glen. However, Drelvish Rangers caught outside the forest received the same treatment from the seven-foot tall warriors of Ooranth as did Drolls and Kiennites. Campfire jargon alleged the Draiths hated Magick and Approximations. Magick was unwanted in Ooranth. Agrarian and Drelves pondered the unwonted black stone, which composed Ooranth's walls and structures.

The Draiths grew powerful.

Agrarian mastered many defensive spells. The Enhancing (Xennic)

Stone enhanced his spells and helped protect Alms Glen. The Bleeding Stone gave him a Circle of Grayness, within which Magick flourished, and the rich red liquid that flowed from the artifact energized him. These effects were manifest only when the Bloodstone was in the presence of the quartet of Elemental Stones.

Tull watched Agrarian grow into adulthood. The old Teacher zealously approached his duties and stewardship of 2 elixirs of longevity, 4 elemental stones, Agrarian's gray bleeding stone… Stone of Enhancement (Xennic Stone) … During the Approximations that occurred at 13, 8, 5, 8, 3, 21, 13, 1, 5,3,5, 1, 21, 34, and 5-year intervals after Agrarian's birth, Tull presided over ceremonies and rituals that dated to the dawn of Drelvedom. Agrarian assisted the Teacher.

# 17.

# Birth of Spellweaver Phyrris, "Fire"

144 years after the birth of Agrarian, Andreas drew near. Gray light concentrated on a tree occupied by Ranger Fonty and his life-mate Danielle. Old Tull and Agrarian made their way to the tree. Midwives expertly helped little Phyrris into the world. The ancient spell book replicated.

*The Gifts of Andreas to the People of the Forest*
ΛΑΡΛΣ
Α& Ω

The babe had fiery red streaks in his silver hair. Drelves were blessed with a second Spellweaver. Fonty looked at the babe's hair and gave him the name Phyrris, after the old Drelvish word for fire. During his nymph hood the tyke was often called simply "fire" because of his vigor. He learned quickly.

On his seventh birthday, Tull and Agrarian led Phyrris to the Old Orange Spruce. The three gathered in the library of the Old Orange Spruce. Tull produced the ancient stones. The Enhancing (Xennic) Stone moved to a central position, and the four elemental stones positioned at four corners around the enhancing stone. Runes appeared on all but the Earth Stone. Auras flashes from the Enhancing Stone to the Fire Stone, Water Stone, and Air Stone. The Earth Stone hovered silently and without auras. Little Phyrris walked around the hovering stones and stared at each. The stones hovered at his eye level. The brilliant colors of the Air Stone captivated the child. He also softly touched the Water Stone and smiled at the Firehorse on the surface of the Fire Stone. The child paused at the relatively plain Earth Stone. Without speaking the child walked into the square area and approached the stone hovering in the center. He reached out his little left hand and touched the stone. The stone shrank to fit into his little hand. The child's orangish skin changed to gray. The little Drelvling stood in the center of the square and looked at Agrarian.

Agrarian said, "I've taken these steps. It seems you have a choice of three, little one. It feels good, doesn't it? Warm all over! Which do you like best, Phyrris?"

Little Phyrris said, "I like them all, Spellweaver Xenn. Which is your favorite?"

Agrarian said, "I'm bound to the Earth Stone. What does the stone in your hand tell you?"

Phyrris said, "Only to choose one, Xenn."

Tull watched intently. Little Phyrris walked to the Fire Stone. The Summoning Stone of Fire (SSF) looked like a rock. The Summoning Stone of Fire (SSF) bore the image of a proud Fire Horse. Runes appeared on the stone's smooth surface.

Ǿ ∞ Ǿ

Phyrris walked to the Water Stone. The Water Stone (SSW) appeared an ovoid watery shape, a prolate spheroid. The curious artifact was like water, or soft clear gelatin. Runes and an ever so faint image of a water horse appeared on the surface of the artifact.

∞ Ǿ ∞

The little Spellweaver went to the Air Stone (SSA), which had the appearance of a rainbow with scintillating colors bent into fattened cigar shape. The object had no weight. Runes appeared on its beautiful surface.

∞ Ǿ ∞

The Air Stone or Wind Stone was sometimes called the Summoning Stone of Air (SSA). Phyrris went to the Earth Stone. The Earth Stone (SSE) shared the oblate spheroid shape of the Fire Stone (SSF), Air Stone (SSA), and Water Stone (SSW), but it looked like a clump of red clay. No runes sat on its surface.

Phyrris returned to the Fire Stone. He took the Fire Stone in his left hand and held the Enhancing Stone in his right.

Tull said, "Quirk of Magick. You choose Fire. A logical choice. The ceremony of the Elemental Stones is completed."

Phyrris learned quickly. He studied the fire spells in the Spellbook. Agrarian tutored the youth often and asked about dreams. Phyrris spoke only of pleasant childhood dreams. At thirteen, Phyrris accompanied Tull, Agrarian, and Flaey to Meadowsweet and Green Vale. During his visit, the Tree Shepherd remained silent. During Agrarian's long life and many trips to Green Vale, the Tree Shepherd had oft communicated with the aging Spellweaver, but the patriarch said nothing in Phyrris's presence. Phyrris returned from Green Vale. The young Spellweaver expressed great interest in weaponry and spent many hours with the bowyers and fletchers. He studied about BJ Aires and Byrum Goodale. Soon he was crafting high quality bows and arrows. Phyrris accompanied the Teacher on every harvest trip. The Tree Shepherd remained non-communicative. In the seventh year after his neophyte trip and after a hard-Light Period's work, the 20-year-old Spellweaver left the armory and walked to a nearby stream to wash the grim away. He reached the stream, dangled his toes in the babbling waters, and acknowledged a tree sprite and rambling bramble bush that passed by.

A feminine voice asked, "Are you tired, Fire Wizard?"

Phyrris turned. A matronly brown-haired she-Drelve stood on the bank behind him.

Phyrris asked, "Who are you? I don't know your face. You are not from Alms Glen and Meadowsweet."

She replied, "My name is Kirrie. I once walked these woods. I was Teacher of the Drelves and betrothed to Spellweaver Gaelyss."

Phyrris said, "Fire Magick seduced Kirrie. That's ancient history. The Teacher Tull urges us to study history so we won't repeat its mistakes. You can't be the Teacher Kirrie. She'd be long dead."

She replied, "Fire Magick sustains me, and I'm not dead. Your choice of the Fire Stone pleases Grayness. I'm surprised you haven't dreamed."

Phyrris replied, "I've had lots of dreams. Know that I have sulfur crushed in my hand."

Kirrie laughed, "You are indeed a Fire Wizard. Tell me, did the Tree Shepherd acknowledge you in Green Vale?"

Phyrris said, "The Teacher tells us not to discuss Green Vale with outsiders. I don't know who you are."

Kirrie answered, "Good to be cautious. The old blighter labeled me Fire Wizard long ago. All I got for saving Alms Glen was banishment and rejection. I'm unwanted and unwonted! Do you seek enhancement?"

Phyrris said, "I am an accomplished sorcerer. I've mastered all the Fire Spells in my spell book. My skills with bows and arrows are second to none."

Kirrie said, "Without enhancement, you'll learn no more than you have now. I offer you power. The power of Fire Magick. How'd you like to make weapons like this?"

She extended a well-made short sword.

Phyrris took the blade and said, "It's nice work, but the Rangers at the meadow's edge carry swords of equal quality. It's not wise to surrender your blade. I could strike you."

Kirrie laughed again and said, "Take the weapon I gave you and scratch your hand."

Phyrris said, "Why'd I do that?"

She persisted, "Are you afraid? It won't hurt much."

Phyrris shrugged and nicked his finger. The wound immediately healed.

Kirrie said, "Now chase me."

She ran away. Phyrris jumped up and ran with blazing speed and soon overtook her. She laughed again and said, "This is the most fun I've had since Yannuvia and I sneaked off to the Lone Oak under the Invisimoss."

Phyrris marveled, "The weapon is enhanced with both *healing* and *speed*. Spells are built into the blade. Few Spellweavers ever learn healing spells. The Haste Spell is easy to learn, but most are reluctant to sacrifice hares for their blood, which is the essential material component. Can you really tell me how to do this?"

Kirrie said, "Sure. All you have to do is take a little trip. I'll have you back in no time at all."

Phyrris said, "Are you a Dreamraider? I'm not asleep! Stories tell that the Lost Spellweaver aged whilst traveling with Dreamraiders."

Kirrie said, "Knowledge has its price. I'm a sister of grayness. Are you interested? Or are you a coward?"

Phyrris said, "I'm no coward. Tell me what I have to do."

Kirrie placed a flat blue tile on the ground and said, "Just step on the blue stone with me. I'll take you to a place where you'll find treasures." The blue tile expanded to cover an area of seven square feet. 84 inchworm lengths on a side!

Phyrris stared at the remarkably attractive older she-Drelve. Her brown hair gave away her maturity, but her flawless light orange skin and clear eyes made her look young. All Agrarian and Tull's warnings for caution left him. Kirrie extended her hand. Phyrris took it and stepped onto the blue tile with her. Blueness surrounded them and they disappeared. Phyrris was vaguely aware of his hand caressing hers as she floated beside him. It was as though their slight orange-skinned bodies and minds ripped through the fabric of space and time. Then… Absolute darkness… cold…void… followed by colors, and energies…his thoughts were spinning violently out of control. Phyrris passed through vortex after vortex of hue and energy. Pain coursed through every nerve ending. He felt the air sucked from his lungs. The only relief came from the inexplicable comforting touch of Kirrie's hand. Then, grayness… Alas! Had he died and entered the abyss? Was there nothing more? His feelings of hopelessness ended when he unceremoniously hit firm ground. His lungs hungrily engulfed warm dry air. He stood with Kirrie in a stone grotto with eerie red walls. Kirrie gently stroked his hair and gripped his hand.

Phyrris asked, "Why am I here?"

Kirrie answered, "You must taste the waters of Fire Lake in order to…"

Her voice trailed away as she steadily pulled on his hand and led him along a trail. The air warmed further as they walked. Eerie red glows flickered on the stone ceiling of the irregular cavern. The pathway widened and they entered a large grotto dominated by a body of liquid. Multitudes of tiny flames flickered mischievously on the surface of the odd lake.

Kirrie pulled a beautiful gem-laced cup from her raiment, bent downward, and filled the ornate chalice with some of the bizarre fluid, and extended the vessel toward the young Drelve and commanded, "Drink this."

Phyrris reluctantly took the ornate twelve-inch-tall cup. Its base was six inches in diameter and stem six inches long. Its bowl held little more than half an average tankard of ale. A faint mauve glow surrounded the chalice. A large upward pointing triangle dominated the bowl. Flowing runes covered most of the bowl of the deep red cup. Pristine stones of all colors lined the rim and also adorned the sides of the cup. The lightweight chalice contained clear liquid. Smoky steam wafted from the cup.

The young Spellweaver marveled, "It's beautiful, but at the same time it frightens me. Still… I can't stop looking at it. The water is smoking!"

Kirrie's voice firmly continued, "Go ahead. It will not harm you. Drinking the waters of Fire Lake will strengthen you."

There was nothing for it.

Phyrris eased the ornate chalice to his pale orange lips and gently sipped the smoky warm water. Goose bumps covered his light carroty skin and he felt chilled to the bone. He tipped the cup and quaffed the remainder of the liquid. Words appeared in Phyrris's mind:

*"I give you my blood through which you will receive all you seek. You in turn give to me your all."*

Ǿ ∞ Ǿ

Phyrris felt strong. Words of terrifying new spells appeared in his thoughts. Powerful Fire Magick!

Kirrie said, "I promised you gifts. The waters of Fire Lake bind us to Fire Magick."

Phyrris asked, "I'm interested in the Magick sword. Is the metal unique?"

Kirrie said, "The metal is adamantine. Quenching it in the waters of Fire Lake bestows greater strength and power. Xennic gemstones bestow the special properties of the sword. Such stones adorn the Chalice from which you just drank. Softer clear ones bestow protection from Magick when crushed and made into an unguent. In this chest, there is a supply of adamantine, a never-empty vessel of the waters of fire Lake, three clear Xennic Gemstones, and a number of brilliant stones. The stones are taken from the depths of Fire Lake. They are the 1/13th the size of an Omega Stone."

Phyrris asked, "What does each stone do?"

Kirrie replied, "They will tell you. Effects are additive."

Phyrris asked, "What do these gifts cost me?"

Kirrie eased over to the Spellweaver, gently rubbed his red-streaked silver hair, and kissed his cheek. "That for one thing. You'll see when we return."

Phyrris asked, "Are there more stones in the lake?"

Kirrie said, "I really don't know… I haven't checked the waters."

Phyrris said, "If the lake is Fire Magick, its waters will not harm me.!" The young Spellweaver dropped Kirrie's hand, slipped off his robe, and approached the water.

Kirrie said, "Wait! No! I don't know what will happen!"

Her warning came too late. Phyrris jumped through the flickering flames into the water. He reappeared on the surface a moment later and shouted, "Come on in. The water's fine!"

Kirrie was disinclined to acquiesce to his request. The Spellweaver swam ashore. His hair changed to fiery red and flames now flickered in his eyes. He said, "I feel great! I also found four more Xennic Gemstones." He opened his hand and revealed a clear, red, yellow, and green stone. The Spellweaver walked over and kissed Kirrie firmly on the lips. She withdrew from him… then said, "What the heck! You're very pretty!" and threw her arms around him and kissed him passionately.

A flash of redness heralded Phyrris and Kirrie's return to the stream near Alms Glen.

Phyrris asked, "When will I see you again?"

Kirrie kissed his cheek and said, "I'm not sure I'm going to leave."

Shouts came from the woods. Kirrie shrugged, dropped the blue tile on the ground, stepped on it, and disappeared in a flash of blueness.

Ranger Rusty ran toward the Spellweaver and said, "I saw flashes of light! Spellweaver! Thank the forest! You've returned! We've searched far and wide. Your father Fonty has not given up the search, though it's been three years since you were last seen. Your hair! It's red! Very red! Drelvedom is blessed! We now have three Spellweavers! Old Tull will be so pleased."

Phyrris said, "Hold on, Rusty. I was only gone for a few hours… maybe half a period. And you said three Spellweavers!"

The Ranger had difficulty containing his joy. He said, "Yes, Spellweaver! We must get you to the common area to meet your brother."

Phyrris said, "My brother. My mother Danielle was not with child."

Rusty said, "Your brother was born during an Approximation two years ago. He's our new Spellweaver Aergin. Teacher Tull says it's the second time for sibling Spellweavers, and the first time the gray light has shown twice on the same parents. The other siblings were twins!"

Phyrris said, "Aergin… the old word for Air. But Rusty… I was only gone…"

Rusty said emphatically, "Three years, Spellweaver! No disrespect intended! Glance in the water, and then please follow me to the common area."

Phyrris looked at his reflection in the clear stream and marveled at the redness of his hair and the maturity in his eyes and face. He looked forty! It made him feel a little better about his liaison with Kirrie. She looked young for her age.

Phyrris said, "So it's two years since the last Approximation. A new Spellweaver arrived! He's my brother! His name's Aergin!"

Rusty said, "Yes to all, Spellweaver, now let's go."

Rusty led Phyrris toward Alms Glen. Phyrris carried the chest he received at Fire Lake. It had remarkably light weight. They passed a few new cottages. When they reached the common area of Alms Glen, all Drelvedom celebrated Phyrris's return. Ranger Rusty carried the chest to the Old Orange Spruce. The Spellweaver rushed to his mother Danielle's tree and found her inside with his beautiful baby brother. Aergin smiled at his older brother. The toddler extended his little fingers and sprayed Phyrris with Dancing Lights. Danielle was overjoyed at the return of her son. Word went out to find Fonty. The searchers found the stalwart Ranger near Alluring Falls. Fonty returned and reunited with his family. Phyrris spent several cycles of Meries catching up on events in Drelvedom. Aergin's birth during the Approximation two tears earlier had been the most celebrated event. Older Drelves had gone to their ancestors and happy couples welcomed nymphs. Teacher Tull groomed young Dina from Grovetown as a possible replacement. Dina had shown enthusiasm for working with Drelvlings. Aergin was quite fond of Dina. Tull insisted on making the trips to Meadowsweet and Green Vale. In turn Elder Coldan and Spellweaver Agrarian insisted the elderly Teacher ride on the horns of a dilemma. Agrarian charmed the chameleon-like bovine with the Summoning Stone of Earth. The rare beast had the ability to adjust the shape and consistency of its large horns. Agrarian suggested the beast form a rocking chair. Old Tull enjoyed "riding in the rocking chair." The folk of Meadowsweet tended the dilemma whilst the harvesters made the relatively short trip to Green Vale. Lovely Dina also made the last two journeys and performed stellar work. Though Phyrris was absent, the Tree Shepherd remained noncommunicative.

Aergin was 21 years younger than Phyrris. Phyrris was 144 years younger than Agrarian. "Fire" became like a second father to the nymph Aergin. Tull was now… very old. Tull now walked with a cudgel. Young Dina constantly attended the elderly Teacher and lightened his load. Tull spent every waking moment teaching. Agrarian spent most of his time with Tull. Elders Coldan and Monty assigned Fonty's brothers Bob and Tim to assist the Old Teacher and they seldom left his side.

A forge appeared in Alms Glen. Its hearth, tongs, hammers, anvil, and slack tub were made of light weight but very hard material. Oil filled the slack tub. There was a supply of odd red rocks that were not consumed by flames. The name Jodie was written across the hearth in letters from Old Drelvish. No one saw the delivery and setup of the work station. Four red-leafed creeping willows volunteered to position themselves around the hearth and interlock their branches to provide a canopy for the work area. The branches intermingled to prevent rainwater from falling onto the forge. The four large mobile trees dug in their roots and left an effective work area of twenty by twenty feet. Phyrris marveled at the quality of the tools and set to work producing fine weapons. The Spellweaver used Fire Magick to superheat the metals and facilitate forming blades. On more than one occasion, his Fire Magick spelled doom for marauding Drolls.

Phyrris's use of Fire Magick concerned Elders Aleya and Vyckie. Some students of the Annals of Drelvedom continued to point out the parallels between Phyrris and the Lost Spellweaver Yannuvia. The Council of Alms Glen requested a meeting with Phyrris. The Annals of Drelvedom detailed the changes in the Lost Spellweaver Yannuvia after he returned from walkabouts. Like Yannuvia, Phyrris had aged beyond his years, but his hair had changed to fiery red in lieu of the browning typical for aging Drelves. During the meeting, Phyrris reaffirmed his loyalty to Alms Glen and particularly his little brother Aergin. Leaving the forge and his work to kowtow with the petty fears of the Council of Alms Glen angered Phyrris. The Spellweaver refused to partake of the Council's meal of fruits of the forest, returned to the forge, worked through the next Amber Period, and returned to his red oak home. On the way, a hare crossed his path. Phyrris zapped the beast with a Magick Missile. He preserved some of the hare's blood to use in Haste Spells and then roasted the coney with a Fire Spell. The beast provided a hearty meal. Phyrris found he was less satisfied with fruits and vegetables and had grown fond of meat. He enjoyed his repasts most often in the solitude of his home. The tired Spellweaver slipped off his raiment and settled down into his soft bed. His mind returned to his travel in the red and blue light with the sultry Kirrie. He pondered the gift of the forge. Then thoughts of the Council's suspicions angered him. He remembered the Tree Shepherd's contempt of Fire Magick. The Tree Shepherd had not felt the comfort of the waters of Fire Lake. Phyrris snapped his left thumb and third finger. Little sparks flew from his digits. He rubbed his thumb and index finger muttered his name "Phyrris" and produced a small flame at the tip of his finger. "Fire" felt warm. Pleasant smoke billowed from the little flame. He remembered Kirrie's warmth and softness. His younger brother and fellow Spellweaver Aergin's progress pleased him. The Spellweaver extinguished the flame by uttering the old Drelvish word for water "Purya." Phyrris closed his eyes and breathed deeply. The smoky air brought back memories of Fire Lake and Kirrie. He found sleep. Redness entered his dreams. Phyrris found the redness pleasing.

Wisps…
Threads…
Threads of Magick…
Threads of fate…
Threads of time…
Threads connecting worlds …
Dreams connecting worlds …

Dreams of Magick…
The Magick of Dreams…
Magick connecting dreams…
Magick connecting worlds…
Dream raiders…
Elf pressure…
Albtraum…
Albträume, elf dreams, nightmares…
Albträume...

Ǿ ∞ Ǿ

Redness cleared. Phyrris hoped to see Kirrie's face. Instead another face entered his dream. Horrific and vaguely female, the creature had fiery red eyes, unsightly wings, and long muscular arms ending in long curved talons, which were covered in dark ichors. The strangely attractive creature pursed her lips, blew the sleeping Spellweaver a kiss, and simply hissed, "Pleasant dreams, Fire Wizard! How do you like these?" The she-beast revealed long curvaceous legs.

Phyrris uncomfortably said, "I am not offended by the title Fire Wizard, Dreamraider. Your visage comforts me and is pleasant to look upon. However, I am needing my rest."

She replied, "Good answer! Your fatigue tells me you are making use of your gift."

Phyrris said, "So your lot is responsible for the gift of the forge. If it means I'm in your debt, you may remove it."

She answered, "The forge is the gift of Grayness and your reward for embracing Fire Magick."

Phyrris asked, "Is your name Jodie? If not, what is the meaning of the writing on the forge?"

She answered, "I prefer the moniker 'Amica.' Or you may call me Good Witch. I did not place the writing on the forge. By the way, you made short work of the Drolls who attacked your folk."

Phyrris said, "They had it coming."

The Dreamraider said, "They did. I've done in a few Drolls in my day. I am not here to badger or chastise you, you are doing well. You have tools to enhance the power of the forge and create items of power."

Phyrris said, "Speak your business and be gone."

The Dreamraider said, "Everything I've heard of you rings true. I am proud to welcome you as a brother of Grayness, of Fire Magick. Know that the Elemental Stones bridge Nature and Magick. Use them with the Enhancing Stone and Bleeding Stone at the forge. The Xennic Gemstones will enhance your creations. You travel the course I'd hoped for, Fire Wizard Phyrris. I've nothing to add, but this."

She moved toward the dreaming Spellweaver and planted a passionate kiss on his lips. Blueness surrounded her, and she disappeared. Phyrris awakened in a sweat. Several Xennic Gemstones were littered around his tree home. Each little stone was shouting a single word from the Old Drelvish language. The stones shouted 13 times. The words identified the properties of the 13 little rocks. Phyrris got up and recorded each stone's message in his spell book. The Spellweaver noted his lips were parched... and slightly burned. He placed the Gemstones in a small sack. The Spellweaver munched on the last of his rabbit and then headed for the forge. His uncles Tim and Bob were waiting. He instructed them to go to the Old Orange Spruce and fetch the exceptional stones.

Phyrris said, "Tell Teacher Tull that I'll be needing them for a while."

Tim and Bob brought the Elemental Stones, Enhancing Stone, and Bleeding Stone to the forge site. The Bleeding Stone rose above the hearth and created a circle of Magick 13 feet diameter around the forge. The Enhancing Stone hovered above the hearth and touched the Bleeding Stone. The adjoined stones sent rays of grayness toward the four elemental stones and the forge. Red liquid dripped from the Bleeding Stone into the forge and burned brightly. Phyrris opened the chest he brought from Fire Lake. The Spellweaver used adamantine quenched in the waters of Fire Lake and a green (healing) Xennic Gemstone. When completed, the wondrous weapon emitted a green glow. Phyrris gripped the short sword. The burns on his lips healed immediately. Next the Spellweaver used a similar length of adamantine and a red Xennic Gemstone and imparted Haste to the second blade. He took a length of Blackthorn and a mauve Xennic Gemstone. He allowed red liquid from the Bleeding Stone to flow over the thin length of Blackthorn. The mauve stone meld with the length of wood. He then added a deep orange Xennic Gemstone to the same wood. The experiment worked! The wood accepted the second stone. Red liquid dripped onto the device. The Wand empowered its wielder with Magick Missile and a limited Fireball Spell. Phyrris retained a large length of adamantine and several Xennic Gemstones. He then went about more mundane tasks. Phyrris placed the brace of exceptional short swords in the care of Fonty and kept the Wand of Magick Missiles and Fireballs in his raiment. After completing his work, Phyrris returned the exceptional stones to the care of Tull and Dina in the Old Orange Spruce. He kept his chest with unused adamantine and Xennic Gemstones in a secret ambry in his home tree. Jodie… the name etched in the hearth meant nothing to the Spellweaver. Until…

# 18.

## Jodie

Some three Dark Periods after the forge appeared, Phyrris worked alone at the forge. A flash of redness surrounded the forge. A feminine form appeared.

Kirrie said, "Hello Spellweaver. Have you been swimming lately?"

The matronly she-Drelve held a wrapped bundle in her arms. Phyrris's mouth gaped. Kirrie moved the blanket and revealed a beautiful infant. The child had light orange skin and silver hair with streaks of red. The infant smiled. Phyrris felt the power of an Empathy Spell.

Phyrris gawked, "Who… what… when… how…"

Kirrie said, "Some deeds have consequences, Spellweaver. Her name is Jodie. She is mine… and yours. She is, as far as I know, the first spawn of two Fire Wizards. Her father is Spellweaver. Her mother is *Spellweaverish.* Though she was not born during an Approximation, Magick touches her. She *is* Spellweaver. A copy of the spell book appeared by her basinet."

*The Gifts of Andreas to the People of the Forest*

ΛΑΡΛΣ

Α&Ω

Phyrris said, "This… has never happened before."

Kirrie replied, "Very unwonted! There's a first time for everything. Would you like to hold your daughter?"

Phyrris awkwardly took the child. He'd enjoyed interacting with Aergin, but the little Spellweaver was already two years old when he first saw him. Jodie opened her eyes and gazed at Phyrris. Blue and red light flickered in the infant's eyes. Phyrris held her for a while.

He said, "What do we do now?"

Kirrie said, "I am not welcomed in Alms Glen. I fear Jodie will not be accepted. We have a safe place to live. Her Godmother Amica assisted my delivery and loves her as much as I do. We'll visit often. It's best you not tell anyone about us. Many forces are at work in this world… and others. We've seen travelers. Some good. Some not so good. I'll be sure she knows her father. It's important."

Phyrris said, "It's so much to absorb… she's beautiful. Just one of her smiles lightens all my loads."

Kirrie smiled and said, "Better be careful, Dad. She is a sorceress. She may be charming you."

Phyrris said, "She has certainly done that. May I hold her for a while longer?"

Kirrie said, "The rest period ends. There is much activity in the common area. It's best we be going. We'll return soon."

Phyrris said with concern, "Won't traveling age her?"

Kirrie said, "For whatever reasons, quirks of Magick, Jodie and I do not suffer the aging effect from traveling in the red and blue light. Amica says it's because we don't leave the World of the Three Suns."

Phyrris bashfully asked, "Might we have some time together?"

Kirrie coyly answered, "I'd like that, too. Maybe soon. For now, stay safe and use well these gifts. We are brother and sister in Grayness above all else. Fire Magick touches us. We must be on our way."

Kirrie took Jodie from him and gently kissed his face. She placed a blue tile on the ground, stepped onto it, and vanished in a flash of blueness.

Fonty, Bob, and Tim arrived with a number of damaged weapons.

Fonty said, "Spellweaver… my son… you seem a thousand miles away. Are you troubled?"

Phyrris answered, "No, father. Looks like I have lots of work to do."

Fonty said, "Yes. We've noted a lot of Droll activity north of the meadow. Sergeant Major France wants all weapons repaired. He's doubled patrols."

Phyrris said, "Stay safe, father."

Most of Phyrris's work involved repairing and forging standard weapons. He had a limited amount of special metal and very few Xennic Gemstones. The Spellweaver still helped the bowyers and fletchers. He spent more time with Aergin as the little Spellweaver grew older. Visits from Kirrie and Jodie recharged his emotions. Kirrie brought Jodie each year on the nymph's birthday. Sergeant Major France's concerns bore fruit. Drolls attacked a Drelvish scouting party near the meadow's edge and killed a young Drelve named Orrby. Phyrris, his father Fonty, Tim, and Bob went into the woods and sought out the Drolls' camp. Phyrris sent a Fire Spell into the wolf-face warriors and killed all but one. The Drelves allowed him to escape to assure word of the attack reached Aulgmoor and the Gap Keep. Agrarian bolstered the defenses around Alms Glen and instructed Aergin. Tull grew feebler, but insisted on continuing his duties as Teacher. Dina assumed a larger role in the day-to-day duties and spent lots of time with Aergin.

When Aergin attained his seventh birthday, Tull presented him with his Spellbook.

*The Gifts of Andreas to the People of the Forest*
ΛΑΡΛΣ
Α&Ω

The old Teacher brought Aergin, Dina, Phyrris, Agrarian together in the library of the Old Orange Spruce for the ceremony of the elemental stones. The ceremony proceeded. Aergin stood in the spacious library of the Old Orange Spruce. Runes appeared only on the Air Stone and Water Stone. Young Aergin predictably chose the Air Stone. He continued to grasp the Enhancing Stone and walked to the lovely Air Stone. The child gripped the Air Stone. His visage flashed the colors of the rainbow. After 13 heartbeats, Aergin's normal color returned and he released the Air Stone and it returned to its position. Little strands of rainbow colors appeared in his hair. He released the Enhancing Stone. After the ceremony, he was oft referred to as "Air."

Kirrie, Phyrris, and Jodie celebrated Jodie's sixth birthday in a secluded spot in the woods south of the wide meadow. Phyrris traveled often to the spot where the ancient hamlet Lost Sons and later a Kiennish fortress had stood. The forest had reclaimed the ground. Rambling bramble bushes, orange triffids, walkabout bushes, shrinking violets, and red-leafed creeping willows provided a secure area for the family gathering. The creeping willows interlocked their upper branches and provided cover for the family. Little Jodie and Phyrris traded playful spells, including Fairie Fire, Dancing Lights, False Auras, and Plant Growth.

Phyrris said, "I'm very pleased with your spells, Jodie."

Jodie smiled and said, "Thanks, Papa, I want to please you."

Phyrris said, "Next year, just eight Dark Periods hence, you will be seven. You'll receive your Spellbook. I have something special planned. It's a surprise."

Kirrie said, "Phyrris, I'd planned on just giving her the book and then coming for a visit. We can't have a ceremony in Alms Glen. What do you have planned?"

Phyrris said, "It's a surprise. Besides, I'm a Spellweaver. I'll do what I want."

Jodie laughed and said, "I love surprises! I'm a Spellweaver, too, Papa."

Kirrie added, "I like surprises, too… sometimes. Your father is full of them."

Phyrris bent down and kissed Jodie's red-streaked silver hair and said, "You are certainly a Spellweaver, Jodie. You're also better than a Mender at healing my ills!"

During visits the following Dark Periods, Kirrie prodded Phyrris for ideas about the secret. Finally, at the last Dark Period's visit before Jodie's seventh birthday, Phyrris said, "Kirrie, on Jodie's birthday, please bring her to the Old Orange Spruce. I will make all arrangements. You may also invite… Jodie's Godmother. Amica. I've met her in my dreams."

Kirrie whispered in Phyrris's ear, "I will do as you ask, but remember I'm not welcomed in Alms Glen. And Spellweaver, just be sure you only meet Amica in your dreams."

Phyrris smiled, "Agreed. As long as you give me some private time."

Kirrie coyly smiled and gave him a lingering kiss. Then she and Jodie vanished in a flash of blueness. Time dragged for Phyrris as Jodie's birthday neared. The Spellweaver visited Tull and Dina privately and prevailed on them for a favor. He spared details, but old Tull nonetheless agreed to assist "Fire."

Phyrris met Tull and Dina at the Old Orange Spruce and the trio descended the stairs to the spacious library. The Old Orange Spruce was much bigger on the inside. Dina removed the invisimoss and produced the ancient stones. The Enhancing (Xennic) Stone moved to a central position, and the four elemental stones positioned at four corners around the enhancing stone. Oddly all four Elemental Stones bore runes. After Aergin's ceremony two years ago, only the Water Stone bore runes. Agrarian, Phyrris, and Aergin had bonded with the other three. Redness filled the library. Kirrie, Jodie, and Amica in Good Witch guise arrived. Amica wore the clinging short white dress she preferred in earlier visits to the Teacher's home. Kirrie gave a copy of the ancient spell book to Tull.

Kirrie said, "Teacher, this appeared the day she was born. She has not yet opened it. It's fitting for you to present it to her on her seventh birthday."

Tull accepted the text. He and Dina said nothing. Phyrris bade Jodie to look at the five hovering stones. Little Jodie walked around the stones and stared at each. The stones hovered at her eye level. She was a bit shorter than Agrarian. The brilliant colors of the Air Stone fascinated the child. He also gently touched the Water Stone and smiled at the Firehorse on the surface of the Fire Stone. The child paused at the relatively plain Earth Stone. Without speaking the child walked into the square area and approached the stone hovering in the center. She reached out her little left hand and touched the stone. The stone shrank to fit into her little hand. The child's orangish skin changed to gray. The little Drelvling stood in the center of the square and looked at Phyrris.

Phyrris said, "It feels good, doesn't it? Warm all over! Which do you like best, Jodie?"

Little Jodie said, "I like them all, Papa. Which is your favorite?"

Dina and Tull reacted.

Phyrris said, "Jodie, you are my equal. I'm partial to fire, but my direction was rather chosen for me. I didn't have the center stone to help me."

Jodie said, "The Enhancing Stone. It's named for Spellweaver Xenn, but isn't Xennic Stones a general term for magic stones?"

Phyrris said, "Teacher Tull teaches so."

Jodie said, "It doesn't really matter, Papa. It's Magick."

Phyrris said, “You are surely wise beyond your years, Jodie. What does the stone in your hand tell you?”

Jodie said, “It’s Magick, Papa.”

Tull, Dina, Phyrris, Kirrie, and Amica watched intently. Little Jodie walked to the Fire Stone. The Summoning Stone of Fire (SSF) looked like a rock. The Summoning Stone of Fire (SSF) bore the image of a proud Fire Horse. Runes appeared on the stone’s smooth surface.

Ǿ ∞ Ǿ

Jodie walked to the Water Stone. The Water Stone (SSW) appeared an ovoid watery shape, a prolate spheroid. The curious artifact was like water, or soft clear gelatin. Runes and an ever so faint image of a water horse appeared on the surface of the artifact.

∞ Ǿ ∞

The little Spellweaver went to the Air Stone (SSA), which had the appearance of a rainbow with scintillating colors bent into fattened cigar shape. The object had no weight. Runes appeared on its beautiful surface.

∞ Ǿ ∞

The Air Stone or Wind Stone was sometimes called the Summoning Stone of Air (SSA)

Jodie went to the Earth Stone. The Earth Stone (SSE) shared the oblate spheroid shape of the Fire Stone (SSF), Air Stone (SSA), and Water Stone (SSW), but it looked like a clump of red clay. Three runes glowed brightly on its surface.

Ǿ ∞ Ǿ

The Earth Stone hummed and emitted faint gray light. Jodie grasped the Earth Stone in her right hand. The stone first shrank to fit her little hand. Then the artifact and the stone in the child’s left hand both disappeared. Jodie’s color changed from gray to muddy red, back to red, and then back to her usual pale orange. Both stones reappeared. Jodie released the Earth

Stone and it floated back to position. Phyrris fought back disappointment. He'd just assumed she'd choose the Fire Stone.

Phyrris said, "Thank you Jodie. You are a sister of the soil. Spellweaver Agrarian would be pleased. You may now release the Enhancing Stone."

Jodie replied, "Not yet, Papa. The Magick isn't finished."

The Teachers and Phyrris were set back. Kirrie and Amica were witnessing their first ceremony of the stones.

Jodie continued to grasp the Enhancing Stone and walked to the lovely Air Stone. The child gripped the Air Stone. Her visage mimicked the effect of Aergin's ceremony and she flashed the colors of the rainbow. After 13 heartbeats, Jodie's normal color returned and she released the Air Stone and it returned to its position. Little strands of rainbow colors appeared in her hair. She still held the Enhancing Stone tightly. The observers remained silent. Next little Jodie went to the water stone. She placed her tiny hand on its watery surface. The stone shrank. Jodie changed to a beautiful blue color. After 13 heartbeats, she changed back to her normal visage, only strands of blue hair appeared on her head. She released the Water Stone and it returned to its position. Jodie held the Enhancing Stone tightly and went to the Fire Stone. She reached out and grabbed the artifact. Red light flashed from the Fire Stone to Phyrris, Kirrie, and Amica. Then red beams flashed from the Enhancing Stone, Firestone, Phyrris, Kirrie, Amica, and Jodie and struck Dina and Tull. Jodie changed to fiery red coloration. After 13 heartbeats, Jodie released the Fire Stone. It returned to its position. Jodie assumed her normal color. The red streaks in her hair grew brighter. Now the child's hair contained very little silver. Reds, blues, and rainbow colors replaced the silver hair of nymph hood. Jodie released the Enhancing Stone and it returned to its position.

Jodie left the square created by the stones, stood by Phyrris and Kirrie, and said, "That was fun, Papa. I feel very good."

Tull said, "You are exceptional, Jodie. I'm honored to present your copy of the Spellbook."

*The Gifts of Andreas to the People of the Forest*

ΛΑΡΛΣ

Α&Ω

Phyrris said, "Earth! Air! Water! Fire! Agrarian, Aergin, Purya, Phyrris in the Old Language! I'm honored to stand with you Spellweaver Jodie. My daughter!"

Dina collected the five stones, carried them to their resting place in the library, and covered them with the plot of Invisimoss.

Tull said, "I'm honored to stand with you, Spellweavers Phyrris and Jodie. I see a spell in my mind. Fire spell! A gift of the Enhancing Stone and its four brethren. The Enhancing Stone granted Teacher Pryam a Healing Spell shortly after its discovery by Spellweaver Xenn. Pryam only managed it once. We've learned the artifact, which we also all the Xennic Stone, imparts a single spell per lifetime to a non-Spellweaver, Detects Magick, Enchants an Item, empowers Permanence, and enhances particular powers of the Elemental Stones. Most powers of the Enhancing Stone are activated only in the presence of the Elemental Stones. Gifting Spells must be a random and unwonted event… given the episode with Teacher Pryam. Quirk of Magick!"

Dina said, "I also see a spell in my mind. A Fire Spell! I am bound by my commitment to keep secret this affair, Spellweaver Phyrris, but how can I keep hidden these wondrous things I've seen and felt. Spellweaver Jodie should serve Alms Glen."

Tull said, "Nonetheless, we must honor our commitment of secrecy. Not since the miracle in Green Vale, when Teacher Edkim and the heroes of the battle of Lone Oak Meadow, has Magick touched Drelves other than Spellweavers. Gray Andreas. Dina… and Jodie. We must use our newfound power wisely."

Jodie said, "One, two, three, four, five, six Fire Wizards."

Tull said, "That's how the Tree Shepherd will see it, Jodie. What are your plans for Jodie, Spellweaver Phyrris?"

Phyrris replied, "Teacher, it was my desire that you present her Spellbook and she participate in the ceremony of the stones. For these things… I am grateful. Spellweaver Jodie is my peer, if not my superior. She will ultimately make decisions about her future. As her father, I'd prefer she remain in Alms Glen and under your tutelage. However, her mother has reservations about Jodie living in Alms Glen. In my mind, Teacher Tull, you are unrivaled, but Jodie has excellent, though unorthodox teachers. She has blossomed in her mother and Godmother's care. Her skills exceed my expectations. She'll, for now, remain in her mother's care... with my blessing."

Kirrie gave a look of surprise. Amica nodded agreement.

Tull said, "It's been my pleasure to oversee this ceremony. Now other duties call. Elders Coldan, Monty, Aleya, and Vyckie have called a meeting of the Council."

Phyrris said, "I was not told."

Tull said, "I'm afraid the meeting concerns you, Spellweaver. Coldan and Monty are very sympathetic and appreciative of your efforts at the forge and in the field with the Rangers, but Aleya and Vyckie worry about your use of Fire Magick. Also... apparently... the farmer Dell saw you smite a coney. The elders note your absence at many community meals."

Phyrris said, "I'm touched the Elders are concerned about my diet. Thank you again for your guidance and hospitality, Teacher Tull."

Kirrie said, "I thank you also, Teacher Tull. Being back in the Old Orange Spruce brings back many memories. Some good... some bad."

Amica quipped, "Thanks, Teacher."

Tull courteously bowed and said, "Dina and I will now take our leave. I invite you to remain as long as you want. Nothing is scheduled today in the Old Orange Spruce." He and Dina ascended the stairs.

Phyrris said, "I'm proud of you, Jodie. We have witnessed events rarely or never before seen in Drelvedom's history. Magick bestowed to non-Spellweavers and a Spellweaver touched by all four elemental stones. The generosity of the enhancing stone overwhelms me. Granting spells to both Tull and Dina."

Jodie said, "Papa. The Xennic Stone didn't give the old Teacher and his pretty helper the Fire Spells. I did."

Phyrris said, "You... you gave the Magick. How?"

Jodie laughed and said, "It's Magick, Papa."

Kirrie glanced at Amica. The Good Witch shrugged her shoulders and shook her head.

Jodie added, "And Papa. I like coney, too, especially if you serve it with taters."

Amica shrugged again and said, "Specialty of the house... and steeped in the waters of Fire Lake."

Phyrris said, "Now that's a dish I'd like to taste."

Amica snickered and replied, "You've already tasted some dishes here, Spellweaver."

Kirrie blushed.

Phyrris blushed.

Jodie said, "I am hungry, mother. Might we have some coney and tater stew?"

Kirrie said, "We really should be going. You've earned your coney stew, Jodie."

Amica whispered to Kirrie, "Would you like a little alone time?"

Kirrie whispered back, "It'd be nice."

Amica took Jodie's hand and said, "Come with me Jodie. I'll fix up that stew for you."

Kirrie winked at Phyrris and said, "Go with your Godmother Amica, Jodie. I'll be along. Take your Spellbook."

Jodie proudly held the book and Amica's hand. Blueness flashed throughout the library and Amica and Jodie vanished.

Kirrie took Kirrie's hand and asked, "Shouldn't you have gone with them? Are you stuck here?"

Kirrie answered, "I can leave anytime. I need no help to *Translocate*."

Kirrie and Phyrris embraced and rekindled the fire that burned at Fire Lake.

Afterward Kirrie asked, "Have you developed a taste for flesh, Spellweaver?"

Phyrris admitted, "Since our visit to and my swim at Fire Lake, I'm ceased being vegetarian and craved a good steak or stew. Many of my former animal friends are finding their way to my table. But, Kirrie, I crave you more. If only you and Jodie stayed in Alms Glen all the time. But you're so far away."

Kirrie said, "You should share meals with us. Jodie is becoming quite the little chef. Amica prepares an excellent coney stew. She really knows what to do with a brace of coneys."

Phyrris stroked her brownish-red hair and said, "I'm getting a little age on me. Traveling to Fire Lake in the red and blue light cost me three years. I lack your and Jodie's resilience."

Kirrie gently rubbed the tips of his fingers. Little blue sparks flashed between them. She said, "Traveling in this world won't age you, Phyrris.

The ancient Fire Wizard Yannuvia and his weak brother Gaelyss learned as much."

Phyrris said, "There you go again. Bad-mouthing the Great Defender. Small wonder you wore out your welcome in Alms Glen."

Kirrie said, "The thanks Amica and I got for saving their sorry *****. My friends and I were exiled. Unwanted Magick! The Tree Shepherd called me out for using Fire Magick."

Phyrris said, "The Tree Shepherd lumps me with you and Yannuvia. The Annals of Drelvedom paint you and the Lost Spellweaver in a poor light."

Kirrie said, "Yannuvia endured tragedy. He exhibited strength."

Phyrris said, "I would have liked to have met him."

Kirrie said, "You are a lot like him. Yannuvia and I shared many adventures."

Phyrris reluctantly asked, "Have Yannuvia and I shared..." He stopped mid-sentence.

Kirrie blushed purple and said, "Me? In that way? No!"

Phyrris said, "I'm... I'm sorry. I just had to know. Another thing... how... how do you maintain your beauty and vigor? You are as lovely as any she-Drelve of any age."

Kirrie squeezed his hand a bit and coyly answered, "Thank you... I think. You are saying I'm pretty good for an old woman. Let's see how old I am. Round two?"

Now Phyrris blushed purple and said, "There's nothing for it."

Kirrie slept in his arms for a bit. Phyrris stared at her and listened to her breathing. When she awakened, the Spellweaver asked, "I'd very much like to share more time with you and Jodie. How'd I know where to go? It's a big world."

Kirrie replied, "We spend time in an ancient cabin in the foothills of the Doombringers. The place really has a history. The view is fantastic, and you'll find lots of coneys and other tasty game. You fight even consider bringing your bow and quiver and giving them a chance. There's not much sport in whacking them with Magick Missiles."

Phyrris said, "Sounds nice, but how do I get there?"

Kirrie said, "I'll give you a Locating Stone. Then you can use the red and blue tiles. We'll be less than a heartbeat away. Why don't you join us in three cycles of Meries?"

Phyrris said, "I certainly will." Kirrie kissed him gently. She gave him a little gray stone about the size of the Xennic Gemstones. The stone bore no markings. Kirrie grasped the stone in her hand and uttered lyrical phrases. She passed the stone to Phyrris. While he grasped the little rock, Phyrris repeated Kirrie's incantation verbatim. Kirrie gave him a thirteen-inch square of blue tile and instructed him to repeat the incantation. Phyrris held the locating stone in his left hand and the blue tile in his right hand. He repeated the incantation.

Kirrie said, "Place the blue tile on the floor. It'll expand. Grasp the locating stone in your left hand and step onto the tile. It'll carry you to the cabin. I must be going. I'm sure Amica has her hands full with Jodie. In three cycles of Meries, my love."

Phyrris released her hand and said, "In three cycles of Meries."

A flash of blueness filled the library of the Old Orange Spruce. Kirrie vanished. Phyrris stood alone for a bit and looked around the myriad of shelves. Drelvedom's history spread out in the volumes. A copy of every Spellweaver's spell book appeared in the library at the time of the Spellweaver's death. Phyrris scanned the volumes. Gaelyss's treasured tome sat in its place. Yannuvia's tome was not among the others. The Lost Spellweaver still drew breath.

Dina and Tull made their way to the common area of Alms Glen. Both suffered mild headache. Dina again expressed her difficulty in maintaining Spellweaver Phyrris's secret ceremony. Tull pondered the nature of the lovely child Jodie. His mind found the phrases of the spell incantation most peculiar. Try as he might, the aged Teacher of the Drelves could not get the phrases out of his mind. His body ached as he leaned onto his blackthorn cudgel. There was so much he wanted to do with his remaining time. Young Aergin had so much to learn. The Spellweaver was 9. Agrarian's invaluable help lightened old Tull's load. Drelvedom had the luxury of three Spellweavers… or was it four? Little Jodie… or five… Dina… or six... himself! In the Battle of Long Oak Meadow, the Kiennish General Saligia bragged of defeating five Spellweaver, when he'd only smote five Drelves touched by Magick in the miracle of Green Vale.

Elders Vyckie and Aleya, over the objections of Spellweaver Agrarian and Tull, did not invite Phyrris to the meeting. Elders Coldan and Monty remained diplomatically neutral in the matter. Heated debate rocked the usually peaceful gatherings. Aleya and Vyckie opposed Spellweaver Phyrris's use of Fire Magick within Alms Glen. The gifted forge set on the outskirts of the conurbation. Ranger Fonty produced the fabulous short sword Phyrris had recently forged from adamantine quenched in Fire Lake and enhanced with green Xennic Gemstones. The Xennic Gemstones imparted Healing Magick to the blade. The wondrous sword emitted a green aura.

Fonty said, "This sword will save the life of its bearer. Never have we had such a weapon to use against out foes."

Elder Aleya argued, "Yes, Ranger Fonty, but have you considered the consequences of the sword falling into the enemy's hand. In the words of the Great Defender Gaelyss, 'The best offense is a good defense.' Creating such weapons through arcane Magick worries me."

The debate continued. Phyrris stood under the Invisimoss that he had taken from the Old Orange Spruce and took in the meeting. The Spellweaver enumerated those who supported and those who opposed him. He remained quiet and away from the others. When Aleya adjourned the heated meeting, Phyrris returned the invisimoss to its resting place in the library of the teacher's home. The invisimoss again obscured the collection of exceptional stones. Phyrris went to the forge, repaired some weapons for the Rangers, used Fire Spells to harden arrow points, added fletching to the arrows, and then went to his home tree.

# 19.

# Mountain Cabin

Three cycles of Meries passed. Phyrris stood in the forge area. He gripped the little locating stone in his left hand and dropped the small blue tile onto the ground. The Spellweaver took a deep breath and stepped onto the tile. Blueness surrounded him. In a moment blue gave way to a flash of red. Phyrris arrived at an unassuming cabin tucked into a mountainside. Kirrie, Amica, and Jodie milled around the cabin. Wondrous aromas filled the room. Stew bubbled in a large pot that sat on a blue flame. Odd blue and red inlays sat in the stone floor. He arrived on a red one. Through a smoky window Phyrris recognized peaks of the Doombringer Mountains and the familiar amber skies of the World of the Three Suns. The Spellweaver glanced into an old looking glass on the wall and saw his reflection. He looked and felt no older.

Jodie squealed, "Papa!" and ran and hugged him. Kirrie smiled coyly and Amica just nodded affirmatively and stirred the pot. Kirrie said, "I… we are so glad you came, Phyrris."

Phyrris said, "Kirrie, this is a beautiful area, but it sits well within the wild woods. Drolls roam unchecked in the Doombringers. Kiennites search this area for wyvern nests. For that matter, this is the favorite breeding ground for wyverns. Is this safe for Jodie?" Kirrie took his hand and answered, "Yes, she loves to play in the woods. She is safe in and near the cottage. Symbols etched in the trees mark the safe boundaries in the forest."

Ǿ ∞ Ǿ

Kirrie continued, "Neither plant nor animal predator will trespass the borders. Within the 1597 Yardley pace radius of the cabin, you will find fruits of the forest and friendly flora. Protection and Hallucinatory Terrain dweomers protect her. But keep the Locating Stone with you at all times. I'll be able to find you. I am now kindred of Fire and Grayness. At the beginning of every eighth Dark Period, Jodie and I revalidate and renew our commitment to Grayness and drink from the Cup of Dark Knowledge. The esyuphee hide sack sitting on the sideboard contains the smoking water of Fire Lake. When the yellow sun Meries reaches its nadir and the dark period begins, the chalice appears on the table. When the chalice appears on the table, we pour smoking water into it until it messages us to stop. We pour four potions from the drawers of the sideboard into the chalice and mix them with the water. The order of the potions must be **U**ncolored, **Y**ellow, **R**ed, and **G**reen. The Cup of Dark Knowledge always demands an item of Magick. The waters of Fire Lake suffice. This maintains and even enhances our power. This is the beginning of the eighth Dark Period since we drank the water."

Phyrris asked, "Won't the little phials and the water will run out!"

Amica answered, "The fluids replenish. The esyuphee sack is Magick. My Master's eye is blinded to Parallan. We are autonomous here. Grayness has touched us. We are sisters of Fire. Your people abandon Kirrie and disrespect you. You are unwanted… and unwonted! You may as well look after number one. You do have us! Kirrie, Jodie, and I are in your corner now."

Phyrris hugged Jodie and Kirrie. He gave Amica a cursory hug. The Good Witch kissed his cheek. Phyrris glanced out the window. Meries sat at its nadir and the Dark Period continued. Purple auras filled the cabin. A beautiful gem-laced cup appeared on the table. The ornate twelve-inch-tall cup's base was six inches in diameter and stem six inches long. Its bowl held little more than half an average tankard of ale. A faint mauve glow surrounded the chalice. A large upward pointing triangle dominated the bowl. Flowing runes covered most of the bowl of the deep red cup. Pristine stones of all colors lined the rim and also adorned the sides of the cup. Phyrris recalled the beautiful cup from his visit to Fire Lake. Kirrie prepared the mixture and drank the beverage. The cup refilled. Jodie eagerly drank the cup's contents. Amica followed. Then Kirrie offered the refilled cup to Phyrris. The Spellweaver drank the liquid down. Words appeared in Phyrris's mind.

*"I give you my blood through which you will receive all you seek. You in turn give to me your all."*

Ǿ ∞ Ǿ

The chalice vanished. Phyrris felt powerful… and hungry. Amica's coney stew filled the cabin with succulent aromas. Jodie dutifully retrieved three shallow bowls from the sideboard. The meat fell off the bone and eliminated the need for knives and forks. Silver spoons did the trick. Jodie, Phyrris, and Amica enjoyed the coney stew and chased it down with booderry and tetraberry juices. Phyrris stared out the window at the magnificent Doombringers. The mountains deserved their name. Only the hardiest adventurers tested their skills on the mountains. Suddenly a thick barbed tail filled the view through the window.

Phyrris shouted, "Woe! It's a wyvern! With a tail that size, it'll test all our skills. Ready Fire Spells!"

Jodie burst out laughing. Amica and Kirrie chuckled.

Phyrris said frantically, "What aren't you getting ready to fight? We're in danger! There's a wyvern on the house!"

Jodie gleefully replied, "That's our friend Fyzer. He's just guarding the house."

Phyrris put his clump of sulfur back in his pocket and relaxed a bit. "Your friend? You're friends with a wyvern?"

Jodie laughed loudly.

Kirrie shrugged and answered, "I've a thing with wyverns. I rode one during the Battle of Lone Oak Meadow. True, I used the Summoning Stone of Fire to lure and control Dallas. The wyvern contributed greatly to Kiennish General Saligia's defeat. I always felt guilty about the wyvern's death. Over time I've gotten familiar with the beasts. I took Fyzer from his mother's nest right after she broke him out of his shell, and he's been with us ever since. He just needs a purple mooler about every other cycle of Meries. Fyzer shows more loyalty than any of the Council of Alms Glen, and he is devoted to Jodie. She's ridden with me a few times."

Phyrris said, "You're a wyvern rider!"

Kirrie said proudly, "It's one of many talents I've acquired."

Amica chuckled and said, "She's pretty good at midwifery, tomb raiding, and roasting Drolls and Carcharians. I'm rather proud of my sister of Grayness."

Jodie hugged Phyrris and said, "You're funny, Papa. Would you like to go for a ride with us? I'm sure Fyzer won't mind."

Phyrris said, "That's OK. I'm good, Jodie. I'd rather just visit with my three favorite ladies. I feel welcome in this cabin and can't say the same for the common area of Alms Glen. A mooler every other day. Huh? Fyzer has a pretty good appetite."

Jodie said, "Some other time, then. I like for you to be here, too, Papa."

Phyrris tarried with Kirrie, Amica, and Jodie. After a period's time, Jodie went to her bedroom. Amica winked at Kirrie and said, "I'm going to see a merchant on the Emerald Isle. I'll be gone about a cycle of Meries. Phyrris, thank you for coming and sharing our meal. Your daughter has enormous potential, but we must protect her from those who would abuse her power."

Phyrris said, "Thank you Amica."

Phyrris and Kirrie shared some personal time. Then Phyrris silently entered Jodie's room and gave her a good-bye kiss. He stepped on one of the blue tiles in the cabin floor and vanished in a flash of blueness. In less than a heartbeat redness flashed around the Spellweaver and he stood alone in his home tree.

Phyrris spent work periods laboring in the forge and assisting in teaching youths when Tull requested his help. Agrarian worked with Aergin and other Drelvlings to prepare them for adulthood. When Elders Vyckie and Aleya weren't looking, Old Tull enjoyed starting campfires with Magick. Dina chastised him. Old Tull laughed incorrigibly.

# 20.

## Aergin's First Harvest Dina's Death

Aergin was 21 years younger than Phyrris. Phyrris was 144 years younger than Agrarian. Jodie was 2 years younger than Aergin. In Alms Glen, only Phyrris, Tull, and Dina knew of Jodie. Tull and Dina abetted Spellweaver Phyrris in performing a Ceremony of the Stones for little Jodie. Agrarian bound to the Earth Stone. Phyrris meld with Fire. Aergin picked the Air Stone. Ranger Fonty rose to the rank of Sergeant Major. Rarely did Rangers achieve this highest rank. Aergin celebrated his 11th birthday. During the festivities, Ranger Tim announced that he and lovely Miranda had decided to join in life-time commitment. Old Tull performed the ceremony in the common area of Alms Glen. Three Spellweavers attended Tim and Miranda's ceremony… an unwonted occurrence. The ceremony was one of Tull's last official duties. The loyal old Teacher joined his ancestors on Aergin's 12th birthday. Dina succeeded Tull as Teacher of the Drelves. Preparation for the harvesting of the Enhancing Root tubers fell upon her shoulders. Tull had taught Dina well, and the young Teacher still kept the secret of Phyrris's daughter Jodie and her own knowledge of Fire Magick. The upcoming trip to Meadowsweet bore particular significance. Spellweaver Aergin was turning 13 and making the trip.

At 13, Aergin went to Meadowsweet and Green Vale. Dina led her first harvest. Spellweavers Agrarian and Phyrris accompanied the Teacher and Aergin. Fonty, Tim, and Bob provided security, along with a contingency of 20 armed Drelves. Dina tentatively led Aergin and the neophytes to the hillock to see firsthand the Thirttene Friends. Phyrris walked away from the hillock and joined Fonty near the exit from the Vale, but Agrarian walked with her. When they stood before the Tree Shepherd, words appeared in Agrarian's mind.

The Tree Shepherd broke his long period of *silent* silence and sent the telepathic message, "Spellweaver Agrarian, brother of Earth, you have walked a true path. Why do you now stand with a Fire Wizard before me?"

Agrarian silently responded, "Tree Shepherd, it's good to receive your thoughts again. But Spellweaver Phyrris, out of respect for you, did not ascend the hillock."

The Tree Shepherd returned the thoughts, "I speak not of Fire Wizard Phyrris. He has no regard for me. I speak of the feminine Fire Wizard that stands beside you."

Agrarian said silently, "Dina. She's merely the Teacher of the Drelves! She is not Spellweaver!"

The Tree Shepherd grumbled silently, "She is a Fire Wizard!"

Agrarian bowed respectfully. The Tree Shepherd did not communicate further. Spellweaver Agrarian finished the tour of the hillock. The geyser erupted and sprayed the young Drelves with its rainbow waters. Aergin received no other messages from the ancient patriarch of Green Vale. Agrarian and Dina led the group from Green Vale to Meadowsweet. After everyone retired Agrarian sought Dina and confronted her. The youthful Teacher fearfully implored Agrarian to send for Phyrris. Phyrris came with Aergin. Phyrris told his brother Aergin and Agrarian the entire story. Dina verified her knowledge of the Fire Spell and confirmed Tull did also. Then Phyrris, Agrarian, and Aergin talked for a long time. Agrarian and Aergin swore to keep Dina and Phyrris's secrets. Only the three Spellweavers knew whether the secrecy was coerced. Phyrris brought Jodie to meet his parents Fonty and Danielle. The child's Grandparents also agreed to secrecy. Kirrie and Phyrris thereafter included the Grandparents in many of their clandestine visits to Alms Glen. Two years later, on her 13th birthday, Phyrris, Aergin, Agrarian, Fonty, and Danielle took Jodie to Green Vale. The enhancing root tubers were immature. Danielle explained the mechanism of harvesting the tubers to her granddaughter, but none of the plants were disturbed. The Tree Shepherd did not communicate. Danielle shared previously harvested and preserved tubers. Jodie preferred coney stew.

Fonty, Bob, and Tim, and other Rangers reported more encounters with Draiths, the inhabitants of the ever-growing black citadel on the plain. Over time, Drolls and Kiennites made fewer attacks against the Draith stronghold. Drolls remained tentative about crossing the River Ornash. Legends of the malevolent river spirit filled their campfire terror tales.

Harvesters encountered Drolls six years after Aergin's neophyte trip to Green Vale. Somehow, the Drolls knew their exact movements and created areas of silence in the ambush area. An odd member of the Droll's party recognized Spellweaver Phyrris and enveloped him with a Silence Spell. The young male accompanying the Drolls was a bit taller and stouter build than Drelves. He was reddish and greenish at the same time and had pointed ears and vaguely Drelvish features. Little red sparks flickered from his eyes. Both Agrarian and Phyrris found him a bit familiar, but the fury of the battle prevented concentration. The areas of Silence rendered Phyrris incapable of using spells in the areas and the spell cast upon him affected the area where he stood. The Spellweaver frantically searched for an area where he could speak. The Drolls outnumbered the Drelves and neared the party. In extremis, Teacher Dina sent a Fire Spell into a group of attackers and saved several young Drelves. The young reddish-greenish male stood in Dina's Fire Spell's area of effect and was unfazed by the destructive Magick. The spell enraged the survivor, who was taller than Kiennites and smaller than Drolls, and he shouted, "I hope it's you in disguise! You'll be sorry you ever drew breath!" He sent an intense mauve ray into the Teacher and ended her life. Phyrris and Agrarian searched for areas to cast spells. Tim fought with Phyrris's Healing Sword. He was wounded thrice in the foray. His wounds healed while he fought. Phyrris moved out of the areas of Silence and blistered the Drolls with Fire Magick. Agrarian cast protective spells. Tim fought his way toward the young male, but three Drolls intervened. The young male disappeared. Blue light flashed in the woods just beyond the battle. Eventually, the Drelves overcame the enemies. Dina and three other Drelves were dead. Over a hundred Drolls fell in the battle.

Agrarian said, "In all my years, I've never seen a Kiennish shaman of such power. Did you get a good look at him?"

Phyrris said, "Only briefly. He looked familiar. He wasn't Kiennish! The Spellweaver Xenn wrote in his Spellbook of dream visitors. Many of us have experienced the invasion of our dreams. Xenn described such a young male… I specially remember the red and green comments. But it was so long ago."

Agrarian said, "I also recall reading Xenn's writings. I agree. We must get the wounded to Alms Glen."

The Council of Alms Glen honored Dina with a eulogy. Survivors of the attack recalled only the furor of battle. None relayed word of Dina's spell to the council. The elders prevailed upon elderly Drelve Dewey to replace Dina. Dewey demanded that he be addressed only as Teacher.

After the attack and fearful of another episode of battling Silence, Phyrris used a precious length of blue wood and a deep red Xennic Gemstone to create a Fire Wand. He presented the wand to the Rangers to be used in travels to Meadowsweet. Four years after the assault that took Dina's life, the wand was stolen.

# 21.

# Purya's Birth

---

55 years after Aergin's birth an Approximation of Andreas produced a beam of grayness that concentrated on the tree home of Tim and Miranda's daughter Natalie and her life-mate Ranger Rabo. Natalie gave birth to a beautiful nymph. The ancient Spellbook replicated.

*The Gifts of Andreas to the People of the Forest*
ΛΑΡΛΣ
Α&Ω

Natalie had chosen the name Barth, but Spellweaver Phyrris asked her to name the child Purya. Four Spellweavers now served Drelvedom. Purya was 55 years younger than Aergin. Aergin was 21 years younger than Phyrris. Phyrris was 144 years younger than Agrarian. Jodie was 2 years younger than Aergin. Phyrris, Agrarian, Aergin, and the Teacher nurtured young Purya. His kind demeanor endeared him to all Drelvedom. When Purya reached his seventh season of the harvest, the Teacher and his fellow Spellweavers met with the fledgling Spellweaver at the Old Orange Spruce. The Teacher presented his spell book and presented the Enhancing (Xennic) Stone and the Four Elemental Stones. The Elemental Stones took their positions. Runes appeared only on the beautiful Water Stone. Purya grasped the enhancing Stone and it shrank to fit his hand. Purya walked to the Water Stone. The Water Stone (SSW) appeared an ovoid watery shape, a prolate spheroid. The curious artifact was like water, or soft clear gelatin. Runes and an ever so faint image of a water horse appeared on the surface of the artifact.

∞ Ǿ ∞

Purya placed his hand on its watery surface. The stone shrank. Purya changed to a beautiful blue color. After 13 heartbeats, he changed back to his normal visage, only strands of blue hair appeared on his head. He released the Water Stone and it returned to its position. Strands of blue hair intermingled with his silver locks.

At 13, Purya made the trek to Meadowsweet and Green Vale. Purya had not mastered any offensive spells. The party was heavily guarded. Phyrris's weapons enhanced the defense. The Spellweaver had not created additional wands. However, before the trip he presented the Wand of Magick Missiles and Fireballs to Purya. The Tree Shepherd did not communicate. The elderly Teacher Dewey ran a tight ship. The harvest proceeded orderly, the visit to the hillock was uneventful, and the group exited Green Vale.

Phyrris relished his visits with Kirrie and Jodie, and did so as oft as possible. Jodie's Godmother was frequently away during his visits. Kirrie mumbled something about family matters, but Jodie let it slip that the enigmatic Good Witch was cleaning up messes and undoing wrongs fomented by her prodigal son. The four Spellweavers coordinated their efforts to defend Drelvedom. Threats remained from the ever-more-brazen Draiths, Drolls, and Kiennites. Mysterious thefts plagued Alms Glen. The treasured Bleeding Stone was taken from its resting place in the Old Orange Spruce. Many blamed the elderly Teacher Dewey. The Bleeding Stone at its own whim bestowed the power of a spell on non-Spellweavers. Kiennites shaman passed abilities along their lines. Kiennites given a spell by the Bleeding Stone passed the dweomer on to their spawn. However, the Stone was just as mysteriously returned after the Teacher dreamed of the Good Witch, who expressed anger at someone named Jar Dee Ans. On another occasion Phyrris arrived at the cabin in the foothills of the Doombringers to find Kirrie alone. Amica and Jodie were away and cooperating in an effort to curtail Jar Dee Ans's activities. The visit afforded Phyrris and Kirrie some alone time. Over time evidence of Jar Dee Ans's meddling diminished. But what damage was already done?

In battle Kiennites sent destructive Magick against the Drelves and also employed artifacts of Magick. But the greatest threat to Drelvedom came from an unexpected place… in the form of a sorcerer named Morlecainen. The Sorcerer of the Lachinor… a survivor of a doomed world of Magick… who stumbled onto the World of the Three Suns quite by accident… via a misspoken spell.

# 22.

## Morlecainen in Donothor

Powerful Magick facilitated the Dark Sorcerer Morlecainen's escape from the doomed world Sagain. The young sorcerer's elderly mentor and the head of the order of Dark Sorcerers Clysis had planned their escape. Morlecainen used an Arrow of Slaying and smote the Head of the Order of Light Sorcerers Kreuseul, the steward of the Orb of Dark Knowledge, and gave the artifact to Clysis. Clysis already held a treasured heirloom of Dark Sorcery, a little ornamental chest that unbeknownst to him contained seven Elixirs of Mastery of Magick. The old sorcerer feared the artifact might fall into another's hand and provide a basis to challenge his leadership of the order. Clysis treasured the chest and guarded it dearly. Dreams guided Clysis. Morlecainen and Clysis constructed a chamber about thirty paces square with a ceiling the height of eight sorcerers and called it "the Room of Wizardry." The Dark Sorcerers filled the "Room of Wizardry" with powerful and rare items, including the Orb of Dark Knowledge, the chest containing the hidden Elixirs of Mastery of Magick, Tome of Translocation, Staff of the West Wind, and staff Maia, the last of the Pleiades, also called the Seven Sister Staves. Clysis's plans proceeded in orderly fashion. The paranoid older sorcerer did not share his knowledge of the necessary spells with Morlecainen. There was nothing left for it. The sorcerers entered the Room of Sorcery. Unbeknownst to Clysis and Morlecainen, the young son of the slain Light Sorcerer Kreuseul stowed away in the Room of Sorcery and traveled with them. As an extra bit of precaution, Clysis applied amber to his left palm and grasped the Staff of the West Wind. Clysis uttered the great spell. The wisest sorcerers of Sagain would have experienced difficulty in deciphering the incantation, but Clysis performed the complex incantation correctly. Sorcerers throughout the doomed world of Magick felt a great foreboding wave on the sea of Magick. The Dark Sorcerers felt their bodies and minds ripped through the fabric of space and time. Absolute darkness... cold... void... then colors, and energies... Their thoughts were spinning violently out of control. They passed through vortex after vortex of color and energy. Pain coursed through every nerve ending. They felt the air sucked from their lungs. Then, grayness...

The travelers arrived in a swamp in a primitive world called Donothor. Casting the powerful spells cost old Clysis his life. Clysis's death left Morlecainen in possession of great treasures and a new world before him. These treasures included the old sorcerer's staff, the Staff of the West Wind. The Staff of the West Wind, one of the thirteen Staves of Sagain and also called the Staff of Stone, had passed along legendary icons of the World of Magick, including Rhiann Klarje, Iyaca Vassi, the wanderer Confusious, the head of the order of Dark Sorcerers Boton Klarje-Jhundi, Bijna Torva, Ross Fizer, and finally old Clysis. The rune "W" of the Old Language was etched into the end of the staff. Four sets of symbols in the center of the staff briefly glowed whenever the Staff of the West Wind was employed. The symbols, **Ǿ ∞ Ǿ,** identified artifacts of Sagain. The relic possessed the innate faculties of the spells Comprehend Languages, Stonewall, Stone to mud, Stone to Flesh, Stone shape, and Petrifaction. The great staff could sometimes reverse the effects of its actions.

The young stowaway, son of Kreuseul, slipped away unnoticed into the swamp with his father's staff Pleione, robe of Sagain, and as much booty as he could carry from the Room of Sorcery. Morlecainen held tightly to his ill-gotten staff Maia.

Morlecainen established a sanctuary he called Ylysis and found a loyal minion in an Ogre named Fange. Fange served without being charmed. The wily sorcerer easily subjugated denizens of the swamp, but the annoying swampland had not been a good source of material spell components. Morlecainen had been forced to seek ingredients elsewhere. The Dark Elves that inhabited the area to the east were endowed with minimal abilities of Magick. Strong forces of Magick manifest deep in the great swamp and north and east of the great river. Emanations of Magick also appeared to the north and west. These were initially minimal but had increased in intensity over the seasons. He had competition. Magick was increasing in Donothor. Dreams troubled Morlecainen. Sleep filled his mind with suggestions. Some he did not understand. Some terrified him. Morlecainen's actions brought him into conflict with the seven clans of Dwarves, Donothor's most successful people. Conflict led to war. The sorcerer underestimated his short-statured foes and didn't figure on a champion in their midst. The Paladin Morganralph Aivendar fought with the Dwarves and enjoyed Protection from Magick. The Paladin was from a hamlet called Lyndyn, known as a minor trading post in the north of Donothor. Following a great battle, Morlecainen used a last resort to escape. The Dwarves had won the battle at great loss of life, including Melnor, brother of the Dwarves' King Travan of Hillesdale. Melnor had felled many of the sorcerer's Goblin and Hobgoblin minions, but the noble prince of Hillesdale had fallen to the Sorcerer's Death Spell. The mysterious Paladin had wielded a great longsword and turned the tide of the battle. Powerful Magick minimally harmed him, and he had almost reached the sorcerer's perch. The most improbable of means felled the Paladin. The sorcerer fired a black arrow from his long bow. The simple wooden arrow passed through the lustrous metal of the Paladin's vorpal weapon, ripped a wide puncture through the metal of the blade, and entered the Paladin's right arm below the elbow. The arrow passed through the blade like a kitchen knife passed through soft butter. The Paladin was lifeless before his body hit the marshy ground. The Paladin's fall gave the sorcerer the opening to escape. Morlecainen's escape had cost him one of four irreplaceable arrows of Clysis, which attained their lethality from their Tuscon feather fletching. Only three remained.

The journey back to Hillesdale was not a joyous one for King Travan. He achieved a tactical victory, but his adversary had escaped and losses were heavy. His brother Melnor and many sons of the Seven Clans were lost. Each captain had the solemn duty to inform families of any in his charge that were lost in battle. It fell upon the king to update the council of the Seven Clans and to inform his brother's wife of his fall. There was the matter of the Paladin from Lyndyn, the hamlet to the east and north. It would be a difficult ten-day journey for the already fatigued king, but he had sworn to get the belongings of the man of great valor back to his family. Morganralph Aivendar had accounted well for himself in battle and had saved the lives of many Dwarves. Perhaps it was time for Dwarves and men to lay aside their differences and work together.

Morlecainen's alliance of Goblins, Hobgoblins and Ogres had failed. He sought other alliances and turned to the Dark Elves. He'd sensed faint emanations of Magick from the deep swamps. He had learned of the rare Dark Elves from Fange and hardier Hobgoblins that had encountered Dark Elves and survived. Goblins exhibited great fear whenever mention was made of the creatures they called "swamp spirits." Many spoke of spell casters among the Dark Elves.

Dark Elves were shorter than Hobgoblins, but taller than Goblins and incredibly handsome with olive skin, delicate stature, well-defined musculature, and perfect complexion. A harrowing journey assisted by painful queries to the Orb of Dark Knowledge brought the sorcerer to Black Dragon's Horn, the stronghold of the reclusive Dark Elves. Morlecainen negotiated a meeting with Dark Elves' King Cellexa and took advantage of enmity between the Dark Elves and Dwarves.

The sorcerer urged Cellexa, "The presence of Dark Elves in my alliance would strike fear into the armies of the Dwarves. I would benefit from a contingent of your people. Accompany me to the Dwarves' homelands. We shall deliver a blow that will generate great riches and glory for both of us."

"I want you to dine with my family," the Dark Elf said, continuing the conversation.

Morlecainen, in his most polite tone, responded, "I am honored, your highness."

"I am the leader of my people. They turn to me for guidance. I do not demand or expect reverence, only respect, obedience and loyalty," Cellexa replied.

Morlecainen was ready to answer when two beautiful Dark Elf maidens entered the room, accompanied by a young male and an older female. The king beckoned them to the table, and the sorcerer stood politely. The Dark Elves seemed puzzled by the gesture, so the sorcerer sat down again.

"This is my mate for life Myrrhna, my son Lexx, and my daughters, Princess Businda and Princess Alluna, who are the lights of my life. This individual is called Morlecainen and we share certain interests," Cellexa continued.

The Dark Elves joined the table and the repast began. The sorcerer was drawn to first one then the other maiden. Ultimately lovely Alluna kept his attention. Three productive days of negotiation produced an alliance between the sorcerer and Dark Elf King. A contingent of a hundred Dark Elves accompanied Morlecainen and Fange back to Ylysis. Prince Lexx and a Shaman led the Dark Elves. Morlecainen gave a bejeweled crown to King Cellexa as tribute. The sorcerer also returned with a gem … the King's daughter Alluna. A room was made for Alluna in the main house at Ylysis. The Dark Elf shaman hallowed the house with soil brought from the Dark Elves' home. The union of Morlecainen and Alluna was already consecrated by Cellexa.

Morlecainen had bolstered his chances. He was driven more than ever. His dreams became more intense when he returned to Ylysis. He was indebted to the Dark Elf King more than he could ever repay. He had created an alliance that would take the battle into the lands of the Dwarves. The young Dark Elf Lexx spent most of his time working in the armory creating arrows for the Elvish bows. The armory of Ylysis was located in a large chamber adjacent to the refectory, the communal dining hall, of the castle. The armory kept the Dark Elves occupied most of the time. They struggled to teach the Goblins to use bows more effectively. Teaching Goblins anything was a challenge.

The sorcerer of the Lachinor needed time to study spell books and practice casting spells to accomplish his goal of mastering Enhanced Teleportation. He had been unable to crack the mysteries of the Translocation Spell that brought him to Donothor. Casting the spell killed Clysis. However, simple teleportation was less challenging. He had managed short distances even in his youth on Sagain. Unfortunately, the spell was designed only for teleporting the corporeal body. Arriving in one's birthday suit, totally nude, in a distant place could be embarrassing, inconvenient, disadvantageous, and perhaps downright dangerous. Hours of pouring over the tomes brought from Sagain had given Morlecainen some ideas on modifying the spell in order to be able to arrive at the new destination with adequate supplies and the preservation of one's dignity. For the next several weeks Morlecainen labored in the Room of Sorcery. The sorcerer had entrusted the hidden room's location to no one, including Alluna. Several times he consulted the Orb of Dark Knowledge. The Orb always demanded a bit of his blood. His sore fingertips became annoying. Images in the device might be hazy or sharp. On other occasions, ideas were planted in the sorcerer's head. One such occurrence involved the appearance of an image of the sap of the amber tree. This short squat plant was uncommon flora in the Lachinor. The Goblins sought it out. Small animals and large bugs became hopelessly entrapped in the sap and an easy meal. Morlecainen sent Fange out to gather some thick yellow sap. The Ogre returned with an ample supply. Morlecainen used a Heat Spell to separate the Ogre's six digits on the hand that gathered the amber sap.

The grateful Fange insisted that his master gorge on fresh meat he gathered from the Lachinor to "keep up his strength."

Morlecainen said to the Ogre Fange, "Bring me a goblin, one that is scrawny and rather worthless."

The Dark Elf Prince Lexx was standing nearby and said, "All goblins are scrawny and rather worthless."

Soon Fange returned with a goblin that would have been thought homely even by other Goblins. Lexx watched curiously.

"Stand here!" Morlecainen commanded the gawky creature. The sorcerer had concocted a thick horribly sticky unguent based on the amber sap. Ingredients that the sorcerer added changed the dark yellow sap to a deep violet hue. He applied a small quantity of the salve to the tattered foul-smelling raiment of the shivering swamp goblin, tacked the garment down to the beast's shoulder, and conjured. A brief flash of light appeared. The goblin and his clothes disappeared.

Lexx stared inquisitively and asked, "Where did he go?"

"Check the courtyard," Morlecainen instructed.

Lexx found the bewildered goblin standing among the flowers of the courtyard. The goblin seemed none the worse for the wear and scratched the area of his shoulder where the unguent had been applied. Inspection revealed a mild rash. Lexx retrieved the vermin and returned to the anxiously waiting Morlecainen. The sorcerer smiled at this early success. He tried longer distances. Most of the trials were successful, but one attempt landed the unfortunate goblin in the great river, where the hapless creature drowned and washed away to the sea.

His next consultation with the Orb disturbed the Dark Sorcerer of the Lachinor. Morlecainen detected strong outpourings of the Magick in both the north and west near the vicinity of the Dwarves' stronghold and also in the north and east. Fear of competition bred a sense of urgency. The strongest forces were confined to the north and west of the Dwarves' lands. He chose to explore this area with the improved Teleportation Spell. The Dark Elves were preparing weaponry far superior to that typically used by Goblins and training Goblins to use the finely made bows and extremely sharp pointed Elvish arrows. Lexx's scouting reported no advances from the Dwarves. Perhaps the vile brutes had been discouraged by the power of his spells in the earlier conflict. Morlecainen fine-tuned his spells with study and practice.

The Sorcerer of the Lachinor consummated his union with Alluna. She was with child and progressing in the pregnancy more rapidly than expected. Alluna's hand maiden had detected two heartbeats coming from the womb of the Dark Elf. Morlecainen instructed Fange and Lexx to continue recruitment of fresh Goblins to replenish the rank and file, production of weaponry, particularly bows and arrows, and training of the conscripts. The Goblins' poor performance against the Dwarves would not be repeated. The Lachinor yielded nothing with the lethality of the Tuscon, whose feathers imparted Death Magick to the arrows created by Clysis. However, one of the lavish plants yielded a malodorous juice that, when thickened by heating, dulled the senses. Lexx's armorers painted the arrow tips with the substance. Non-lethal wounds still poisoned the victim.

The sorcerer commanded, "I shall be working in my study for some time. I am not to be disturbed for any reason. If my spouse inquires, tell her that I am seeking more gems for her. Make ready our forces. The sea birds have been raiding the vegetable gardens. Have the Goblins use their slingshots to rid us of the pests. Leave no tern unstoned."

"Yes, master," Fange said obediently.

"Prepare, prepare! When do we fight?" Lexx fumed.

"Have patience. You'll return to your father a victor. When I am finished with my current preparations, the time will be near," the sorcerer added.

Morlecainen dismissed Lexx and Fange, and when he was sure that they had departed, he uttered the phrases, "Ylysis forever" and "Neniacelrom". A secret door appeared on the north wall of the study, the glyph deactivated, and the door opened. Morlecainen used information gained from the Orb of Dark Knowledge and painstakingly created a map of the land above the river. The best of Magick was not as accurate as eyeballing an area. The sorcerer placed the map upon the large table in the center of the Room of Sorcery. He positioned a bloody finger on the map at a location just beyond the area north and west of the Dwarf lands, concentrated heavily, and thought only of this area. He sweated profusely. He gathered small bags of ingredients, placed them in a small mortar, ground them together into a powder, and poured a green liquid over the powder. A fizzing sound and pleasant-smelling green smoke filled the room. Morlecainen deeply inhaled the vapors and felt light-headed for a moment. A warm feeling encompassed the sorcerer. The sorcerer applied a quantity of the amber tree unguent to his shoulder, left hand, bow and quiver, and lastly to his precious staff. He could not risk traveling without the staff. He inhaled again deeply and then exhaled the last of the green smoke from his lungs. He again placed his finger on the map at the location north and west of the Dwarf land and resumed his concentration.

# 23.

## A gate between worlds

Morlecainen then said succinctly, "Go now. Leave here and be there. The return command is 'Return to Ylysis'."

Excruciating pain coursed through his body. His head throbbed. He sensed a passage of great distance and saw surreal images of the Room of Sorcery, Castle Ylysis, the swamp, the great River Luumic, the mist-shrouded forests, mountains, and lastly a large castle made of dark gray stone. The journey seemed to last forever, but the position of the single small yellow sun did not change in the sky. No appreciable amount of time actually passed. In a few hundred heartbeats, he had experienced enough pain to last the changing of a season.

A loud thud filled his ears.

The sorcerer was lying on the ground when suddenly the sky above him became a vortex. The world was spinning violently. An irresistible force pulled and lifted him into the air about the height of a man. The force released and dropped him to ground covered by reddish grass. Faint amber light surrounded him. An area of rectangular shape roughly the height of a man and two arm-lengths breadths shimmered brightly beside him. He breathed clear air. The odd color made orientation difficult.

Morlecainen surveyed his surroundings. He feared detection, felt the need to be out of sight, and rushed behind a nearby tree with yellow bark and reddish foliage. The only ingredient required to use the Orb of Dark Knowledge was his own blood. The amber light renewed his strength. Pain left his body.

Casting Detection of Magick required only an owl's eye as material component. The sorcerer pinched a dried eye, gestured, muttered the incantation, and turned in a circle. Faint emanations of Magick appeared in an area in the dense red forest to his right. Otherwise, the area was devoid of Magick. The shimmering rectangular light stood out in the sea of reds, yellows, and oranges. Morlecainen brought out the Orb of Dark Knowledge, used his knife to cut his index finger, and allowed his blood to drip onto the orb. The sorcerer muttered," I give to you my life's blood. I ask of you how I may return."

The sorcerer the eased over to the rectangle, held the orb in the direction of the shimmering light, hazarded a peek into the rectangle, and saw green grassy ground. An image formed with in the orb and words entered his mind. "Donothor lies before you. Traversing the *Gate* requires Protection from Magick."

Morlecainen reached into his robe, removed a piece of dried bark, uttered a brief incantation, and chewed the bark. The sorcerer felt the familiar prickly sensations associated with the Protection of Magick Spell which he had known and cast proficiently since boyhood. He gingerly placed a finger into the shimmering light. He felt warmth, then the sensation of cool damp air on the other side. He placed one foot into the shimmering light and then stepped through with the other foot… thump!

The sorcerer fell the distance from the *gate* to the ground and hit hard. The Gate was about the height of an average man above the ground.

He grimaced and cursed his clumsiness. "Fool!" The only thing injured was his pride. He held up the Orb. The doorlike outline shimmered about six feet above the ground. A simple Levitation Spell would work. He threw a small feather into the air and muttered another brief incantation. He slowly began to rise into the air and reached the base of the Gate. The towers of the dark black-gray castle at the base of a great mountain appeared in the distance. Unseen forces pulled him through the shimmering door-like shape. From Donothor side the *gate* was evident only by Detection of Magick. The Detection of Magick and the Protection from Magick spells that he had cast were still in force. From the other side, the shimmering lights were nigh blinding.

Questions appeared in his mind. Whilst attempting to create an Enhanced Teleportation Spell, Morlecainen had opened a Gate to another world. The creation of the Gate was a quirk of fate… and Magick.

Unwanted and unwonted… those touched by Magick felt the creation of the portal between worlds that opened in the propinquity of Briar Garden, the Donothor home of the irascible mage Roscoe. Roscoe had put his studies aside to help the Dwarves and labored to bolster the defenses of the Dwarves' citadel Hillesdale, which expected an imminent attack from the forces of the Lachinor. In Hillesdale, the Mage feared the powerful emanations that created a massive wave on the sea of Magick. In her freehold the Fane of the Setting Sun, the Priestess Knarra of Donothor felt the opening of the portal and expressed her concerns to the Captain of Donothor's Rangers Ordrych Aivendar. The Priestess dispatched the Captain to Lyndyn to apprise his father King Eigren Aivendar of her concerns for the kingdom's safety. Others felt the opening of the portal with great interest. The Dream Master's minions met in council. Dreams troubled many Drelves, including the four Spellweavers.

The sorcerer Morlecainen felt much weaker on the Donothor side of the portal. His strength returned after he passed into the new world. The newfound strength brought back memories of Sagain. Morlecainen placed the Orb of Dark Knowledge within the deepest pocket of his robe and pointed his staff toward the shimmering Gate.

"Diminish."

"Fade."

"Be hidden."

The Command Spells failed. The Gate shimmered brightly. The point of the blade was against his back before the sorcerer could react. He could not see the blade bearer, but his three companions appeared in front of the sorcerer. Their raiment and orange-yellow coloration blended perfectly into the surroundings of the strange place. They had similar appearance and stature to the Dark Elves of the Lachinor. One spoke.

Morlecainen's ears only head gibberish, and he shook his head negatively and said," I don't understand." Then the aura of the Comprehend Languages Spell surrounded a short sword carried by one of his captors. The sword's red-orangish elfish bearer spoke, and the sorcerer understood, "Do you serve the Draiths, or do you serve the forest?"

"I serve no one," the sorcerer answered.

"What manner of shaman are you? What is this ruse?" the inquisitor continued and pointed toward the shimmering lights defining the portal.

Morlecainen fumed. Shaman indeed! The weapon at his back prevented his taking action to defend his honor. The Protection Spell did not save him from harm by weapons and non-Magick attack.

The creature's fine features hardened. "You must think us fools, spy of Ooranth. We are Drelves, protectors of the forest. We cannot have you fetching flaming doors out of the sky."

"I know nothing of Ooranth. I am a peaceful traveler from a faraway land," Morlecainen answered.

"Secure his hands," the speaker commanded.

Two of the creatures shouldered their bows and approached the sorcerer. They removed his staff from his hand and patted him down. He smiled inwardly at their inability to detect the myriad of hidden pockets that filled his robe of Sagain.

"He carries only the staff and a small ornamental dagger, Seilvre. His robe is similar to Agrarian's. I'm fearful of digging deeper into it." one of the searchers informed the apparent leader.

Seilvre replied, "Lots of shaman wear robes. His is dingy gray. Agrarian's is the color of the forest."

The examining creature said, "The fabric feels the same, Seilvre. I've touched the Spellweaver's garment."

Seilvre said, "Bind him."

The Drelves bound the sorcerer's hands with a fine rope and did not note the pinch of yellow powder that he had managed to sneak between the third and fourth fingers of his left hand as they were taking his staff. Morlecainen's Protection from Magick Spell was still in effect.

"We'll take him to the Teacher and the Spellweavers," the leader said.

Morlecainen did not resist and elected to go along to learn more of his current state of affairs. His journey for new knowledge had taken an unexpected turn. The ogre Fange had used the expression "roll with the flow" when he talked of traveling the rivers and streams of Donothor.

The Drelves scurried across the reddish meadow, splashed through a shallow stream, and quickly led him into the cover of the forest. The leader signaled comrades hidden in the trees. Several other Drelves descended from perches and joined Seilvre's troupe. Eight heavily-armed Drelves quietly led the sorcerer rapidly along a threadlike pathway deeper into the beautiful alien forest. Morlecainen recognized none of the dense flora.

Paths opened before them. Bright orange bushes literally uprooted and moved aside the clear the path. The skilled guide negotiated each cluster of plants. Morlecainen had no concept of direction or time. When he looked back, the path had closed behind them. When their path crossed with that of an exotic bird or a small animal, the Drelves paused and allowed fellow creatures to pass. The leader Seilvre paused and talked with an orange, rotund furry creature. The Drelves blended into the forest completely, and their gentle steps respected every blade of the reddish grass. Finally, they reached an area with visible paths. More of the Drelvish people peeked from behind or within some of the larger trees. His muscles ached after the lengthy trip. He had difficulty measuring direction, distance, and time. Soft yellow light bathed him, but the thick orange-red-yellow canopy obscured the sky. The party reached a clearing and paused. Morlecainen was afforded a chance to study the skies and the world's three suns, a huge black unmoving spiral, a tiny bright yellow dancer, and an inconspicuous distant speck of grayness. This third sun intrigued the sorcerer most. When he stared at it, he felt familiarity and strength. Plush dense moss of a myriad of colors covered the ground. Stepping on the mostly orange and red moss gave the sensation of walking on air. Several great red trees dominated the area and towered over the surrounding forest. Except for their coloration, they were similar to the great oaks of the central forests of Donothor and the black oaks that grew on the slopes of Mt. Airie on Sagain. Drelves literally passed through the red bark of the breath-taking red oaks. An edifice constructed of large rocks and covered by the ever-present moss filled the center of the cleared area had been constructed to minimally disturb the environment. The party leader Seilvre led Morlecainen into the clearing. A hundred Drelves surrounded him. Smaller Drelves had silver hair, whilst the older Drelves had brown locks. Rather fetching females bore resemblance to his Dark Elf mate Alluna. The Drelves were an extension of the forest. An older Drelve carrying an oaken cudgel and wearing a crown of woven vines emerged from the largest tree in the central area.

The leader of the quartet Seilvre addressed the older member of the community, "Elder Dilan, we have a spy of Ooranth. He seems to be a spellcaster of weak ability and was fomenting mischief. He is not ugly enough to be a Kiennite and almost as ugly as a Droll. He is pale, though not as pale as a Mender. He most resembles an emissary of Ooranth."

The older Drelve nodded and said, "We know little of affairs within the black walls of Castle Ooranth."

The Elder Dilan said, "Russell, no spell casters serve Ooranth, but as the Approximation approaches, even the most mundane of the world's creatures may develop skills of Magick. He seems too big to be Kiennite. Are you Kiennish?"

Morlecainen did not answer.

"It is a question for the Spellweavers and Teacher. I hate to trouble them. This is important," the old Drelve Russell continued. Russell pulled back his long brown hair and settled onto a chair. Russell was a neophyte in Green Vale with Agrarian and now older than most elders.

The captors led Morlecainen to a small chair, unceremoniously deposited the sorcerer, and reinforced his bindings. At least the blade was gone from his back. Lovely females brought nourishment to him. Younger faces sported fully silver hair. Brown hair interspersed with the silver in older Drelves. Orangish brown locks covered the heads of the Elder Dilan. After a while, the exact amount of time was hard to assess, several important looking Drelves approached.

Four wore elaborate bejeweled crowns and carried cudgels. The oldest wore a orangish robe that looked similar to Morlecainen's robe of Sagain. A fifth older and simply dressed Drelve emerged from a large orange spruce tree at the far end of the cleared area. A very young, somewhat less attractive Drelve and Seilvre accompanied them. Seilvre carried the blade that produced the Comprehend Languages Spell at the meadow. Introductions were given, and the names were very complex. The four were Drelvish Spellweavers. The oldest was the Teacher. The youngest was an apprentice named Ramish. The apprentice lacked the beauty typical of the Drelves.

The Teacher said. "I am the spiritual leader of my people. I have great knowledge of the World of the Three Suns and never encountered one such as you. Where do you come from?"

"I am a light sorcerer. I was trying to cast a spell to protect my lands and peoples from a marauding army of Dwarves when I stumbled upon your lands. I know naught of Ooranth or Kiennites. I am a peaceful man," Morlecainen said in his most subservient voice.

"I do not trust him," Seilvre quickly interjected.

A Spellweaver with bright orange tresses held Morlecainen's Staff of Sagain and then spoke, "An advocate of peace would not carry this complex staff. It's too intricate to be the staff of a simple spell caster. Why don't you tell us who you really are?"

"Why don't you tell a simple traveler more about where fate has taken him? I am the one that was dragged away at sword point. I've wronged no one here," the sorcerer replied.

The Teacher continued, "You ask a fair question. The light of three suns bathes our beautiful world. We never have darkness as total as that of the subterranean caves. The greatest sun, the dark Giant Orpheus, never completely dips below the horizon. Dark periods occur at regular intervals. We experience one such period now. Equal amber and light periods occur repetitively and coincide with movements of Meries, the small yellow sun. Reaching its lowest point in the sky creates lesser amber light. Brighter light periods occur when the little sun is at its peak and alternate with amber periods. Our dark period occurs once every hundred and twenty amber and light periods and lasts thirty amber-period lengths. Meries sits at the horizon during dark periods. The average Drelve will see twelve hundreds of these dark periods if he is blessed with good health. This period is important to all of the peoples of the World of the Three Suns. It is during this time that the enhancing root tubers, which are so important to our rituals and wellbeing, must be harvested. The Teacher, neophytes, the keepers of the arts, must accomplish this mission. The light of the gray Wanderer, Andreas, bathes the land unpredictably. On rare occasions, the Gray Wanderer comes very near the land. The Approximation of Andreas is a time of great Magick power.

"The Draiths inhabit the lands to the center of our world by the way we measure direction. They are a hardened people who have struggled to gain total dominance of these lands for many generations. Their wars with the Drolls and Kiennites have cost our world dearly. Drolls and Kiennites are our ancestral enemies. Draiths are more recent foes, but may be the deadliest of the lot. The nomadic Drolls consider their domain to be the lands near the Mountains of the Great Sea. The Drolls are tribal, but unite with Kiennites to strike against the Draiths or other foes. Many times, my people have faced the armies of Aulgmoor. The Kiennites match our stature, but their features are hardened. They bear enmity against all other races, particularly my people. Kiennites disdain Drolls, but they unite out of convenience. Kiennites number spell casters among them. My Rangers wonder whether you serve Aulgmoor. On occasion, our people have encountered non-Kiennish spell casters in raiding parties. You are alone.

"We are a peaceful people and rarely become involved in the great struggles among the other peoples, though we are frequently victimized on an individual basis and our lovely forests are purged by the battles. Only the skills of our Spellweavers in the creation of weaponry and our allegiance with the forest keep the evils at bay. Alms Glen, where we stand, is the center of Drelvedom. "

The sorcerer's clear view of the sky confirmed the distal gray sun had moved nearer.

The older Spellweaver, who wore the elaborate Robe, spoke, "You are strengthened by the nearness of Gray Andreas. I can see it in your eyes, Sorcerer. You are no simple shaman. Be advised that any attempts to cast harm here will be dealt with severely."

"I am besieged by hordes of Dwarves. I seek remedy," he answered concisely.

"What are Dwarves?" a younger appearing Spellweaver named Purya asked. His hair remained silver.

"You are blessed that your world is not infested with them. They are despicable brutes with no regard for nature. They mine indiscriminately and violate the land. If they had their way, no forest would stand in my world. They search for me now. Can you help me?" Morlecainen pleaded.

The Teacher said, "You are welcome to rest and regain your strength. But we must know your plans and intentions and assure you are a friend of the forest. Seilvre and Ramish will take you to a guest tree. We will have council. I will safeguard your staff."

Morlecainen continued the ruse of being the underdog and released the sulfur granules from his fingers and furtively returned them to their resting place in his robe. The older orange-haired Spellweaver Phyrris smiled wryly. Was he telepathic? Did he know the sorcerer had the Fireball

Spell at ready? Rarely sorcerers of Sagain enjoyed mind-reading. Keeping on the sheep suit seemed the best option at the moment. Weremen of Donothor wore fleece in order to sneak into farmer's flocks and rob them of sheep.

Morlecainen offered," I'll help you harvest your enhancing root tubers."

Seilvre grumpily loosened Morlecainen's bonds and led the sorcerer toward a large red oak. Morlecainen paused.

Seilvre muttered, "What are you waiting for? Go on through!"

Morlecainen touched the hard-red bark. Ramish gave him a gentle shove, and the sorcerer passed through the thick bark and entered some very cozy quarters inside the great red oak. She-Drelves brought tea and fruits of the forest and left the sorcerer alone. Morlecainen stretched out on a comfortable mossy bed and closed his eyes.

The Teacher and four Spellweavers walked toward the Teacher's home, the Old Orange Spruce. One by one they entered the tree. The Teacher Shayne retrieved an old tome. The Spellweavers Phyrris, Purya, Agrarian, and Aergin settled around the foyer.

The Teacher Shayne said, "The Annals of Drelvedom tell us of a foreign sorcerer that arrived at the time of the birth of the Great Spellweaver Xenn. He departed as mysteriously as he arrived and never returned. Rangers Birney and Mikkal detained him for a time, and he bartered for his life with the brace of elixirs that Teachers have safeguarded all these years. Our people were overjoyed by the birth of the Spellweaver and made little notice of him. No known harm came from his visit. That's not to say our current visitor is harmless. He must be tested. "

Phyrris asked, "How do you mean to test him?"

The Teacher replied, "We do not know him and will test his truthfulness. He'll accompany me on my quest for the enhancing root. The tubers are maturing. The Gray Wanderer draws slightly nearer. We may be blessed with an Approximation at harvest time. The annals tell of wondrous things happening in such circumstances."

The cautious elderly Agrarian said, "I worry about taking this newcomer to the confines of Green Vale and the proximity of the Thirttene Friends."

The Teacher answered, "We have four Spellweavers, the approaching grayness of Andreas, and the Thirttene Friends. He is one person. I want to learn more of these Dwarves that he says threaten us."

Phyrris gently rubbed the hilt of his sword and replied, "We have Draiths, Drolls, Kiennites, and beasts of the wood to worry about. Invaders of our dreams have set upon us. Strange occurrences plague the Drolls whenever they cross the River Ornash."

Morlecainen slept well and awakened to a soft touch on his shoulder. The young Drelve Ramish pointed at the foyer wall. Ramish lacked the gentle features of most Drelves. His features were hardened and brought to mind some of the better-looking Goblins from the Lachinor or Kobolds from Sagain. Morlecainen stood, walked over to the wall, took a deep breath and stepped through the thick red bark.

The Teacher, Four Spellweavers, Seilvre, and several heavily-armed Drelves waited in the common area. The Teacher said, "You may have your staff."

Seilvre handed the staff to the sorcerer. It felt good in his hand. The light was dimmed. The gray sun had drifted nearer. Morlecainen asked, "Is this an Approximation?"

The Teacher answered, "Andreas the Wanderer follows no order. It oft toggles nearer the world. Only when the gray sun fills the sky do we receive its wondrous gifts of Magick. It's time to proceed to Meadowsweet and Green Vale to harvest the enhancing root tubers. Are you committed to serve the forest?"

Morlecainen answered, "I want to learn more of your world. I seek aid in my struggle against the dwarves. If I fail, it's only a matter of time till they find their way to your lands."

The red-orange haired Spellweaver Phyrris chided, "If they find their way to the World of the Three Suns, it's because you led them here through your nebulous opening. Why don't you close the Gate so they can't follow?"

Morlecainen honestly answered, "I cannot. Though closing the Gate would trap me in this world, I'd choose that over enslavement by greedy dwarves.'

Morlecainen noted a mauve aura around him. The Spellweaver Purya completed some gestures. The aura faded. Purya said, "The Detect Lie Spell confirms he speaks the truth."

The Teacher spoke, "I hope you are rested. Are you ready to accompany us?"

"I feel well rested and look forward to learning more about you and your lands," the sorcerer answered.

"Then let us be away. We have much to do this period," the Teacher added.

"How should I address you?" Morlecainen asked.

"You may call me Teacher," the old Drelve answered tersely. Since the time of the Teachers Tull, Dina, and Dewey, Drelves had taken to addressing the Teacher simply by the title. Learned Tull had stressed commitment to Drelvedom superseded personal ends, including the use of one's given name. The current Teacher's given name was Shayne.

"What does the root do for you?" Morlecainen asked.

"It replenishes us, gives vitality, supplements our diet, makes us stronger mentally and physically, and is a rock of our foundation," the Teacher answered.

"Do your sorcerers use enhancing root tubers in their spells?" Morlecainen inquired.

"No. I am not empowered with the skills of sorcery. I am only entrusted with the continuation of our heritage. You should ask the Spellweavers about their skills. It is their power that in the end protects us from the more physically powerful enemies of our lands," the Teacher stated.

The party traveled to Meadowsweet, an ancient Drelvish community. The Elders of Meadowsweet greeted the group, accepted the Teacher's decision to bring Morlecainen to the community, and entertained with a feast of the forest. Morlecainen spent another rest period in a stately red oak. Drelves of Meadowsweet joined the group. Many Drelves who had seen thirttene seasons were making their pilgrimage to harvest the tubers. Morlecainen learned only the most promising Drelvlings made the journey. The group made the short trek to Green Vale. The path ended in a cluster of red oaks. During the journey, the sorcerer was an exemplary member of the party. Nevertheless, forces forbade his entering Green Vale. The ancient Protective Magick that surrounded the island of greenness in the orange-red-yellow world prevented his entry. Quirk of Magick… Morlecainen dutifully waited for the harvesters to complete their work and accompanied them back to Meadowsweet. Morlecainen 's behavior was model. The sorcerer sat with the Teacher after the meal. Morlecainen asked, "Tell me about your Spellweavers."

The Teacher answered, “Spellweavers are born at the time of the Approximation of the gray sun Andreas. Approximations occur at irregular intervals. Our Annals of Drelvedom records intervals of 1,2,3,5,8.13.21.34.55.89, 144,233,377,610, and 987 years. Our year consists of one season of growth of the enhancing plant tubers, which is 600 Days. We define a “day” as the length of one Amber Period and one Light Period. In terms of Magick’s most consistent measure of time, the unvarying minute minuteman heartbeat, a “day’ is 57,600 heartbeats. Not every Approximation brings a Spellweaver; some generations of Drelves neither walk with a Spellweaver nor witness an Approximation of Andreas. Four Spellweavers serve the current generation. These four Spellweavers are given the Drelvish names of Land, Wind, Water, and Fire… Agrarian, Aergin, Purya, and Phyrris. The four elements of nature dictate the direction that life leads all forest dwellers. Their skills differ. “Fire’s skills are highly touted. He is unsurpassed in the creation of weaponry. Even his younger brother “Water” has extensive abilities. Drelvedom saw twin Spellweavers on one occasion. Conflict developed between the twins. The Great Defender Gaelyss long served Alms Glen. The Lost Spellweaver Yannuvia trekked the path of Fire Magick and disappeared with his most loyal followers. Other than Gaelyss and Yannuvia, Phyrris and Purya are the only known Spellweavers born to the same parents, and the only ones born in differing Approximations.”

It required many excursions into the forests for Morlecainen to learn of the Drelves and the Spellweavers. The enhancing root tubers were harvested annually and only in Green Vale. The Teacher sought many other fruits of the forest. Delicious tetraberries and foul-smelling gray berries were prized. The gray berries were used in many Drelvish concoctions, and the tubers harvested from gray berry plants made surprisingly good soups and teas. He maintained his diligence and cooperativeness throughout the excursions. The Teacher was called by no other name by the other Drelves. The old Drelve was elated each time they found the small bush with the gray berries on the forest floor. He would carefully harvest the berries, and then diligently remove the small plant from the ground, carefully keeping some soil around the frail roots. He would snip a small piece of the root from each plant, then carefully replace the plant with kindness and tenderness. He smoothed the rich dirt around the plant after replacing it. The Teacher reacted as if he had uncovered a wagon load of gems. Morlecainen did not fully understand.

Morlecainen learned the extent of the Spellweavers' weaponry skills on the next trek into the forests. The affair started uneventfully, but after half a time period, which seemed about four "hours", screams from the young Drelves who were gathering herbs and roots in the periphery of the group announced trouble. Four huge wolf-faced creatures accosted the young Drelves.

"A Droll raiding party!" the Teacher exclaimed.

A small Drelve Ranger charged into the fray with his short sword drawn. The Drolls seemed amused, but their mirth only lasted a moment. The Drelve moved with blinding speed and slashed the life from the nearest Droll. The blade easily penetrated the beast's thick hide. The three remaining Drolls descended upon the Drelve defender, and the fight was over soon. The Drolls fell before the sword in short order. The seven-foot-tall beasts had no chance against their four-foot-tall outnumbered opponent.

When it was over, Morlecainen went over to the defender and said, "I thought you were doomed, but you defeated them easily and before I had time to help."

The young Drelve smiled and said, "I owe my survival to the blade. This is the work of our Spellweaver 'Fire.' He imparts speed to the blade."

The Drelve allowed Morlecainen to hold the blade. The weapon had little weight and split the air with a humming sound. Gorgeous gems adorned its hilt. Morlecainen had no training in swordsmanship, but he felt comfortable with this blade.

"This is remarkable. It is so light. Have you been trained in swordsmanship? Have you been trained in fencing?" the sorcerer asked.

The youth answered "I am barely beyond a neophyte. I accompanied the Teacher to Green Vale last year. The strength comes from the blade. Any of my contemporaries could have yielded it as well as I did. We must defend the forest."

"Speed and accuracy are the attributes of this blade then," the sorcerer surmised.

"Yes," the Drelve replied.

The young Drelves gathered roots and herbs and returned to Alms

Glen. Another nourishing meal and comfortable night within the great red oak followed. The next "day" he was awakened and, after breakfasting, the Teacher gathered another group of students with different defenders with different armaments. The Drelves were sending additional guards as a precaution. Four guards were armed with swords. A different young Drelve held the blade that had saved the previous party. The others carried similar ornate blades. The young gatherers carried well-made self-bows. The Spellweaver "Water" Purya and young Ramish accompanied the elderly Teacher.

"Are you expecting something big today?" Morlecainen asked.

"We are just being cautious," Purya answered. "Drolls don't travel far in small numbers. What attacked yesterday was a hungry scouting party. There is likely a larger group in the area. Food must be scarce in their lands this season; otherwise they would not venture this far into our forest. They certainly are up to no good."

The Teacher motioned for them to move forward. The larger group moved remarkably quietly through the forest and soon were in new areas to harvest the roots and herbs. Purya posted guards in the periphery. One of the archers ascended a red oak. Spellweaver Purya stood diligently in the midst of the group.

The harvesters worked without interruption for a full period. Then they paused for nourishment and moved to another area. A shrill call from the lookout interrupted work. Purya drew a short wand from beneath his cloak and made ready. The guards positioned themselves to defend the harvesters, who in turn made ready their small bows.

Morlecainen stood by the Teacher and whispered, "What have we encountered?"

"Drolls. Quite a few, and they are unexpectedly accompanied by Kiennites. Drolls and Kiennites only ally in times of war against a common enemy. Otherwise, they dislike each other too much to cooperate. Kiennites rarely venture this far from their lands. Something is afoot. If you have a means to protect yourself, you should make ready," the old Drelve confided.

The Drelves blended well into the forest surroundings. Morlecainen stood out like a sore thumb. He only needed a pinch of sand and a brief incantation for an Invisibility Spell. The sorcerer cast the spell, faded from view, and said to the Teacher, "I'll stand by you so as not to become a casualty by one of your archers."

Several seven-foot tall wolf-faced beasts came into view. The Drolls were sniffing loudly, looking all around, and detected the Drelves' party. A gaunt creature in their midst reminded Morlecainen of an undernourished Goblin. The humming of Drelvish bowstrings produced a chorus of howls from the front rank of the advancing Drolls. Two fell lifelessly to the ground. Wounds only angered others. The Kiennite raised a wand and muttered garbled phrases. Flames came from the end of the device and struck the Drelvish lookout, who fell screaming from the tree. One of the Drelvish swordsman shouted and charged the Kiennite. Six Drolls were in position to intercept the suicidal Drelve. The blade of the charging Drelve's sword emitted a greenish glow in the amber light. The first Droll struck him with a heavy blow and opened a deep wound on his shoulder.

"That's a mortal wound," Morlecainen surmised. The Drelve shouted and returned the attack. His blade sank deeply into the towering Droll's side. The blade's glow deepened, and the angry wound on the Drelve's shoulder closed. The huge Droll fell to the ground. The Kiennite pointed his wand in the direction of the charging Drelve. A ray of white heat struck the small warrior and knocked him to the ground. The air filled with the smell of burning flesh. The Drelve staggered to his feet and faced two more Drolls. The first Droll thrust a huge blade into the Drelve's chest. The four-foot tall warrior ignored his wounds, persisted in his attacks, and slew the first Droll with an upward stab into his chest. The Drelve's ugly wounds disappeared again, and he turned to face the second Droll. The huge wolf-faced warrior also fell to the Drelvish Ranger's glowing green blade. The Drelve was now about thirty paces from the Kiennite. Spellweaver Purya pointed his wand toward the Drolls on the right side of the clearing. The wand sent a Fire Spell that enveloped and smote twenty Drolls.

Invisibly, Morlecainen said to himself' "I can't be left out of this."

The sorcerer raised his staff and shouted a command. A lightning bolt left the end of the staff and killed the Kiennite. The offensive actions made the sorcerer visible. He moved to the left and prepared another spell. The brave Drelve swordsman wielded the glowing blade, fought like a legendary Berserker, and slew two more Drolls. A second Kiennite appeared and threw a Flame Spell in the direction of the Teacher and young Drelves. A strong smell of burning flesh and cries of pain again filled the air. Three gatherers fell lifelessly to the ground, and the Teacher received burns to his forearms. Luck placed Morlecainen just outside the spell's area of effect. Purya directed his wand in the direction of the second Kiennite and fired a mauve ray. The unerring Magick Missile ripped through the vile creature and ended its life. The few remaining Drolls retreated. Only the moans of the wounded Drelves and fading wails of the retreating Drolls broke the silence. Four Drelves were dead. Although he had endured three wounds that should have been lethal, the Drelvish Ranger bearing the glowing green blade appeared unwounded. The sword still emitted a deep green glow. The Teacher comforted the young. The air was heavy with smoke. In short order, several Drelves arrived. A flash of blue light and a clap of thunder heralded the arrival of Spellweaver Phyrris, "Fire." "Fire" was capable of Enhanced Teleportation.

Phyrris, Purya, and the Teacher had a brief discussion. Phyrris commanded, "Gather the dead. Collect items with the fallen Kiennites. We must return to Alms Glen immediately."

The Teacher's hands were burned rather badly. The young Drelve who had so bravely advanced against the Drolls gave the green blade to the old Drelve.

"Hold this, Master," the youngster said.

The Teacher smiled and said, "I'll take this gift of 'Fire'."

Spellweaver Phyrris, "Fire" acknowledged the compliment with a nod. The features of the greatest Spellweaver of the Drelves hardened as he concentrated on the horizon.

Phyrris, "Fire" lifted his staff and queried, "Enemies?"

The Spellweaver glowered at Morlecainen.

Morlecainen dismissed Phyrris's scowl and said, "Do you detect any more of those beasts. I've been trying to concentrate on my most evil thoughts, hoping that if there is a spell user among them that he will sense that I am powerful and evil."

Phyrris asked, "*Are* you powerful and evil?"

Morlecainen did not immediately answer and grew uncomfortable.

Spellweaver Purya intervened, saying, "The stranger slew the second Kiennite shaman with a Thunderbolt Spell. I was barely keeping the large number of Drolls at bay. Our losses would have been much greater had he not intervened."

Purya's words lessened Phyrris's suspicion of the Drelves' mysterious visitor.

Phyrris asked the Teacher, "Are you well enough to travel, Master?" After he held the glowing sword, the severe burns on the Teacher's hands healed. The Teacher answered, "Spellweaver Phyrris, not even your great skills can fully heal these old bones. I am grateful, nonetheless. Yes, let us make our way back. I am also grateful to you, Morlecainen. This could have been an even more baneful day." The Teacher returned the *healing sword* to the young warrior and gathered the youngsters for the journey back to the Drelves' sanctuary Alms Glen. Rangers recovered two wands from the Kiennish shaman. The weapons had been taken from unfortunate Drelves in earlier battles.

Phyrris said, "It's nice to regain these old friends. I'd worried since they fell into the Kiennites' hands. Whether these weapons rest in our hands or our enemies, the grayness of Andreas energizes them."

Rangers assumed the lead and hurriedly organized the group for the return trip. Everyone kept vigilant. Soon the beleaguered party reached the wide meadow at the fringes of the forest around Alms Glen without further mishap and then reached Alms Glen proper. The news of the dead brought great outpouring of grief. Rangers increased the guard at the edge of the red meadow. Seilvre supervised the guards. Young Ramish stayed by Morlecainen. The Spellweavers cast many defensive spells.

*"Air"*, who responded to Aergin, stared at Morlecainen and then conferred with Phyrris. Both Spellweavers looked in Morlecainen's direction. The tall sorcerer tried to look busy.

The skies grew darker, but the darkness did not approach the blackness of the night of Donothor. The gray sun inched closer. Morlecainen pondered his state of affairs in the World of the Three Suns. The approach of the Drelves' four Spellweavers interrupted his musings.

Phyrris spoke, "We appreciate the assistance that you gave in the fight against the Drolls and Kiennites. We now must concentrate all our energies in determining their next moves. Their alliance usually means a hard time for all in our world. We can no longer afford the luxury of monitoring you. You radiate evil. I do not understand your fundamental nature. We ask that you leave Alms Glen and the World of the Three Suns. Our people will escort you to the gate that you created. What say you?"

Truth be known, Morlecainen wanted to ascertain the status of his operations in the Lachinor and slyly answered, "I will do as you ask. I pose no threat to you. My cooperation should convince you. I recognize the seriousness of your situation. I would like to return one day and learn more of your skills of weaponry. I face terrible adversaries in my world. Will you answer some questions? Will you tell me why each weapon imparts a different power to its wielder? Can healing, speed, and accuracy be imparted to a single blade?"

"You ask many questions, sorcerer. The Grayness of Andreas grants the powers of weaponry creation. It's too complicated for you to learn. You will depart after resting." Phyrris said categorically.

Morlecainen acquiesced. Winning the support of the Drelves required more work. He bowed smartly to Phyrris, Purya, Aergin, and Agrarian and returned to the red oak to have a rest. Slipping through the thick bark got easier each time. The tree accepted him. The sorcerer snuggled into the thick mossy bed and found sleep. A gentle touch awakened him. The lovely she-Drelve took an enhancing root tuber from a wooden tray she carried. She stroked the tuber gently and brought it to her lips. An iridescent tear fell from her cheek and struck the enhancing root. The plant opened immediately when the tear fell upon it. The she-Drelve removed the pulp and passed it to Morlecainen, He munched on the luscious fruit and likened the taste to a crunchy strawberry. The she-Drelve smiled and led him through the tree's thick red bark. Several young Drelves came to escort him to the forest edge.

# 24.

## Return to Donothor

Morlecainen reached the Gate and cast Feather Fall and Protection Spells. The Feather Fall Spell enabled him to float gently to the ground. He crossed through the portal without discomfort or injury and returned to the refreshing darkness of Donothor. The area was undisturbed. He checked and reconfirmed that the portal's location was revealed only by Detection of Magick. The cold season was upon the land. He had been away for weeks. His Return Spell placed him at Ylysis in an instant. Castle Ylysis was bustling in the absence of its master. Prince of the Dark Elves Lexx relished his role as master of the house in Morlecainen's absence. The Ogre Fange obediently went about obtaining new recruits from the Lachinor's Goblin population. The Goblin ranks swelled. The Dark Elves trained the unruly Goblins as best they could.

When Morlecainen's spell opened the Gate, Roscoe avoided Magick to spare detection, traveled conventionally to Briar Garden, and arrived in a week to find nothing disturbed. In coming days Roscoe traveled back and forth between Briar Garden and Hillesdale several times. He had not again felt the presence of unknown forces north of his castle and utilized his Teleportation Spell to save time. For several weeks, he had kept *shadows* posted in the area. The ethereal guards only saw birdmen. There had been no attacks on the Dwarves' lands and no emanations of Magick from the Lachinor. The Mage Roscoe had not felt the presence of the Old Sorcerer Clysis's apprentice for weeks. Could rumors of Morlecainen's demise or departure be true? Magick was the sum of its parts. A part was missing. Or was just inexplicably distant? The Mage completed tasks in Hillesdale and returned to Briar Garden for a few days. Roscoe worked feverishly on many projects. The fatigued Mage anticipated a trip to Hillesdale the next morning and retired to his bedchamber in Briar Garden. A disturbance of Magick awakened the mage from a sound sleep. He had sensed Morlecainen's return to Donothor through the Gate and danger just to the north of Briar Garden. Roscoe jumped up, grabbed his robe, and summoned his guards. The Mage conjured, cast Detection of Magick and perceived nothing. Morlecainen had teleported back to Ylysis. Teleportation caused a mere ripple in Magick's great sea. Roscoe went back to bed.

Morlecainen's return through the Gate disturbed Knarra's sleep. A sense of evil gripped her. The fear left quickly. Knarra went back to bed. Neither Roscoe nor Knarra slept the remainder of the night.

Morlecainen returned to Ylysis and happily noted his burgeoning forces. Dark Elves bolstered his ranks. The young Dark Elf Lexx had yearned for action, felt that the sorcerer had been gone a lifetime, and was champing at the bit. The Dark Elf asked sarcastically. "You said you would be working for some time. We have not heard or seen you in weeks. Your wife, my sister, asks for you daily. Are you interested in the status of your family?"

Morlecainen glowered at Lexx and muttered, "I won't suffer insolence! Tell me of my spouse!"

Lexx swallowed his pride with a big gulp and timidly answered, "Yes, Sorcerer. Your daughters were born a fortnight ago. They and my sister are well. Word has been sent to my father King Cellexa. We are preparing for his visit."

Morlecainen rushed to his mate's chambers. His spouse Alluna looked radiant as she sat by the fire. Two small basinets were new to the room. The Sorcerer of the Lachinor walked over to the small beds. The infants were sleeping. The first had flaming red hair.

The sorcerer said, "Chalar."

The second had dark hair.

He said smiling, "Theandra."

Morlecainen raised the Staff of Sagain and quietly uttered a simple incantation. Mauve light filled the room. Markedly strong emanations of Magick came from the girls. The Sorcerer of the Lachinor had progeny.

He smiled and looked into Alluna's dark eyes. The Dark Elf beauty returned the gaze. Only the breathing of the tiny twins interrupted the brief uncomfortable silence.

Finally, Alluna said, "They cry very little. Where have you been in my hour of need?"

The sorcerer said in his most sincere voice, "I've been seeking greater treasures for you, my love. I may have found even greater riches than those of the vile Dwarves. Here is a sample."

Morlecainen produced a number of brilliant gems that he had taken from the Drelve sanctuary when the owners were occupied with other things. The baubles pleased Alluna. The Dark Elf leaned against his chest. The sorcerer excused himself from his consort and rushed to his first love, the Room of Sorcery. Morlecainen desired more from the World of Three Suns and told no one of the Gate Spell. The spell needed work and he hoped to perfect it, but there was the matter of the conflict with the Dwarves. Preparations continued. Cellexa's upcoming visit should enhance his position. His forces were better trained and stronger. He endured the discomfort of cutting his finger and allowed his life's blood to flow onto the smooth surface of the Orb of Dark Knowledge. Consulting the Orb gave no insight as to how the Enhanced Teleportation Spell transformed into the Gate Spell. Morlecainen labored all night. Exhaustion overcame him and he slept until a clamor from the courtyard awakened him.

King Cellexa had arrived from Black Dragon's Horn with a large contingent of his people. Morlecainen and Alluna proudly presented Chalar and Theandra to their grandfather. Lexx strutted about and demonstrated to his father the training that he had given the Goblins and weaponry that the Dark Elves had created in the armory. Great feasting and celebration followed. Morlecainen presented the Dark Elf liege with multiple elaborate trinkets and treasures. The visit went well. Five hundred Dark Elves joined Morlecainen's forces. Five shamans with skills of healing and five more with skills of Dark Magick accompanied the skilled Dark Elf warriors. Lexx insisted on remaining as commander of the Dark Elves' forces.

The Dark Elf King wished Morlecainen well and departed for Black Dragon's Horn deep in the Lachinor. The King planned another visit after the upcoming harvests.

Morlecainen sent for Fange. Fange grinned widely. An ogre's smile likened to a painful grimace.

"Welcome, Master!" the massive Ogre yelled enthusiastically. "I make the Goblins stronger for you. You are daddy now. What is your will, my Master?"

The sorcerer ordered, "Go to the goblin chief Phazymme. The time is nigh. Have you done as I ordered with the cork trees?"

The Ogre replied, "I don't understand, Master, but the squares of wood are assembled as you desired. The six-legged horses have arrived from the elf-lands as well. We have prepared them near the river bend as you commanded,"

Fange's command of language and culture had dramatically improved since Alluna's arrival. The Ogre Fange on Morlecainen's order had commanded the construction of enough twenty-by-twenty-armlength squares made of the cork tree wood to span the mighty Luumic. Light weight cork wood floated and tied together well. The assembled cork units would allow a huge force to move across the river rapidly and be upon the Dwarves on the other side in great numbers.

"Getting there first with the most" was a successful military tactic attributed to Phazymme. The Goblin Chieftain had actually said, "Get there fustest with the mostest."

Fange left the sorcerer, grabbed his spear and pack, and was away. Morlecainen went into the Room of Sorcery and studied furiously. In two days Fange returned with Phazymme and a huge goblin force. Phazymme was as ugly as but a little smaller than Fange. He had a nasty reputation as a cruel dude, was noted for ferocity, and had a weakness for trinkets. Rumor held that he liked the taste of Dwarf. Phazymme's entourage added eight thousand Goblins to Morlecainen's army. Most goblins carried crude swords, but some were skillful archers.

The Sorcerer of the Lachinor had assembled a great force. Dwarves had also had the opportunity to regroup and time to recover from their wounds. A great battle loomed. Morlecainen's forces attacked Hillesdale, but the Mage Roscoe's defenses proved too strong. The sorcerer was wounded in the leg in the fray and ordered a retreat. Morlecainen and Lexx reached the Luumic River in two days. The remnants of the invading force traveled hastily through most of the night. The Dwarves feared additional attacks and did not pursue the retreating party. Morlecainen and Lexx reached the river with two hundred and fifty Dark Elves and about as many Hobgoblins and Goblins that were commanded by Fange. The Hobgoblins had been specially trained by the Ogre to serve as a rear guard to defend the Sorcerer of the Lachinor. Now the sorcerer faced a decision about the bridge.

"We will not provide them a means of crossing the river," Morlecainen said. "Get everyone across."

Once the party had crossed the river, the sorcerer raised his staff and conjured. The bridge burst into flames and Fire Magick consumed it quickly. Goblins were instructed to maintain a watch from the southern side of the river. The company faced no other adversity during the remainder of the return journey to Ylysis. The mental anguish of his defeat hurt more than the wound to his leg. Fange had removed the arrow and provided rudimentary care to the wound. The Dark Elf shamans had fallen. Morlecainen tried to think positively. Items at the Room of Sorcery would help his recovery. Thoughts of his twins and Alluna's touch comforted him. Lexx had proven himself in the campaign and the Ogre Fange was intensely loyal.

Fange said, "In the future, we will recruit more of my people. Things will be different. Goblins are not strong enough to fight Dwarves." Morlecainen considered his options. Ogres and Giants were an untapped source of alliances. Ultimately the day had been lost because of his wound. The arrow struck his leg and ruined a calamitous spell intended for the mage allied with the Dwarves. When his wound healed adequately for travel, Morlecainen planned another journey to enhance his chances.

The two toddlers and Alluna greeted the sorcerer. Chalar and Theandra had grown in his absence. The girls were as beautiful as their mother. He spent a few moments with them, making every effort to hide the extent of his thigh wound. Eventually he made his way to the Room of Sorcery, retrieved some ointment from a small jar within one of the cabinets, and applied the unguent to the angry wound. The unguent relieved only his physical anguish. The sorcerer muttered every expletive known to Sagain. Then he caressed the Orb of Dark Knowledge, which felt unusually heavy in his hand. Morlecainen scratched the surface, gave the device its meal of blood, made many inquiries, and received vague and evasive answers. He studied in the room many hours. Goblin emissaries reported no pursuit and that the river was quiet. Morlecainen worked until fatigue made continuing impossible. He placed the orb within its chest, reactivated the glyphs, and left the Room of Sorcery.

Deeply within the orb, its consciousness stirred. Coolness and faint humming filled the Room of Sorcery. The phantasm slipped through the sleeping castle and reached the nursery where the twins slept. The Orb's spirit left the beautiful dark-haired child undisturbed and entered the dreams of the mischievous red-haired child. The Orb of Dark Knowledge preferred red. Chalar grimaced as the force entered her dreams. The child did not awaken. This was the first of many such encounters. Dreams troubled Chalar.

The Ogre Fange found few goblins and pressed some shapechangers into service. Shapechangers were tricky and untrustworthy. A mischievous shapechanger mimicked Morlecainen and tried to gain access to Alluna's bed chamber. A Protection Glyph preserved the purity of their relationship. Morlecainen forced the perpetrator to assume the form of a horse's backside and face ridicule from its cohorts. Guards posted at the River Luumic reported no activity on the other side.

Morlecainen spent long hours in the Room of Sorcery and had little time for Alluna and the twins. He studied tomes, practiced spells, and often consulted the Orb, which always demanded a bit of his blood. Alluna queried about his sore fingers. When he returned from the work room a few nights after his return from the disastrous Hillesdale campaign, she said, "Your work consumes you. You miss the changes in the children. Today Theandra changed a dark weed to a bright yellow flower. Chalar changed the flower back to a dark weed. They quarreled for an hour. Little puffs of smoke came from their ears as they squabbled. The power of Magick is strong in both of them. Chalar spends much of her time playing in the hallway near the armory. When I ask her why, she says 'My friend is there.'"

"I had imaginary playmates when I was a child," the sorcerer mused. Memories of his mother and the family retreat, Ylysis, returned.

"Why do you seek dominion over the Dwarves?" Alluna asked.

"There is great bounty to be had in this world. I am not content to rule in this swamp. I want more for you and the girls. I think I may have found a way to do so. It will mean another journey. I may be away for some time," Morlecainen answered.

"Why must you go? The Dwarves are not coming for vengeance. Lexx said they suffered massive losses. My father has dispatched five hundred of my people to guard us. Two Black Dragons patrol the river. The girls hand feed them when they return to Ylysis. My father has given great offering to the Black Dragon Lord Xollos. The Dragons report no enemy activity. The Dwarves fear you," Alluna pleaded.

"I fear that they will seek vengeance for our attack upon their citadel. I must make adjustments to my defenses. I must protect you and the girls. I must assure dominance," the sorcerer continued.

A night of intimacy followed.

# 25.

## Ruse and Deception

The next morning Morlecainen made his way to the Room of Sorcery. Fange arrived midday with three shape changers. Morlecainen cast Charm Spells on the amorphous weak-willed creatures and instructed the shape changers to assume the shape of armed Dwarves. Three pseudo-Dwarves stood before the sorcerer. Morlecainen prepared Fange and the shape changers for enhanced teleportation. He had perfected the spell after great practice and drowning a few goblins in the Luumic. The spell worked flawlessly as the five arrived at the location of the gate to the World of the Three Suns. He prepared them for passing through the portal by casting Levitate and Protection Spells. He placed Invisibility and Silence Spells on Fange and told the Ogre to remain three Ogre paces behind him. The five floated into the air, stepped through the gate, and stood on the other side. The light of the three suns was at its brightest. The gray sun, looming much closer than it did during his last visit, dominated the sky.

Morlecainen felt immense strength. The Drelves had told him that the power of Magick was enhanced with the approach of the gray sun that they called Andreas the Wanderer. Morlecainen looked at his entourage. The three pseudo-dwarves were quite obedient. Fange was doing very well to remain quiet. If he spoke, the Silence Spell which would be ruined. The Invisibility Spell hid the Ogre from sight. Morlecainen broke into a run. As they had been commanded, the three shouting and screaming "Dwarves" pursued him. The sorcerer headed for the edge of the forest. As the sorcerer had correctly anticipated the Drelves were watching the gate. A volley of arrows flew through the air and felled the three shapechangers.

Morlecainen performed a brief incantation and incinerated the shape changers with a Fire Spell to prevent their assuming amorphous form with their deaths.

Fange had held back and had remained out of harm's way. The big Ogre watched as his master was approached by several of the forest dwellers. Then he placed himself about three paces from Morlecainen.

"Thank you. I was pursued through the gate by the perpetrators. I am weakened because I have been involved in a great battle with them. They have found their way to your world. I used the last of my energies of my staff to burn them. They might have brought pestilence and contaminated your world. You must take me to your Spellweavers. I know how to defend you," Morlecainen urged.

The young Drelve Lignis led the watch party. He insisted, "Hurry then. I will take you to Phyrris."

The party divided leaving several archers to watch the gate. Lignis and three others took Morlecainen to the common area of Alms Glen. The Drelves moved fluently and quickly through the forest. Morlecainen was familiar with the area. The trip seemed faster. The closeness of the gray sun gave him energy.

The obedient Ogre followed a few paces behind them. His last dinner worked against him and he had to relieve himself. The Silence Spell was effective in covering the noise, but the Drelve in the rear stopped and sniffed the air.

"What is it?" Lignis commanded.

"A foul smell permeated the air for a moment. I can see nothing," the young Drelve answered.

"Do you smell anything now? Does anyone sense a danger?" Lignis asked.

"No. There is only the wind. The forest seems secure. I see nothing and I hear nothing. I detect no threat," the young Drelve replied as he completed his assessment.

Lignis led them to the sanctuary of the Drelves. Soon the four Spellweavers and the Teacher appeared; personifications of fire, air, water, and soil. Lignis informed them of the events leading up to the return of the Sorcerer of the Lachinor to the World of the Three Suns.

"You grace us again with your presence, sorcerer," Phyrris said in a subdued voice.

"I come to you to serve both our ends. I have fought long with the foul creatures. They have made allegiance with a powerful sorcerer. I would have ended his life but my Magick could not protect me from their physical attacks. My wound prevented my victory. He exposed the healing wound on his thigh. I lack the skills of manufacturing weapons. I seek your assistance in the creation of a weapon that heals such as I witnessed during my brief respite here. They know the way to your world. Their sorcerer will come. I cannot defeat him without your help. Give me what I seek and I can defend your world," Morlecainen said in his most convincing voice.

Phyrris responded, "We are four. We do not fear this potential threat, sorcerer. I don't understand your motives. Why should you care what happens to us? You do not seem to be the gratuitous type, sorcerer. Why should we trust you with a vorpal weapon that we could not ourselves defend against?"

"I have served you well. I return in my own hour of need. I am exhausted. May I rest?" Morlecainen asked.

Phyrris turned to the others. He addressed the sorcerer of the Lachinor saying, "You may have refuge. We saw that you were pursued through the gate that you probably created. If our world lies in jeopardy, it is likely that your deeds led in part to it. We will discuss our options."

"Don't tarry. The Dwarves ally with a sorcerer. He is powerful. My greatest spells did not affect him. He may come here himself, but he seems to be mostly inclined to bolster the strengths of his foul minions. They know of your world. He knows the most powerful Magick. I urge you to assist me," Morlecainen pleaded.

Phyrris was obviously the greatest in power and influence. Morlecainen was led to the great red elm that contained the "guest room." The Silence Spell disguised the Ogre's heavy steps. The activities of the busy compound would have likely obscured the sound anyway. He joined the sorcerer within the great red elm.

Morlecainen said, "You may break your silence."

"How may I serve you, Master?" Fange asked.

"They are comfortable in their numbers, my loyal servant. We must reduce their confidence. Do you still carry the Dwarves' blade?" Morlecainen asked.

"Yes, master. I carry it, but it does not yield as much force as my axe. By speaking, I broke my Silence," Fange answered.

Morlecainen said, "Not to worry. I'll place another Silence Spell on you. I feel your presence. Speak no more till you complete my instructions." Morlecainen conjured. Fange again fell silent. Morlecainen touched the invisible Ogre's forearm and uttered incantations for Silence and a second spell. Fange did not detect the second spell and failed to notice that his head did not hit the ceiling of the room.

"Good. I want you to go to the dwelling from whence we came. I want you to impale the first of the four forest Spellweavers that exits the room, if he is alone. Use the Dwarfish blade! Reducing their numbers will lower their confidence. Wait for surprise. I do not want you to be seen. I will again hide you if you are successful. If there is not an opportunity, wait for one. I must convince them that the Dwarves are a great threat to them," the sorcerer continued.

Fange exited the cramped space. Fange stood nine feet tall in his furry feet and bent down when he entered the tree to avoid bumping his head on the eight-foot ceiling. The naïve ogre maintained his bent over posture.

Morlecainen realized that he had not been lying when he had said that he was weary. His muscles ached. The wound was healing but there was a distinct throbbing in his thigh. He silently cursed the Dwarves and their sorcerer. Dwarves were supposed to shun alliances.

The four Spellweavers and the Teacher gathered in counsel after the exit of the stranger.

Phyrris, the Spellweaver of Fire, did most of the talking. "I do not feel that we can trust this chap. His alignment is difficult, if not impossible, to determine. His aura is not discernible. Magick blocks my efforts to detect evil or malice within him. He carries devices within his robes. I cannot determine their nature. I cannot do as he asks. We should rid our people of his presence as soon as we can. The Approximation of Andreas is near. I feel the strongest that I have ever felt in my life. I do not feel that we have anything to fear from the distant sorcerer and his Dwarves. His story is suspect."

Aergin (Air) said, "I respect your wisdom, Phyrris. However, our guards witnessed the pursuit of the Dwarves. Our archers slew them. They were few, but he speaks of thousands. We are strained to maintain our safety from the fiends of our own world. Could he speak the truth?"

The eldest of the four, Agrarian (Soil), then added, "My seasons are long. I have seen many dark periods. I have witnessed the Approximation of the gray sun. There are few of us that have done so. The powers of Magick will amplify beyond your wildest dreams. Even the small animals of the forest will be able to influence their world. I do not have a feel for this strange traveler. He did help us in the attack by the Drolls and Kiennites upon our people. Perhaps we should consider his words. If what he says is true, we would help ourselves by helping him."

Purya (Water) added, "I am the youngest among us. I feel my strength grow as the gray sun nears. I don't understand the powers of weaponry that you possess, Phyrris. I shall support your decision. I am going now to instruct Lignis to increase the guard at the portal of entry from the other world. "

Phyrris followed by saying, "That would be a good idea. We will discuss little more this period. The decision may be easier after rest."

Purya exited.

Agrarian said, "Could you construct such a weapon even if you wanted?"

Phyrris replied, "Yes. I have labored long on a device to protect our peoples from the assaults of the Drolls, Kiennites, and most importantly the Draiths. We can battle the Drolls and Kiennites effectively. However, the Draiths resist our spells. I have labored to create a vorpal weapon that would be particularly effective against them. I have been unable to finish it. The nearness of the gray sun strengthens me. With the approximation of Andreas and the powers of the Xennic gemstones, I can add Magick to the blade. I would have to add a protection for our people and the creatures of the forest if I ever considered placing such a blade in the hands of a non-Drelve. Now I am tired."

Agrarian reached deep into his raiment. He extended his hand to Phyrris. He opened his palm and revealed a simple rounded gray stone. He said, "This is a Rock of Andreas. It has passed down from my family for generations. Legend tells that it is a fragment of the Gray Wanderer, cast off during a long distant Approximation. Look at it. See the radiance. The gray light spreads out from it. This only occurs during an Approximation. Place the Rock of Andreas within the hilt of the blade and concentrate on your desire that the blade be unable to harm the ilk of the forest and our people. I'm told by tradition that this deed will produce Magick as powerful as a Permanent Wish Spell."

"No Spellweaver has ever been capable of casting a Wish Spell, let alone one of Permanence," Phyrris questioned.

"No other Spellweaver has had access to a Rock of Andreas during an Approximation," the older Spellweaver said reassuringly.

"So be it. I shall also wish for added power against the Draiths. A device that could not be wielded against our people but had great baneful for our strongest enemies would easily be my greatest accomplishment and would leave a legacy that any Spellweaver would cherish. Rest will serve us all. My brother, we will begin our efforts after a rest period," Phyrris added.

The three grasped forearms and made ready to retire to their respective rest areas. The others sensed Phyrris's zealousness.

Purya walked from the meeting into the quiet common area and inhaled the sweet, clear air. The gray sun Andreas almost filled the sky. It was a great dark period to be alive. Most Drelves were resting. He sensed a brief rancid odor. A heavy hand covered his mouth and prevented his crying out. The point of the blade burst through the front of his chest and impaled him from the back. The Spellweaver died quickly.

The act of treachery exposed its perpetrator. Fange was only a little taller than the creature that he had slain. The Dwarves' blade had filled his hand perfectly. He heard a voice screaming.

Morlecainen yelled at the top of his lungs, "Treachery. The Dwarves attack."

Too late Fange realized the ruse. The Ogre did not detect the Transformation Spell that had followed the Silence Spell. He looked like a dwarf, held a Dwarves' blade, and was standing over the body of the fallen Purya. Drelves were filling the common area.

Fange shouted angrily and ran toward Morlecainen with blade extended. Unfortunately, this completed the ruse. Many bows hummed. Arrows pierced his transformed body. He fought the pain and neared his quarry. Then he was struck by three spells. Phyrris had cast a Flame Spell which enveloped the unfortunate Fange, Agrarian had thrown a

Slowing Spell, and Morlecainen completed his treachery with a Fireball that consumed the body of his former and loyal servant.

"I can get another Ogre," the tall sorcerer thought silently and covered a sarcastic chuckle. "The poor fool didn't even realize that he was the victim of the Transformation Spell. It's a miracle that his smell didn't betray me."

The Drelves gathered around the fallen Purya. Agrarian, Phyrris, Aergin, the Teacher Shayne, and elders tried in vain to revive him.

"So young to fall," old Agrarian mourned.

Lignis lamented, "How could he have not seen the vile creature?"

"I was enjoying a walk in your beautiful common area. I saw Purya leave the meeting. He had no warning! The Dwarf cast no shadow. He was invisible and made no sound. I tell you that the Dwarves have a mighty ally. You can see that they have access to your realm. You are not safe and will be overrun. Again I ask your assistance. If I can defeat the Dwarves and their sorcerer, I will gain the means to close the portal that connects our worlds. It must have been the creation of their ally. I cannot defeat him with my spells, but he has no weaponry skills. With your help I can defeat him," Morlecainen said in his most sincere tone.

Phyrris answered, "Leave us to grieve, sorcerer. We have suffered a great loss. We will have counsel after the next rest period."

Morlecainen did as he was asked and returned to the sanctuary of the guest tree room.

"That could not have gone much better," he mused.

Teacher Shayne, Phyrris, Agrarian, and Aergin left the mourning to the other Drelves. The three Spellweavers and Teacher entered the Old Orange Spruce.

Phyrris said, "I reluctantly fear that there is some truth in the ramblings of this spell caster. We have no knowledge of his world. I can add protective Magick to what I will call the Draithsbane. I can cast a Locating Spell that only the three of us would be able to follow, so that we can regain the blade after the sorcerer has his day with the Dwarves. He can protect himself as well as our people from the attacks of these greedy creatures that he describes. He says that he will gain the power to close the portal between our worlds if he can defeat the Dwarves and their sorcerer. What are your thoughts?" Phyrris asked.

"I don't fully trust him. I agree that we are compelled to assist him in his conflict," Agrarian said.

"I will help you, brother. I lack your skills. My studies are not complete. But I feel great strength from the gray sun and I feel that I can contribute in our people's hour of need," Aergin added.

Phyrris went to the corner of the room. He uttered a complex series of phrases and a small chest appeared. He removed the protecting glyph, disarmed the poisoned needle trap, and opened the chest. He removed several brilliant gems of varying colors.

"The Xennic Gemstones. They carry the powers of many Approximations of Andreas and hold the Magick of many generations. The hammers of our fore fathers are here as well. The greatest bowyer and fletchers of Drelvedom, BJ Aires and Byrum Goodale used these hammers. They were not Spellweavers, but their weaponry skills were unsurpassed. With these we can try to secure the safety of our people. The gray stone that Agrarian has entrusted to me will place a control on the weapon that will prevent the blade from harming the ilk of the forest and those of Drelvish blood. The other stones will provide powers of attack and healing to the weapon. The Draithsbane will be a loan to this sorcerer. It will be my legacy to our people. It will take at least fourteen periods to complete the task. If the Approximation occurs, I could forge the weapon anywhere. Otherwise, we'll use the Elemental Stones and Bleeding Stones to create the circle of Magick. I will tell the sorcerer to return to his world and come back at the appropriate time to retrieve his prize. I don't want this individual in our world for any longer amount of time than is absolutely necessary, particularly during the Approximation," Phyrris added.

Phyrris removed two hammers and the brilliant stones and closed the chest. He replaced the glyph and the chest again disappeared from sight.

Lignis and a small party of Drelves escorted Morlecainen through the forest to the area of the portal gate. There was great activity in the sanctuary as the Drelves prepared the death pyre to honor Purya.

# 26.

## Plans at Ylysis

Morlecainen cast Protection from Magick and Feather Fall spells and entered the gate. The sorcerer soon was breathing the air of Donothor on a moon lit night. Floating from the portal to the ground was becoming familiar to him. There was no activity in the area. He did not tarry. He cast the Teleportation Spell and returned to Ylysis. Lexx greeted him.

"Where is the Ogre?" the Dark Elf asked.

"He was killed by a beast in the forest," Morlecainen answered flatly.

"The Dragons report that a force gathers at Hillesdale, the stronghold of the Dwarves. What are your commands?" Lexx asked.

"Do all you can to protect the household," the sorcerer answered. "I will prepare for them. Post guards at the river. It will take them several days to march to the river. Crossing the Luumic will delay them as well. We have time to prepare. Send the Dragons, Dark Ash and Gray Wind, to scout their progress."

The young Black Dragons scouted the lands above the River Luumic and reported back to the Sorcerer of the Lachinor. The Black Dragon Lord Xollos's granddaughter Dark Ash discovered the advancing dwarves' army. The Mage Roscoe spotted Dark Ash. The dragon flew far beyond the range of a longbow. The Mage Roscoe raised his Staff and sent a streak of blue light from the tip of the staff through the clear morning sky. The spell found its mark. Dark Ash howled, briefly fell downward, eventually righted herself, and flew rapidly toward the Luumic. The force was discovered!

Morlecainen noted great activity in the inner ward of Ylysis. The young Black Dragon Dark Ash was writhing on the ground with a badly wounded wing. Several Dark Elves were aiding the stricken wyrm, and Prince Lexx was communicating with her.

Lexx turned to Morlecainen and said, "I hope your secret labors are nearing completion. Dark Ash tells me that a large force comes from the north. This army is composed of not only Dwarves but also armed and robed men. They carry great quantities of materials and construct redoubts, small fieldworks to provide refuges for their soldiers outside their stronghold. They have reached the river. The north bank of the Luumic is abuzz with activity. Should I mount an offensive?"

Morlecainen quickly answered, "No. Our numbers are too few. I've not had time to recruit! Make ready the castle. Protect my mate, your sister, and the children at all costs. Organize what forces that we have left to make a stand in the valley just before the hill upon which Ylysis stands. I will be briefly away. I have studied their plans. I think that they intend to build an outpost on the northern side of the river. That will take some time. We will give them that. Attend to the Dragon's wounds. Dark Ash is old Xollos's favorite granddaughter. I do not want Xollos upset with us. Send word to the Dragonlord that his granddaughter was attacked by a sorcerer of Donothor. I don't mind if Xollos is upset with him."

Dark Elf Prince Lexx cautioned, "The Black Dragon's wound is likely mortal. She lost much of her foul ichor in returning. My healers lack skills to aid injured Dragons. I would not risk deceiving the Black Dragon Lord. Xollos is legend in the deep swamp. His years are long and his cunning and wisdom are great."

Theandra did not share her sister's curiosity about the area of the house where Chalar spent much of her time. Theandra preferred playing out-of-doors to hanging around the foyer and her father's study. Chalar spent her play time making life miserable for small forest creatures. Goblins avoided being subjected to her annoying spells by bringing her victims. Goblins considered the creatures a sources of food and didn't understand the child's actions. Hunger drove Goblins to kill. Chalar seemed to enjoy the beasts' suffering. Dreams told Chalar not to kill them quickly.

Theandra did not pester the Goblins and was grateful that the gnarly swamp denizens supplied her with "subjects" for her gentle spells. Theandra used her budding Magick skills to augment the natural attributes of the fauna and flora. She enjoyed making a flower blossom brighter, a lizard faster, or a bird's song more melodious. Chalar often teased and taunted Theandra, but the dark-haired child held her own.

Theandra slept well at night. Dreams troubled Chalar. The little red-haired sorceress complained to Alluna. The dreams only came when her father was home and never when Morlecainen was away. When Morlecainen was home, the Orb of Dark Knowledge sat within its chest in the Room of Sorcery. He carried the Orb within his raiment when he traveled. Chalar stopped complaining about the dreams. The dreams did not cease. Chalar began to enjoy them and complained when her father was away. Alluna wrongly thought her red-haired child was missing Morlecainen.

Morlecainen went to his heavily protected personal chest. Inactivated the warding glyphs, and carefully removed his bow and three Arrows of Clysis. He returned to the Room of Sorcery. took the Orb of Dark Knowledge from its case, and felt for the first time a slight burning in his fingers. The object had gotten noticeably heavier. He yearned for more information about the scrying device. His mind raced. Had his ruse worked? Were the Drelves convinced Dwarves threatened their lands? He missed the Ogre Fange's influence in dealing with Goblins. Lexx used the threat of retribution and on one occasion threatened an unruly goblin with calling Chalar. The Goblin cooperated immediately. Morlecainen found this amusing. The girls were certainly following their father's footsteps. He fondly recalled his childhood on Sagain and the joy of pulling feathers off a Phoenix.

# 27.

# The Draithsbane

Agrarian grieved Purya most and immersed himself in teaching his apprentices. Agrarian had taken under his wing a young Drelve with weak ability of illusion named Ramish. Ramish was neither strong in Magick nor a Spellweaver. Ramish had been conceived when a foraging Kiennish Shaman forced copulation upon a young Drelvish maiden. Ramish had inherited rudimentary powers of illusion from his Kiennish father. The young Kiennite-Drelve studied hard and possessed a strong work ethic. Ramish practiced particularly hard during Dark Periods and Approximations. Kiennites were an unscrupulous immoral lot. Kiennites born during the Approximation of Andreas had powers of Illusory Magick and passed their abilities down to their progeny. Their illusions were particularly effective against less intelligent opponents. Gangly goblin-like Kiennites were usually not a serious threat unless accompanied by powerful wolf-faced Drolls. Ramish's Kiennish father did not long survive the attack upon his mother. Drelvish archers discovered his treachery and slew him and the Drolls that had accompanied him. Ramish's birth occurred during an Approximation of Andreas, ended a long and difficult gestation, and cost his unfortunate mother her life. His Kiennish blood harvested power from the Grayness of Andreas and his Shaman father's bloodline. Ramish's power equated to the offspring of a Kiennish shaman born during an Approximation. Such Kiennites gained some spells like Magick Missile and modest Fire Spells. The half-Drelvish, half-Kiennish child had been taken in by the Spellweaver Agrarian's great, great nephew Tyler and his life-mate Carin. His adoptive parents had treated him kindly.

His appearance was not pleasant, but most Drelves considered Ramish better looking than Drolls, Kiennites, and the tall, mysterious visitor Morlecainen. Insensitive Drelvlings ostracized and mistrusted the different-looking Ramish. Some adults were wary of his vaguely Kiennish traits and feared consequences of his Magick. Ramish inherited rudimentary powers of illusion from his Kiennish father. Agrarian welcomed Ramish under his tutelage. The exceptionally quiet Drelvling oft did not reveal his inner thoughts and emotions. Agrarian also tutored the elder Dilan's son Magrian. Precocious Magrian possessed no skills in Magick. Many young Drelves had been fascinated by the Approximation of Andreas. Agrarian had sought each birthing during the Approximation in hopes of finding a child blessed with the skills of Magick. Unfortunately, he discovered none. In the periods immediately after the time of great Magick, the small Drelve Magrian had taken to Agrarian. Magrian was brilliant and learned quickly. All Drelves matured quickly, but young Magrian exceeded his peers and approached learning zealously. His motto became, "Let learning be cherished where Drelves are free."

Perhaps his high intelligence and rapid growth was accounted for by the fact that he had taken his first breaths when the gray sun was precisely at its closest point. The spark of Magick was not there, but the timing of the Drelvling's birth was unique. Magrian quickly joined Ramish as apprentice to old Agrarian. There existed some jealousy among the other young Drelves and even Ramish. None of the others shared Ramish's paternally derived skills of illusion.

Andreas drew near. An Approximation was imminent and fortuitously augmented the Spellweavers' efforts. The three Spellweavers and Teacher Shayne met at the Forge. Phyrris had reluctantly agreed to forge the weapon. Agrarian's contribution of the Rock of Andreas, the Approximation of gray Andreas, his brother Aergin's willingness to help, and finally the inflation of his own ego had ultimately led to his decision to complete the blade. Phyrris determined the necessary Xennic Gemstones and sequence of spells necessary to create the vorpal weapon. Phyrris filled the fire pit of the forge with fire rocks from Fire Lake and ignited them with a Fire Spell. Agrarian placed the four elemental stones equidistantly from the forge. Agrarian then took the Bleeding Stone in his hand. Runes appeared on the artifact.

Ǿ ∞ Ǿ

Gray light spread from the Bleeding Stone to the four elemental stones. Runes appeared on the four stones.

Ǿ ∞ Ǿ

A circle of thirteen-foot diameter formed around the forge. Red liquid flowed from the Bleeding Stone. Agrarian took the Enhancing (Xennic) Stone and touched the forge, the Bleeding Stone, and the Elemental Stones. The Bleeding Stone eerily rose to thirteen feet above the forge. Red liquid dripped from the stone into the fire pit. Each drop intensified the fire and heat. Phyrris placed several beautiful gemstones, the gray family heirloom from Agrarian, three locating stone, and two hammers on his work table.

Agrarian spoke first, "It is the time agreed upon. Can you finish the blade this dark period? The Gray Wanderer will get no closer."

Phyrris responded, "It will be finished. I have determined the sequence of the stones and added an Illuminating Spell that will cause the runes to glow whenever the blade is held by one of the forest. The Locating Spell will give the location of the blade. Only the three of us have the knowledge to invoke the Locating Spell. These three stones match the three locating stones that I will impress into the blade. Are you going to share this knowledge with the half-Drelve? I advise against that."

Phyrris distributed three translucent stones. Agrarian and Aergin accepted the artifacts. Phyrris kept the third.

Aergin interjected, "The sorcerer requested that all three of us be present for the transfer of the blade. He insisted that we had a great reward in store and that we would receive what we had coming to us."

Agrarian said, "I will not remain at the Forge. The fire is hot and ready. I can do no more than fuel the Forge. The Gray Wanderer enhances the heat far beyond anything that we could create even with our Magick. Strike your hammers well and place the Xennic Gemstones, Locating Stones, and the Rock of Andreas in the required order. My time will be best spent trying to enhance Ramish's meager abilities while the Wanderer fills the sky. I will tell young Ramish nothing of our dealings with the sorcerer. I have no interest in dealing with the sorcerer again. You may accept my reward. I still grieve Purya greatly. If this sojourner had not interrupted our peace, young Purya would still live, and we could still hear his loving voice. I hope that this period will be the last that our world is befouled by the presence of this sorcerer from the other world."

Phyrris and Aergin remained at the Forge. Teacher Shayne and Agrarian met Ramish at the Old Orange Spruce. All manner of celebration filled Alms Glen. Andreas filled the sky. The Approximation arrived.

The two Spellweavers Phyrris and Aergin labored over the heat of the forge. Sweat fell profusely from their noble dark brows and the muscles of their forearms tensed with each strike of their hammers. Many beautiful gems were being forced into the shimmering elongated object that was slowly taking definition as a result of their physical and mental labors. The silence of the evening air was repeatedly broken by their voices, but the arcane phrases would have been understood by only a few.

Aergin muttered between incantations, "Why do we concern ourselves with the conflicts between Necromancers and Dwarves? These labors tire my spirit."

Phyrris replied, "We have never been so encumbered by their conflict. You know the hold the wizard has over us. Do you want to remain obliged to do his will? Do you want Dwarven hordes traversing and foraging through our world?"

Disgruntled, Aergin continued his verbal protest by adding, "Do we want to empower the wizard more? Could he not challenge us more than an army of short-statured and ill-mannered brutes?"

"Nothing is certain, my brother. The wizard reached our domain, and the Dwarves managed to follow. As a result, Purya lies dead," Phyrris replied bluntly.

"He is a wizard," came the reply from young Aergin.

They worked on into the grayness, bathed by the ever-diminishing light of the three suns. Incantation followed incantation and strike after strike of the hammers fell. Slowly the vorpal weapon was taking shape.

After a time of great effort, Phyrris finally answered his complaining companion, "I am instilling in the weapon the force of healing its wielder just as he requested. But I also impart in the blade the inability to harm those of our ilk. It shall not spill the blood of the forest. He will have his power over the dwarves, but he will not harm us with the blade. We can protect ourselves from the effect of his unrefined Magick. This weapon will serve our people long after his time. He won't possess the blade for many time periods. There is little for us to fear."

After hours of grimy work, the two stood over a shimmering blade adorned by many jewels. The elder Phyrris painstakingly etched runes and symbols into the hilt and the blood groove of the weapon. When Aergin raised the blade, the runes etched on the sword began to glow intensely, illuminating the area around them. He quickly placed the blade beneath his raiment to avoid exposing their unwonted work area to unwanted eyes that might be drawn to the bright light. He noted that several small scratches on his fatigued forearms had fully healed in the brief moment that he fanned the air with the blade. The two marveled at their own creation.

"How do you impart these qualities to the blade?" the younger Aergin added quizzically.

"Because I am taught well by the Teacher and I am the son of my mother. Look above you. The Gray Wanderer, the third sun Andreas, fills the sky. The Approximation sometimes occurs only every several lifetimes. Do you not feel the waxing of the energies within you? It is youth that prevents you from feeling this. You will learn in time," his older brother Phyrris replied. "Let us deliver our tithe so that we can be rid of our debt to this wizard and perhaps rid our world of him."

********

Morlecainen set his mind to the tasks before him. The Spellweavers had agreed to meet Morlecainen in a fortnight. He gathered up his staff and ingredients for his spells. Finally, he donned his robe and placed the Orb of Dark Knowledge within the largest pocket of his thick outer raiment. This time he would go beyond the portal alone. The ill-fated Fange had lowered the odds. With Purya's death, only three Spellweavers remained. Without the power of their Spellweavers, the Drelves could do little to impede him. He could exploit the resources of the World of the

Three Suns. If everything went according to plan, Morlecainen could have two worlds to domineer.

The Sorcerer had arranged a meeting place with the Drelves' Spellweavers. Phyrris had finally been convinced that a threat existed and had agreed to his terms. Morlecainen had requested the creation of a weapon that would make him an accomplished swordsman and heal his wounds. As soon as he dealt with the Dwarves, he planned to turn his attention to the World of the Three Suns. His greatness would surpass old Clysis.

Morlecainen reached the portal without incident. Casting a Protection from Magick Spell and using the amber paste more sparingly made the journey less painful for the sorcerer. He had perfected passing through the gate. He cast an Invisibility Spell before he left Donothor, but he waited until he was on the other side of the gate to cast a Silence Spell.

On the other side of the portal, the still air was energizing. The pale light of the gray sun reduced the sky's amber color. The net effect mimicked summer twilight on Sagain. The gray sun Andreas almost filled the sky. Morlecainen basked in its rays and felt stronger. He passed the guards at the perimeter of the forest unnoticed. They had not seen his arrival. Casting the Silence Spell involved only the invocation of a single phrase, which resembled a low-pitched whistle, and did not betray his invisibility. Magick was finicky. If he had cast the Silence Spell first, casting the Invisibility Spell would have revoked the silence. Speaking aloud broke Silence Spells. Aggressive or offensive actions negated Invisibility Spells. The Silence and Invisibility Spells could also be cast over areas, affecting all characters within the area. If an invisible character cast a Silence Spell upon his own character, an existing Invisibility Spell would not be lost. If an invisible spell caster attempted to silence opponents, the sorcerer sacrificed his invisibility. Silence and Invisibility Spells always worked on willing recipients. If the spells were used offensively to cover an area, the area was always affected by the spell, but characters within the spell's area of effect could leave the area and escape the spell. The power of level of the spellcaster determined the area of effect and duration of the spell. The relative strengths of the spellcaster and his intended victims determined success or failure of spells. Magick had many quirks, vexing complexity, unwonted effects, oft unwanted effects, and a never-ending learning curve.

"It's Magick" oft answered the questions "Why?" "How?" "Who?" "What" and "When?"

Nearness of the Gray Wanderer energized Morlecainen mentally and physically. The possibility of expanding his powers enthused him. The World of the Three Suns was at his mercy. Morlecainen knew nothing of the Draiths, the self-proclaimed Masters of the World of the Three Suns.

********

Phyrris and Aergin left the steamy forging area and entered onto the pathway leading to their prearranged meeting point. The brothers arrived first and waited impatiently. Their friend the forest was remarkably quiet as they continued to await the arrival of the magician. The elder brother Phyrris had planned so well. But he could not have fully appreciated the wizard's treachery. A soft swish filled the air. Aergin noted with horror the Arrow of Clysis that tore through his brother's chest. The elder Phyrris fell to the floor of his beloved forest without uttering a sound. The younger Aergin did not have time to incant or to draw sword before the second arrow pierced him. Aergin also dropped to the ground when the magical force of the arrow struck him. He could not find the strength to grasp the blade before the Magick of the unerring arrow ended his existence. The stillness of death blended into the silence of the forest. Morlecainen determined that the brothers were alone and triumphantly moved to their bodies and retrieved the blade. His Silence and Invisibility Spells had been negated when the released the first of the rune-covered arrows. The advantage that he had gained was insurmountable.

"Is this the best this world has to offer?" the wizard mused, managing a smile. "And the fools thought that I would actually close the Portal Gate. I would not do that even if I had the knowledge to do so."

Morlecainen inspected the magnificent sword. Fine runes were etched into the weapon. The blade shimmered in the amber darkness, but the area was too dark to allow Morlecainen to study the runes. The wizard used his Orb of Illumination to read them. The ever-approaching moon-like object was choking out the rays of the other two suns. But it was not a moon. Moons did not radiate gray light. Morlecainen witnessed the Approximation of Andreas for the first time. His mind bristled with energy. Oh, to meet the Dwarves' sorcerer ally at this moment!

Silence bathed the area. The denizens of the forest were respecting the fallen. He could interpret many of the elvish runes etched into the blade, but the forgers had included some arcane symbols that were foreign to the wizard.

The wizard incised his palm with the point of the blade. Brief lancinating pain came as he anticipated, but to his delight, the wound quickly healed as he gripped the blade. The evidence of the wound was manifested only by the few drops of his dark orange blood that had fallen to the ground near the slain Drelves. The wizard sheathed the blade within his robes and began the journey homeward. Even though the light ebbed, he could see well enough to traverse the path. He was getting accustomed to the strangeness of the fauna and flora.

Morlecainen reached the portal gate and uttered a brief incantation. A mauve glow surrounded him. He traversed the portal. The darkness of Donothor's night comforted him. He uttered "Ylysis" and stood upon the ridge overlooking his once modest castle. In the distance, the multitude of campfires of the Dwarves' army flickered in the darkness. At the foot of the ridge glimmered the few fires of his own conscripts, mercenaries, and rogues, a paltry force gathered to defend this last bastion of the wizard's domain.

The sorcerer grasped the hilt of the sword and said smugly, "Let them come now."

All his remaining personal guard had been dispatched to the force awaiting the Dwarves' certain attack. It only took a moment to disengage the Fireglyph from the castle doors, and only another moment to reengage the Magick lock. Morlecainen then entered his abode. His lovely Dark Elf mate Alluna sat silently near the open fireplace. A warming flame flickered, but there were no logs. She was knitting a garment for the girls. He stored his staff, the sleek bow, and the realm's only remaining Arrow of Clysis and secured the lock on the chest. The treasure had been well worth the cost of the other two arrows. He could only cause one inevitable death with each arrow, but the Magick Sword would empower him greatly in battle. The sorcerer activated another Fireglyph with a single phrase. Morlecainen trusted no one, including his mate. The wizard walked to the children's room and peered into it. The twins slept serenely as he watched. Morlecainen marveled at the precociousness and beauty of the girls. Would

Chalar or Theandra succeed their father when the time came? The journey had tired him. The sorcerer dropped down onto his soft bed and rapidly fell asleep.

Morlecainen was rested when Alluna entered, awakened him, and said icily, "Many Dwarves and men occupy the fields before the castle. My brother Lexx seeks to speak with you urgently."

The sorcerer replied, "I will see him now."

Morlecainen felt surprisingly sore from the efforts of his journey and struggled to his feet. He left the bedchamber and found Lexx waiting in the dining area. Breakfast was waiting on the table.

The Dark Elf queried, "Were you successful?"

Morlecainen answered, "Our chances for success are favorable."

Lexx replied, "They outnumber us ten to one. We have no Dragon support."

Morlecainen said, "What are you saying?"

Lexx said, "Dark Ash, the young she-Dragon, died. The other Gray Wind flew away to the south, I assume to inform Xollos of his loss."

Morlecainen asked of his lieutenant, "What is our strength?"

Lexx summarized, "We number five hundred of my people, but I have stationed them to the rear to guard the castle as you ordered. Their bows and few spells will be of no value there. We have seven hundred mercenaries and Hobgoblins at the base of the hill. The few Goblins that are not involved in the running of the castle fled into the forests."

Morlecainen said confidently, "Your people will stay as they are to protect my family. Should the need arise, they can carry Alluna and the girls to your father Cellexa. The paltry force we put on the field is simply gambit. I only want to draw the Dwarves into battle. I will crush their morale and they will bow down before me."

Lexx sighed, "What would you have me do?"

Morlecainen answered, "Stand by your sister Alluna, my betrothed. You will command the retreat to Cellexa in the unlikelihood I am proven wrong."

Lexx warned, "Our scouts say there are many men among them. The sorcerer is likely one of them."

Morlecainen replied curtly, "I hope that he is."

Lexx added, "I anticipate that they will attack in the morning. They have been positioning archers upon the higher ground to cover any charge by our forces."

Morlecainen said, "You have served well. Your father can be proud of you. Now I must see your sister and nieces."

Lexx bowed and left. Morlecainen went into the main living area of his dwelling and found his mate and daughters. He watched the girls cast Magick and marveled at Chalar's ability to learn new spells and Theandra's ability to procure spell ingredients from the forest. The children eventually tired, and Alluna put them to bed.

Chalar pleaded, "Please don't leave, father. I want to dream."

The sorcerer thought his presence reassured the child and smiled. Mauve light flickered deep within the Orb of Dark Knowledge.

A deafening howl of dismay filled the heavy air of the deep Lachinor. Young Black Dragon Gray Wind informed the Black Dragonlord Xollos of the death of his granddaughter Dark Ash. The aged Dragonlord fumed, "The Sorcerer of the Lachinor vowed to protect my granddaughter! He will pay for his incompetence! Vengeance will be mine!"

# 28.

# Conflict in the Lachinor: the Power of The Blade of Fire

Four thousand Dwarves faced Morlecainen's paltry force of seven hundred mercenaries and Hobgoblins. Lexx held the Dark Elves in reserve. The commanders of the Dwarves and their allies made ready. The Mage Roscoe sprinkled some fine sand, waved his staff in the direction of the castle, and reported that there were no invisible defenders.

The sorcerer reported, "What you see is what we are against."

Dwarf King Travan said, "There must be a start to it. Send forward the first ranks."

The first ranks moved forward. Five hundred paces separated the foes.

Prince Ordrych Aivendar of Lyndyn said, "I will join them."

King Travan said boldly, "The honor of leading falls to me."

The Dwarves moved forward at a steady pace. The guarding force held their ground. The center of the defensive line parted, and a single tall figure started to move toward Travan's army. He wore no armor and carried no shield. Flames flickered from the longsword he carried.

Roscoe looked through his Magick prism and dumbfoundedly said, "This is the sorcerer. He radiates Magick, but he casts no spells. He is committing suicide!"

Dwarf Sergeant Saultzo queried, "What is suicide?"

"He seeks self-destruction," Roscoe answered bluntly.

Grizzled warrior Dann Rocherr boisterously exclaimed from his position in the front rank "I'll be glad to oblige him."

Pirmis, a young Curate from the Fane of the Setting Sun added, "He carries no staff. I detect no illusion."

Four hundred paces separated the foes. Roscoe raised his small prism, pointed his staff at Morlecainen, threw a snail shell into the air, and uttered an incantation. A pink ray streamed from the end of the staff and bathed the lone advancing enemy. He continued forward.

The mage uttered dejectedly, "He radiates great Magick. There are no effects from my Slow Spell."

Roscoe then threw a piece of coal into the air and spoke the arcane phrases of the Darkness Spell. A black cloud left the staff's end. The cloud dissipated over the advancing tall figure.

Roscoe confided, "There is no effect from the Darkness Spell."

Three hundred paces separated the foes. Roscoe then threw a precious piece of sulfurous rock into the air and uttered a harsh incantation. The smell of rotten eggs filled the air. The Fireball exploded around the advancing tall figure and incinerated twenty of the fighters behind him. The spell had no effect on the advancing figure.

Roscoe surmised, "He has cast many Protective Spells upon himself. I doubt that I will be of much help in this fray. Why does he not use spell attacks?"

Two hundred paces separated the foes. Travan raised his shield hand and stopped the advance. The tall figure continued to move forward.

Travan spoke to the archer beside him, "Ophirr, he comes to within bow range. End this affair now."

Ophirr said, "There's no honor in this."

The young archer then drew taut his bowstring and then the bowstring hummed. The arrow arched high and flew toward the steadily advancing target. Ophirr's aim was impeccable. The arrow struck the figure in mid-chest. He did not fall. Instead he raised the flaming blade to the sky and repeated a phrase three times. The impaling arrow fell from his chest. He moved forward. A roar swelled from the men and Hobgoblins behind him, and they ran forward at a rapid pace, soon overtaking and passing him. One hundred paces separated the foes. The Dwarves held their ground.

King Travan urged, "Prepare to battle!"

The heavy sounds of metal on metal filled the air. The outnumbered mercenaries fought with tenacity. They were buoyed by the their leader's show of resistance.

Ordrych Aivendar urged, "Seek out the sorcerer. Beware of his spells."

Morlecainen reached the conflict and engaged Pamalar, the first Dwarf he encountered. Veteran of many battles, Pamalar wielded his blade well and defended with his shield. He struck the sorcerer, but the blow did not burden Morlecainen. The sorcerer wielded the flaming blade with astounding speed and made no effort to parry. Brave Pamalar was the first to fall before the Blade of Fire. The blade blazed with red flame during the heat of battle. In quick order, the sorcerer proceeded to his next foe. His opponent's blade struck him repeatedly and opened his flesh, but blood did not flow from the sorcerer's wounds. There were many stalemates between the foes, but Dann Rochen, Ordrych Aivendar, and King Travan had more success. The experience of earlier battles gave them advantage. The numbers of defenders trickled. Morlecainen was leaving a wide swath of death as he drove deeper into the Dwarves' lines. Two, three, four, five, six, seven, eight, nine, ten, and eleven… Dwarves fell before him. He advanced in a purposeful course. A young Dwarf named Ellavel watched his best friend fall, disregarded the honor of combat, and thrust his blade into the tall figure's back. The sorcerer flinched, turned in a blinding circle, and slew Ellavel with a single blow. Ellavel's blade fell harmlessly to the ground. Twelve, thirteen, fourteen, fifteen, sixteen… the numbers mounted. Ordrych Aivendar ended his enemy's life and grasped the hilt of his telepathic sword Exeter.

Exeter detected enemies and warned her bearer of his greatest threat. The sword communicated, "Clearly the most dangerous foe is twenty paces to your right. He nears King Travan. I …"

Roscoe went to the rear after his spells failed and stood with Curate Pirmis just beyond the carnage. The mage watched the castle intently and said, "I still fear the castle. There are other Spell Casters in the castle. Great Magick remains there. Why have they not attacked? Why does he fight with a blade? What is the nature of this weapon? It radiates much power."

Pirmis surmised, "He cannot cast spells when he wields the blade. He can only slay us one at a time. Nothing comes from the castle. Our warriors are thinning their ranks."

Roscoe added pessimistically, "We only number four thousand. Our blows do not wound him. My Magick did not affect him. It will take him awhile but at this rate he will destroy us all."

Travan felled another of the mercenaries and readied himself. The tall figure approached and snarled, "Prepare to meet your doom, miserable little creature." Travan raised his shield just as the blazing longsword arced toward him. The shield resonated from the force of the blow and the king staggered backward briefly. Travan felt the heat of the flame. He landed a blow from his axe upon the tall sorcerer's leg. The blow had little effect.

Sergeant Saultzo screamed, "To the aid of the king!" Saultzo bravely dropped his shield, swung his axe with both hands, and scored one direct blow to Morlecainen's right shoulder. Nevertheless, the sorcerer attacked Travan again. The king again parried the blow but was unable to counterattack. Suddenly shimmering lights covered Travan. The king then faded from sight. Roscoe's Invisibility Spell had worked and saved the king at least temporarily. Morlecainen cursed loudly, slashed his blade wildly through the air, and struck nothing. Angrily he lunged toward Saultzo and struck the Dwarf's helmet. Saultzo lost consciousness and fell motionlessly to the ground.

Ordrych Aivendar called to the sorcerer, "Face me if you will!"

Morlecainen turned and sneered. The blood of his victims stained his robes, and his eyes brimmed with blood lust. All around were ongoing shouts and sounds of battle as men, Dwarves, and Hobgoblins struggled to destroy one another. Morlecainen and Ordrych became oblivious to the other conflicts. Ordrych grasped Exeter. Exeter's feminine voice communicated, "I detect intense auras from the sword. I can find no weaknesses. Good luck." Morlecainen attacked like a berserker from Valhalla and furiously landed blows. Ordrych skillfully parried the blows but could not match Morlecainen's incredible speed. Morlecainen never parried. Exeter found the sorcerer's flesh often but drew no blood.

Pirmis said to Roscoe, "How can we wound this man?"

Roscoe answered, "The weapon empowers him! I cannot determine the nature of the blade."

Pirmis quickly replied, "Nor can I. What should we do?"

Ordrych parried many blows. His energies faded, and he no longer attacked. The weight of his shield encumbered him, and he threw it aside. Throwing the shield aside quickened his hands, and he rapidly moved

Exeter to parry the sorcerer's blows. Exeter blocked the sorcerer's blinding blows. Morlecainen sensed that his opponent was no longer an offensive threat, but he could not determine how long the stalemate would last. His own forces were dwindling, but more of the opposing warriors were stopping their own conflicts to watch the marathon struggle between Morlecainen and Ordrych. The sorcerer pummeled Ordrych, but Exeter's metal withstood the blows. Morlecainen slowed his attack, grasped the flaming blade with both hands, drew the weapon back over his head, and swung downward with all his might. Ordrych parried the blow but was knocked to one knee. The sorcerer again raised the blade. With a loud clang Travan's axe struck the sorcerer's blade hand and severed three fingers. The Dwarf appeared behind the sorcerer. Roscoe pointed his staff at the same hand and threw a Magic Missile Spell which struck a moment after the Dwarf. The King and Roscoe's efforts separated the weapon from Morlecainen and the blade fell to the ground seven feet away. Drops of blood fell from the sorcerer's severed fingers. Ordrych mustered enough strength to raise Exeter to deliver a fatal blow. Suddenly an orange ray of light hit the tall Donothorian and knocked him backward. Another orange light struck Travan and knocked the King down. The diminutive hands that had cast the Stun Spells were standing high upon the hill outside the castle. Theandra and Chalar had disobeyed their uncle Lexx and mother Alluna and were surveying the battle. Both had mastered Stun Spells. Morlecainen struggled to his feet and tried to reach the blade. "Clear away from him," Roscoe shouted. "See to King Travan and Ordrych."

Nearby Dwarves dragged Ordrych and Travan away. Roscoe reached into his robe, removed a small rounded object, hurled it through the air, and uttered arcane phrases as it flew. Purplish fumes erupted around Morlecainen and covered an area of about ten yards. The sorcerer fell and began to cough. He had no protective Magick to defend against the Stinking Cloud Spell. Roscoe created the new spell using the dung of the Leicat. The blade lay now five feet away from the incapacitated Morlecainen. A brazen Dwarf warrior named Zoffolt drew a deep breath and rushed toward the sword. He reached, grasped the hilt. and triggered the Death Glyph. The powerful explosion destroyed his hand and he fell lifelessly within the vapors of the Stinking Cloud.

"He has cast Warding Glyphs upon the blade. We cannot utilize it,"

Roscoe surmised. He turned to face the castle. Pirmis successfully placed a Silence Spell upon the twins. The girls panicked and ran back into the castle.

Ophirr screamed, "Let me end his evil!"

The archer fired his bow toward the prone sorcerer. The first arrow struck Morlecainen in the right leg. Ophirr fired again, but the fallen sorcerer managed to reach the blade with his uninjured left hand. The arrow struck his back in the mid chest, but no blood came forth.

Roscoe stared at the castle upon the hillock. He raised the prism before his eyes, scanned the area, and stated, "We do not know what other attacks may come from the castle. This is a battle that we cannot win. We must retreat to fight another day. I don't know the length of the Stinking Cloud Spell. I have never used it before. He still crawls and twitches. I didn't kill him and he has regained the blade. Given the incapacitation of King Travan, I command that we retreat."

Quickly the Dwarves' forces organized and assisted the wounded. The dead were by necessity left.

"We will honor them," Dwarf Sergeant Royboy insisted.

Too few of Morlecainen's forces remained to impede the retreat. The battle had destroyed most of the sorcerer's support. He grasped the blade with his left hand and lapsed into unconsciousness.

Several hours passed before the Morlecainen was able to sit up. His lungs ached, and he was coughing and sweating profusely. He reached out and grasped the blade. The bleeding from his wounded hand had stopped. He was able to find two of his severed fingers. He grasped the hilt of the blade with his left hand and the fourth and fifth fingers of his right hand mended. The middle finger was missing. This was the permanent price of this battle. Many warriors lay upon the field. His enemies were gone. His castle and his family had been saved. Once again, the conflict had almost cost his life. Morlecainen stood on wobbly legs that suddenly became strong. He lifted the blade. It gleamed with the blood of his enemies.

"Why was I not killed when the blade fell from my hand?" he asked himself. He looked at his right hand. Quirk of Magick…

Travan and Ordrych recovered from the effects of the Stun Spells. Neither debated Roscoe's decision. They reached the River Luumic without incident. Three thousand returned. Four thousand had started the campaign.

# 29.

# Chalar and Theandra

The young black dragon Dark Ash died. The vengeful black dragon lord Xollos faulted Morlecainen for not keeping the young dragon safe, disguised himself, stole his way into Ylysis, and kidnapped Morlecainen's life-mate Alluna. Ultimately the sorcerer faced the ancient spellcasting Black Dragonlord, bested him with the help of the Flaming Blade of Phyrris, and recovered Alluna. The kidnapping of Alluna had been a painful ten-year lesson. Morlecainen brought her back to Ylysis and gathered his family. Now when he spoke to Alluna, Theandra, and Chalar, he addressed a beautiful matron and two mature Sorceresses.

"There must be a means of escape for you, if I should fall. There is another place. Hold to my robes tightly," he commanded.

Morlecainen had become very proficient at casting the Enhanced Teleport Spell and eliminated the painful sensations associated with the spell. He uttered the familiar series of phrases. The Sorcerer of the Lachinor, Alluna, Chalar, and Theandra disappeared in a flash of light, instantly stood near tall mountains in the northwest area of Donothor, and breathed cool, crisp air.

"Please hold onto my robe again," the sorcerer requested. He cast a Protection from Magick Spell and gave the "Fly" command to his staff. They rose a few feet into the air. The sorcerer's family looked through an opening like a window to a reddish-yellow landscape.

"Please step through the gate," he suggested. The foursome stepped through the opening and stood in a meadow covered by plush reddish grasses. The sky was dominated by a huge black sun that stood directly overhead. There was a brilliant yellow sun to their left and there was a gray speck in the distant sky to their right. Reds and yellows dominated the very different landscape. A clear stream ran through the grassy meadow. Trees laden with red, yellow, and orange leaves surrounded the wide meadow. A group of large purple bovines grazed near the far edge of the field. Orange rabbits and red grouse scurried across the field.

Morlecainen spoke, "This world can serve as a sanctuary for you. I feel that either of the girls can dominate the weak beings here. No one in our world Donothor knows of this opening."

The Sorcerer of the Lachinor conjured and scattered soil from Ylysis's gardens onto the ground. He touched Alluna, Chalar, and Theandra.

Morlecainen continued, "I give you a Word of Return. Chalar and Theandra, say the word "Sisyly" and cast Teleportation if you are in great jeopardy. Magick will return you to this place. Alluna, in extremis, you should seek one of the girls. You must have some command of Magick to safely traverse the gate. The Protection from Magick Spell is easily learned, girls. You must learn the Teleportation Spell. Utter 'Sisyly' and cast Teleportation and you'll stand before the Portal Gate. You must learn the Spells of Levitation and Protection from Magick. Your mother will require your help to escape. All she need do is hold to you dearly. You must learn this Magick well. The spells must be second nature for you. I do not want any of you vulnerable to the scourges of the world that we inhabit. Let's return to that world now and stabilize our home."

Alluna nodded understanding and grasped Morlecainen's hand.

Theandra said, "I'll help Mother."

Chalar huffed, "The precaution is unnecessary, Father. We'll crush our foes in Donothor."

The sorcerer and his family crossed back through the gate. Torches flickered in the dark night and drew nearer. Morlecainen quickly cast the Teleportation Spell and whisked them to Ylysis. Roscoe and three shadows arrived at the area near the gate but found nothing. The sorcerer looked all around and found no one.

"There was Magick here," he uttered.

Roscoe removed his small prism from his robe and looked through it. The prism detected Magick. He did not look overhead and saw nothing. The shadows said nothing. They never did.

Morlecainen spent his days within the Room of Sorcery. Chalar spent her nights there. Thrice Theandra saw her sister sneaking down the corridor after their father retired to his bedchamber. On the fourth night, curiosity won out, and Theandra cast an Invisibility Spell upon herself and secretly followed her sister down the hall. Chalar uttered the complex incantation and manipulated the opening mechanism to gain entry to the Room of Sorcery. Theandra entered the room behind her preoccupied sister. Chalar went immediately to the chest and removed the Orb of Dark Knowledge. She paid the tithe of blood. Purplish gray auras surrounded the Orb and enveloped Chalar's hands. Chalar concentrated, communicated silently with the artifact, and began conversing.

Theandra seized the opportunity and gathered items; a cute little violet bag, bright red bag, and third black one. The three bags were made of odd, smooth material. She reached into the bags and didn't find a bottom! Joyous! Next a simple jewelry box caught her eye. A simple latch secured its lid. A quick check confirmed Chalar immersed in thought with the Orb. Theandra waved her left hand, whispered a three-word incantation, and found no Magick. It was merely a mundane, pretty box. She raised the lid and peeked into the empty box. It was odd that such a simple chest would be among the priceless treasures brought from Sagain. Theandra's mother Alluna oft chastised her for not storing her hairpins properly. The pretty box would serve the purpose and also look good on her chifforobe. She filled the little box with gems. An old weathered, dust-covered staff leaned against the wall in the back of the room and had obviously not been moved in years. Morlecainen had left old Clysis's staff in the Room of Wizardry after the old sorcerer died and seldom used his own staff since the great Blade of Phyrris had come into his possession. Theandra placed the staff and jewelry box in the red bag and then placed the red, black, and blue Bags of Concealment within her garments. Alas! She dropped a stone. The sound alerted Chalar. The red-haired sorceress immediately used the Orb of Dark Knowledge and cast a Hold Spell in the area of the sound. Being invisible was no defense against it. The power of the Orb required no incantation. Chalar said aloud, "Show me the intruder's face."

The Orb emitted dense grayness and sent a mauve ray toward Theandra. Theandra's face appeared. The rest of her body and the things she held remained invisible.

Chalar fumed, "Very funny! Interpreting my words literally! Not to mind, I see her. Hello, fairy princess." Chalar pulled an ornamental dagger from her belt and continued, "I ought to mark that pretty face. Our father might not like you so much then. Mother always liked you best, too! But I am better than you! I know more spells than you can imagine. This room is mine. I'm going to make it so that you can never return to this room. The Tome of Banishment has taught me the spell. If you reenter this room, you will die. If you ever tell our father that you have found me here, the spell will teleport you here and you will be utterly destroyed. No spell of Magick can save you, if you ever return to this room. Get ready for some pain, sweetie. I'm going to teleport you as you are with your clothes and items. It'll hurt more!"

Theandra could neither move nor speak. Simply breathing was difficult. The Hold Spell froze her fingers around the three bags filled with items. The Orb's macabre interpretation of Chalar's command left only Theandra's head visible. Chalar uttered a complex incantation of old forgotten phrases. Only the most powerful sorcerers of Sagain commanded the nefarious Banishment dweomer. The spell was beyond Clysis and Morlecainen's comprehension. The incantation flowed meticulously from the glowing Orb to Chalar's lips.

High Priestess Knarra of Donothor awakened from deep sleep with a severe headache. Great waves disrupted the sea of Magick! Impossible! Even the great Light Sorcerer of Sagain Gwindor was incapable of casting the ninth level Spell of Banishment. The Tome detailing the spell had been lost! This had to be a terrible dream. Roscoe felt the power of the spell. Morlecainen oft felt emanations from the Room of Sorcery and attributed the disturbance to the Orb of Dark Knowledge.

Chalar completed the spell. Theandra's head macabrely passed through the wall of the Room of Sorcery. Chalar laughed hysterically. The Banishment Spell teleported Theandra and everything she carried from the Room of Sorcery to her bedchamber. Carrying items increased the victim's pain. Chalar completed her work and left the Room of Sorcery. She parted the double doors and peered into the quiet study and then down the dimly illuminated hallway. Chalar sneaked down the quiet hallway, paused at Theandra's door, and heard sobs coming from the room. Chalar fought back a chuckle.

Every muscle in Theandra's body ached. She removed large pins from her hair and prepared for bed. She opened her new jewelry box to store her hairpins. The gems in the box made putting the hairpins inside the box awkward, and she had to push one of the pins. There was a click! The hairpin found the miniscule latch that had been hidden for ages. The latch sprang and revealed the false bottom of the little box. It contained seven phials of liquids. An aura of Magick filled her bedroom. Mauve light bathed Theandra. Thoughts appeared inside her consciousness and defined the small Elixirs. The box contained two Elixirs of Enhancement, two Elixirs of the Stars, two Elixirs of The Future, and a single Wish Elixir.

The Elixir of the Stars gave the imbiber of the contents of the phial the ability to transfer to a fifth dimension, the Astral Plane. The user would remain capable of casting spells and regulating the flow of Magick in the four dimensions from whence he came.

The Elixir of Enhancement enabled to the imbiber to cast spells of higher difficulty, the ability to cast more quickly, and less fatigue associated with spell casting. The Enhancing Elixir bequeathed True Seeing, Detect Lie, Detect Magick, and Comprehend Languages. Casting spells of greater power while maintaining vigor afforded tremendous advantage in conflicts with other spell casters.

The Elixir of The Future enabled the imbiber to see possible courses of the river of time. Too many possible turns in the great river and too many tributaries made compromised any attempt at gazing into the future.

The Elixir of True Wishing was the greatest Magick. Sorcerers of all means and alignment coveted the power of a Wish. The Elixir granted the power of a single Wish. Theandra's tomes told of no successful Wish Spells. Theandra smiled. She replaced the cover over the false bottom, closed the box, and placed it in the black Bag of Concealment. The painful night had brought rewards. A child's hairpin had uncovered treasures hidden from generations of sorcerers. Theandra never returned to the Room of Sorcery. She kept secret the items she took from the chamber. Chalar obsessed over the Orb and paid little mind to the rest of the room's contents. Morlecainen concentrated on his plans to conquer the Dwarves and defeat their sorcerer. The Blade of Phyrris never left his side. Theandra spent more time away from the castle in the woods. Her Uncle Lexx insisted guards accompany her, but the dark-haired sorceress easily escaped them.

# 30.

## Areniel Nightshade

Areniel Nightshade awaited the maiden's return. The Gray Elf scout had watched her frolic in the meadow for many days. Each time he had resisted the great urge to approach her, but his resistance was weakening. Areniel was assigned duty to monitor activities of his folk's ancestral enemies, the Dark Elves. At least three thousand Dark Elves under the royal banner of King Cellexa had bolstered the garrison at the ever-expanding fortress Ylysis, but the Dark Elf King was not present. Great numbers of Dark Elves oft meant trouble for Gray Elves. The assembling force had fomented no aggressive actions, but a storm cloud usually unleashed a downpour. Areniel sighed. The maiden arrived just after the sun reached the highest point in the sky. She was wearing a brilliant red dress that accentuated the darkness of her hair and eyes. She stepped into the meadow and uttered a few phrases that he could not understand. A small purplish cloud appeared, covered the flowers of the meadow with the purplish hue, and then dissipated. She smiled broadly. There was nothing for it.

Areniel stepped into view. The maiden stood, stared at the Gray Elf, and started to conjure. Areniel looked directly into her eyes and did nothing. The maiden interrupted her spell and looked back into his gray eyes. The two stood silent and motionlessly. Areniel took a step forward; she took a step backward. They stood twenty feet apart.

"Why do you watch me? Who are you?" Theandra asked.

"I am but a simple servant of the forest and grateful observer of your Magick. I am clay in your hands; mold me as you want. I am your pawn," the Gray Elf warrior answered.

A pawn was a weak piece of attack in a child's game that Gray Elf children enjoyed. Theandra did not know of pawns. She was intrigued.

"Why should I not destroy you for spying on my father's lands?" she asked.

"If you choose to do so, I won't resist. I can no longer watch you without revealing myself. I have never beheld such beauty. I will do anything you ask. I am a candle and you are the flame. I have lived all my life in darkness, and you are light that I have seen for the first time. Since my eyes first beheld you, all I need is the air that I breathe and to love you. I am at your mercy," Areniel replied. The Gray Elf lay down his bow and short sword and stood helpless before the raven-haired maiden.

Theandra kept her index finger pointed in the direction of the mesmerized Gray Elf. A single phrase incantation detected that he held no Magick items. He had shown no aggression and had a very pleasant appearance. Her curiosity was raised.

She said coyly, "I will listen to you. You are pleasant to gaze upon. Tell me why you are here."

"I love the forest and the plants and animals that live within her. My people live within the forest and serve her as well. We are curious about the affairs of this area. Many armed warriors gather at the fortress. We pose no threat to anyone. I only want to know you," Areniel answered.

"Can you sing? I enjoy singing," she answered playfully.

Areniel nodded, shrugged, and sang a love ballad in his melodious voice. The gentle breezes and sounds of the forest carried and augmented his words. Theandra did not understand all the lyrics, but she did recognize, "Just one look at you and I'm hypnotized. I'm drowning in your eyes and fascinated by your smile; if I were king of the forest I would still be captivated." The lyrics blended beautifully in the elvish tongue. She allowed him to sing for a few minutes and then raised her hand.

She added. "You sing beautifully. You are very pretty. In many ways, you remind me of my mother's people, the Dark Elves. Your eyes… are different. Such depth… grayness."

Areniel stood quietly. He would have preferred *handsome.*

Theandra walked toward him, stood on tip-toe, and gently kissed his cheek. She cooed, "Thank you for the song. I will be back tomorrow. If you are here, I would love to hear another song." She smiled, turned away, glanced back alluringly, and asked, "What is your name?"

He stuttered. "I … I am Areniel. I am called Areniel Nightshade."

"I am Theandra. Now I must be going. Good-bye, Areniel Nightshade," she added.

The encounters continued daily for two weeks and lasted longer each time. Gentle embraces lasted longer. The couple spent quiet moments in a secluded hideaway used by the Gray Elf scouts. Areniel had found the love of his life.

Tensions grew in the Lachinor. Theandra discovered her Dark Elf Uncle Lexx plotted against the Gray elves. Morlecainen promised Lexx dominion over the western Lachinor, which included the Gray Elf lands. Theandra chose Areniel over her Uncle Lexx, sister Chalar, and father Morlecainen. Theandra created several ruses, feigned her kidnapping by denizens of the Deep South region of the Lachinor, charmed information out of a Hobgoblin named Dark Raider, and clandestinely placed a Locating Spell on Lexx. She reached Areniel and his stalwart Gray Elf friend Merinde and relayed her intelligence, "Your people are in jeopardy. My uncle Lexx plots against you. He gathers a force of three thousand of his people bolstered by over a thousand Hobgoblins and at least fifty Ogres from the Iron Mountains. My sister will accompany him. Although she is young, Chalar is experienced. She is an accomplished sorceress and has neither conscience nor compassion. Cruelty is her strongest suit."

Areniel and Theandra returned to the hideaway. Exhausted Theandra fell asleep. Areniel lay down beside her and inhaled deeply. The air was fragrant near her; he felt her warmth as she slept. He had allowed her to become involved in the conflict. She had chosen *him* over her blood line. Areniel took her to Detlor, the home of Gray Elf elders, for their ceremony of life-long commitment. The ceremony was simple but beautiful. Theandra wore a simple white dress and floral crown; Areniel stood by her. Grey Elf elder Garnett placed their hands together; the couple interlocked their fingers. Garnett symbolically tied a garland of flowers around their joined hands. The Elder sang verses speaking of love and commitment in the native Gray Elf tongue. The entire ceremony lasted about ten minutes and concluded with melodic verses rendered by the Gray Elves. Garnett smiled and wished them well. The uncertainty of the state of affairs in the

Lachinor dampened enthusiasm, but Areniel and Theandra were extremely happy for the moment. The maiden had become a matron. Merinde returned to the hillock overlooking Ylysis to monitor events. Theandra's ruse seemed to have worked. Merinde carried a Locating Stone, which was paired to the artifact Theandra had placed in her Uncle Lexx's armor. The Locating Stone indicated that Lexx was still in the Deep South searching for Theandra.

Areniel's mother Esthra welcomed the union of her son and Theandra. Esthra was a healer and possessed a wealth of knowledge of all things natural. It did not take Esthra long to recognize that Areniel's life-mate was with child. The old Gray Elf matron brought herbs and fruits of the forest to Theandra. Areniel spent much of his time going back and forth between Detlor and Ylysis. The Dark Elf prince Lexx and the Sorcerer of the Lachinor traveled the deep reaches of the swamps searching for Theandra. A year passed and they found no sign of her. Theandra's ruse bought time for the Gray Elves and gave her and Areniel precious time.

In Detlor, Theandra's female child was borne uneventfully. She shared the dark hair of her mother and strong features of her father. She flourished under the guidance of Esthra. Her father Areniel was overjoyed. The baby soon was able to sit up in her nursery. Whenever she laughed, the little girl, who was called Cherilynn, revived wilting flowers in the nursery. Magick had come to the Gray Elves.

War came to the western Lachinor. Lexx and Chalar led a formidable force against the forces of Detlor. Carnage ensued. Both sides suffered heavy losses. Chalar sent many horrific spells against the Gray Elves. Then a Gray Elf archer's arrow found Chalar's leg. The red-haired sorceress fell and dropped the Orb of Dark Knowledge. Areniel Nightshade found himself in position to end Chalar's life. Chalar trembled. Areniel kicked the Orb away from her hand and pressed his short sword tightly against her throat. Over three hundred of his people had fallen to her spells. It was time to end her cruelty. The Gray Elf looked at his fallen brethren, drew back his blade, and started to strike a hard blow. Sunlight reflected from Chalar's necklace… identical to his life-mate and her twin sister Theandra's heirloom… and made the Gray Elf hesitate.

Areniel lowered his blade and said, "I cannot take your life. You share the bloodline of the one that I love dearly. Let's end this bloodletting and make peace. I'll help you stand and take you to our healers; the healers will attend the wound on your leg."

Areniel sheathed his bloody blade, leaned forward, and to reached down to her. He winced and uttered a simple groan. The point of a sword ripped through the front of his chest. Areniel dropped to his knees and silently fell to the ground. Lexx appeared behind the fallen Gray Elf. The Invisibility Spell was spent when he made his surprise attack.

Lexx smugly said, "Arise Chalar. This day is not lost. I left three hundred warriors at the campsite we chose last night with orders to march three hours behind and reinforce us. They will soon arrive. I just killed their Captain. We will crush the remnants of their defenses."

Areniel's friend Merinde was just returning to the fray and witnessed the treachery. He yelled in rage and charged toward Lexx. The Dark Elf prince readied his defense. Chalar had bled heavily from her leg wound. Casting many destructive spells fatigued her. The Orb had left her hand. At the moment, she was helpless.

Though an expert swordsman, Lexx had never faced a foe who had just witnessed the cowardly murder of his truest friend. Merinde fought like the legendary berserkers of the Iron Mountains and scored often. After many melees, the Dark Elf prince fell. Merinde turned toward Chalar. The sorceress had crawled to within arm's reach of her precious Orb.

The Orb's voice appeared in the red-haired sorceress's mind, "The unfailing Word of Return requires no energies of Magick."

Chalar extended her arm to the fullest, touched the Orb of Dark Knowledge, screamed "Sisyly!", and vanished.

Chalar's Return Spell robbed Merinde of his vengeance. The Gray Elf lieutenant had heard Lexx say that three hundred fresh Dark Elves were headed to the field of battle. He gathered the remaining Gray Elves and set up what defenses that he could with seventy archers and four swords.

# 31.

# Theandra's Revenge

Merinde ignored his own fatigue, lifted the body of his fallen friend, and carried Areniel the short distance to his mother Esthra and life-mate Theandra.

Theandra was distraught. She ran from the room and screamed to Merinde, "I have the strength to finish this day's battle."

Merinde ran after her. Theandra reached the hillock overlooking the battlefield. Three hundred Dark Elf reinforcements soon arrived. Theandra drank down the contents of three small phials of liquid. Intense gray auras bathed her with each imbibing. Merinde looked into her eyes, saw only two cold, black, and lifeless spheres, and felt chilled. Theandra reached into a Bag of Holding, obtained red powder, threw it into the air, and growled three phrases. A red cloud developed over the advancing Dark Elves. The poison in the gas immobilized immediately but took hours to kill the victims. Anguished screams rose from the suffering victims. Theandra stood emotionlessly and watched. The three hundred Dark Elves died.

Theandra extended another small bag of holding to Merinde and said, "Give this to my daughter Cherilynn. Note well the staff that lies within. I no longer require it to cast my Magick. Harden her heart, Merinde, I do not want her to feel the hurt that I have felt."

The Bag of Concealment contained many things, was much bigger on the inside, and weighed almost nothing.

Merinde worriedly asked, "Where are you going?"

"I have a date at Ylysis," she said point-blank and began to walk away.

Theandra walked through the night. An unfortunate bearcat heard her footsteps and attacked her. Theandra blasted it into oblivion with a Lightning Bolt Spell. The aching in her heart overshadowed the fatigue in her body. Icy coldness replaced the warmth that had lived in her heart. She reached the Gray Elf hideaway and found it still intact. Areniel's skill kept it undetected, even though foraging Hobgoblins had scoured the swamp. She entered the place where she had shared the best moments of her life with Areniel. The embittered sorceress uttered a simple incantation. A reddish hue developed underneath the plush plant bedding. She reached into the area, removed another little Bag of Concealment, and took spell components from the bottomless bag. She had removed three Bags of Holding from the Room of Sorcery. One was tied to her waist band; one was entrusted to Merinde and Gray Elf Elder Garnett to keep for her daughter Cherilynn; the third was hidden in the hideaway. She had not even revealed to her beloved Areniel that she had left the items of Magick. She removed spell components.

Theandra removed the small black box from the Bag tied to her waistband. She had always kept the box taken from the Room of Sorcery on her person. Theandra had serendipitously discovered the small latch that revealed the box's secret compartment. The mundane latch was simply mechanical and had evaded the eyes of many sorcerers. It yielded its secrets to a hairpin. The hidden compartment had contained seven phials that were filled with liquids of varying colors and consistency. Runes on the bottom of the inner lid of the box identified the contents of the phials. The runes were not evident until the inner lid was removed. Two phials contained "Elixir of the Stars." Drinking the clear effervescing elixir allowed one to use Magick and remain in contact with the physical world while one's essence was in another plane. Physical attacks were not possible. Two phials contained "Elixir of Enhancement." Two held "Elixirs of The Future." The box contained one "Elixir of True Wishing." Theandra had imbibed the contents of one "Elixir of the Stars," "Elixir of Enhancement," and "Elixir of The Future." Her Magick became much more potent. The liquids in the phials had given her the energy to reach the hideaway in just over a day. She had left three identical phials with Merinde. The Elixirs were protected in a Bag of Concealment and to be given to Theandra and Areniel's daughter Cherilynn when she reached maturity. Enhancements bequeathed by the Elixirs of Mastery of Magick passed to progeny. Only one True Wish phial now remained within the little box. The inestimable power of a single unrestricted Wish Spell...Ninth Level Magick... remained at her disposal. Theandra placed the box back into the Bag of Concealment.

Theandra quickened her pace and within an hour was standing within sight of the walls of Ylysis. The wall walk on the outer curtain of the massive fortress teemed with movement. She uttered another brief incantation and conjured up an opaque globe of shimmering spheres. The colors appeared in the order of red, orange, yellow, green, blue, indigo, and violet. The different colors flashed in a repeating pattern every heartbeat. The brilliance of the colors blinded anything in the immediate vicinity of the ten-pace diameter sphere. She moved about within the sphere and commanded it to move forward. She conjured and crushed a small clay shield in her left hand. A large translucent shield appeared and moved two paces in front of her. She began to move forward. The guards upon the wall-walk surrounding Ylysis witnessed the formation of the Shimmering Spheres. The colors were beautiful but unnerving at the same time. The general appearance was that of a rainbow rolling toward the castle. Ogres used trebuchets to hurl flame rocks against the spheres. The Magick shell deflected the fire rocks. Archers fired longbows. The arrows penetrated the nebulous spheres but the translucent shield stopped the projectiles. From Ylysis's allure two robed figures rained more than two score spells upon Theandra's spheres and only minimally weakened them. Theandra counterattacked and sent torrents of Fire Magick against the defenders. Ogres fell screaming from the allure. Trebuchets burst into flame. Secondary explosions ripped the enceinte of Ylysis as fire rock exploded. The taller robed figure left the wall walk. The sorcerer of shorter stature persisted with three more spells, and then disappeared.

Theandra moved forward. A single figure walked toward her. Her father Morlecainen approached and carried his treasured flaming blade. Deep red flames erupted from the long sword's blade. The young sorceress advanced toward the castle. The sorcerers stopped ten paces apart. The Shimmering Spheres steadily shifted.

Morlecainen spoke first, "This is a battle that you cannot win. Many defensive spells are cast within the castle. I am aware of the Banishment Spell that Chalar cast upon you. If you step upon a Teleport Spell hidden by Conceal Magick, you will be carried into the Room of Sorcery and immediately destroyed by Death Magick. Your wall of colored spheres will not protect you. Although the Shimmering Shield cannot save you, I am impressed by your use of the spell. I have read of it, but I have never been able to master it. You must have found the ability to Enhance your Magick. I would pay dearly for that."

Theandra answered, "You had the ability for years. You are too quick to overlook the simple. I have no more of the Elixir."

She lied. There was another phial within the Bag of Concealment left with Merinde for the infant Cherilynn.

Morlecainen said, "Theandra, our family has suffered greatly. Let's not prolong the suffering further. There is another world for you to explore. You can dominate it easily. I will give you a lion's share of the bounty from the black dragon Xollos. Will you consider my offer?"

Theandra asked, "My dearest father, your compassion touches me. My loving family! Were you and Chalar not just trying to destroy me with torrents of Magick from the castle wall? Why should I ever trust you now?"

Morlecainen answered, "I thought you were coming to harm your mother or me. I didn't know the depth and breadth of the rift between you and Chalar. The rift also grows between your sister and me. I know she threatened you and understand your silence about her betrayal. Chalar violated my confidence and disrupted my work. Theandra, dreams trouble your sister and flaw her reasoning. Let's reconcile our differences."

The dark-haired sorceress answered, "The name Theandra means nothing to me. I will be called by another name. The Gray Elves' phrase 'anectrus phineas' means 'harbinger of death.' Anectrophinea is now my name. I am empowered by longevity, enhancement, true seeing, and foresight. Much of what you say is true. Chalar has had time to cast many traps within the Inner Ward. I must bring death to my sister. Will you reveal her location within the castle?"

The Sorcerer of the Lachinor said, "You cannot defeat her. There are too many traps within the castle. She has great assistance from Dark Sorcery. You cannot defeat me. The Sword of Flames brought down the Black Dragon Lord Xollos. You have seen its powers when I fought the Dwarves. I carry the sword and cannot assist you in your conflict with Chalar. I can assist your transition to the World of the Three Suns. I implore you to stand down."

Theandra asked, “If everything that you say is true, why cannot you assist me against her evil?”

“If you will trust me enough to extend you forearm through the walls of the Shimmering Sphere, I will show you,” Morlecainen requested. “I’m not asking you to leave the sanctuary of the sphere and risk Magick attack. If I had desired, I could have entered the sphere before now. The sword protects me from harm. Shimmering Spheres does not create a physical barrier. It deflected the Magick fire rocks but not the Ogres’ arrows. Those Ogres were very hard to recruit. I’ll have to go to The Iron Mountains, one of my least favorite places in this world, to replace my great hairy servants.”

The power of the Elixirs told her he was speaking the truth. She gingerly extended her left forearm through the sphere. Morlecainen slowly moved the sword toward her, touched the smooth skin of her forearm, and scratched her. Theandra felt no pain and the weapon did not draw blood. The shallow scratch quickly healed.

Morlecainen said, “The same thing will happen if I attack Chalar with this weapon. It will not harm members of my family. It’s an unwonted effect and quirk of Magick! I don’t know how the Magick is given to the blade. It was not made by those of this world.”

Theandra was silent. Morlecainen extended a small bag toward her. The Bag of Concealment was brimming with treasures from Xollos and her most treasured possessions.

“How many of these bags do you have?” she asked.

“Enough,” he replied.

Theandra sighed and replied, “I know that I cannot defeat her at this time. I foresee this. There are too many traps within the castle. I know that you cast spells from the wall. If you knew of the existence of the Shimmering Spheres Spell, then you likely knew the sequence of spells that could disable it. Yet you did not cast them. I believe your words and accept your offer. There will hopefully be a time that I can return and gain revenge against the red-haired evil.”

Theandra accepted the Bag of Concealment. She said,” Sisyly,” triggered the Word of Recall Spell that Morlecainen had taught her, and vanished.

# 32.

## Drelves in Donothor

Drelvish Rangers discovered Morlecainen's treachery. Phyrris and Aergin lay dead and the blade was missing. The Council of Alms Glen declared a time of mourning. Rangers watched the portal constantly. Angry voices called for revenge and the weapon's return. Ramish demanded vengeance. Calmer heads realized powerful Magick had struck down mighty Phyrris and Aergin. The Drelves had no counter to such power. Agrarian, the Teacher, and Elder Dilan feared the sorcerer's return and advised taking all possible defensive measures. Rangers on duty employed all weapons Phyrris had created. Lookouts used "toot-and-see-scrolls" to survey the area. Archers kept self-bows trained on the portal. The just-ended Approximation of Andreas had not resulted in the birth of a Spellweaver. Unbeknownst to the Drelves, Morlecainen had his hands full with first the Dwarves and then the vengeful Black Dragonlord Xollos.

When Phyrris failed to show up at the mountainside cabin, Kirrie and Jodie came to the Old Orange Spruce. The Teacher summoned Agrarian, and the old Spellweaver had the solemn duty of telling them about Phyrris and Aergin's murders. Jodie wailed inconsolably. Kirrie angered, ran to the portal, and sent torrents of Fire Magick into the shimmering rectangle. Agrarian reassured the Rangers guarding the meadow's edge and monitoring the portal. In Green Vale, the ancient Tree Shepherd muttered, "Fire Wizard." In Donothor, powerful Roscoe, Knarra, and Morlecainen felt nothing. The Dreamraider Amica appeared in a flash of redness. Amica inspected the portal and uttered several spells. She said, "Wait for me to return. There's nothing for it" and stepped into the gate. Protection from Magick and Globe of Invulnerability Spells protected her.

The Good Witch returned in a while and confided to the others, "The sorcerer hides his location. Aberrant Magick created the portal. Unwonted Magick. Unwanted Magick. The gate is an unwonted effect or quirk of Magick and difficult to predict. Jodie and Kirrie, I advise you avoid the Gate. Powerful Magick struck down mighty Phyrris and Aergin. Don't move against the sorcerer without extensive study and precaution. Phyrris will be avenged. Now is not the time."

Kirrie and Jodie clandestinely supported the defenses of Alms Glen and helped Agrarian with studying the Spellbooks. Jodie used the Elemental Stones, Enhancing Stone, and Bleeding Stone to facilitate their work. The forge's utility died with Phyrris. Ten seasons of the harvest passed and the sorcerer did not return. The old Spellweaver Agrarian lacked aptitude for Fire Magick. Jodie and Kirrie helped Agrarian with the Spellbooks. Ramish was a more willing student. The sorceresses managed to augment his meager skills. Then Kirrie and Jodie were called away to another place.

The Teacher and Agrarian had to take breaks and lead harvest trips to Meadowsweet and Green Vale. Over time Agrarian strengthened his defensive skills. Time did not quell Ramish's thirst for vengeance for Phyrris, Purya, and Aergin. Many leaders called for retrieval of the blade. Agrarian also deeply longed for the return of Phyrris's definitive work. Long ago the Mender Fisher presented the Drelves with 'the Keotum Stone' and revealed it protected from Magick. The lone surviving Spellweaver Agrarian did not know whether the artifact's protection extended to those passing through the gate. Agrarian, Magrian, and the Teacher Shayne persistently advised against attempting retrieval of the weapon. Agrarian labored at the tomes of his forefathers, studying the spell books of Gaelyss and Xenn. His apprentice Ramish made up for his lack of talent with enthusiasm. Scholarly Magrian read and reread incantations to Agrarian.

Agrarian slowly came around to Ramish's thinking. Drolls and Kiennites were more brazenly entering the forests, and the Draiths were sending more scouts from Ooranth. Andreas faded to a gray spot in the sky. Elderly Agrarian bore the weight of responsibility. Each dark period made his people more vulnerable. Ramish and Magrian did what they could to lighten his load.

Most of Agrarian's skills were in defensive Magick. The old Spellweaver found casting spells of destruction difficult. He had great knowledge of the Xennic Stones and gemstones. With Kirrie, Jodie, Ramish, and Magrian's help, Agrarian finally had labored and mastered the protective Magick required to traverse the gate to the other world. Phyrris had used Locating Stones and created a perfect means of tracing the blade. Locating Stones were Xennic gemstones. Phyrris placed three in the Draithsbane and distributed their mates to Agrarian, Aergin, and himself. Agrarian's locating stone rested in his raiment. Its mate rested within the great weapon. Phyrris and Aergin had carried their locating stones the baneful night when the blade and their lives were taken. Agrarian returned those stones to the chest that Phyrris used to store Xennic Gemstones. Agrarian now retrieved the stones and entrusted them to Magrian and Ramish. Agrarian crushed a soft opaque Xennic Stone and created an unguent that would allow them safe passage through the gate. Agrarian met at length with the council. Conservative voices pointed out that the sorcerer had not returned in ten years. Others pointed to the increased aggression by Drolls, Kiennites, and Draiths, and pressed for the return of the Draithsbane as a means of bolstering defense. After extensive preparation, Magrian chose his team. He would be accompanied by Magrian and Ramish and a skilled archer named Prosca. The four Drelves cautiously approached the gate. Draith patrols were increasingly frequent in the area. The Masters, as they liked to call themselves, were becoming more blatant. The Draiths had inspected the shimmering rectangular portal but had not understood its significance. Several had died while trying to enter the portal. The quartet reached the gate without incident, and Agrarian applied the greasy ointment to their skins. The balm had a pleasant aroma. The Drelves noted that minor injuries healed when the old Spellweaver applied the balm.

"This is an unexpected but welcomed effect," Agrarian mused. "The Keotum Stone serves us well." They successfully passed through the portal. The discomfort was tolerable. The Drelves were startled when they reached the other side. None of them had ever experienced the darkness of night.

Agrarian, Ramish, Magrian, and Prosca employed everything at their disposal to get around in the strange new world. Darkness fell regularly and left them no alternative but to camp. Hungry beasts roamed the green forests. Every animal in the sorcerer's world evidently preferred

Drelve as a meal over anything else. Their locating stones gave them a general direction for the blade, but intense Magick in the south made pinpointing the weapon difficult. Truth be known… Morlecainen carried the blade on his ten-year quest to find and defeat Xollos and regain Alluna. The Sorcerer of the Lachinor via the Room of Wizardry possessed great means of distorting Magick. The Drelves did quite a bit of wandering and brought to mind the old adage, "most of those who wander are lost." The quartet discovered the sorcerer's worlds changing seasons. Winter was quite difficult. For two weeks, they had followed a group of Dwarves hoping they'd lead them to their goal. The Dwarves stopped for the night at a tavern called the Halfway Inn. The four Drelves constructed a campsite overlooking the riverside inn. Agrarian produced enhancing root tubers and trail mix from one of the many pockets in his robe. Young Magrian brought spring water and brewed herbal tea. The four munched and exchanged stories. Most of the time the experienced Spellweaver Agrarian dominated the conversation. The younger Drelves relished his many tales. Ramish described vivid dreams and alleged a red-haired sorceress visited him. Many Drelves had experienced disruptive dreams, but the half-Drelve actually anticipated the dreamy visits. Prosca volunteered to take the first watch. Ramish quickly fell asleep and hoped for another visit from the vixen. Agrarian and Magrian huddled by the fire and remained awake.

Agrarian spoke, "I have seen the Approximation of the Gray Wanderer twenty-three times in my long life. The Approximation has no fixed interval. On average, Drelves witness the Approximation twice in their lifespan. I have seen many seasons. There has never been a time of greater need for our people. I have found no other with the commitment that you demonstrate, Magrian. Your youth and vigor are refreshing. I offer you one of my greatest treasures. Generations ago, I drank this elixir."

The old Spellweaver removed a small phial from his tattered inner raiment. The phial contained a silver mercurial liquid. Its consistency was that of the sap of the everred tree during the coolness of the dark period.

Agrarian continued, "This is the last phial of the Elixir of Longevity. It was created by great Sorcerers of another age. We have labored, used the Enhancing Stone, Bleeding Stone, four Elemental Stones, and all combinations of Xennic Gemstones, but we have been unable to duplicate the formula. I have already tasted its Magick. It can do no more for me.

I want you to drink the contents of the phial. You must survive this adventure, return to our people, and teach them of their past and the realm of the forests. You will become the Teacher of our people and survive long beyond your expected lifespan."

Magrian accepted the phial and turned it up to his lips. The thick, bitter liquid shared the aroma of old shoes. The elixir left no aftertaste. Magrian felt a sensation of warmth and burst of energy; however, his appearance did not change.

Agrarian then said, "I also want you to take my robe. Drelvedom's future will fall on your shoulders, should you return. I am very old."

Magrian resisted, but the old Spellweaver insisted. Agrarian passed the Robe of Sagain to Magrian. The robe adjusted to fit him perfectly, and its color changed to match Donothor's green forests. Agrarian smiled, leaned backward onto his blanket, and soon slept. Magrian's mind raced and sleep evaded him. The young Drelve relieved Prosca and allowed the others to sleep through the night. Magrian awakened the others when he saw the party they were following preparing to leave the Halfway Inn.

# 33.

## Gift of the Death Arrow

The red-haired sorceress Chalar clandestinely communicated with her father's treasured Orb of Dark Knowledge. The Orb oft invaded her dreams and fomented plans. She sliced her finger with an ornamental dagger and allowed her blood to drip onto the Orb's surface. She groaned, "It's much less painful for you to enter my dreams."

The artifact sent the message, "You pay a small price. I'm your true ally and friend. Your father cares little for either of us now that he has the Fire Blade."

Chalar face reddened. She responded to the Orb's prodding, "I understand. My compassion for him ended long ago. He slobbers after my sister Theandra, his fairy princess. However, I have seen my father in battle. He heals more quickly than wounds can be created. I have seen him walk through spells of fire, ice, and lightning. Since he obtained the great blade, ancient Dragons fall before him. I have poured over the tomes in the Room of Sorcery, but I can find no spell to overcome the power of the sword. He ignores *you*!"

The voice replied, "He seldom carries me and gives me his blood. There is a way. The same way that he acquired the blade. There can only be one attempt. There is but one Arrow of Clysis. There are those who seek the blade and hate your father for his prior deeds. We can let them serve us."

Chalar responded, "I am aware of them. I sensed their passing through the gate. Passing through the portal sends an unmistakable wave across the sea of Magick. They have wandered the north lands aimlessly and are not getting any closer to the blade. They cast weak Magick which barely creates a ripple, let alone a wave, upon the sea of Magick. Some who wander are hopeless. My father has cast so many spells to disguise his location that even a blood cat would have difficulty finding him."

The Orb's voice asked, "There are no blood cats in this world. How do you know of the legendary beasts that tracked the lawless on Sagain?"

Chalar said, "I have read everything in the Room of Sorcery. I have read more than my father. The tomes speak of the great cats. I would have enjoyed one as a pet."

The voice followed, "Hunters allowed blood cats to eat the heart of harvested victims. The beasts became too vicious to roam among the population, and they were destroyed. A blood cat was not a very good pet."

Chalar muttered, "I'm in no mood for a bestiary lesson. I will cast a Beaconing Spell upon the castle or send a Thought Spell to the spellcaster among them. He will feel overwhelmingly intelligent. I will guard their way to Ylysis. Their simple illusions will not keep them alive."

The Orb responded, "Your father will detect the Beaconing Spell. The Thought Spell is a better choice. If they reach Ylysis, they can serve our needs."

Chalar rambled, "I don't have full knowledge of my father's travels. I mainly know what you've told me, but I have seen the native world of these beings. They traversed the portal. They hate my father and seek the blade. I suspect that my father attained the blade through some devious act in their world. I don't know how to defeat my father and hope to learn from my adventure with my Uncle Lexx. Being away from Ylysis will benefit me."

The voice said comfortably, "You will have to obtain the Death Arrow. It rests within his chest in his bedchamber and is guarded by glyphs. I'll tell you the sequence of phrases that will disarm the glyphs. He checks the chest every night. You must wait until the moment is right. Mastery of this world awaits you."

Chalar placed the Orb into a Bag of Concealment that she had taken from the Room of Sorcery. She reclined and futilely tried to sleep. She welcomed the morning light, dressed, picked up her bag, and went to the dining area. Her mother greeted her.

Her Dark Elf Mother Alluna said, "Your Uncle Lexx awaits you. You are following your father's footsteps. Have you learned anything of your sister? She took my betrothal dress from my chamber and I would like to see it returned. If you must follow your uncle please be careful."

Chalar gave her mother a courteous hug. She left the inner ward and walked into the quadrangle. She found Lexx and her father in the enceinte, the enclosed area of Ylysis. Morlecainen gave her a small sack. The sack was brown and was made of a shiny material. The sorcerer of the Lachinor said, "It contains extra ingredients for your spells. You can't have too much material spell components. Please stay close to Lexx and the First Guards."

The First Guards were longest serving and most loyal Dark Elves. Their primary mission was protecting Lexx and Morlecainen. Chalar accepted the items and gave her father a tentative hug.

The sorceress concentrated and cast the Thought Spell. Her thoughts touched Ramish's mind. Ramish was dreaming when the red-haired vixen appeared to him.

"I know what you seek," she said tauntingly.

"How can you know?" he asked.

"It's Magick," she answered.

"Where is the Draithsbane?" Ramish asked.

"The weapon lies in the great swamp. You can find the sword and your vengeance at a place called Ylysis," she answered. She gave Ramish detailed directions to Ylysis.

Ramish awakened his companions and said confidently, "The blade rests in a large castle to the south in the great swamps. I know the directions."

Agrarian asked, "How do you know this?"

"I don't know. I think it's Magick," Ramish confided.

"That is as good an answer as any. We have roamed this world aimlessly for what its citizens call a year. The Locating Spell has not been effective. We have no leads. Let's follow your lead," Agrarian said.

"Why are you following Ramish's suggestion?" Prosca asked.

"I don't have any other ideas right now," Agrarian said honestly.

The red-haired sorceress Chalar gained knowledge of her father's lone remaining Arrow of Clysis. While the sorcerer was occupied with a disturbance outside the castle, Chalar slipped into Morlecainen's chamber, placed a Forget Spell on her mother Alluna, followed the instructions of the Orb, disarmed the warding glyphs on Morlecainen's chest, and usurped the deadly arrow. The sorceress carefully avoided the black fletching.

Agrarian, Prosca, Magrian, and Ramish followed the course given Ramish and traveled through the swamps. Ramish's directions were accurate. The Drelves reached the large fortress in the swamp. Great confusion surrounded the castle. The defenders had endured a great battle. The doors were ajar. Agrarian placed Invisibility Spells on the foursome and they made their way into the castle. The Old Spellweaver told them to keep an invisible hand on the shoulder of the Drelve in front of him and maintain silence. They assumed an order of Agrarian, Ramish, Magrian, and Prosca. Within the castle, the foursome made very slow progress. Agrarian detected Magick at each footstep. Teleportation traps, Magick Mouths, and Warding Glyphs threatened every step. Agrarian led them at a snail's pace. Footsteps approached. Agrarian stopped them. An attractive red-haired maiden approached the archer Prosca, carefully extended a dark arrow with a black fletching, and gave him the arrow.

"How can you see me?" the startled Drelve asked.

"Simpleton, I can detect invisible creatures with the wave of my hand. Who do you think guided you here?" Chalar said condescendingly. She had always known the four Drelves' location.

Ramish said, "The woman from my dreams!"

Agrarian asked, "You speak our tongue perfectly. How do you do this? Why do you lead us here?"

She sorceress answered, "We seek the same end, the destruction of the sorcerer. You are a means to that end. Place this within your bow and find the source of your agony within the great hallway of the castle. Do not touch the fletching." she added.

Prosca said, "How do you know I won't shoot you?"

Chalar glared in his direction. "I didn't kill your Spellweavers. You have one chance for vengeance. Take it!" she demanded.

Agrarian led them away from her and into the foyer. The Sorcerer of the Lachinor approached. Morlecainen drew the Blade of Phyrris. Flames crackled from the blade.

"I can see you, vile creatures. I have enough wrath left to destroy you. I'll finish what I started eleven years ago. Come to your doom," he snarled.

Prosca filled his bow with the Arrow of Clysis. From the distance, it looked like any other arrow.

"You cannot harm me fool," the sorcerer taunted. Morlecainen grasped the blade with his right hand. With his left hand, he directed a Death Spell toward Agrarian. Mauve lights left the outstretched fingers of the sorcerer and struck the old Drelve in the chest. Agrarian fell and breathed his last. The four Spellweavers of the Drelves were lost.

The reliable archer Prosca aimed and released the Arrow of Clysis. Morlecainen shuddered as the arrow ripped into his chest. The Sorcerer of the Lachinor clutched the hilt of the Blade of Phyrris… to no avail. Morlecainen's robe of Sagain defended Death Magick, but the lethality of the Arrow of Clysis derived from its deadly Tucson fletching. The Blade of Phyrris healed wounds but afforded no defense against deadly arrow. Morlecainen fell and breathed his last. The Blade of Phyrris clanked loudly to the floor of the hallway. His staff fell from his back to the floor. Ramish grabbed the blade. Flames ripped the length of the artifact. Small scratches and abrasions of Ramish's arms and legs healed. Magrian directed Ramish to place the hilt of the sword in Agrarian's hand. There was no response. Agrarian was dead. They could do nothing or him. Prosca started toward the staff of the sorcerer, but Magrian warned against the action. He feared enchantment of the device. Ramish cast an Incendiary Spell which rapidly consumed Agrarian's body. Magrian, Prosca, and Ramish fled with the Draithsbane, the Blade of Phyrris.

Chalar entered the foyer. Her father's lifeless body was laying on the floor.

"I am the Sorceress of the Lachinor," she uttered confidently.

"You have many enemies approaching," the Orb's familiar voice informed her.

In a great battle, Mage Roscoe, Priestess Knarra, Gray Elf Merinde, and their allies vanquished Chalar and used three Staves of Sagain to destroy the Orb of Dark Knowledge. Destroying the Orb freed its prisoner.

Magrian, Prosca, and Ramish hurriedly traversed the swamp. Ramish smote several swamp denizens with the Sword of Phyrris, which the Drelves called the Draithsbane. The trio made the River Luumic and fashioned makeshift rafts from abandoned corkwood. They crossed the river at dusk and made their way to the fringes of the Misty Forest, which was the most direct route back to the Gate between the worlds. The Drelves made camp. Prosca fell asleep.

Magrian looked at Ramish and asked, "How are we to tell our people that Agrarian fell? All the Spellweavers have fallen!"

"We return to them with a greater defense than they ever had. I am here now. I have the Draithsbane," Ramish answered confidently.

The young half-Drelve fell asleep immediately and did not hear Prosca's garbled sounds as shapechangers garroted him. One of the amorphous beings next ripped Ramish's throat, but the Drelve slept with his hand gripping the Draithsbane. The grievous wound healed as rapidly as it was created. Ramish quickly swung the sword and hewed the amorphous beast. Magrian cowered near the fire. Ramish quickly destroyed the remaining seven shapechangers.

"You *are* the greatest Drelve warrior of all time," Magrian said in awe.

The two Drelves did not sleep further. Ramish cast an Incendiary Spell upon the Prosca's remains and the vile shapechangers. The treacherous Misty Forest of Donothor posed no further lethal threats to the two travelers, and they reached the portal gate. The Gate was not evident to the naked eye, but Ramish knew well its elevated location and used Levitate Spells to get them to the portal's level. Magrian wore Agrarian's robe and Ramish carried the Draithsbane as they passed through the gate. Ramish and Magrian passed through, endured some pain, and welcomed the amber light. The Gray Wanderer Andreas was a gray speck low in the horizon. They sped across the meadow and found the security of the forest that they loved. Prosca did not live to see the adoration given to the Blade of Phyrris's returners, but campfire songs praised him as the "Wizard's Bane."

# 34.

## Theandra in Parallan

Theandra arrived in the World of the Three Suns moments before Magrian, Prosca, Ramish, and Agrarian reached Ylysis. The dark-haired sorceress uttered the reversal of the Return to Ylysis Spell and instantly stood before the gate between Donothor and Parallan. Her father Morlecainen had fomented foul deeds against the forest people to obtain the weapon he treasured and placed above treasures from his native Sagain and his family. Theandra's enhanced True Seeing spell penetrated the Sorcerer of the Lachinor's mind and analyzed his thoughts. The Blade of Phyrris made him feel invincible. She peered into Morlecainen's inner thoughts and learned the full extent of his treachery against the people of the new world as they talked near the battered outer curtain of Ylysis. Power motivated the Sorcerer of the Lachinor. True… the sorcerer had searched far and wide throughout the Lachinor for her mother Alluna. But was defending his self-image the greater reason? Black Dragonlord Xollos had entered Ylysis and stolen from Morlecainen. Morlecainen's union with Alluna solidified his alliance with the Dark Elves and secured resources to reach his goals. He had sacrificed his most loyal servant, the ogre Fange, to further his goals. Theandra felt no true love from her father and gave none in return. She had become his rival. His greatest concern was taking her out of the equation whilst he struggled with Chalar and the Dwarves' alliance. Sending her to the World of the Three Suns got her out of the picture and likely put her out of the frying pan and into the fire. Morlecainen's deeds created a hostile environment for anyone traversing the gate into the odd red and yellow world. Extra precautions were necessary. Oft when Theandra cast spells, words appeared in her thoughts.

*"I give you my blood through which you will receive all you seek. You in turn give to me your all."*

Ǿ ∞ Ǿ

Theandra said, "When I pass through the gate, I am no longer Theandra. I am Anectrophinea."

She cast Invisibility upon her person and faded from view. She cast a Protection from Magick Spell. The Dark-haired sorceress then cast a Rope Spell and ascended the fiery rope that appeared. She stepped through the gate and stood in the amber light of the World of the Three Suns, where the shiny gate stood at ground level. The sorceress learned a bit of the new world's geography and peoples from her probing Morlecainen's thoughts. The Drelves lived mainly in the central forests. Great red, yellow, and orange trees stood to her right. Thick underbrush made passing between the trees nigh impossible. To her left the left the flora was less dense. Small animals scurried about the wide red-grass covered meadow. Tall mountains beckoned in the distance in three directions. Toward the Drelves' forest only the isolated peak Mirror Mountain rose into the amber sky. The little yellow sun danced high in the sky and the large unmoving dark sun kept its steady position. The third sun… she didn't see it. Theandra walked invisibly across the wide meadow and approached a road leading to the north. She detected activity to her right, turned, and noted a contingent of Drelves exiting the forest and approaching the shimmering gate. Curiosity compelled her to investigate. The Drelves neared the shimmering gate. Theandra quietly listened a few paces from them.

Sergeant Major Seilvre led the party to the cursed gate. The newly promoted veteran carried in his left hand a well-made sword that emitted a green glow. Veteran Ranger Lignis, Elder Dilan, Elder Tyler, Elder Carin, and a score of heavily armed Rangers stood about twenty paces from the portal. Elders Tyler and Carin were Ramish's adoptive parents. Lignis carried a bow with a nocked arrow at ready. Elder Tyler and Elder Carin carried wands in their left hands. Tyler was the Spellweaver Agrarian's great, great nephew, and Carin was Tyler's life-mate. In the absence of the

Spellweaver and his apprentices, the Elders had assumed more active roles in Drelvedom's affairs. The elderly Teacher spent most of his time in the Old Orange Spruce. Already one harvest had passed since Agrarian's group passed through the gate. Rangers constantly watched the portal. Every other period the Drelves performed the current ritual. Suddenly Seilvre stopped, turned his head around to face Theandra's position, and sniffed the air. Theandra quickly squeezed a lavender berry and filled the air with its fragrance. She remained invisible. Crushing a lavender berry did not constitute an offensive action… unless one was a lavender berry.

Elder Tyler asked, "Seilvre, what is wrong?"

Seilvre said, "I thought I detected an odor… I thought I smelled… no… it's nothing. I get edgy when I get near the gate."

Elder Carin said, "Understandably! I long to see Spellweaver Agrarian, my adoptive son Ramish, Magrian, and Prosca return through the portal. With or without the weapon…"

Elder Dilan said, "I understand your angst, Elder Carin, but Agrarian, Ramish, Magrian, and Prosca chose this course of action. They knew the risks. We must maintain our hope for their success in regaining Phyrris's blade. Now we must get on with the task. This is close enough, Seilvre."

Seilvre said, "Proceed, Elder Tyler. Our scouts saw a Draith patrol near the old Kiennish fort site north of the meadow two periods ago. Let's not tarry."

Elder Tyler extended the rune-covered wand in his left hand and said, "Always, we must thank Phyrris for his gifts of these artifacts. Also, we must remember young Purya who carried this device." Tyler muttered an old Drelvish phrase. A mauve ray left the end of the wand and passed into the shimmering gate. The portal did not react.

Young Ranger Landry asked, "Why use the wand? Why not fire an arrow into the light?"

Elder Dilan said, "Purya's wand sends a Magick Missile into the aberration. Magick to Magick! Agrarian advised against sending anything of our physical world into the portal. The point of the exercise is to disrupt any monitoring from the other side. Quite honestly… we don't know whether it does any good."

Sergeant Major Seilvre added, "Besides, arrows are finite resources. Our bowyers and fletchers spend long hours creating them. Agrarian asked us to perform this ritual. I just hope we don't hit him… or one of the others."

Elder Carin then pointed her wand toward the gate and sent a ray of white heat into the gate. The shimmering portal did not react. She commented, "Ironically, the sorcerer Morlecainen helped turn the tide in the fight with Kiennites when this wand was recovered. It was taken from us earlier. I honor Aergin every time I use it."

Seilvre said, "I understand the sword and bow. I'll continue to follow Spellweaver Agrarian's directions. Now I suggest we return to the safety of the forest. I… I still feel we are being watched."

The Drelves sang a brief lament honoring Phyrris, Purya, and Aergin. Then Elder Carin threw a three-leaf red clover into the gate. The gate sizzled. Young Landry asked, "Why'd you throw in the clover, Elder Carin?'

Carin smiled and said, "Just sending luck to Ramish, Agrarian, Magrian, and Prosca."

The Drelves turned and walked back toward the forest. Theandra followed at a distance. Seilvre reached the edge of the forest. Two orange rambling bramble bushes separated their interlocked thorny branches, uprooted, and opened a path. Other plants separated behind them. Many Wall of Thorns Spells reinforced the natural flora around the big trees.

Seilvre waited for the others to enter. He asked Elder Tyler for Purya's wand. Seilvre turned quickly and rapidly sent Magick Missiles from the wand across the open meadow. Theandra dove to the ground. One of the Magick Missiles grazed her left thigh. The sorceress grasped the invisible wound with her hand, muttered a command under her breath, and closed the wound with a Healing Spell. The self-administered Healing Spell did not violate her invisibility. She crawled on her knees for a bit, then stood and ran toward the road to the north. Seilvre shrugged his shoulders and gave the wand back to Elder Tyler. The veteran Drelve walked out onto the meadow and found a few drops of Theandra's blood on the grass.

Seilvre said, "I heard footsteps behind us. Someone was watching and following us. I sent the missiles toward the sound. Someone learned a lesson about Drelves' hearing."

Theandra's thigh throbbed. She muttered, "I should have killed all of them!"

She didn't see the hundred archers stationed in the trees. Once she reached the perimeter of the meadow, Theandra cleared a small area, removed *invisibility*, and attended her leg. Visualizing the wound made attending it easier. An enhanced healing spell mended the wound. Words appeared in her mind,

*"I give you my blood through which you will receive all you seek. You in turn give to me your all."*

Ǿ ∞ Ǿ

The sorceress had barely completed the healing spell when her keen hearing detected gruff voices. A group of bronze-skinned, unarmed seven-foot tall muscular blokes moved stealthily through the woods. She used her childhood spell "Tree" and transformed to a sturdy sapling. At the last moment, she remembered to present red foliage. One of the Draiths sniffed around her and went so far as to touch her "bark." The spell wasn't illusory. Theandra was a tree!

The Draith muttered, "We've passed this way many times. I don't recall this tree. It could be Kiennish or Drelvish tomfoolery!" The powerful warrior drew back his strong hand and struck "Tree-andra" with an open-handed blow. The force of the blow shook her foundation and fomented horrific pain. She struggled to maintain the spell.

Another Draith said, "I hope you didn't hurt your hand, Dontax. It's what you get for thinking you know every tree in the forest!" Three other Draiths laughed.

Dontax growled, "Go on and laugh a******! If I'd been right, when we turned our backs, we'd be scorched by Magick." The incredibly handsome warriors moved on after a time and moved toward the meadow.

Theandra caught her breath, fought back tears, and scorched the five Draiths with an enhanced Fire Spell. The Draiths held on much longer than Dark Elves. Dontax crawled most of the way back to her and died at her feet. Words appeared in her thoughts,

*"I give you my blood through which you will receive all you seek. You in turn give to me your all."*

Ǿ ∞ Ǿ

In Green Vale, the ancient Tree Shepherd muttered, "Fire Wizard."

Shouts rang out from the meadow. A large party of Drelves ran toward the site of the spell.

Theandra said stoically, "There's plenty more for you."

She conjured and sent a ray of fire toward the Drelves. Fortunately, Seilvre carried the Keotum Stone and Lignis held the Xennic (Enhancing) Stone. Theandra's spell enveloped the Drelves. The forest folks suffered non-lethal burns. Seilvre organized a rapid retreat into the forest. Seilvre brought Alms Glen's defenses to high alert. Dilan, Tyler, and Carin feared the tall wizard Morlecainen's return. Theandra studied the Drelves' forest. Odd Magick kept her prying mind at bay. From what she'd gathered from Morlecainen and seen in the meadow, the sorceress felt little more to gain by remaining in the propinquity of Alms Glen. Morlecainen yielded information about other peoples and places. Theandra disdained invisibility and walked up the middle of the road. A wailer charged out of the woods toward her and screamed. Theandra screamed louder and sent the beast running back toward the forest. She killed it with a Magick Missile before it reached safety. Further up the road, a noir skat peaked around a red oak. Theandra smote the shy beast with another Magick Missile. She camped neared the gap in the Peaks of Division. Her Bag of Holding contained ample supplies. The land never grew dark… the sky became less yellow every eight hours. Eight hours later it grew bright again. Lack of darkness made sleeping a challenge. Morlecainen revealed every sixty cycles of the little yellow sun the land entered 15 cycles of darker light… but never darkness. The sorceress returned to the road and headed toward the mountains. She reached the River Ornash. Ruins of an ancient destroyed Kiennish outpost littered the field. Crude outriggers and hollowed out giant yellow bamboo logs served as transportation for Drolls and Kiennites. Legends of a dark equine river spirit reduced river crossings in less than large groups. A small bridge again spanned the river. Theandra crossed the river. A group of figures approached her. She made no effort to leave the road. Seven seven-foot-tall wolf-faced warriors and a gangly goblin-like bloke with carroty-orange skin approached. The Drolls were actually rather handsome. The smaller creature barked commands. The Drolls circled Theandra, who continued to walk forward until she bumped into the largest Droll.

The Kiennite said, "What is this? Who are you?"

Theandra scoffed.

The largest Droll said, "She's not Drelvish. Perhaps an ally of Ooranth?"

The Kiennite drew a short sword, pushed it against Theandra's chest, and said, "Unlikely. Why'd she be here alone? If she is alone? Check the trees!"

The Drolls quickly rummaged through the bushes, sniffed the air, and howled. The largest reported, "She's alone, Henery. What do we do with her? There are Draiths in the area, least you forget."

The Kiennite Henery said, "Let's get her off the road, Uthgar. I want to interrogate her."

Theandra went along. The biggest Droll Uthgar grabbed her arm and dragged her into the brush. Henery said, "Start talking, sweetheart. I don't have a lot of time. Who are you and why are you traipsing along my road?"

Theandra laughed and said, "Your road! You scrawny a******! What gives you the right?"

Henery said, "Watch your tongue, ******! You are addressing warren leader Henery the Eighty-eighth. Uthgar leads the Korcran clan of Drolls. You are on borrowed time. Start talking!"

Theandra said, "Why should I want to talk to you? Who is your leader?"

Henery the 88th fumed, "I am the most powerful warren leader since the time of General Saligia and Delano. My warren seized power over Aulgmoor when old Saligia died… a long time ago. Even the Draiths fear my name."

Theandra pulled a strand of her dark hair nonchalantly and said, "I doubt it."

Henery said, "You insolent b****!" I should have Uthgar rip off your head and s*** down your neck!"

Uthgar nervously looked around and said, "I'm ready to do it, boss. Let's be rid of her and get going."

Henery said, "Not so fast, Uthgar. We haven't seen hide nor hair of those Draiths. Granted, this **** is not a looker like the Belles of Thabell, the prettiest ladies of all Kiennitedom. Still… I might want to have my way with her… if you know what I mean."

Uthgar said, "Well, make your mind up about it, Warren Leader Henery. She's looks rather plain to me. I'd as soon have a Drelve."

The other Drolls howled.

Theandra said, "You arrogant little piece of ****! You'll not touch me!" The sorceress had enough of the dawdling and moved with blazing speed. She hit Uthgar with a Power Word Stun and the big Droll stopped in his tracks. She uttered Death Spells in rapid order and smote the six Drolls. Henery the 88th dropped to his knees and tried to crawl away.

Theandra said, "Not so fast, **** for brains. I have questions for you now."

Theandra grabbed his shoulder and utter the icy phrases of a Spiritwrack Spell. Henery wailed in pain. Theandra said, "I'm going to let you suffer for a while. Then you're going to answer all my questions, and later you and pretty boy Uthgar will take me to your leaders."

Henery the 88th wailed. His cries brought several predators. The predators met grisly deaths. Theandra asked questions and Henery gave answers. The torment continued for hours. When she was satisfied he'd spilled all the beans, Theandra placed a Hold Spell on the Kiennite. She aroused Uthgar and placed an enhanced Charm Spell on the hulking Droll. She released the Kiennite and threatened another Spiritwrack. Henery quickly pledged fealty. Uthgar and Henery the 88th led her to Aulgmoor. Henery summoned the warren leaders and Uthgar gathered the Droll chieftains.

Theandra addressed the gathered warren leaders, "I am now your queen. You may call me Anectrophinea. If that's too hard to remember, just call me Death, because that's what you'll receive if you disobey me. I want all efforts put into turning this s*** hole into a decent fortress. You will dominate this world. Everybody's got to serve somebody. You've got to serve me, but in return you will dominate this world. The Draiths and Drelves will fall before us. If anyone refers to me as anything but Anectrophinea or Death Queen, his penalty will be death."

Theandra became Anectrophinea. The name came to mean death in Kiennish. Legions of wolf-faced Drolls followed her. The scrawny, weak-willed Kiennites venerated her. Anectrophinea ruled with an iron fist and fashioned a stronghold upon a craggy rock. She cut the fortress out of the stone of the mountain with powerful spells and created a circumferential glacis. The glacis was composed of the rubble created by the blasting spells. She also called her fortress Aulgmoor. The fortress sat on the site of General Saligia's stronghold, which had been attacked and weakened by Draiths. The gate could only be approached by a narrow stone walkway. She unpacked her Bags of Concealment. The contents filled many rooms. She created a library which stored the knowledge that she had carried from the other world. Enhanced Magick was known for the first time in the absence of the Approximation of Andreas.

The Draith Dontax, who she killed in the forests, was son of the Draith monarch Nargan the Red and heir to Ooranth's throne. Drolls threw Dontax's remains at the base of Ooranth's towering black wall and proclaimed the spectacle a gift of Aulgmoor's new queen Anectrophinea. King Nargan demanded vengeance for his son. He'd been the most successful Draith leader in regard to fighting the Kiennites, Droll, and Giants. He sent his forces against Anectrophinea time and again. The Kiennite Death Queen's Magick leveled the field.

# 35.

# Anectrophinea and the Cave Dragon

While Uthgar and Henery the 88th's charges busily bolstered Aulgmoor, Anectrophinea explored the castle's dungeons and discovered access to the underworld cave system. She used Rock-to-Mud Spells to expand passages beneath the castle in order to have some escape route. During her exploration, Anectrophinea stumbled on the lair of the Cavedragon Phanres. Phanres was over eighty feet long and stood almost sixty feet tall when reared upon its hindlegs. Small vestigial wings on its back served only to aid in warding off blows, for they would never hoist its bulk into the air. Where was there to fly in the caverns anyway? Magick did not touch Phanres. The dragon held great contempt for those who used Magick. The great beast had long since abandoned the practice of going above ground for prey and treasures. The caverns supplied it with more than enough even for a dragon's standards. Old Phanres dominated the dark caves beneath Parallan. Anectrophinea heard the beast's heavy breathing and detected the scent of its lair. She quickly cast Invisibility and peered around the corner.

Phanres sniffed and said, "Aha! A snack! Invisibility won't help you, sorcerer! This old nose knows right where you are! Ha ha ha! I made a funny! My nose knows! Please don't run. I'm going to catch you anyway, and it'll be over much quicker for you."

Anectrophinea said, "You aren't going to eat me, you blowhard!" She stepped around the corner and dispelled Invisibility. She was in full view of the massive Cavedragon.

Phanres said, "Aw, it's a pretty girl. I bet you taste better than you look, too. Come on over here and jump in my mouth."

Anectrophinea replied, "I was thinking how much my warriors would enjoy Cavedragon stew!" The Cavedragon snapped its maw at her. She quickly moved aside.

Phanres laughed, "It's pretty and funny. But I sure am hungry. Aw shucks, I missed! Hold still! I'm going to eat you sooner or later."

The sorceress tried a subtle Charm Spell. Phanres said, "I'm too hungry for that, pretty wizard."

She tried Power Word Stun. Phanres guffawed.

Anectrophinea tried Hold Monster, Sleep, Minimize, Fumble, Confusion, and Suggestion… to no avail. Phanres said, "I just love to hear your voice, but my belly is growling loudly now. I don't want to forage for cave rats and cave divers. I've not had fresh giant in weeks. Not many of the big blokes come this way these days. Come to me, pretty snack."

Anectrophinea pulled a red diamond from her Bag of Holding, augmented the dim light with Illumination Spell, and said, "I have a better idea. What can't we be friends? I can send you lots of morsels. And treasure too. Look at this red diamond. It's from a long dead world. Irreplaceable. You'll be the only dragon in the World of the Three Suns with one."

Phanres said, "Easy decision. I'll just eat you and then take the pretty red rock."

She replied, "Silly, the point is that I can give you lots of shiny things. And victims. If you eat me, you'll be hungry again soon. Let's be friends."

Phanres inched toward her and said, "Nope. You look too tasty!"

The sorceress said, "Wait a second! What's your favorite food?"

Phanres smacked its lips and said, "Dark-haired sorceress! Yum!"

She moved back a few steps and said, "No, silly, what do you really like?"

Phanres replied, "Oh, purple mooler, I guess, but they don't come down here and are too heavy for my friend to carry. Come on! Don't be difficult! I'm going to get you sooner or later! Might as well get it over with!"

She countered, "What if I left now and brought you back some purple mooler tomorrow?"

Phanres smacked his lips again and said, "Why put off eating till tomorrow what you can eat today! Get over here!"

Anectrophinea remembered the little chest that always rested in her ever-present Bag of Holding. The Bag always gave you what you wanted when you stuck your fingers into it. She removed her favorite hairpin and said, "Beware, mighty dragon! This is Dragonsbane! It's been the death of many dragons. You know I'm a powerful sorceress. You've seen my Magick. I'm not bluffing!"

Phanres laughed and said, "You tried lots of Magick. None of it worked on me. When I saw my 100$^{th}$ Approximation of Andreas, most Magick quit working on me. Besides, that just looks like a hairpin."

Anectrophinea said, "Suit yourself. Risk it! But this is not a Magick spell. It's death Magick for dragons. All I have to do is nick you, and you'll be dead in a *minute* minuteman heartbeat."

She pointed the hairpin toward the dragon and took three steps forward. Phanres backed up a step and said, "Maybe... we could negotiate. I like the red rock... and you said you'd bring mooler... and I could always eat you later."

Anectrophinea said, "All true. What do you say, noble Phanres? Regain some of your glory. Join me."

Phanres said, "What the heck! Be sure to bring the mooler."

Anectrophinea said, "It'll be here tomorrow, and you may also eat the Kiennites that bring it to you."

Phanres said, "Kiennite is not good eating!"

Anectrophinea said, "Silly dragon. I could have gotten away anytime."

Phanres said, "Nope. Nobody knows these passages like me and my friend. We'd have caught you."

Anectrophinea uttered, "Hairpin!", activated her Word Of Recall Spell, and instantly stood in the privacy of her bedchamber in Aulgmoor. She smirked and said, "Valuable ally. I must inquire about his friend."

Seven Kiennites carried fresh mooler to the Cavedragon. None returned. In return for treasures, Phanres gladly carried out many of the Deathqueen's death sentences. Its alliance or at least coexistence with the Kiennite stronghold at Aulgmoor provided the beast with both treasures and the flesh of Aulgmoor's enemies and cast-offs. Few defenders were required to guard Aulgmoor from foes foolhardy enough to try to gain access to the stronghold through the caverns.

# 36.

## Jar Dee Ans

Anectrophinea reversed her Recall Spell by saying "Nipriah" and returned to Phanres chamber. Several cavedivers flew about the chamber and with their chittering announced her arrival. The sated Cavedragon burped and said, "Thanks! You even sent young Kiennites, so they weren't so tough."

She waved her arms, shooed cavedivers away, and said, "Why do you keep those disgusting bat-like beasts around?"

Phanres said, "Do you mean my alarms? I keep them around to warn me of interlopers, and sometimes as a snack. A dragon can't be too careful these days, with folks trying to steal treasure and dark-haired sorceresses showing up and all."

Anectrophinea said, "Fair enough! Tell me about your friend."

Phanres said, "He's been around a long time. Like me, he's stuck down here. Did something to make his mother mad and she confined him to these caverns. He's not very happy about it. We talk a lot in my dreams. He says its good practice for him."

Anectrophinea asked, "Where is he now?"

A male voice said, "I'm right here."

The largest cavediver swooped down and sat by Phanres. The image shimmered and changed to a young male a bit shorter and stouter build than Anectrophinea. He was reddish and greenish at the same time and had pointed ears and vaguely Drelvish features. Little red sparks flickered from his eyes. He continued, "My name is Jar Dee Ans. I prefer Dee. Some refer to me as Adjuster. You may call me Fire Master, or simply Master. I have tried to enter your dreams. You are a Spellweaver, but you are not

Drelvish. Quite a barrier guards your mind and thoughts, even when you sleep."

She asked, "It doesn't look like you are trapped. Why don't you just fly out of here."

Jar Dee Ans gave a gruff laugh and said, "You don't know my mother. She confined me! Her own son! Just for hassling her precious Drelves! I was just having some fun. I only scorched a few of them and gave the Kiennites a little help. I might have taken old Arachnis's favorite scrying device and given it to the Draiths. Mother accused me of using it to spy on... ladies."

Anectrophinea asked, "Did you say you helped the Kiennites?"

Dee replied, "Yes, and they surely need it."

Anectrophinea added, "I can't argue with that. But I'm confused... how are you confined. Are you a simple shapechanger?"

Jar Dee Ans shimmered. His visage now mimicked Anectrophinea. He snapped his fingers and created a flame that burned from his fingertips. He said in *her* voice, "Do you still think me a simple shapechanger?"

Phanres said, "Hold on now, Dee. I won't know which one of you to eat!"

Anectrophinea said, "Don't even think about it, Cavedragon! Magick touches you, Dee. All the more reason you should just leave."

Jar Dee Ans solemnly answered, "I can't fight the power of the pentagram. My own mother! She constructed the cursed figure, wrote my name in it, and confined me to these caves. I cannot use Magick outside these underworld labyrinths. I'll appeal to my father when he awakens... provided I can contact him. These caverns do not connect to his realm."

Anectrophinea said, "But they connect to my castle. My dungeons open directly into the caverns and follow paths in the other direction all the way to Alluring Falls. You have talents I could use."

The Adjuster said, "Why should I help you? You look like dragon food to me! However, you are quite pretty."

Anectrophinea shrugged and answered, "Suit yourself. Keep wallowing in cavediver s***! It might be valuable someday! In some worlds bat guano has value! Or you can have access to my castle and its amenities... at my discretion, of course."

The Adjuster smugly asked, "If suns light hits me, I'll be in violation of my confinement. Where is your bedchamber? May I share your bed?"

Anectrophinea answered sharply, "Uh… no. I sleep upstairs. You'd best stay in the dungeons."

Jar Dee Ans replied, "Can't blame a guy for asking. I must adhere to the terms of my confinement. I cannot leave the underground caverns, use Magick outside the caves, and invade dreams outside the caves. Phanres and I have worked out a symbiotic arrangement. Oh, mooler s***! What have I got to lose! I'll join your team, sorceress. Maybe you'll change your mind and put a bed in the dungeon."

Anectrophinea said, "Don't hold our breath, Adjuster. I will send some Belles of Thabell down to you. They're the best the Kiennites have to offer. However, you'll have to stop your 'symbiotic partner' from eating them."

Phanres said eagerly, "Are you sending more mooler?"

The dark-haired sorceress said "hairpin" and vanished.

Jar Dee Ans smugly said, "I've got to do something about that."

Phanres said, "Good luck with that. I'm still hungry. Lead some of those dumb bats in here."

# 37.

# Fates of Ramish and Magrian

Ramish and Magrian returned to Alms Glen with the Draithsbane, the Blade of Phyrris, and received a hero's welcome. News of Agrarian's passing saddened Drelvedom. The Drelves had lost four Spellweavers. Ramish had inherited rudimentary powers of illusion from his Kiennish father. The young Kiennite-Drelve studied hard and possessed a strong work ethic. His spell capability had grown with exposure to the Elemental Stones, Enhancing (Xennic) Stone, and Gray Bleeding Stone. Teacher Shayne broke tradition and gave Ramish a copy of Agrarian's Spellbook. Unfortunately, most of the spells were beyond the scope of the half-Drelve's understanding. Ramish practiced particularly hard during Approximations. Dreams troubled Ramish during his sojourn to Donothor and after his return to Alms Glen. He no longer saw images of the red-haired sorceress. Instead, a dark-haired woman of equal beauty drifted into his dreams and taunted him with visions of power and the Kiennish stronghold Aulgmoor. Ramish did not discuss his dreams with Magrian. Elderly Shayne yielded the role of Teacher to Magrian.

After their return to Alms Glen, Ramish and Magrian zealously protected the Drelves. Ramish wielded the Draithsbane, escorted harvesters to Meadowsweet and Green Vale, and repeatedly brought down attackers. Magrian led many harvests. Ramish fearlessly waded into large parties of Drolls or Draiths and smote the foes. He usually fought Kiennites till they submitted and then spared them, a fact noted by Magrian. The Drelves enjoyed relative safety for many dark periods because of the half-Drelve's diligence. Drolls, Kiennites, and even Draiths gave the Drelve lands a wide berth. Massive campaigns between the forces of Aulgmoor and Ooranth occupied the enemies. Unsettling and powerful Magick aided the forces of Aulgmoor. Magrian and Ramish explored the World of the Three Suns and sought the source of the Kiennites' newfound strength. Magrian created a detailed parchment map. The adventurous Teacher and Ramish explored dangerous caves near Alluring Falls, discovered winding extensive passages that drew dangerously close to Aulgmoor, and narrowly escaped the caves with their lives. Arcane forces were at work in the dark underworld. Magrian immersed himself in the role of Teacher and became the greatest teacher of the Drelves. Bolstered by imbibing the Elixir of Longevity and protected by Agrarian's gift of the Robe of Sagain, the sagacious Teacher lived far beyond his peers and attained age usually seen with Spellweavers.

Ramish unsuccessfully sought a life-mate among the Drelves. She-Drelves shunned the half-Drelve, half-Kiennite. Ramish did not receive the high regard of the people that he had anticipated. He was instead feared and ostracized socially. His isolation ultimately alienated him. Ramish heard rumors of the rise of a new leader of the Kiennites. Loneliness drove him to his father's people; he yearned for companionship and acceptance; his illusionary skills stagnated. He never yielded the Draithsbane to any other Drelve. Ramish left the Drelves to try to reach the stronghold of the Kiennite queen Anectrophinea. The half-Drelve, half-Kiennite tried a shortcut through the caves of darkness and encountered a massive Cavedragon. A large cavediver betrayed his position. The ancient beast's aura overwhelmed Ramish. The half-Drelve dropped the Draithsbane. Ramish fell to the great Cavedragon Phanres and became the beast's dinner. The Draithsbane joined Phanres's treasure pile.

# 38.

# The Spawn Curse: the Deathqueen's Wish

Anectrophinea grew powerful, relished the title "Deathqueen," and warred with the powerful Draiths. Many Draith Lords opposed the Deathqueen. Nargan the Red was the greatest Draith Lord. Nargan the Red's grief over the death of his son Dontax spurred the Draith King's efforts. After many battles, the Draiths neared the total ultimate victory. The Giants had been decimated and their leaders slain, the race never again to be a power. The army of Nargan the Red was perched at the very stronghold of the Kiennites' Deathqueen; thrice the wicked wizardess threatened to ruin the race of the Draith King if the battle did not cease, but thrice Nargan crashed his forces against the walls of the castle. The walls were about to fall. Within the castle, Anectrophinea knew she'd exhausted her resources. Cave-ins had closed her escape route into the caverns. Phanres and Jar dee Ans could not help. She's used many spells. Even her enhanced Magick had limits. Her armies and spell components were decimated. The Deathqueen reached into her nearly empty Bag of Holding and removed the little box. She used her precious hairpin, opened the latch, and removed the last phial. The last Elixir of Mastery of Magick was the Phial of True Wish. She sighed. The Draiths victory would be bittersweet. Some things were more painful than death. Nargan the Red would see the end of his people. Male Draiths would share the loneliness she endured after Areniel's death. Anectrophinea opened the phial and imbibed the liquid. Draiths banged on the castle doors. Her last defenders fell. She concentrated. Wording was everything. Keep it simple. She said icily,

"It is my wish that every female member of the Draith race be stricken and die. Every feminine child fathered by Draith men shall die at birth. Females fathered by Draith males born to women of other races will die at birth. Magick shall offer no remedy to the Draiths. Not even by true wish may Magick remove my spawn curse."

Nargan's ears heard the wailing from the homeland those thousands of paces to the south, and the tide sustaining the Draith onslaught ebbed. The land was filled with a chill and brief blackness. As the light returned, Nargan knew that a baneful lesson was upon him. The Kiennite Deathqueen used her ultimate power and denied Nargan the victory. Anectrophinea caused the immediate death of every member of the female gender of the Draith race. Telepathically she communicated to Nargan that the males would be next, and the Red King had no way of calling her bluff. She also assured the Draith King that the genetic curse applied to any feminine child sired by Draith males and born to women of other races. Nargan did not call her bluff. Her threat to destroy the males took Nargan's thoughts went to his three young sons in Ooranth. Truth be known… the great Magick had so weakened Anectrophinea that she sat helpless within her castle. True Wish cost the spell caster a goodly portion of her *enhanced* Magick. Her full powers never returned. An ancient staff disappeared from her Bag of Holding. Magick did not touch Nargan. He didn't comprehend the cost of casting the True Wish. Nargan could have walked through Aulgmoor's weakened walls and slain all within, including the helpless Deathqueen. Instead Nargan retreated to Ooranth.

Everyone touched by Magick felt the great wave created by Anectrophinea's spell.

Anectrophinea used the Phial of Wishing to cast the Spawn Curse upon the Draiths. Death instantly claimed all feminine Draiths. All Draith female children were doomed at birth. An unexpected effect came from the Spawn Curse. "Magick shall afford no remedy for the Draiths" indeed prevented any spell from ending the Spawn Curse. It also imparted remarkable Magick resistance to the surviving male Draiths.

Unwonted and unwanted effect! Quirk of Magick! Draiths were forced to steal the maidens of other peoples to perpetuate their race. Draith traits dominated in the hybrid male offspring. Every feminine child died at birth. Draiths kidnapped and tortured Kiennite spell casters, who had been empowered by the Deathqueen. The tortured Kiennites yielded the secrets about the portal. The boon of the stolen scrying stone and their newfound Magick resistance enabled Draiths to cross the portal and seek victims. Disappearances plagued Donothor and Parallan. Nargan opened the doors of Ooranth to Menders and merchants from the Emerald Isle. Midwives were welcomed and treated well in Ooranth. Many elderly females of other ilks sought the positions. Draiths bartered with pieces of the Stone of Ooranth, which was virtually indestructible. Of course, individual stones required the Rod of Ooranth to replicate. For a time, Drelvedom benefitted from the weakened Draiths, Drolls, and Kiennites. Eventually the Deathqueen regained much of her strength, Droll and Kiennite numbers increased, and the Drelves faced their old enemies again. Approximations of Andreas occurred but brought no Spellweavers. Rangers searched in vain for Ramish and the Draithsbane. Ramish had carried the locating stones paired to the Draithsbane. Draiths frequented the wide meadow and traversed the portal. Draiths had difficulty maintaining their numbers and assumed mainly defensive posture. Nevertheless, Ooranth grew stronger over time. Drolls, Kiennites, and Anectrophinea's Magick lacked the power to bring down the fortress walls. Drolls and Kiennites remained wary of crossing the River Ornash.

********

Drelvish Elders ordered constant vigil of the portal to the other world. The shimmering rectangle's luster endured and did not fade. She-Drelves mysteriously disappeared never to be seen again. Rangers watching the portal saw Draiths approach and traverse the gate. Often Draith scouts stood on the meadow's fringe and stood by the gate. Without Spellweavers and having lost the power of the Draithsbane, Rangers could do little more than watch. Rangers gave the seven-foot tall bronze-skinned warriors a wide berth. The Draiths paid little attention to goings on in Drelvedom. Draiths returned through the gate bearing females of otherworldly races.

The worlds of Donothor and the Three Suns were again intertwined… through the broken hearts of the kidnapped maidens' families.

***********

In Donothor, following Theandra's instructions, Gray Elf Lieutenant Merinde had carried the Bag of Concealment containing the three Elixirs of Mastery of Magick to Detlor and gave them to the wise Gray Elf Elder Garnett for safe keeping. Merinde took a life mate and joyously accepted the task of caring for Theandra and Areniel Nightshade's daughter Cherilynn. The child was surrounded by love and nurturing. She grew lovely and shared the most positive traits of her mother Theandra and father Areniel. When she matured, Merinde and Garnett gave her the staff and the Bag of Concealment as Theandra had asked him to do. She drank the phials of liquid as she was instructed. The Elixirs of Mastery of Magick were spent. Cherilynn took a life mate from her new people, and she was blessed with children. The powers gained from the phials were passed to her female progeny. The traits of her mother were always dominant; beauty and power grew with succeeding generations. This was an unexpected effect of the "Elixir of Enhancement."

One day, a descendant of Cherilynn was tragically taken from her family. The Gray Elf Prince Vannelei relayed the sad tale to Prince Eomore of Donothor:

"A young elven woman disappeared under the cover of darkness without a trace. Only her crying infant son and torn body of her guard dog remained when her husband returned from the hunt that evening. The woman was called Mariniel, the most beautiful of her generation. Mariniel was endowed with great power of Magick. She was the first sorceress that our people were graced with in many generations. The husband was the then elven noble and now king, Cyratiel. Yes, the infant son was I. Of course, I have no memory of what happened. My father searched for years and grieved greatly over her. He left me in the care of relatives and combed the lands for his lost mate. But never a trace was found. My mind's only picture of Mariniel, my mother, comes from the image in the small portrait enclosed in the Luck Amulet that was blessed by the High Priestess Knarra and given to me by my father when I was a nymph. Eventually the love and grief which drove him yielded to reason, and Cyratiel returned to his people. On the death of his father, he became the figurehead "ruler" of our people. Of course, Eomore, you are well aware that we consider individual freedoms paramount, and our council of elders with the "king" at its head only convenes when the community is threatened. I must admit that is rare, for we exist peacefully for the most part."

Vannelei continued, "We do not hoard treasure, so the goblins have no real reason to attack us, and we remain geographically separated from our greatest racial enemies, the orcs, hobgoblins, and the many races of giants. However, we have again been struck by tragedy."

"On his return to his village, the bereaved Cyratiel was befriended by an elven woman named Corri, who had been widowed when her mate was slain by a nightmare, one of the demon horses that served the arch evil Chalar, on a hunting trip deep into the Lachinor. Eventually the couple fell in love and married, and the union was consummated with the birth of a daughter eighteen years ago. Heather was a beautiful child and she brought great joy to her father. He felt so blessed that he named her for our most revered plant. She proved to be remarkably intelligent and was a ready student of the forest. Plants seemed to flourish whenever she walked by. It seemed that the Spirits of the forest had in some small way tried to repay the just Cyratiel for his years of grieving through this child. As she grew into womanhood, Heather became loved by all the peoples of our village and the surrounding communities. She accompanied her beaming father on many of his trips to the council meetings.

"Oh, but the cruel hand of misfortune has struck again. Some six weeks ago our Heather was taken from us. So many of the circumstances were like those of forty years ago, only this time there were unfortunately elven witnesses. On the dark starless night, much like the one just past, Heather was staying the night with friends, when the unthinkable happened. The account is given by the only survivor of the tragedy, a thirteen-year-old girl who saved herself through an invisibility potion. There was great mirth in the house as they celebrated the visit of the elven princess. From the outside, there was a growl from the faithful watch hound, then a painful yip, and silence. When the patron of the home opened the portal to investigate the noise, he was struck a single blow to the throat by a great dark hand and fell lifelessly back into the room.

"Through the door came a number of creatures who were as dark as the night and who moved as silently as wraiths. They systematically began to eliminate all the occupants of the room. The fallen man's eldest son managed to reach his short sword but the dark raiders merely turned back the blade as the young, but quite strong elf struck. He then fell as his father to the crushing force from the blows of the great fist. There was one last hope. The matron managed to get an arrow into her husband's long bow, and the taut string hummed, but the perpetrator caught the missile in its flight and angrily snapped it in half. The killers then went into a frenzy, and killed all within the dwelling except the survivor and the Princess. A great arm lifted up the princess in a single, effortless motion, and they then left as silently as they had arrived, bearing their quarry with them. Half in shock over witnessing the wanton slaughter of her family, the girl still managed to reach a neighbor's home to relate the grisly tale. Then she collapsed. The neighbors quickly ran to the site of the tragedy and unfortunately confirmed the story of the hysterical child. Eleven of our people lay crumpled on the floor."

By quirk of fate… Draith raiders took Mariniel, a woman of enhanced Magick. By quirk of Magick… she gave birth to a half-Draith son. Enhanced Magick passed to her son Calaiz.

One-day one of Cherilynn's Gray Elf line joined in life time commitment with a dark Elf princess. The couple welcomed a lovely child named Cara. Grayness surrounded the little dark-haired girl. Cara was born in Detlor, in the western Lachinor region of Donothor, in the light of a single simple sun. Yet, a copy of the ancient spell book of the Drelves appeared by the Elfish child's bed.

*The Gifts of Andreas to the People of the Forest*
LARLS
A&W

The ancient tome replicated when a Spellweaver was born. Cara Nightshade bore striking resemblance to her ancestor Theandra. Little Cara learned to pat her tiny hands together in response to children's rhymes. Tiny sparks flew from her tiny fingers.

In Green Vale, the ancient Tree Shepherd muttered, “Fire Wizard.” Unwonted gift of Magick! Quirk of Magick…

Ǿ ∞ Ǿ

Albträume

Printed in the United States
By Bookmasters